The Gap Between Us

Enjoy the read!
Norelle

Norelle Smith

ACKNOWLEDGEMENT

To my husband – Thank you for being my 'Loren'.

To my kids

My oldest – Through every hard time and obstacle that has been put in front of you, you've remained one of the most generous and kindest people I know.

My middle – The one who has blessed me with my beautiful grandkids. They couldn't have asked for a better mother. You're amazing with them.

And my youngest – Looking back on my life, I wish I would have had my head on straight like you always have. You've been a great role model for so many.

The three of you have been inspirational to me.

And my best friend 'Polly' – If not for your input, Marcel's character would not have developed the way he did. And… Thank you for *everything*. No one should walk through life without a friend like you.

DISCLAIMER

The content in this book is a work of fiction. The characters and incidents are a product of the author's imagination. Any resemblance to any person living or dead is purely coincidental. Apart from "Pastor Archie". This character is fictional, however was created and written to honor a pastor I knew long ago. He, along with his wife laid a foundation under my feet that changed my life.

Copyright © 2021 by Norelle Smith

TABLE OF CONTENTS

Chapter One

Norma

My neighborhood had always been a quiet one, known for its laid-back, relaxing atmosphere and the magnificent buildings found on every street. But on that day, I wasn't admiring my neighbors' yards or the beautiful buildings on either side of the road like I usually would have. My mind had been on other things.

A couple of kids were shuffling by on their skateboards—laughing, while the adults watched them with fond smiles. None of this held my attention, however. I was too focused on the dream—more like a nightmare—I'd had the previous night.

It was…bizarre to say the least. Every stitch of detail was still buried deep in the recesses of my mind. Even now, I couldn't figure out what had led to it, but I guess that's one thing about dreams, we can never tell how one starts.

I tried to make some sense of it. So far, I hadn't come up with anything. And for the life of me, why had the mere thought of it cause me to shiver and make the hairs on my body stand up straight? I shuddered as the images of the dream emerged in my mind's eye, sending a disturbing chill down my spine —

The wide expanse of the lush meadow was captivating under the brightness of the sun. I'd never seen grass so green before. Overcome by euphoria, I ran through the tall grass, enjoying the brushes of the towering leaves against my fingertips, enjoying the warmth of the summer sun on my olive skin—the feeling of being sun-kissed.

I wished my parents, and my siblings were here. It hit me then, where were they anyway? Pausing in my steps, I looked around, searching through the blades of grass to find them. With my minuscule height, it was hard to see anything much—never have I ever wanted to insult my petite size more, but I didn't give up.

"Norma!" a voice suddenly screamed.

Startled, I called out, "Dad? Dad, is that you?" That was the first question my brain commanded. It didn't really sound like him, but who else could it have been?

"Norma." the voice called again, a bit softer this time.

My fear gave way to curiosity. "I'm here." I called back, standing on the tip of my toes. "Where are you?" I questioned.

"I'm over here." This time, it was almost a whisper, and yet I could still hear him clearly. There was something about it that I could not explain. I walked towards the voice, my heart palpitating, hammering like it wanted to burst through my chest. Who was this person? Why did I feel compelled to go to him?

My contemplation halted when a string of explosions went off all around me. Were those...gunshots? The sudden change in the atmosphere caught my attention. The sky that had been blue and clear a second ago had turned a haunting grey as dark clouds gathered around. Even the luscious green of the grass began to fade. Slowly, they all withered, dropping down dead. Dread like I had never felt before crept up my spine. I turned to run, but it was as though an invisible force held my feet firmly to the ground. I tried again, but it was to no use. Left with no choice, I stood there, panting, my heart pounding, wondering what was going on.

"Norma," the man's voice whispered to me again and I turned back in the direction it was coming from. "Run. Run and don't look back." He urged. Odd that I could hear that whisper over the blasts. What struck me was that his instruction scared me even more than the explosions. That not finding him would be my death sentence.

"No, I won't leave you!" I shouted, surprised at my own words.

—

"Norma. Norma?"

This time, the voice was different. It was…feminine.

Effectively slapped out of my reverie, my head turned in every direction, trying to locate the voice's owner. A ghost of a smile touched my lips when I caught sight of my best friend, Betty Ann.

"Norma," she called once more, jogging toward me. When she caught up to me, she threw her arms around me briefly.

"You're looking good," I commented, eyeing her knee-length blue dress and cute sandals. "You wouldn't have a date tonight, would you?" I teased.

"Ha-ha," Betty Ann replied, tipping her head and shaking it. "I wish, but not today, girl. And thank you." She added looking down at her dress before her attention zoomed in on my face. "Are you okay? I called out your name like five times, but you were so lost in your thoughts, you didn't even hear me."

I offered her a broad smile in an effort to reassure her that all was well. But of course, being my closest friend for more years than I could even remember, she wasn't fooled.

She frowned; I didn't have to ask. I knew she could read the worry lines on my forehead. "Is this about that issue with your mother?" she probed.

I let out a long sigh.

The 'issue' was one I didn't like to talk about, or even remember. It happened almost three months ago but even to this day, the utter humiliation of it was still eating away at whatever thread of dignity I had left. Every time Betty Ann mentioned it, I wished for the earth to swallow me even if just for a few hours so I could hide my shame. But to no avail.

How could I have been so foolish? More than anything, I knew better than to put myself in that kind of situation, and yet I had done it anyway. Had my young adult hormones been so out of whack that day? Honestly, making out in my bed with a boy I'd only just started dating? What had I been thinking?

The most dreadful part about that afternoon was the shock on my mother's face when she walked into the room and saw Brian's hands caressing my body. I'd been so caught up in the moment, I hadn't seen her until she had firmly said, "What on earth is going on here? Out."

Honestly, there had been no better chastisement than that look in her eyes.

Needless to say, the experience seemed to have built a wall between my mother and I, so much so that she didn't talk to me for the rest of the afternoon. I literally became a shadow of my former self. Fear of seeing my mother's disappointed face kept me hidden in my room. The guilt of what I had done tore at my delicate heart.

After several hours, I realized I could no longer keep myself in isolation, and went to seek for my mom's forgiveness. I promised her the incident would never happen again.

"I'm sorry, mom," I muttered, with tears streaming down my cheeks. "Please, forgive me."

She did; however instead of feeling better about it all, I ended up feeling worse. I still felt like I couldn't regain my footing. It was almost like I'd lost a part of myself that I couldn't get back, no matter how hard I tried.

"Hey." I jumped a bit, startled by the sudden call.

Betty Ann's prompting pulled me out of my thoughts. When our gazes met once more, I realized she was still waiting for a response to her question. I forced a half-smile. "Everything's fine. I told Brian I couldn't see him anymore and I haven't talked with him since. I'm not even sure why or how I allowed myself to get into that situation. He doesn't even believe there is a God. I mean, that's how we ended up connecting anyway. I was trying to convince him that God was real; I really botched that one. What a terrible example I set." I told her. Then added, "He was a great conversationalist though…" I dropped off.

"And he was cute," Betty Ann added. "But I think you made the right decision."

I chuckled. "Right. Anyway, I was trying to be that girl who could change him, but he had affected me more than I him. I never should have allowed things to go on the way they did since he wasn't even a Christian."

"Unequally yoked and all that jazz," Betty Ann said. "I get it. But it's time to let it go. God has forgiven you. Your Mom has forgiven you. Now it's time for *you* to forgive yourself." She locked her elbow with mine. "Come on. Let's get to the meeting before the others start to wonder if we've ditched them."

Together, we walked inside the little white church that had been our spiritual home since birth. The pint-sized conference room where we usually met for our youth committee meeting was at the extreme back, close to the church office. When we got to the room, the other members of the Youth Committee were already seated and waiting. In no time, the meeting began, and I put away all thoughts of my dream from last night, as well as my unfortunate experience with Brian.

Betty Ann, the youth leader tabled her plans for the upcoming fundraiser for our summer camping trip. Thereafter, she asked everyone to make relevant contributions regarding the fundraiser. Everyone seemed to be in a passionate mood at the beginning, but thirty minutes into it, the energy in the room began to wane as people got lost on ideas to bring forth. Alyssa, one of our newest Youth Committee members, stood and we all turned to hear her.

Hard as I tried, I could no longer keep my concentration on Alyssa and the discussion. *I wondered what that dream meant, though. Is someone in trouble? Am I going to lose someone close to me? If only I could interpret dreams like Joseph in the Old Testament—but that was not the case.*

"Great!" Alyssa practically squealed, pulling my attention back to the meeting and discussion at hand. She looked like she wanted to do a lap or two around the room. The majority had voted for her idea. Thankfully, she retook her seat, resigned to only dancing in her chair like a kid. I laughed. Shaking my head, I quickly typed the plans on the word document making sure to save the changes. The meeting only went on for a few minutes longer, with everyone now in high spirits, contrary to the earlier pensive moods.

"This meeting is adjourned," Betty Ann announced when the last topic on our agenda was wrapped up. She turned her sights on me yet again. "Norma, will you please say the closing prayer for us?" I nodded. Despite not liking the center stage, I enjoyed praying whenever asked. Perhaps, because my eyes were closed, and I didn't have to see anyone looking at me.

"Heavenly Father," I started. "Thank you for giving us another day and another opportunity to work for You. We're grateful for Your mercies toward us even though we don't deserve them…"

I went on to pray for our youth, the committee, and the plans we'd managed to come up with. By the time I was through, the room itself felt lighter.

As I stowed my laptop, I waved at a few of my friends who were heading through the door. One thing I loved about our church was that we were like one big, happy family. Not that we didn't have our share of shady characters, but for the most part, we loved each other despite our shortcomings. Nothing was more precious to me than that.

Slinging my tan bag over my shoulder, I headed for the door. My house was only a few blocks away from the church. And since it was the early days of summer, the air was a little warmer, allowing for a nice evening stroll. I was thinking of all the tasks I needed to complete before I called it a day when I heard someone call out to me.

"Wait up, Norma." Betty Ann was after me again. The girl was my best friend, but I seriously hoped she didn't want to continue that discussion about the 'issue with my mom,' as she called it. I turned and waited as she ran towards me. Her long, curly blonde hair bounced with each step she took. She was much taller than me, but then again, almost everyone was. At only five feet, most people towered over me.

Despite my exasperation with my friend, I knew she meant well in everything she did. We always looked out for each other, and that was what mattered. We had been friends since we could walk and from that time, her bright, cheerful personality remained constant. My lips quirked up as she came to a halt in front of me.

"Hey, what's up?"

She tilted her head slightly and smiled. "Well, some of us girls are going out to eat and we would love it if you came along."

"Oh, that's nice," I replied. "I'd love to, but I can't. My parents are expecting me to be home for dinner." I stared at her, hoping she would understand my point.

"Oh Norma, you never go out with us anymore. Are you still punishing yourself because of that thing with Brian? Geez. You made a bad decision. You can't put your life on hold because of it," Betty Ann whined, her pink lips in a sad pout. "Now, come with us. I'm sure your mom won't mind if you miss dinner tonight."

I shifted from one foot to the other. I hated having to disappoint my friends. The plan was to just head home, eat mom's famous *caponata* dish with my family, then do some studying for my final exam before falling asleep. Nothing fancy, but it was slowly becoming a pleasant routine for me. Not only that, but it kept me in my mother's good graces.

"Come on. It'll be fun." Betty Ann pleaded, giving me her puppy-dog stare. I let out a sigh, my determination weakening. Lord knows I wanted to go out with my friends and have some fun. But it had been on one of those 'fun' occasions that unfolded the whole Brian thing.

Knowing I could not make the decision on my own, I told her, "Let me call mom first." Before Betty Ann could get a word in, I pulled out my phone from the side pocket of my bag and started dialing the number. If my mom didn't like the idea, then Betty Ann wouldn't probe further. My mother answered on the fifth ring, which meant she was probably finishing up with cooking.

"Norma, *Tesoro*, are you on your way home for dinner?" Mother's Sicilian accent was beautiful and filled with delight.

"Hi Mom," I replied. "Umm, I wanted to ask you something. Betty Ann and a few of the girls are going out to eat. They invited me. I was wondering if you would mind if I went with them. I know how much time and effort you put into our meals and—"

"Norma," my mother said, cutting me off. I could hear the smile in her voice when she said, "you're twenty-one years old. Of course, you can go out with your friends. You don't need my permission. You're a smart girl and typically have a good head on your shoulders. Go on, have fun. Just do your mom a favor and stay away from unsuitable boys."

Though I knew she didn't mean anything bad by that last statement, I cringed. "Thanks Mom. I have to go. I love you."

"I love you too, *bambina*."

"Well, what did she say?" Betty Ann asked as soon as I hung up. Though she was taller than me, she looked like a little puppy waiting for a go-ahead sign.

"She said I'm old enough to go out without asking her," I admitted.

"Well, no surprise," Betty Ann said, laughing. "You're the only one who seems to think your parents are going to hate you if you miss dinner. You made a mistake, let's move on." She took my hand and pulled me toward the waiting group. "Now, let's go."

The girls all turned to look at us as we approached. Trudy, a pretty and curvy redhead, said cheerfully, "Welcome back, Norma. Let's get going already. I'm starving." She rubbed her stomach with a sour look to prove her point. Some of the other girls nodded in agreement.

“Here, here,” someone said before we all started for the parking lot. The drive to the restaurant was lively, with TobyMac on the radio and the girls mostly chatting about the last time they’d gone out together and the fun they’d had. I felt like an intruder overhearing their conversation. Betty Ann had also invited me, but I’d declined.

Staying on my mother’s good side was my current focus. For the past few months, I’d been putting her first. She’d been right. I should never have disrespected her and my dad the way I had. Knowing how much she cherished family time, I’d made it my point not to miss dinner over the past couple of months. Marissa Tesoriere was an incredible mother, and I would have done anything to make her happy, even if it meant not doing what other young adults my age did. I needed her to trust me again.

Replaying in my mind the conversation we had earlier, it seemed I had reached my goal. There had been no reservation in her voice whatsoever. Mom trusted me. That should have made me happy. Instead, the pressure of the expectation that came along with that trust; I needed to remain focused. I wouldn’t let a handsome boy distract me again. I didn't care if I looked prude in anyone's eyes.

The restaurant was nearly packed when we arrived, with only a few tables available. We opted for one close to the glass window. As soon as we took our seats, our waiter appeared. “Good evening, ladies,” he said. “What can I get you? Oh. Norma, hi. How are you?” Hearing my name called with such familiarity, my head snapped up to look at the waiter.

I could tell right away his face was familiar. Still, I couldn’t place where I knew him from. Not wanting him to pick up on my struggle, I smiled. “Hi. I’m great, thanks.” It wasn't the first time someone had approached me and I couldn't remember where I'd met them. The trick was to just offer a kind smile with a simple reply.

But he figured it out quickly, “You have no idea who I am, do you?” He laughed and I could feel my cheeks heating up.

“I’m sorry. My brain is clearly not working today.” Was all I could think to say.

“I’m Alan,” he answered. “We go to the same Art School,” he said. “Remember me now?”

I did. Though I was surprised he knew me. It wasn't like we spoke or anything. It was mostly the usual friendly greeting that was exchanged whenever we passed in a hall. “That’s right. Sorry,” I said with an apologetic smile.

“It’s okay,” he replied with a smirk. “Anyway, what can I get you ladies?” Even though his question was directed at everyone, he was still looking at me. I could feel my friends’ eyes on us, watching to see what would happen next. My discomfort grew with each passing second and it took all my willpower not to squirm in my seat. I really didn't like when people stared at me for so long, I always felt they should be able to sense how uncomfortable that was and stop. But Alan’s eyes wouldn't leave me. Mom’s words from earlier replayed in my head.

Just do your mom a favor and stay away from unsuitable boys.

Old-fashioned as my mother was, I wasn’t inclined to go against her wishes. Not that Alan looked “unsuitable.” He looked like one of those clean-cut kids with professional parents who taught them how to save and prepare themselves well for a bright future. Funny enough, Brian also had that look going for him. And we all knew how well that turned out.

Thankfully, Betty Ann broke the silence and placed her order. The others followed suit. I was the last to put in my request for a burger, fries, and a soda.

As soon as our waiter was out of earshot, Trudy didn't waste any time to blurt, “Oh my gosh, Norma, he likes you. And he’s so cute." The entire table erupted into giggles. Usually, I'd be laughing along with them. Today, it wasn't the same. I kept my cool.

"Seeing as you both go to the same school, maybe you should hang out with him," Trudy suggested. "You don't know what the future may hold for you." She lifted her left hand, dangling her fingers. The girls made an 'oooooh' sound before going into another round of snickers.

That made me smile a little. These girls were crazy, and I loved them all the same. "Cute," I replied. "But I'm not interested in a relationship right now, and I'm definitely not looking for a future partner at the moment." I vaguely remembered hearing a conversation when he said he was not a believer.

"That's a shame," Trudy said with a disappointed look. "Look at him. He's adorable. Can't you at least invite him to church? Maybe he'll show up, get saved and then you can marry him." I pressed my lips together in an effort to look serious, but in a matter of seconds, I broke out into laughter. The other girls started cackling as well.

"You're ridiculous," I said through my laughter. She reminded me of those crazy matchmakers I'd seen in TV dramas. "Since you're so smitten with how attractive he is, maybe you should be the one to invite, convert and marry him yourself."

"I would, except it seems he only has eyes for you," she replied, batting her eyelashes. I was about to cover my eyes with the palm of my hand at the desperate look in her eyes, but instead I gave a small smile.

"Here he comes," Betty Ann announced. I was tempted to look but if I did, he would know we were talking about him or think I was interested in him, I didn't want to give off the wrong impression, so I kept my gaze locked on Betty Ann.

"Here we go," Alan said as he distributed our food. "Enjoy ladies. Please, let me know if you need anything else." He said with one last look at me, with that, he left to provide service to a couple two tables away from us.

"He really is handsome." One of the other girls said.

"And Norma doesn't want him. Can you believe that?" another teased. I shook my head and opted not to answer. To my relief, someone changed the subject. Unwrapping my burger, I opened my mouth to take a huge bite of the delicious juiciness when movement outside caught my eye.

It was already dark but soft lights from the street gave just enough illumination for me to spot three men standing in the parking lot. Their attention was glued to a fourth man who was considerably larger and more muscular than the others. I gasped at the sight of him.

Big.

That was the word that came to mind. He was like a bear looming over every other creature around him. So much so, that it took me a minute to notice the man he was holding by the collar, firmly pressed against a dark van.

The big guy pulled the much smaller man away from the vehicle, only to slam him back into it. The impact made me wince, even though I was a good distance away. Big Guy leaned in close, whispered something in the man's ears, then stepped back, releasing him. The poor man collapsed to the ground, more than likely in fear. Big Guy was giving me the shivers, and he was not even near me.

My throat started to close when Big Guy lifted his head and looked in the direction of the restaurant. It felt like he was looking directly at me, though to be honest, I was so small he more than likely could not spot me from where he stood. His face was rough, angry. My throat went dry just looking at him, my food still close to my mouth. I hadn't taken a single bite.

When Big Guy started in the direction of the restaurant, my heart began to race. He looked like a panther, dark and menacing and on the prowl for his next prey. I could not take my eyes off him, even as he made his way through the glass door. He was decked out in dark blue jeans, dark shoes, and a white t-shirt. He also had a gold chain with a cross as the pendant, around his neck. His hair was ink black and he had a black and grey bandana tied around his crown.

He terrified yet fascinated me at the same time. I couldn't seem to tear my eyes away from him.

Big Guy walked toward a table about fifteen feet away from ours. There was a girl sitting there, arms folded across her half-exposed chest. Her arms pushing her cleavage even more in view for anyone to see. She wore a short red dress that didn't leave much to the imagination. Even with all the make-up on her face, I could tell she was a teenager, maybe the same age as my sister, Luna. She pouted, ignoring Big Guy by turning her head to the side, a stubborn look on her face.

"Get up," I heard him say. "Now." he commanded as he stared down at the girl. His voice was low, but the heavy bass in it made it project farther than he'd probably intended. I took a quick glance around the restaurant and noticed that there was no one else paying attention to them. Was I the only one interested in the drama?

I touched Betty Ann's arm to get her attention. "Hey, what do you think that's about?" She followed my gaze to the table.

"I don't know," she answered. Though, now it had gotten her attention, I could hear her own curiosity seeping out in her reply.

"Get up," Big Guy repeated, and I shuddered. I was even more surprised by how unaffected she was by him. The girl, whoever she was, glared at him, but did as she was told.

"Walk," was his next instruction. She did as she was ordered, though it was obvious she didn't want to. This left me wondering, who this man was to her. She undoubtedly had more boldness than I did because I would have been brought almost to tears at the first command. I could not recall a single time my dad had ever used such a harsh tone with me.

Apparently, the girl was not fast enough for him because he suddenly took hold of her upper arm. "Marcel." she protested through gritted teeth. "Slow down. I can't walk that fast in these heels. Stop embarrassing me." My eyes went down to the killer heels. They were so high; I couldn't imagine taking one step with them without twisting my ankles and falling face flat on the floor.

Pausing, he scowled down at her. "Do I look like I care?" he growled. "You're a kid. You shouldn't be wearing them in the first place." He didn't give her time to respond but continued at an even quicker pace toward the front door. For the entire time, I couldn't keep my eyes off of them. When he pulled her into the parking lot, they disappeared between the rows of cars.

Who was that guy? And why was he reprimanding that girl like a father would a daughter? Even with all his ruggedness, I could still tell that he was young. Way too young to be her father—he couldn't be much older than me—but he had to be something to her.

"They obviously know each other," Betty Ann whispered. "Maybe he's her uncle, or boyfriend."

Something about that last word turned my stomach.

I frowned as I stared into the parking lot. "Yeah, maybe," I murmured, my eyes still stuck outside. Betty Ann lightly bumped her shoulder into mine.

"Hey."

Knowing she was checking up on me, I prepared a smile before turning to her. "Let's eat, it's none of our business. You're right, it's probably her uncle or another family member." I nodded and made a show of biting into my burger. I barely tasted it, but I moaned around the mouthful. That seemed to satisfy her and she returned to the conversation with the girls.

My eyes returned to the parking lot on their own accord.

Marcel, the girl had called him. So rugged, so daunting, so…handsome. His face and everything about him were now imprinted on my mind. Smooth olive skin, austere cheekbones, that angry mouth, even the muscular ridges of his physique. It was all there, trapped in my very soul.

I froze when I realized what was going on. It was happening all over again. I had just seen this stranger, who obviously didn't even know of my existence and here I was, still thinking about him.

Sighing, I looked down at my plate. This was exactly what I'd wanted to avoid. It was even worse this time because that guy, Marcel, was no doubt a gangster. Everything about him spelled it. I wanted to slap myself silly for finding him attractive.

As I took a second bite of my sandwich, I silently thanked God that at least we never had a face-to-face meeting. Now, if only I could get his image out of my mind. Especially those dark intriguing eyes.

Chapter Two

Marcel

My entire body was shaking. Not from being cold, as the weather was warm, the telling sign that summer was here. My tremor stemmed from anger—raw, untainted rage. And it was all because of the little girl next to me, who insisted on driving our entire family up the wall. In a state like this, I could not find the right words to say to her, so I stuck to short, clipped instructions as needed.

"This is all you ever do, embarrass me," Sofia ranted, as I pulled her toward my ride in the parking lot. "I'm not a child anymore. I'm fifteen-years old." I rolled my eyes. Even with the makeup on her face, a man who'd lost his glasses could see she was just a child. "I can do whatever I want with my life..." she went on, "and you, of all people, have no right telling me what to do."

Her words only fueled my anger. Still, I ignored her and continued on my way. That didn't mean my sister was going to give up. She went on. "You know, you should really learn to mind your own business, Marcel. Stop being such a control freak."

"When you stop being foolish and do what's right, then I will stop being what you see as a 'control freak', but for now, be quiet," I simply said. We were getting strange looks from passersby, but honestly, I was used to that already. This wasn't the first time I was dragging Sofia's butt back home.

"You have a problem." She continued. "A big one. *You* come judging *me* like you're one of the good guys? But we both know you're far from that. Every time you paint me as the black sheep of the family, we still all know that it's you."

I knew this game well enough. She was trying to get me to lose my temper. Sadly, for her, tonight I refused to play. This was no game. Sofia was walking down the wrong path, just like my mother had feared, and I would rather chew off my arm than let her continue. Somehow, I needed to get this girl under control.

"Say something!" she yelled, growing frustrated with my silence. She let out an angry growl when she saw I was ignoring her.

I shook my head and continued dragging her along. When we reached the dark blue Honda that belonged to my boss, I opened the front passenger seat and shoved Sofia inside. She moved to fold her arms again, but I pulled the seatbelt across her, locking it in place.

Once she was secured, I slammed the door shut and stormed off to the other side of the car. All I could think about was throttling my little sister. But I knew better. I'd never hurt a girl in my life and wasn't going to start now. Moreover, I didn't want any of my sisters growing up thinking it was okay to let a man hit them.

Inconspicuously, I glanced at her once again and my heart cracked a little bit more. This kid used to be so sweet, so kind, so loving. Now, she was becoming unrecognizable. I wanted nothing more than for her to snap out of this ridiculous behavior and start being the responsible daughter my mother needed her to be.

Scotty and the new guy my boss Johnny had picked up a few days ago, were waiting for me on the driver's side. "Give me an hour," I told them as I opened the door.

"Make it thirty minutes," Scotty said. "We're already behind schedule, the delivery is in less than an hour." The fact that this was brought to my attention irritated me even more. Sofia was notorious for pulling stunts like this and always at the wrong time. It was as if she was dying for attention, which was just ridiculous and sad.

Lips pursed, I nodded in acknowledgement. "Alright, thirty it is." I jumped into the car and peeled out of the parking lot, not bothering to put on my own seatbelt. I didn't slow or look at Sofia again, until we reached the first stoplight.

I slightly shifted my gaze toward her. "Tell me something, Sofia. Do you like to see our mother in pain, weeping over you? Do you get some kind of sick satisfaction in knowing you're turning her hair grey at an early age, because she's wondering if you're dead or alive?"

Sofia met my glare with one of her own. That look could probably have broken a weaker man, but I wasn't just any man. I was a criminal—a hardened one, despite being only twenty-five years old. I'd been at this for close to ten years, and more than once I'd had to deal with much worse than my little sister's scowl. To me, she looked nothing but silly.

"Sofia," I called again when she wouldn't answer.

"I'm not trying to hurt anyone. Don't you get it?" she snapped. "I just want to live life and have fun. Is that too much to ask? Other girls my age are doing it, why can't I do the same?" That was the most ridiculous defense I'd ever heard. It was funny she thought *that* was a good explanation as to why she'd been sneaking around with men twice her age. It was like she just didn't care anymore, as if she'd blocked every little pore where common sense could seep into her brain. Sometimes, when I looked at her, I didn't even recognize her anymore. Especially now, looking like—well, like the girls I hooked up with for one-night stands. But this was my sister. I didn't want that for her. I wanted to protect her from that life. From men like me.

"See, there's a bit of a problem with that," I hissed. "You're not an adult yet. You're a young girl. You shouldn't be doing things just because other girls are. You're different. Do you know what that means? It means you do not get to live your life the way you please. You don't get to sleep with men who are old enough to be your father. In fact, you shouldn't be having sex at all. You're fifteen-years old."

She rolled her eyes, giving a little scoff. "I can do whatever I want."

"I don't know what those men are saying to deceive you. They want just one thing from you, nothing else. Considering how sharp-mouthed you can be, you're surprisingly naive," I said. And it was true.

"Piss off." She looked hurt by my words, but I couldn't care, not now. She needed to understand that what she was doing wasn't right, and if I went soft on her, she would never change.

I let out a cold, bitter laugh. "You know, the only reason I didn't break some of his bones was because of our location. Not to mention you were there and, as self-centered as you've been lately, I'd never want to traumatize you like that. But if you lied to me, I will find him and I will beat him to a pulp, do you understand me?"

Out of the corner of my eye, I watched Sofia shudder, and her eyes widened in shock. "He didn't touch me, Marcel. I swear," she said quickly, fear laced in her voice.

"You swear, huh?" I raised an eyebrow in question. "Wouldn't be the first time. You swear so much nowadays, it's become like your second language."

"Brother, I'm not lying to you. Don't hurt him. He didn't know I was fifteen. I told him I was eighteen," she confessed, her cheeks heating from embarrassment.

The light turned green, and I continued on my way, refusing to look at or speak to her anymore. Eighteen? What kind of buffoon would even think she was eighteen? Even under all that makeup, Sofia still looked too young. That man knew she was underage, yet he'd still propositioned her for sex. He was nothing but a pervert—a sick pervert that would be half-dead by now, if only I wasn't so busy.

Maybe I should go looking for him after all, I thought.

We were home in a matter of minutes. Not wasting any time, I exited the car, opened her door, took her arm, and led her into our apartment building.

Our apartment was on the third floor, so we took the old elevator up. Even though she was no longer struggling, I refused to let go of her. It was irrational, but some part of me feared if I relaxed my grip, she would disappear from my sight—wouldn't be the first time.

When the elevator flaps squeaked open, I dragged her toward our door, much like I did in the restaurant. Our neighbor—a girl about Sofia's age who lived with her father—stepped out, holding a large plastic bag I suspected contained the daily garbage. Her eyes widened when she saw us approaching. She took a step back. It seemed and looked like she wanted to run back through her apartment door. Sofia eyed her as we passed, but I knew she was embarrassed, not about how she looked, but to be caught being dragged like a child, since she didn't want to be seen as one. She didn't complain though, but I could feel her frown on me.

Like I care.

Inside, I found my mother sitting on the old gray sofa in our living room, with my two other sisters, Isabella and Juliana. Both on either side of her. Mom's eyes were swollen, her shoulders shaking as she wept, and her hair was ragged.

She lifted her head when she heard us. The sight of my mother in this rumpled state made my heart drop. I loathed seeing her in pain, especially an emotional one. For a moment, her red-rimmed eyes widened, and she jumped up from where she was sitting, running over to us. When she got to where I stood with the defiant Sofia, she wrapped her up in her arms.

"Oh, my baby," Mom wept. "I thought I had lost you for good." I expected her to dive into another round of sobbing. Instead, she pulled away from Sofia, holding her at arms' length.

"Have you lost your mind, Sofia? Two days! You've been gone for two days, with no word whatsoever of where you are. Why do you continue to do this to me? Are you trying to send me to an early grave?"

I didn't have to look at my sister to know she was scowling at her. Sofia always acted like she was irritated when my mother questioned her, even though she had given her every reason to do so. Thankfully, she didn't argue. There was only so much that I could take. Plus, my mother had already gone through enough. She didn't need Sofia disrespecting her under her own roof for simply trying to protect her.

I wished Sofia would open her eyes to see how much she was hurting our family. I wanted her to turn the switch off. She was always giving off the 'bad girl' vibe, acting like she didn't care about the outcome of her actions, but deep down I knew she did, I just didn't fully understand why she insisted on staying that course.

Knowing she was off guard, I reached over and snatched her cell phone from the side pocket of her skimpy red dress. Sofia whirled to grab for it, but it was already too late. "What do you think you're doing?" she snapped when she couldn't get a hold of it.

"You're grounded," I told her. "Go to your room and get out of those dreadful clothes. I don't ever want to see you wearing that dress again." I wasn't even kidding. No girl her age should be wearing her definition of the word clothes. I knew my mother didn't get it for her so she must have borrowed it from a friend.

I saw the rage in her eyes build, almost in slow motion. "How dare you?" she screamed. "Who do you think you are trying to put me on restriction? Even my dad has never grounded me before. He adores me and lets me do whatever I want when I get to visit him," she said, her breath coming out in angry puffs, her chest heaved, syncing with it.

I shrugged. "That's because he has never lived with you. He doesn't see what you're doing. He only sees what you want him to see. How often do you see him? Once every couple of months? And even when that happens, how long do you stay? A few days? Never even a week." I retorted.

"Oh. Big man, preach to me. This coming from Saint Marcel who doesn't even know his father," she shot. Ten years ago, that would have hurt, but now I didn't care about the man she called my father. "Maybe I should go and live with him," she continued. "No one wants me here anyway." The last part was just a call for pity. She acted like this wasn't her home, or we didn't care enough for her. When she'd first started using this tactic, it would break my mother, so she would soften up but Sofia had pulled that line for so long, we were all tired of it.

"No one wants you here?" I closed the distance between us with a small step. "Go to your room." I ordered. I've had too much from her already and I needed to leave, remembering Scotty was waiting for me.

She faced me and smiled mischievously, crossing her arms before her in a rebellious manner. "Why should I listen to you?" She cocked her head to the right, a daring smile on her face. It was obvious that she was enjoying this; she pushed and pushed just to see how far she could go before I snapped.

"Sofia, *stop*. What's gotten into you?" Mom said. Having witnessed my rage before, I imagined my mother was probably worried that I *would* snap, maybe toss my little sister over my shoulder, and take her to her room myself. But I wasn't into her games tonight. Isabella and Juliana were still sitting on the sofa, observing us with wide eyes full of fright. I hated that they had to grow up to this, and even worse, the fact that they were probably used to it.

Lowering my head so I was nose to nose with Sofia, I told her in my calmest voice, "There's so much you don't understand right now. But I promise you, when you grow older, you will appreciate Mom and I for all we're doing to protect you from the world around us."

A look of guilt crossed her face. It disappeared as quickly as it came and she put a glare on her face, hissing. "I do appreciate Mom. She works hard for us. I love her. But you… You're a hypocrite, Marcel."

"You love her?" I scoffed in disbelief, standing back to my full height. "Well, look at her, does she look happy to you?" Sofia looked away, avoiding my eyes. "When you love someone, wouldn't you do everything you can to make them happy? So far, all you've done is show how immature and ridiculous you can be."

She held out her hand. "Can I have my phone back? Give it back and I'll gladly go to my room."

"So, you can go around, texting older men again?"

"Are you going to give it to me, Marcel?"

I ignored her question; I wasn't going to give her the phone just yet. "If you ever, and I mean ever, pull another stunt like this again, I'll not only take your phone, but I will also *lock you up* in that room." I threatened. Maybe then she would finally realize how much she was hurting the people who genuinely cared for her. Not only us but hurting herself.

With nothing else to say, she turned around and stormed down the hallway.

"I don't understand," Mom cried as we watched Sofia leave. "Where did I go wrong with her?" She shook her head, her shoulders slumping. My chest tightened seeing her looking so defeated. I stepped up closer to her and pulled her into my arms.

In times like these, that was the only thing I could do, offer comfort. My mother really did a good job raising Sofia, but then Sofia got involved with the wrong crowd.

"Don't blame yourself, Ma," I said to her. "It's not your fault. You raised us well, even without a man there to support you. I couldn't be any prouder of you."

She sniffed, her tiny hands circling my waist. "Thank you, son."

I looked over at Isabella and Juliana, giving them a small smile. "Ma, I have to go. I have some business I need to take care of." I told her. The moment the words left my lips, I felt my mother struggling to free herself from my hold, so I let her go. She looked up at me, her dark eyes searching mine. They were hard now.

"Girls, turn on the television," she said in Isabella and Juliana's direction. She didn't acknowledge their reply but grabbed my hand and led me into the kitchen. She didn't want them to hear what she was about to say. I could already tell what this was about, and I braced myself for it. It wasn't the first time we were having the talk.

"You're still hanging out with that gang, aren't you?" Mom said, her tone accusing.

I sighed. "Ma, relax. They're just friends."

Her eyes narrowed and she all but screamed. "Son, you can't keep throwing your life away like this. Don't you think it's hypocritical of you to be living that kind of lifestyle while berating Sofia for not being a good girl? You must lead by example, Marcel."

My mother was right, and I knew it. Still, things were not as clear cut as she made them out to be. "I'm sorry, Ma, but I don't have a choice. I've told you this before. I can't just walk away. Please don't worry. I'm doing this to help our family."

"I don't want your blood money!" she barked. "I don't want your money when it's gotten from dirty deeds. I rather eat once daily and live an honest life than have a feast before me, eating with guilt in my heart."

I rolled my eyes, just like Sofia had done earlier. “Stop with the dramatics, Ma. I don’t go around killing people, if that’s what you think. It’s a business, it’s my job. And it pays well.” She scoffed. “I have to do what I can to help us get by, you know that Ma. With the money I earn, you don’t have to worry about getting swim gear for Isabella, or the classes she’s supposed to start soon. As for Juliana, you don’t have to think about getting her a new violin…”

Their laughter from the living room caught my attention, stopping me midway. I could hear the auto-tuned voice of a cartoon character; mom looked in the direction of the living room before facing me again.

She exhaled. “You think I don’t want those things? Of course, I do. But not like this. It may seem like a good idea now, but in the end, you’re going to get yourself killed or in jail. And where would that leave us?”

“Ma, don't start with this.” I rubbed my forehead tiredly, this conversation was draining my energy, but I couldn't walk out on her.

She put her palms on her waist. “Start with what? You know it's the truth. I don't want you to end up like your father.”

That ticked off something in me. I hated when she compared me to him. I knew I wasn't on the right path, but at least, I would never abandon my children. “I'm not my father. Can you stop bringing that guy up? We might as well forget his existence, just as he’s forgotten about ours.”

“Don't speak like that.” She sighed. “I don't want you to rot in jail, Marcel. I wouldn't be able to bear it. What would I tell the girls if that happened?”

I didn't know how to explain to my mom that I had decided to just live in the present-day. Deep down, I knew that my crimes might catch up with me one day, but I wasn't going to let something that hadn't happened yet bother me. I already worried so much about my family, I couldn't also carry the burden of thinking about what my future would look like. If there was one thing Johnny had taught me, it was to live only in the present—perhaps it wasn't the best advice; but it was the guidance I had decided to make my own.

I sighed. "None of that is going to happen," I said. "I would never do that to you." I pushed a lock of her messy dark hair away from her face.

I knew that what I told her was a bag of boloney, and she knew that too. But what else could a guy tell his mother in a situation like that? I kissed her forehead and backed out of the kitchen. In the living room, my sisters were still seated on the couch with their eyes glued to the old television.

Making my way over to them, I kissed them each on their foreheads as well. Before I could pull away, Juliana reached for my hand. "You're leaving again?" she asked.

"I have to work, sweetheart," I told her softly.

"Oh." A sullen look took over her features. "When will you be back?" she asked. "I really miss you."

"I know. I miss you too. Both of you. I have to leave for a few days. But I'll be back before your birthday. And I'll make sure to bring you each a gift."

That made Juliana's face light up. "Really?" she asked excitedly.

"Really." I nodded. It was the least I could do after being away for so long.

This brought big smiles on their faces. "Yay! I can't wait." She rose from the couch to do a little dance and I had to laugh. Isabella looked on, giggling at her sister's antics. Even though they were twins, Juliana was the younger of the two. They were nine going on ten in another week. I knew I had to make their birthday extra special for them. The two girls were such a contrast to each other.

While Juliana was expressive, Isabella was reserved. Nonetheless, both were sweet, good girls.

Unfortunately, the three of us didn't have our fathers in our lives. I was told that my father had been in and out of prison for drug related crimes. The twins' dad had walked out on our mother not long after they were born. According to his goodbye note, he couldn't deal with the pressure and financial demands of having twins, as well as helping to care for Sofia and me. I was fifteen at the time.

I turned towards the kitchen, where my mother was. Over the years, she had grown into an incredibly strong woman. Sofia's dad was still in her life but lived in another state. He was always asking my mother to let Sofia come to live with him, since he was in a better position to support her. But my mother refused every time, simply because she wanted to raise all her children together. He'd even gone as far as denying her child support, just because of the stance Mom had taken.

She had done her best to keep this away from Sofia. Still, I was convinced she knew about it. In fact, I was certain she blamed Mom for her father not stepping up and supporting her the way he should. There was also another issue that seemed to eat away at my sister's heart. The twins and I shared our mother's last name, while she had her father's. Somehow, she thought she was less loved, and often referred to herself as the outsider who didn't belong.

It had more than likely contributed to her being so defiant.

To be quite honest, I couldn't understand her pattern of thinking. The twins and I were the ones without fathers. I didn't even know what mine looked like. There was a time in my life when it bothered me that I didn't know him or bear his name. But that longing for him was gone. I had no time pining after a man who didn't want me in his life. When the twins' dad walked away, leaving Mom to fend for us all on her own, I knew it was time. It was time to step up and be a man. It was time to become the father figure that my little sisters needed. That was how I ended up working for Johnny at the age of fifteen. I needed a way to help provide for my family. Johnny found me on the streets one day and recruited me just like that. Said he saw something in me. What exactly, I still wasn't certain. But after his very convincing speech, I joined his gang. The rest was history.

Pulling my gaze away from the kitchen, I eyed the twins, giving them a smile. After another round of kisses, I headed for the front door. Before my hand touched the handle, I felt tiny hands tugging at the back of my shirt. I turned around to find Isabella there, looking up at me with concern in her big brown eyes.

"Marcel, be careful. I don't want you to die," she said, her voice small, vulnerable even. I swallowed hard on the lump forming in my throat. No matter how much I tried to hide what I did from the younger girls, they were smart. Maybe Juliana hadn't figured it all out yet, but Isabella certainly had.

"I will, don't worry," I told her, ruffling her dark hair. "Take care of Mom and your sisters while I'm away, alright?" Despite her age, the situation of things has made Isabella much smarter than one would expect for someone so young.

She nodded, a brave look on her face. "I will."

"Good girl." With that, I exited our apartment with my heart forcing its way up my throat.

As I started the engine of my boss's car, I thought about our business transaction for that night. When it came to this type of business, nothing was certain. One minute everything could be going right, and then one bad move could make everything go wrong.

I don't want you to die.

Isabella's words sliced through me like one of my enemies' daggers. Still, all I could do was hope that there would be no shootout that night, and that I would make it back to my family in one piece. I couldn't afford to die and leave my mother in more pain than she was already in. I wanted, needed, her and the girls to be happy and safe.

Before driving off, I typed out a quick text to Mom.

Marcel: *I'll be back soon, don't worry. I love you.*

After sending the message, I made a quick call to Scotty. He picked up on the first ring. In spite of my concerns, I placed all the confidence of a gangster in my voice as I told him, "I'll be there in two. Be ready and let's get this done."

Chapter Three

Norma

The crowd was loud. Normally, I didn't enjoy large groups of people. Nevertheless, when it came to football, I hardly minded. It helped that my little brother was on the field, dominating like the incredible athlete he was. I knew well enough that Rico was more than a little embarrassed whenever Mom and Dad screamed and cheered excitedly throughout the games. He tried to force a smile for their benefit, but I could see his struggle.

I giggled.

Luna and I held up a banner we had made at home with Rico's name on it, shouting cheers as well. But even together, we could not be as loud as our parents. We were no match for them. I glanced over at them and found that Mom had leaped up from her seat and was doing a weird celebration wiggle. I tossed my gaze in Luna's direction. She was already breaking out in laughter.

"Oh no, Rico must be dying from humiliation out there," I shouted in her ear, above the noisy crowd.

"We should join in," she replied with a cheeky smile, her dimples poking out. I almost keeled over laughing. *Poor Little-Coco.* A sweet memory of the nickname Luna had given him when she was a toddler momentarily distracted me and I fell into another round of hysteria. But that sweet memory, as I watched him, made me burst with pride.

When our brother made the winning touchdown, we had to cover our ears to keep from going deaf; not only did our parents go wild, but also the rest of the fans around us. In another few seconds, we completely lost sight of Rico as the crowd rushed onto the field to congratulate the team on their victory. Dropping the banner, we followed the tide of people.

"There he is!" I heard Dad shout over the crowd. He pointed in the direction of a group of players. Rico was among them, and his friends were all patting his back, giving him the respect due to him.

"Son!" Dad called out to him. His earlier embarrassment had disappeared, and he was grinning from ear to ear. He pushed away from his friends and accepted Dad's waiting embrace. "You were great out there, kid! I'm so proud of you!"

"Thanks, Dad!" Rico shouted back over the noisy crowd. Luna and I forced our way in to congratulate him as well.

"You killed it out there, little brother," I told him. He smirked and ruffled my hair as if I were the little one. Technically, I was physically smaller. At only five feet tall, I was unquestionably the tiny person compared to his almost six feet. I slapped his hand away but still laughed.

His friends had already arrived to get him by the time mom got her hug in. "See you later!" he shouted as the boys lifted him and stole him away. We were used to it by now. It would be another hour or so before Rico would be ready to leave. He was the star player on the team and everybody wanted to shake hands or bump fists with him before he made his escape.

"I think this is his best game yet," Luna said as we made our way to the parking lot. "Too bad none of the scouts from any of the Universities were here today. I know Rico has his heart set on Stanford." It had always been his dream.

"True." Dad nodded. "But I'm not worried," he said, he was always the one to think positively. "When the time is right, they'll be here to see my boy play, and they're going to be begging him to sign with them." He had a proud look on his face.

Mom nodded. "I couldn't agree more," she said, standing beside him. I beamed, knowing they were right. Rico was good, and as long as the right people watched him play, he would be going places.

I was about to slip into our Suburban and plop myself on one of the seats when I felt my bladder calling. "I need to use the restroom," I told my parents with a sheepish look.

"I'll go with you," Luna said as she laughed, "The bottle of coke and water I drank earlier is taking its toll on me too."

"Go on, you two," Mom told us. "We'll wait here," she said, as we moved to get out of the car.

We made our way to the restrooms, cautious to avoid overly enthusiastic fans who appeared to be a little tipsy. As far as I knew, drinking on school grounds wasn't allowed. "Just ignore it. People sneak in alcohol all the time." Luna said, dragging me along to go faster.

"You know, back when I used to attend school here, that would never have happened." I remembered the time a boy in my science class had brought a bottle of Vodka to school that he and his friends were planning on drinking up on the roof during lunch break. He was caught and had gotten suspended for a week.

She shrugged. "A lot has changed since then," Luna commented. "People now do things that are a lot worse."

"I can tell," I murmured dryly as I eyed a couple displaying their affection without a care of who was watching. I had nothing against couples showing their affection in public; holding hands and a kiss, I found it sweet. But then, there was something about a full make-out session out in the open that made me feel embarrassed for them.

Luna noticed. "Ignore them," she said. "Those two do that all the time. Sometimes even worse than that."

I nodded, looking away from the couple. "Let's just get to the restroom."

"Whoa," I heard Luna say. She came to an instant halt, making me almost lose my balance. I grabbed on to her elbow to steady myself.

"What's going on with you, Luna?" I asked, surprised.

"We can't go over there," she said, looking in the direction of the restroom. There was a group of four girls standing at the entrance, but they looked pretty harmless as far as I was concerned, though their attire made me raise an eyebrow. It wasn't *too* provocative, but it's unlikely those were the clothes they wore when they left their homes today.

"What do you mean we can't go over there?" I questioned, looking from them to my sister who seemed tense all of a sudden.

She turned to face me. "I mean we can't. Do you know who those girls are?" she asked in a fierce whisper, turning to face them again. "They're bullies, all of them. See that tall, dark-haired one that looks like a model?" I looked at the one she was talking about. The girl was wearing a mini skirt with a matching black crop top that showed off her pierced navel. If she leaned over at all, everything would be exposed for the world to see. She had the matching mean-girl attitude—with the aid of her heels—she towered over the girls around her. "Her name is Sofia Johnson," Luna continued. "She's their leader and the worst of them. She's mean and pretty much destroys everything in her path. I mean, no one even wants to cross her, everybody stays clear of her."

I pulled away from my sister so I could get a good look. "You're being bullied at school?" I asked, hoping she wouldn't confirm that.

She sighed. "Only if I get in their way—and I don't," Luna said with a shrug. "Sofia brags about being untouchable. Rumor has it she has an older brother who would never let anyone hurt her, he's part of some gang or something. She just bullies people as she pleases."

"Are you serious?" I shrieked, shocked at this news. "Why didn't you tell me? Or Mom and Dad? We could have helped you."

The moment she heard my words, Luna reared back as if I had slapped her. "Are you crazy? I can't tell anyone. That would only make things worse. They're already calling me a 'Jesus-freak', just because I tried to share the Gospel with some of my classmates like Pastor Archie had challenged us to do. That was the worst decision of my life and I wish I'd just kept my big mouth shut."

My heart faltered just hearing those words coming out of her mouth. "Oh Luna, don't say that. Telling others about Jesus is a good thing, even if other people think it's foolish. You should be proud of yourself, and they might not realize it now, but if you continue the good work, slowly they will see."

Luna's shoulder's slumped and she groaned in frustration. "You don't understand. Back when you were in high school, most of your friends were already Christians. I, on the other hand, don't have many of those friends. And some of the kids who are hide it because of the mocking." She looked at me nervously, as if wondering if she should say her next words. "That, by the way, includes Rico," she added.

I blinked twice, wondering if I had heard right. "Rico?" I frowned. "Do you mean *our* Rico?" I asked.

Luna moaned. "Yes Norma, *our* Rico," she said. "He doesn't talk about religion either. According to him, it's not 'cool' amongst his friends."

"What do you mean not cool among his friends?" When has he ever cared about that? "Are you sure Rico said this?"

"He told me himself when I questioned him. He said he didn't want to embarrass himself, so it was best he didn't bring his religion up," she said. "Well, it's his decision, I can't exactly force him to do what he doesn't want to."

My heart ached to learn this about my brother. I had, for a while, notice how withdrawn he had become and how Mom and Dad had a hard time getting him out of the house to go to church with us. Still, I had never really taken it seriously. After all, he was a seventeen-year-old boy going through his adolescence. I was sure this was just a phase. I knew that a lot of teenagers got to this stage where they had to fight peer pressure. Rico, being on the football team, had been exposed to far more, and been influenced in more ways than I could have imagined. Surely things would soon go back to normal like they had with me.

Right?

I made a mental note in my head to talk to him about it. In the meantime, my irritation was bending toward this Sofia Johnson girl and her cronies. How dare she bully my sweet sister? I wasn't one for confrontation, but I felt obligated to do something about it.

I'd never really experienced bullying. Sure, when I was in high school, I wasn't on everyone's good side, but then, people for the most part minded their own business. It pained me that a girl who probably wasn't even sixteen was exercising some sort of cruel power over her classmates—especially when one of them was my sister.

Before I could talk myself out of it, I grabbed Luna's arm and continued toward the restroom. "Norma, what are you doing?" Luna squeaked, her eyes widening in panic.

I gave her a look like it wasn't obvious enough. "We're going to the restroom," I told her. "If this Sofia girl doesn't like it, that's her problem."

"Please, Norma, don't do this," Luna nearly wept when she saw I wasn't backing down. I ignored her.

I was on a roll, and I was not going to back down. The moment we got close enough for the girls to hear, they all turned to look at us. My feet faltered when I caught sight of a familiar face. She was still wearing a skimpy dress and heels but looked different without all the extra makeup and a different hairstyle. However, I could still tell it was her.

That same girl I'd seen two weeks ago being dragged out of the restaurant by that bear of a man. My eyes widened and all the willpower I felt three seconds ago wilted out of me. So, this was Sofia Johnson. She also had that commanding presence about her that pinpointed her as the leader. She scowled at me as I paused in front of her.

"What are you looking at?" she sneered, lips curling back like an angry animal. I felt my face heat up. More than likely, I was as red as a tomato.

"Nothing," I replied, my voice too small for a twenty-one-year-old woman. "Could you excuse us please?" I asked her politely, hoping my friendly words would soften her cold heart and that she would move out of the way.

Though I didn't see anything amusing in what I had just said, her friends started giggling, making me feel uncomfortable. I shifted nervously, but I tried not to let it get to me.

Sofia looked at Luna then to me, as her brows lifted. "Sorry," she said in a sugar-coated voice that held nothing but malice. "But you're going to have to find some other bathroom. This one isn't open to freaks." The statement sent the other girls surrounding her into snickers. I glanced at each of them, baffled by this ridiculous behavior. Luna was right. I did not understand. I had never been bullied before.

Sure, there had been annoying kids in my days, but the overwhelming majority of my classmates had treated me well. This blatant attack was unfamiliar territory to me. An assault like this should have had me running. Thing was, this was not about me. It was all about my fifteen-year-old sister who was being harassed by these girls.

Luna standing behind me only hardened my resolve not to back off. Luna was too bright, too patient, and too peace-loving to go through this kind of harsh treatment. I needed to help her.

Thoughts racing through my mind, I came up with the perfect angle to strike back. I recalled that gangster's name. *Marcel.* Shrugging, I decided to try my luck and see where it would lead me. Maybe hearing his name would send her packing and leave my sister alone.

Tilting my head to one side, I told her, “You know, I highly doubt Marcel would approve of you treating good people like that.” I watched as the smug look slipped away, and a look of uncertainty passed over her face. It didn’t last long, however.

Sofia folded her arms across her chest and scowled down at me. Of course, like most people in the world, she was taller than me and had the privilege of looking down at me like I was a bug under a microscope.

“Just who are you and how do you know my brother?” Sofia growled.

For some odd reason, I felt relieved that Marcel was only her brother. My thought stunned me and for a second, I delayed in my response, which only deepened Sofia’s scowl.

“Don't let her get to you, Sofia,” one of her minions said. She was the smallest in the group, but she looked older than Sofia; they all looked older than her. She was probably the youngest but held the power.

“I’m Norma Tesoriere,” I told her. “Luna and Rico are my younger siblings. You must be Sofia Johnson.” I gave her one of my most polite smiles. Sofia looked like she had no idea what to make of me.

“You didn’t answer my question. How do you know my brother?” she asked again. “As far as I know, Marcel doesn’t talk to freaks.”

“I’m sure your brother talks to everyone and doesn’t pass judgment on people,” I tell her. “You should probably borrow a page from his book.” I was aware that I was not making any sense, because I didn’t even know the guy. But something told me I was right about my assessment of him.

Sofia did not seem to agree. She laughed, throwing back her perfectly straightened black hair. Soon, there were tears springing from her eyes. “What did you say your name was again? I have to tell my brother about you. *Seriously*.”

It was my turn to turn ghost white. I felt the color drain from my face as I slowly stammered, “You don’t need to do that.” I hated the tremble in my voice. Sofia gave me an evil grin when she noticed my hesitancy.

“Go ahead,” she finally said, as she stepped out of the doorway. “It’s all yours, Norma Tesoriere,” she added, articulating my name in a mocking tone. With another bark of laughter, Sofia walked away, her minions right behind her, shooting daggers at my younger sister.

“Norma, I told you not to get involved, now look at how things escalated. What am I going to do?” Luna looked worried as we watched the girls walk away.

“They can't do anything to you, Luna,” I answered, even though I was a little worried for my sister after what I had just witnessed. “If they give you any trouble, you need to report it to the school. Tell the principal or tell Mom, or Dad.”

“You don't know what those girls are capable of, especially Sofia,” Luna said as we proceeded into the restroom. “She's the closest thing to evil that I've ever come across, that's why I stay clear of her. Anyone who crosses her path lives to regret it.”

Good Lord. How had things gone so bad so quickly? One minute, I was fighting on my sister’s behalf, the next, the entire plan was blowing up in my face. As I watched Luna, I couldn’t help but wonder what I’d gotten myself into.

So much for trying to save my sister. Now I was the one who needed saving from a gangster named Marcel.

It was just a little under an hour when Rico finally made it back to the car. I was eating a hot dog Dad had bought for me earlier when he came strolling up, his face still glowing with excitement.

Despite the whirlwind in my mind, I smiled at him. "You were so amazing out there," I gushed, giving him a big hug. Mom and Dad perked up when they saw him finally arrive.

"Thanks," Rico said. Our parents were about to smother him again, but he took a step back. "Mom, Dad, please, no. Let's just get home." He glanced around as if to make sure none of his friends were watching.

"Do you hear that? No more kisses for Mom," our mother said, but probably only half teasing. "Disappointed, but I'll be okay." I bit the insides of my cheeks to stop from laughing. Luna, who didn't care at all, laughed uncontrollably. Rico grimaced at her and shook his head. And just as we expected, he leaned over and gave Mom a quick peck on the cheek. If he hadn't pulled back quickly, I was sure my mom would have pulled him in for a hug. Rico was lucky he escaped that one.

"Don't worry, little brother. I kept watch for you. You're safe." He tried to maintain the cool guy and got in the car.

Seatbelts secured in place; Dad drove our white Suburban out of the parking lot of my former high school. For the duration of the ride home, Mom and Dad sang the high school theme song at the top of their lungs in honor of today's win. This happened after every successful game. Rico ducked his head to hide from any passer-by, embarrassed by their antics. As for Luna and I, we joined in, singing with them all the way home. I enjoyed embarrassing my brother and it was a welcome distraction from my thoughts.

The drive home should have taken about twenty minutes, but it took more like forty, seeing there was heavy traffic on the road. When we got to our house, I noticed that there was someone sitting on our porch. It was Betty Ann. I unbuckled my seatbelt and pushed open my door as soon as Dad came to a stop.

"Betty Ann, hey," I called out with a questioning tone. "What are you doing here? Is everything okay?" It was late already, and she hadn't called to say she was coming, so I was surprised that she was here.

She stood up when she saw me, her nose scrunched up as she looked at me perplexed. “We talked about us hanging out, yesterday. Remember?” She asked, placing her hands on her hips.

I tapped the palm of my right hand on my forehead. “Sorry. I totally forgot.” Stepping closer to her, I pulled her into a quick hug, then asked. “Oh, how did the meeting with Pastor Archie go?” Remembering she had gone to the church to talk to him about the upcoming talent show.

“Betty Ann, hi. How are you?” My mother questioned before my friend could give me a reply.

“I’m doing well, thank you.” Betty Ann passed her eyes over all four of us as if taking note of our dress code for the first time. We all sported two stripes of blue and white painted on both sides of our cheeks, which was the color code of Rico's team. “Another wild game, I suppose?”

“You bet,” Mom told her, chuckling. “You should have seen my baby out there. How do you youngsters say it again?” She snapped her fingers. “Right. He was on fire!”

“Mom,” Rico started to moan, his cheeks turning a pinkish tint from embarrassment. He palmed his face, shaking his head.

Betty Ann smiled. “Congratulations, Rico. You’re definitely going places. Remember me when you’re famous and playing pro-ball.”

“Thanks,” he replied, before disappearing inside. Dad and Luna greeted Betty Ann as well before they all went inside, leaving us alone.

“So, to answer your question,” Betty Ann started, “it went fine. He loved all our ideas.” She said with a bright smile.

“That’s great!” I exclaimed. I tugged at her hand. “Let’s go upstairs so we can chat more.” Once we got inside, I disposed of the uneaten half of my hot dog then collected two bottles of water from the refrigerator. I handed one to Betty Ann as we headed for the stairs.

In my room, I plopped down on my bed and took a healthy drink. When I lowered the bottle, I noticed that Betty Ann was staring at me with a curious look. "What?" I asked, wondering if something was on my face, maybe some mustard from my hot dog. "Is there something on my face?" I was already cleaning my chin before she could reply.

"No," she said, walking over to the bed. She licked her lips before sitting down beside me. "Remember that guy we saw at the restaurant? The one who was scolding that girl?"

Marcel.

His image came into my mind the instant the words fell out of Betty Ann's mouth. My heart rate picked up. Ever since that encounter with Sofia Johnson, I'd been doing my best to avoid thinking about him. That girl had threatened to tell her brother about me. I tried not to think the worst of it, but my mind had already succeeded in conjuring the worst thoughts of what could happen.

Would he really come after me?

My throat went dry. It was silly to think he would drop everything he was doing just to come looking for me, but then, the things Luna told me about Sofia flashed through my head and she looked dead serious while laying the threat. I took another swig of my water before replying to her. "Uhm, yeah. Why?" I cleared my throat.

Her brows pulled together. "I think I saw him yesterday. He was in a group with some other rough looking guys, and it got me wondering who he was to the girl and if he had hurt her. Maybe we should have stepped in and helped her. Those guys looked like trouble; you should have seen them."

"No. I found out that's her brother," I told her. Instantly, she looked at me in surprise.

Betty Ann squinted. "Really?" She raised an eyebrow in question, obviously surprised by my reply. "And how did you come by this information?" She leaned forward curiously, her body shifting fully to face me now. She was in bloodhound mode.

"All a crazy coincidence," I chuckled nervously with a shrug. The room fell silent for a few beats, as we both engaged in a staring contest until I finally sighed in defeat. Knowing she would push for more, I proceeded to tell her about what had happened earlier, right after the football game.

"What? That's crazy!" she exclaimed, after hearing the story.

"Crazy barely even covers it," I sighed. "Do you think she'd really tell her brother about me?" I thought about it again. "Maybe she was just bluffing." I hoped.

"Yeah, maybe. But then again, maybe not." She shrugged, half teasing.

"Not helping," I exclaimed, as her last words had done nothing to calm me down. Reaching for the nearest pillow, I threw it at her. Betty Ann threw her head back in a laugh and fell back on the bed.

"I know, I'm just joking. But seriously, I don't think it's anything you need to worry about. She probably just said that to look tough because her friends were watching. Forget about it." She paused and sat back up, giving me a curious look. "But I saw the way you looked at him at the restaurant. You're fascinated by him, aren't you?" Her stare dug into my soul. I flew off my bed, suddenly feeling…I'm not sure what. Awkward? I wasn't sure what to do, so I headed over to my window to open it.

I welcomed the cool breeze that gently touched my skin, breathing in the fresh air. I suddenly found interest in an old tree that had stood before my family's house for ages. While staring at it, my mind travelled back to the restaurant where I had seen Marcel for the first time.

"Norma?" Betty Ann called, pulling me out of my thoughts. "I know you heard me. I'm not wrong, am I?"

I turned to face her. "Don't be ridiculous, Betty Ann," I said. "That guy is obviously a gangster. You said yourself the other day, that he's trouble, which means he's bad news through and through. After what happened with Brian, do you really think I would be stupid enough to let myself be dragged into an even worse situation?"

Betty Ann did not respond right away. Instead, she pressed her lips together as she continued to watch me. My heart's speed kicked up another notch. Guilt swallowed me whole because deep down, I knew that Betty Ann was right. He intrigued me. Why was I so engrossed with this guy?

"Okay," Betty Ann finally replied with a nod. I forced a smile and sat back down, relieved that she would drop the topic, at least for now. Because deep down, I was scared. Not only because of what this gangster might do to me if he showed up, but also from that bubble of excitement I felt every time I thought of him.

I know I say this often but, *Help me Jesus.*

Chapter Four

Norma

There was something refreshing about spending time in the presence of God. It didn't matter what kind of problems we had to face out there, once you took a step inside, it was like being in a whole new world. At least, that was how I felt as Pastor Archie led us on another journey through God's Word that night.

The man had a way of digging deep into the endless depths of the knowledge and wisdom of God and teaching it to us, his congregants. It was one of the characteristics that made him such a fitting pastor for our little church. I took a quick glance around me. Everyone seemed to be enjoying the study as much as I was. I liked when Pastor Archie made little jokes or shared funny life experiences that tied in with his sermons. I couldn't have been any happier to have this entire group of people in my life. This was home away from home.

As always, Pastor Archie ended the night's Bible study with prayer. Usually, I would listen and agree with his prayer. Tonight, I felt the need to whisper it in my heart. Truth was, I didn't have the best day. Guilt was weighing me down more than it had in a long time, and I knew exactly why. On my way home from school, I'd spotted Brian. He had been busy talking to another girl, so he didn't see me. However, I had felt so ashamed, I'd ducked my head and whizzed past as quickly as my feet could take me.

Even though I'd already prayed a hundred and one times, begging for forgiveness, I had to do it again. I had to…

Will you stop?

My eyes flew open when I heard those words. The voice sounded like mine, but I knew I hadn't said them. With my brows pulled together, I eyed the people beside me. Their eyes were closed which meant none of them had spoken to me. Shaking my head, I closed my eyes and went into prayer again.

I'm so sorry that I messed up. I'm sorry that I didn't make the right decisions. I failed my parents, I failed myself, but most of all, I failed you...

Stop apologizing. You are already forgiven.

Just like before, my eyes popped open. Again, the voice sounded like mine. By this time, Pastor Archie had ended his prayer. "Thank you, everyone, for coming out this evening," he started to say. Then he added, "And remember, if we confess our sins, our God is faithful and just and He will forgive us and cleanse us. Good night, everyone. God bless." With a final wave, he stepped off the podium to meet and greet his congregants one by one.

I blinked at him in surprise. Like lock and key, everything seemed to click into perspective right then and there. I stared at my hands when I felt tears springing to my eyes. "Thank you, Jesus," I whispered. Somehow, I managed control of my impending tears. When I trusted myself to lift my head again, I reached for my Bible and tote bag.

Swinging the bag over my shoulder, I took a peek out the window and noticed it was already getting dark. The study had gone on a little longer than usual. But I didn't mind. I had enjoyed every bit of the study and that was what mattered. As I headed toward the exit, I took note of how much lighter I felt inside. Knowing that God had forgiven me was such a relief. But I should have known. All my life I'd been taught that whenever I confessed my sins before God, He would forgive me. Yet there was nothing like being weighed down with guilt.

It was in that moment that the image of a certain gangster resurfaced in my mind like dense fog on a cold winter morning. No matter how hard I tried to hold it at bay, it stood there, demanding my attention. I had managed not to think about him for the past hour and a half. But now that the study was over and it was time to head back home, thoughts of him were invading my world. *Again.*

My mind drifted back to the scene at my former high school. Why, oh why had I mentioned his name to his sister? Sofia's promise to tell her brother about me had me worrying all week. No matter where I went, I found myself looking around every corner and checking every alley, just to make sure I was not being followed.

It had been a dumb move to mention Marcel, and I'd regretted it every moment since. I was just relieved that school was out for the summer and Luna would not have to see Sofia and her minions for a couple of months. Perhaps by then, the entire confrontation would become a distant memory.

It had been over a week since the altercation, and nothing had happened. In addition to asking God to forgive me for what I'd done with Brian, I'd also taken the time to thank Him for keeping Marcel away from me. For more reasons than one, I needed him to stay away. I believe the main reason I'm often attracted to nonbelievers is because some of the guys in my church, although nice, were immature or not always the person they portrayed themselves to be. And I know that's wrong for me to do. I mean look at me. I make my own mistakes and bad decisions.

Each day since the confrontation with Sofia, I comforted myself with the distinct possibility that she had forgotten about me already and had not bothered to mention me to Marcel.

But what if that bear of a man was already out there searching for me? That thought sent quivers shooting up and down my spine. I vividly recalled his facial expression that evening at the restaurant. He was someone who could easily tear me apart, without hesitation. Despite my nervousness about him finding me, I promised myself that I was not going to miss Bible study, just because there was possibly a gangster out there watching me, waiting to strike when the time was right.

That night, I was going to walk home alone. Rico and Luna were out of town visiting with our aunt, mom's sister. I should have been on that trip as well, but I had a few assignments at school that I needed to complete before leaving.

As for my parents, my father was down with a cold and my mother was nursing him back to health.

Continuing to make my way to the exit, I waved to a few people here and there, pausing only twice for a short conversation. I was almost at the door when I felt a hand touch my shoulder. "Norma."

I spun to face my friend, already smiling. "Hey Betty Ann. I didn't see you earlier."

"Yeah, I came in a little late, so I sat at the back. Tough day at work. Anyway, a few of the girls and I are going on a weekend trip to Trudy's parents' vacation house. It's that beach house they have. You want to come?"

She said it so casually, but I could see the pleading in her eyes. My lips lifted in a smile. "That sounds exciting. When is it?"

"Next week. It's going to be so much fun." Her excitement was starting to slip out. My heart fell a little.

"I wish I could, but I can't," I told her. "I'm going to visit my aunt that same weekend. Sorry."

Betty Ann sighed, her shoulders slumping. "I understand. We're really going to miss you, though. Dinner was a lot of fun the other night."

"It was," I agreed. "I hope we can all get together again when we're back in town. And thanks for the invite." Overwhelmed with gratitude, I pulled my friend into a tight hug. Betty Ann let out a little squeak of surprise, then giggled before returning the hug.

"Hey, do you want me to give you a ride home?" Betty Ann asked when we broke apart. "It's close to dark out there and I noticed you came alone tonight."

I followed her gaze to the exit where the evening light was getting dimmer and dimmer. "No, it's fine. It's a nice evening out and it's only a few blocks. If I leave now, I'm sure I'll get home before it's totally dark. Thanks for the offer, though." I ignored the split-second feeling of uneasiness. Instead, I reminded myself it wasn't far. The quiet walk home would be nice.

Betty Ann seemed undecided about allowing me to walk. I expected her to demand that I get in the car, but she nodded as if coming to some resolve in her head. "Alright. If you're sure. Text me when you get home, okay?"

"Sure thing." With one last hug, she exited through the double doors, walked down the steps, and headed to the parking lot. Going in the same direction as she did, I stepped out into the evening air. I couldn't wait to be back home. I hastened my steps, wanting to be safe before it got even darker.

As I walked, I tried to focus on my schoolwork, instead of Marcel. But before heading down the street, I lifted my gaze toward the little white church that had been my place of worship for as long as I could remember and smiled. We were a small group, compared to many other churches throughout Atlanta, but this place? It was home. A sanctuary of safety. Not just for me, but for anyone who walked through its doors.

Within my periphery, I spotted Pastor Archie talking to one of our church mothers a short distance away. As if he could feel my eyes on him, he looked at me across the parking lot and I waved. He said something to the church mother, who smiled and nodded before walking off. He waved back, then started walking toward me.

"Norma."

"Pastor Archie," I replied, coming to a halt.

"You're alone tonight?"

"Yes. My Dad isn't feeling well so my mom stayed home to take care of him. Luna and Rico are out of town visiting our aunt."

"Ah." He nodded in understanding, his smile bright and sincere as usual. "I must say, I love that you're so committed to the services and growing in your faith, Norma. Don't ever lose that."

"Thank you, Pastor Archie. I won't," I replied with a grin. "I have to go before it gets darker. I'll see you on Sunday."

One more wave, and I was off, walking across the lawn and veering left toward my home. The transition between night and day brought out the natural colors of the evening sunset dancing across the sky and I took a moment to admire its beauty.

When I thought about it, God had indeed blessed me with a good life. Quite frankly, I'd had it pretty easy. I realized as well that I'd never gone hungry a day in my life. Not to mention I had the best parents on the planet. Growing up, my siblings and I had had everything we had needed.

As I turned left down another street, this one seemed a little lonely, but I didn't mind. I was in my happy place. And I found myself softly singing one of my favorite songs.

...whatever the fear...whatever the cost...You always draw near...

My words were cut off when suddenly, I felt myself being shoved by big, manly hands. The force of the push sent me crashing into the window of a car, leaving me stunned. For a moment, I was confused, unable to comprehend what was happening.

Glass shattered around me, and I felt something warm trickle down the side of my face. Blood. My blood. Before I could grasp what was happening, I felt a hand wrap around my throat. My attacker was so close to me now, I could feel his breath against my ear. My heart was pounding. What was happening? Salty tears burned their way down my face, mingling with the blood from my forehead.

Looking in the partially shattered window, the first thing I noticed was how small I was and how big he was standing behind me. Then I caught a glimpse of my attacker's eyes. His eyes were wild.

Was he high on drugs?

Jesus help me!

I'd walked this route more times than I could count, and even on the darkest, loneliest nights, nothing had ever happened to me; I always felt safe.

Fear gripped me, I tried to scream. In vain. My neck burned under his grip. I scratched him, but he slammed me hard against the car again. More blood trickled down the side of my face. My vision blurred.

"Give me everything you have. Now." He growled in my ear. I didn't get a chance to comply because another man appeared to my right and ripped my tote back from my arm. A bone popped and I was certain he'd dislocated my shoulder. The pain was unbearable. Tears spilled from my eyes and down my cheeks.

I watched the second man toss all my stuff to the ground. He snatched up my purse as soon as it fell out and my tears increased.

Just when I thought things couldn't get any worse, another guy appeared to my left. He didn't look as wild as the other two, but he was grinning, perhaps enjoying my torture. He reached for the Bible I was holding in my other hand. My heart stuttered. That Bible had been a gift from my dad for my sixteenth birthday.

Jesus. I cried inwardly. I could not believe my eyes. This could not be happening.

The man with the Bible flipped through it and his laughter grew mocking as he began to rip page after page from the book. The pain from my arm seemed to dim as the one in my insides took precedence.

Stop it! I wanted to yell at him, but I couldn't talk. The first man was still holding me hostage. He started digging through my pockets with his free hand. The distraction must have been what loosened his hold on my neck. I quickly inhaled some air before he could notice.

"I...don't...have...anything...else...Let...me...go!" That seemed to have angered him further. He tightened his fingers around my neck.

"Please. I can't breathe." The words came out muffled even to my ears. My body went into fight or flight mode. Ignoring the ache in my arm, I kicked and swung, trying to escape his grasp. My captor spun me around in one swift move before sending a huge fist into my stomach.

The pain and impact seemed to take all the air from my lungs. I crumbled to the ground in a boneless heap. Despite the pain, I tried to crawl away on my hands and knees. I felt a boot hit my ribs. My lips parted as I tried to call for help. No sound came to my lips.

My vision started to darken around the edges. Is this the night I would die? There were no witnesses.

Oh God. I don't want to die. I have dreams and plans for my life. Jesus, no, not yet. I cried.

Like a broken record the words spun around in my mind. How did I end up in this situation? Being the next murder victim.

My vision grew darker. Consciousness was slipping away from me with every passing second. I desperately tried to keep my eyes open, but I was losing the battle.

Just before my eyelids closed, I caught sight of him. As he drew closer, I recognized his bandana. My heart raced, my breathing grew more ragged. Then everything went black.

Marcel

I'd been following this girl, Norma Tesoriere, around for the past few days. It was not like I didn't have better things to do. In fact, this little activity was keeping me away from my job. But after what Sofia had told me as soon as I got back into town, I knew I had to check her out.

According to my little sister, Norma Tesoriere knew my name. She also knew I was involved in some shady business. How could she have possibly known that? We had never met before. In fact, until a few days ago, I didn't know she even existed.

At first, I had been worried she was a cop. Or, someone who was sent by a rival gang to spy on my activities. I had questions, and only Norma Tesoriere had the answers. That was, until Sofia told me she looked like she could barely crush a fly.

"She's Rico Tesoriere's older sister," Sofia had gone on to explain.

Rico Tesoriere. I knew that kid alright. He was Sofia's school's star football player. Still, I'd never met anyone in his family. There had never been any reason for it.

After following his sister around for days, I found that Sofia's assessment of her was on point. Norma Tesoriere was nothing more than a church girl. She worked part time at a hardware store and attended a local art college. Whenever she wasn't at school or at work, she was at church.

That was kind of cute and all, but what I wanted to know was how she knew my name or the things I was involved in. Based on my research, her father was a software engineer, and her mother was a housewife. They had nothing to do with law enforcement.

It was Thursday. I should have been out with some of the boys today running business errands for the boss and doing what I did best. Instead, here I was, tailing this girl like an idiot. This had to stop. I had determined that as soon as she got to the church doors,

I would walk away and never look back. I was a man of my word. Everyone knew that.

So that was what I did. I left Norma Tesoriere behind and went to meet up with the boys at Johnny's club. When I got there, they were all looking at me as if they thought I was going to blow a gasket. To be fair, I'd been in a bad mood for several days, even before returning to town.

I forced a smile, hoping it would help them relax. "What's up? Is Johnny around?" They all tilted their drinks at me in acknowledgement, but it was Danny who replied.

"Not yet. Said he wanted to see you, though."

"Of course, he does," I grumbled, waving the bartender over for a drink. Johnny had been watching me for days. In fact, he had always had his eyes on me. There was a time when I thought he did not trust me, but as time went by, I realized that he was assessing me. Though I was one of the youngest among the boys, I was one of his best.

For the next half an hour, I did my best to focus on the conversations swirling around me. Nothing registered the entire time. My mind was consumed with thoughts of Norma, an innocent church girl, who knew a little too much about me.

I was peeved. For one, I hated that this girl was invading my mental space. I also despised the fact that I wanted to see her again. I had not yet seen her face up close and that left me curious. Since following her around, I'd managed to keep a fair amount of distance between us so I wouldn't be discovered.

Would it make sense to approach her? We were from two different worlds. Surely, the very sight of me would probably terrify her. No matter, I knew myself well enough that I would not be able to put her behind me until I solved the mystery. I needed to know more about the girl, and how she knew my name.

"I have to go," I announced, standing. The conversation around me died and just like before, they were all looking at me.

"What about the boss?" Scotty asked.

"What about him?" I gritted out. He flinched a little but managed to catch himself before backing away.

"I told you, he wants to see you."

"Tell him I'll be back in an hour." I didn't bother waiting for his reply. Instead, I headed for the exit. Almost twenty minutes later, I was leaned up against the wall of a building across the street from the little white church where I had last seen Norma Tesoriere.

It seemed I returned right on time because people were starting to file out of the building. Trying not to seem obvious, I pulled out my cell phone to randomly browse apps I had not even so much as looked at before. To any passer-by, I was positively caught hook, line, and sinker by what was on my screen. But all my attention was really on that door, biding my time, just to get another glimpse of this girl.

After what felt like an eternity later, I saw her. She stepped out of the building right after a blonde who was heading for the parking lot. My feet urged me to walk up to her, but I knew better than to do something so careless. So I watched from a distance. Just as I had been doing all the previous days.

Her dress was some shade of blue, and very modest for a girl her age. For some reason, this fascinated me. I continued to watch her as she started down the steps, waving at a few of her friends. At one point, she stopped to look back at the church. That was when she was approached by an older man.

They talked for only a couple of minutes before she waved goodbye and walked away. I expected her to head to the parking lot, but she moved toward the road, veered to my right, then began walking down the street by herself. My mouth dropped to the ground.

Was she walking home by herself at this hour of the night?

This girl is crazy, I thought, frowning. Not only was she poking her nose in my business, but she also had no sense of danger. If I wanted, I could easily walk up to her and do as much damage as I desired before walking away, and no one would be there to witness it.

Silly and naïve. That was what she was. Why hadn't she let one of her friends take her home? Didn't she realize how dangerous these streets were? Irritated, I straightened from the wall, slid my phone back inside my pocket and started following her, though from a distance.

It was crazy how small she was, yet her lady-like walk made it obvious she was all-woman. I had to fight against my own need to catch up to her with my much longer legs. Her dark hair hung down to her midriff, swaying in the light wind behind her.

There was no doubt about it. Norma Tesoriere was beautiful. I didn't have to see her entire face to know that much. This little fact sent alarm bells off in my head. It was all the more reason to keep my distance from this girl. I could not allow myself to lose sight of the fact that we were extreme opposites. Day and night. She was pure, as far as I could see. I would be poison to her. Stepping into her world would only destroy her, while leaving me with more guilt than I already had to bear.

This realization made me pause. Literally. My feet came to a sudden halt, and I contemplated just walking away now instead of escorting her home. I needed to do the right thing and leave this girl alone. Still my curiosity was eating me alive. Not only that, but I was already starting to imagine all the things I would say to her, just to charm her. She looked so sweet, so innocent, and I wanted to…

"No," I scolded myself. "You need to walk away now. Walk away and don't look back." My legs grew heavy, determined to stay rooted to the spot. Still, my willpower was not so easily conquered. It took me a minute or two, but I finally got them to turn and walk in the opposite direction of Norma Tesoriere.

This was for the best. There was a gap between us that kept us worlds apart. It would have been stupid of me to try to scale that wall, knowing it was a hopeless feat. The temptation to look back was strong but I didn't. Instead, I picked up the pace.

I was almost in front of the little white church again when my breathing grew ragged. I wasn't tired and I wasn't ill. But my heart was racing a mile a minute simply because every distance I was putting between Norma Tesoriere and I was killing me.

"You've got to be kidding me," I groaned.

I had to do it. I had to go back and talk to her. It was the only way that I was going to satisfy this attraction to her. Maybe after meeting her, that longing would wane. She was a church girl after all. There couldn't possibly be anything about her that could keep me interested.

With that resolve, I headed back in the direction I had just come from. It didn't take long for me to get to the street where I had left her earlier. As soon as I turned the corner, the sight hit me, I almost staggered to my knees. Shocked at the scene in front of me, my mouth fell open. That feeling was instantly overcome by fury. With my hands balled into fists, I bolted across the street toward the terrible scene playing out before my eyes.

Norma was on the ground, curled up in a fetal position. There was a guy standing over her, kicking her. Two other guys were standing there as well, one rummaging through her bag while the other was ripping apart some book and snickering. I came to a sudden halt, realizing that I knew these guys.

The Rioters.

I knew right away that this was not a fight I belonged in. Even so, this was an innocent girl. The rage I was feeling was too much. Before I could talk myself out of interfering, I rushed toward the idiot who kicked her in the stomach. Grabbing him by the throat, I squeezed. Hard.

He looked at me then and that was when I noticed how vacant his eyes were. This guy was high as a kite. With every ounce of strength I had, I tossed him against the wall of a nearby building. Though he was twice her size, I was bigger. He was no match for me. He went flying into the wall with a crunch, then crumpled to the ground, unconscious.

Gone was the humor from his friends. The other two glanced at each other, fear seeping from their faces. The one who was ripping Norma's book cleared his throat. "You're Marcel, one of Johnny's boys," he started. This surprised me, though it really shouldn't have. I had a reputation out there, after all.

"If you know that, then you should be running, not talking," I told him. His gulp was audible. The other one standing beside him scowled at me.

"We're from the Rioters," he growled. "Our gang and yours have a peace treaty. Now go and mind your own business."

"She *is* my business," I said, then glanced at Norma on the ground. She was bleeding from her forehead and her nose. She was also pretty much unconscious. An image of my sisters flashed in my mind, and I saw red. The third guy pulled a blade from his waistband, clearly to prove his point. What he didn't know was that I'd defeated men who'd had guns pointed at my head. A knife was the least of my worry.

Before he could swing the blade at me, I landed a solid punch in the centre of his face. Just like his other friend, he crumpled to the ground, his blade clattering on the concrete beside him. Before I could take a hit at the last man standing, the coward dropped Norma's purse and ran, leaving his buddies behind.

I could have gone after him, but I was too worried about this girl to even consider it. Kneeling beside her, I pushed her hair aside, and caught a good look at her face. Though bleeding and starting to bruise, she was enchanting, just like I'd imagined. Full lips, a small delicate nose and long lashes that fanned her high cheek bones. She was a vision.

This wasn't the time to think about that, though. She needed a doctor. Fast. I reached out to check her pulse. It was weak. But I'd been grateful when I found she had one. Seeing as I was a person of interest to the cops, there was no way that I was going to make a call to the authorities from my own cell phone. There was only one way that I could help her.

Snatching up her phone from the pile beside her, I dialled the number for the ambulance and left the line open. In a couple of minutes, this place would be crawling with cops. It annoyed me that I had to leave her there alone on the cold pavement. But there was nothing that I could do about it. If the cops saw me, I would most likely be arrested. With that in mind, I pulled away from her and headed across the street to hide and watch from an alley.

Not too much time passed before Norma was placed on a stretcher and lifted into the ambulance. As soon as the ambulance took off for the hospital, I slipped further into the darkness away from the flashing lights.

When my phone began to ring in my pocket, I didn't have to look to know that it was Johnny. More than likely, he had already learned about what had happened with the Rioters.

I knew this wasn't going to end well. But honestly, I couldn't get myself to care. Norma Tesoriere had needed me, and I had helped her. If Johnny didn't like it, I was prepared to face the consequences of my actions.

Chapter Five

Marcel

Why are you going in there? This is a terrible idea...

In spite of my self-admonishment, and the reprimand I'd gotten from Johnny, my feet still took me right through the glass door of the hospital entrance. After, I'd forgotten most of the obscenities Johnny had shouted into my ears the moment I stepped out of his house. Then walking into the hospital, I ignored all the voices in my head telling me to turn around, but I was too stubborn for my own good; I wasn't going home.

Norma.

I would never understand the feelings she stirred up in me. If someone had told me a year ago, or ever for that matter, that I would someday find myself chasing after a church girl, I would probably have laughed hysterically and called it garbage. I needed to stay away from her. I *should* have stayed away from Norma Tesoriere from the start. I'd left my boys in a risky spot with the Rioters because of what I'd done the day before.

Two of their members, the ones I'd beaten up, were in police custody. They were still lying in the spot I had left them when the cops arrived on the scene. This made the Rioters' boss Toby furious, and he laid his complaints on Johnny. That, in turn, infuriated Johnny, though I got the feeling his anger was directed more at the Rioters than at me. He did not take kindly to threats, especially when it was coming from an inferior rival. Still, it would have been smart to stay away from this girl. Getting too close to her could potentially put her in harm's way, but then, the other night had proven that maybe that was the only way to keep her out of danger. I felt trapped between conflicting interests.

I paused in my steps when I saw the nurse at the front desk. I wondered if she would call me to question me. I looked down at my clothes. They weren't that bad, though my tattoos were visible, and I knew I put off a certain vibe, one that was mostly frowned upon. Luckily, she got distracted by an elderly man dressed in a black suit, who had just arrived at the desk. Seeing as she was busy answering the man's question, I took the chance.

Just five minutes. I just want to make sure she's okay.

This was what I told myself as I walked past the front desk. Since the incident last night, sleep had completely eluded me. Whenever my head touched my pillow, thoughts of Norma clouded my mind. I kept wondering if she had regained consciousness yet. Even my mother noticed that something wasn't right, but I couldn't bring myself to tell her that the cause of my sleepless night was a girl whom I had never even spoken to in my life. A girl who I had been following around town like a dog on a leash.

As I walked, I realized there was no point in stopping to ask where her room was. Since I wasn't family, that information would not have been divulged to me. In fact, one look at me and they would have been convinced that I had been involved in the attack that had put her there in the first place. Security, or more likely the police, would be called to take me out before I could say another word, and I couldn't leave until I had laid my eyes on her and seen that she was alright.

I got strange looks from people I passed. I creased my lips and faintly shook my head as a woman eyeing me pulled her son closer to her, protectively. The little guy peered up at me with curiosity, then offered a big smile, showing me his full teeth, as he waved wildly. This small gesture warmed my heart; children really were precious. Before I knew it, I was smiling and waving back at him, until his mother noticed it. This time she grabbed his hand and walked to another area to sit. I sighed and continued to walk down the hallway. As I did, I took random peeks into different rooms, hoping to find her.

The first room looked like a party room. A teenage boy was lying on the bed surrounded by his friends who were laughing and joking while eating fries out of a brown bag. In the next room an elderly woman was sleeping. I nodded at anyone who looked my way, putting on the best smile I could summon to try to make them feel comfortable in my presence. After roaming the halls for about ten more minutes, I almost gave up on the task.

"Where are you, Norma Tesoriere?" I murmured to myself. I was starting to think I was in the wrong hospital or something. Was it possible that there had been no room available for her, so she had been transferred elsewhere? Maybe she had never been brought here in the first place, but I decided to look around, just a couple more rooms.

I came to a door at a dead end and stopped. I was about to palm the wall closest to me out of frustration when I glanced through the glass window in the door beside me. I sighed, relief washing over me. There she was. She was wearing one of those white hospital gowns, her dark hair spreading all around her like a halo.

Her eyes were closed, and it made me wonder if she was still unconscious or just sleeping. A woman was sitting at her bedside, clasping Norma's hand in her own. The other hand was in a cast. I remembered how bad the arm had looked when I had seen her lying on the ground. I groaned, hating myself for having taken so long to get to her the previous night. I never should have walked away in the first place. I'd thought leaving her would be the best option, yet the result was this.

It did not take any stretch of the imagination to know that the woman at her bedside was her mother. They had the same dark hair and petite figure. I noticed her mouth was moving. At first, I thought she was talking to Norma. Then, I noticed that her eyes were closed. This woman was praying. An odd sight, though I already knew they were Christians. I couldn't recall ever seeing my mother pray.

After a while, Mrs. Tesoriere opened her eyes. I could see she had been crying. She placed her daughter's hand back to her side; she stood, leaned over, and ran her fingers through Norma's dark strands. She mumbled something to Norma, then kissed her forehead. With that, she straightened up and started heading for the door.

My heart jolted in my chest. On quick thinking, I turned and knelt down to fiddle with my perfectly tied shoelace to avoid any suspicion. It seemed to have worked because Mrs. Tesoriere moved down the hall without a second glance at me.

I straightened myself as soon as she turned around the corner, and I pushed open the door to Norma's room. She was in the same position her mother had left her, still as a statue. Beat up as she was, Norma was still a sight to behold. Her dark lashes were naturally long and laid against her olive cheeks with perfection. Her lips, though dry, were pink and full. She had high cheekbones fitting for a model, not a simple church girl. Since her eyes were closed, I couldn't tell what color they were, but I imagined them to be dark or some shade of brown, since she was of Sicilian descent. Until the night of the attack, I had never gotten this close to her, and even then, there hadn't been time to admire her beauty.

I looked down at the frail but gorgeous figure lying motionless on the hospital bed. The cut on her forehead was stitched together, reminding me of the awful ordeal she'd gone through. My gaze dipped lower to look at her neck. There was a handprint there, purple green and ugly looking. A new wave of fury filled me. My fists tightened at my sides as I scowled at the marks.

I should have done more than knock that lowlife unconscious. I felt disappointed in myself for letting go of him just after a single hit. I would have loved to see him beg for mercy. He should have gone through twice what this innocent girl had. How could a man beat up a woman like that and live with himself? I just couldn't comprehend it.

A gasp registered through my rage, and my eyes lifted back to Norma's eyes. I was stunned to meet a pair of the most magnificent hazel eyes looking back at me. My throat went dry. She was awake. Just when I thought she couldn't look any more beautiful than she already was. I stood still, not knowing what to do. I had come all the way here to see her, but I hadn't thought this through. In fact, I'd been glad when I'd seen she wasn't awake yet, because then no words would be exchanged. Even though I'd imagined and wished for this moment, I still didn't know what to say to her.

At first, her eyes were unfocused, disoriented, like she was still trying to figure out if she was dreaming. But as the seconds ticked by, recognition showed in her gaze, as realization seemed to hit, and a huff escaped her lips.

"Please don't hurt me again." she whispered, her voice so low, I could barely catch her words. It was obvious she was struggling to speak.

Her words stunned and confused me. Perhaps I hadn't heard her correctly. Hurt her *again*? I threw my head back. She thought I did this? As if in slow motion, her eyes widened. Wincing, she struggled to push herself up on one hand, trying to pull away from me.

Without thinking I reached for her. With fear in her eyes, she looked at my hands on her shoulder in shock, then back at me. "Hey, relax. If you keep doing that, you're just going to hurt yourself more." I tried to calm her down.

Norma ignored my words. She coughed slightly, still trying to push me away. "It was you," she whispered. "I saw the bandana and I…" Her voice trailed off, she looked around the room, eyes coated in panic as she seemed to be looking for someone to help her. Although I'd hoped this wouldn't happen, I had somewhat expected it. I couldn't bear to see her so frightened of me. I needed to assure her I would never do anything to hurt her. I also couldn't be here for much longer; I didn't know where her mother had gone, and anyone could walk in at any minute.

I took hold of her good wrist, making sure not to add too much pressure. She jumped when she felt my touch. I thought she would snatch her hands from mine, but she kept still, looking at me with fearful eyes. She looked so fragile it broke me inside.

I gently massaged her wrist. It had been the first time I'd touched a woman like this. Her low whimpers brought me back from admiring her pure beauty. I cleared my throat. "Norma, it's okay. I'm not going to hurt you. You're in a hospital. I just came by to check on you and make sure you're alright." I paused, then added with a grimace, "You identified me just by my bandana?" I still found it really surprising, but then, it was a bandana I wore almost everyday. She must have seen me with it before.

Her lips trembled as she opened her mouth to speak, but when no words came out, she stared down at our hands which were still locked together. "Please don't hurt me." She murmured once more.

My heart ached each time I heard it. I shook my head. "What are you talking about? I didn't do this."

She raised her head. "How do you know my name?" she asked, stuttering a little in her words.

"My sister told me." I answered, holding her gaze. Her eyes widened even more when she heard me mention my sister. I didn't know much about what had gone on between her and Sofia, but knowing my sister, I assumed the exchange hadn't been exactly pleasant. If I heard she'd been mean to this beautiful girl, Sofia would be getting a piece of my mind later.

"Your sister?" she asked almost inaudibly. I was only able to catch the words because I was staring at her beautiful lips.

"Norma." I whispered gently. "It's okay."

She raised her head once more, looking into my eyes. "I'm sorry I ever mentioned your name," she said quickly, tears crowding her now glassy eyes. She turned to look at the emergency button signalling for the nurse, but seeing it was too far for her hands to reach, she turned back to me. "Please, don't."

I'd saved her life, yet she thought I'd orchestrated the attack.

Don't hurt me again, echoed through my head.

"No, no," I said, ready to defend myself with every part of my being. "Norma, I didn't do this to you." I tried to caress her hand with my thumb, but she snatched it from me and tried to move away. The little hospital bed restricted her movement, and she had no choice but to listen as she wasn't strong enough to get out of it yet. I reached for her hand again; this time she didn't pull it away.

"I saw you. You were with them—"

I interrupted her. "No," I shook my head. "I saw the men attacking you and ran to help you; I was the one who called the ambulance."

"You…you helped me?" She spoke the words slowly like she was still wrapping her head around what I had just told her. "Those men...the ones who attacked me, they don't...they don't work for you?"

I shook my head. "No, they don't. Two of them are in police custody at the moment, and one got away, but I'll make sure they never lay a finger on you again," I promised. "I wish I hadn't left you that evening. Maybe if I had intervened earlier, those guys wouldn't have hurt you. I'm going to let you go now," I told her. "No more flailing. I don't want you hurting yourself." She blinked up at me with those wide, innocent eyes and then shook her head. Trusting she would do as she was told, I let go of her, then took a small step back. I realized that I had been a little too close, I didn't want her to feel like I was crowding her. She didn't want to be anywhere near me, and I totally understood why.

Norma's lips parted. I waited in anticipation for more of her words, but only a hoarse, dreadful sound escaped her this time. She rubbed her throat with her good hand, wincing. I cringed. That had to be painful. Forget hurting, I should have just killed that guy and been done with it.

Glancing at the nightstand by the bed, I found a glass of water sitting there. I reached for it and brought it to her lips. "Small sips," I instructed her. "You don't want to make it worse." When I was satisfied that she'd had enough, I pulled the glass away and put it back on the nightstand.

"Better?" I asked.

"A little." The gruffness was still there, but at least this time her voice did come out.

"Good." That look of skepticism was still in her eyes. I waited, knowing the questions would come.

"How did you find me?" she asked. My brows lifted.

What exactly was I going to tell her? Give her more detail about how I'd been stalking her since the moment I'd laid my eyes on her? How I had gone off to gather any information I could on her, or the feelings and desires that rose each time I set my eyes on her? I couldn't tell her that. If I did, then she would see me as nothing more than a creepy stalker. Frankly, I was already feeling like one.

I nervously scratched the back of my head, trying to avoid her eyes as she peered up at me, still waiting for my answer. I folded my arms across my chest with a shadow of a smile on my lips. "I have my ways," I said simply.

She scoffed. "I'm sure you do," she replied. Even though she was no longer backing away from me, the mistrust was still evident in her eyes. I hated that.

"Don't worry, I'm not your enemy," I tried to convince her one more time. "I have no reason to hurt you." Then, without being able to keep the words inside my heart, I softly added, "I would never hurt you."

She held my gaze. I could see the wheels turning in her mind.

I suppressed my smile. Despite her apprehension, I needed to find out how she knew my name and what kind of things I was involved in. I took a single step forward before going on, my voice lowered. "Since you're not well, I won't demand anything of you right now, but when you get better, I'm going to need you to tell me exactly what you know about me and how you came by that information. Do you understand?"

Norma swallowed hard, as her eyes filled with fear again, like a steel band, wrapped around her. It was not my intention to scare her, but if that was what it took to find out what I needed to know, I was not going to back down.

"Good, I'll leave now." Unable to resist, I ran the back of my hand down the side of her face, once again noting how smooth and perfect her skin was. Replacing the fear, a blush crept up her cheeks. It only made her more mesmerizing than she already was.

"Wait," she said, reaching out to grab my hand just as I was about to go. "Why did you save me?" She let go of my hand once I was facing her again.

Why did you save me?

"What do you mean?" I asked.

"I mean, you could have turned a blind eye. You don't need to say it for me to somewhat understand what kind of man you are and since you..." She pursed her lips. "I just never expected such an act of kindness from someone…well…like you. I thought you were out to hurt me. I just want to fully understand why you did...why you helped me."

I understood where she was coming from. I was the guy that had put many people in a hospital bed and had driven a few almost to the point of death. But I still had a heart and no matter the things I'd done, I still cared. Especially when it came to innocent women and children. It was my weakness. I had no pity for men who hurt innocent people. I wouldn't think twice about dealing with them.

If these guys ever did touch Norma again, I'd make sure pain would be the last thing they would ever feel.

I blinked, coming out of my thoughts. Then I realized she was still staring at me, waiting for an answer. "I just had to," I told her. It wasn't the best answer, and she was probably expecting more than those four words, but she looked satisfied with it. I was grateful she understood that I wasn't willing to say more, because that might have somehow led to these uncertain feelings, I had brewing for her. She didn't need to know until I knew exactly what they were.

She gave a small smile, "Thank you," she said.

I hoped she didn't see how pleased I was to hear those words. Like I needed anyone's acknowledgement or gratefulness. I knew she still didn't completely trust me and the only reason she hadn't reached for the call-button was because she knew I was the one who had helped her. "You're welcome."

I straightened up. It was time for me to go. Turning on my heels, I headed for the door without looking back. If I stayed in that room another minute, I was going to do something stupid, I was certain of it.

Like kiss Norma Tesoriere.

It was a fantasy that had been playing over and over in my head. I felt the burning desire to know how her lips would feel, taste, move against mine. Yet I feared I would never know. But for now, at least, I could leave with the satisfaction that she was alright. This wasn't the last time I would see Norma Tesoriere. I knew that for sure. I didn't know when our next encounter would be, but our paths *would* cross again.

Just as I stepped out, I ran into a girl I had seen outside the church the previous day. I was grateful I'd left as soon as my instincts had told me to. If I had stayed a little longer, she would have probably walked in on me kissing Norma. She stared at me, slowing down her pace. A series of emotions passed over her face.

Shock. Confusion. Fascination. It looked as though she wanted to say something but decided against it. Then, with quick feet, she hurried past me and slipped into Norma's room. Could this get any more interesting? I couldn't wait to have that conversation with Norma Tesoriere.

Norma

Don't worry, I'm not your enemy. I have no reason to hurt you. I would never hurt you.

Marcel's words replayed in my head like a scratched record. It was hard to wrap my mind around the idea that he had been my guardian angel, not one of my attackers. This was the man who had caused me to live in constant fear for the past couple of weeks, wondering if he would come out of nowhere, and do God only knows what, for having mentioned his name to his sister.

He'd come like I'd thought, but had saved me instead, something I had least expected.

My lips curved up in a small smile. Just then, the door to my room flew open, and my best friend appeared. "Oh my gosh, you're okay. You scared me." I cringed at how loud her voice was. Marcel had only spoken to me in gentle tones. My ears were not prepared for the sudden change in volume. She walked over to me, leaning down to embrace me. I groaned as pain shot through my body. "Oh, I'm so sorry," she squealed, letting go of me instantly. "I hope I didn't cause too much pain?"

"It's okay," I croaked out. Betty Ann winced at the sound of my voice. I couldn't blame her; I know how horrible my voice sounded.

Betty Ann's face was suddenly set in a deep frown. "Next time, let me give you that ride, crazy girl." She scolded, waving her index finger before me. “I thank the Lord you're alright Norma. You could have been…” she paused, clearly finding it difficult to complete that sentence.

Killed. I finished for her in my head.

This thought made me shiver. An image of what my memorial service would look like flashed through my mind. I could already see my parents and siblings drowning in grief. A part of me wished I could turn back the hands of time, and I would have followed Betty Ann to her car when she had offered.

Betty Ann shook her head as if to rid herself of the horrible thought, then sat beside me in the chair next to my bed. “Anyways, where’s your mom? I thought she’d be here.” She said, as she looked around the room.

I shook my head, indicating that I had no answer to that question. I had woken up to Marcel.

Betty Ann nodded. Her eyes faltered a little before lifting to meet mine again. “I saw that guy from the restaurant just now. He walked past me in the hallway leading to your room. You wouldn’t know anything about that, would you?” She inquired.

I feared the questions would start coming. So, I asked her, “Can you please get me some water? My throat hurts.” I didn’t need it, since Marcel had taken care of that earlier. But honestly, I didn’t want to talk to Betty Ann about him. I hadn’t even started to figure out this guy for myself yet. Not only that, but my heart kept pounding in my chest whenever I heard his name, and it wasn’t only from fear—at least, not anymore.

Marcel wasn't who I had pictured him to be. He seemed to have two sides to him. I thought he was still involved in questionable business. An image of the first time I had seen him raced through my mind. He had looked so terrifying then. But the guy I had seen here today, the one who had caressed my hand so gently and spoken to me so softly, he made my whole insides feel as though they'd been invaded by butterflies. That Marcel was the one who had saved me.

"Okay," Betty Ann replied, getting up from the bed. She snatched up the small cup that Marcel had handed me earlier. She walked over to the small pitcher tucked away in a corner and filled the cup. When she handed it to me, I took small sips like Marcel had instructed earlier. For the entire time, I could feel Betty Ann's gaze burning a hole into my skull. I knew she was waiting for me to finish with the water so she could finally get her answer. But that wasn't going to happen today.

I placed the cup back on the nightstand. "I'm glad you came, Betty Ann, I really am, but I'm tired. Could we talk about this later?" I hoped she wouldn't push further. My throat was still hurting. It felt like someone was gently poking my vocal cords with needles each time I spoke.

She sighed, the questioning look on her face disappearing. "Hmmm," she murmured. "Of course, but only because you're not completely healed yet. And from how bad your throat sounds, I'm sure it's painful." She hesitated then added, "Well, I'm looking forward to this." When I met her eyes, there was that familiar look of determination sitting there.

Great. Now I had two persistent people bent on plucking information from me. Suddenly, the prospect of a speedy recovery seemed less appealing.

Chapter Six

Norma

Today was the day. The day when I finally got to leave the hospital. My excitement knew no bounds. Even though it had only been a couple of days, I was already over and done with this small, confined space as well as the smell of antiseptics akin to hospitals. I needed fresh air. I was also desperate to sleep in my own bed. Honestly, I'd sleep on anything soft and comfortable, rather than the hard bed my butt was on. Not to mention, I missed my friends and, most importantly, going to church.

"You're free to go," the doctor informed me after checking my vitals again. Doctor Garcia reminded me of physicians you might come across on television. He had that perfect smile. The one they gave you even when they knew you were probably about to die anytime soon. Luckily, death wasn't knocking on my door. My mother sighed in relief. The doctor turned to my parents. "Keep an eye on her and let her rest for a few more days. No overdoing it."

Mom nodded in response, while my dad stood there, lost in thoughts. When the doctor was finished with his instructions, my parents pushed me out of the small hospital room. Sitting in the wheelchair I was told I had to leave in, I said my silent goodbyes to the nurses by smiling and waving at them. I didn't want to worry my parents by the strange sound of my voice. I had made friends with a few of them who had checked in on me.

Outside, a bright sun and a soft breeze greeted me. I wished I could spread out my arms and just dance under the sun, but I wasn't quite feeling up to that yet.

"Easy," my mother said as I stepped into the car. I smiled at her, reassuring her I was okay. Dad started the car, and we began our journey back home. It was a quiet ride, as I was supposed to rest my voice for a few more days. My parents didn't do much talking either. The few times Dad spoke, it was to apologize for not having been there to protect me. My mother kept throwing occasional glances my way, no doubt still worried. I didn't like that my dad was beating himself up over something he couldn't have known was going to happen. I was actually the one to blame. I wished I could turn back the hands of time, shove down my stubbornness, and accept Betty Ann's ride.

But at the moment, my mind was stuck on a certain gangster. I had expected him to visit me again at the hospital, but he hadn't. I wanted to see him again, talk to him, and ask him questions about the night I was attacked. Like why he was there. There were parts of the ordeal that remained a blur to me. Although, maybe it was best I forget about the assault. Maybe then the nightmares would stop, and I could just move on with my life.

When we finally arrived home, my mother beat me to the door handle of the car before I had the chance to reach for it and open the door myself. She reached out a hand to help me and I took it, not wanting her to feel bad. To be honest, I was already feeling overwhelmed by my parents' constant attention, but I didn't complain. They were both just upset by my near-death experience and loathed the idea of ever leaving me alone again.

Given the beating I'd received, one would have thought my body was more broken than it actually was. But the bruises on my body and throat, the two cracked ribs, as well as the broken arm, were not the only things I had to be concerned about. These nightmares were horrible.

My left arm was to be confined to a cast for the next couple of weeks. Thankfully, my right arm was unharmed. I would still be able to finish up my assignments for school.

"Take your time," Mom said as she led me to the front door of our home. Again, I didn't complain. After all, my body was still sore. The only reason the pain was bearable was because of the medication still pumping through my system.

When we got inside, she led me to the couch and directed me to sit. I did as I was told. My dad came inside right after, his hazel eyes filled with sadness. "Oh sweetheart," he started once again. "I'm so sorry. I hate that I wasn't there to defend you." This was at least his tenth apology since the day had started. He'd been miserable at home with a cold and fever while I was out there getting beat up. He seemed to think that it was his fault that I was attacked. I could never blame him, or anyone else for that matter. Those guys were the ones at fault, and they were the only ones who deserved to be punished for what they had done. I admit it hadn't been my wisest decision to walk the streets alone at night.

Not wasting any time, mom headed for the kitchen to make me a fresh pot of chicken soup. Soon enough, the house was filled with the heavenly scent, and I found my stomach twisting in knots, begging to be fed. I was grateful when she finally brought me the bowl. I was about to take it and feed myself, but my mother wouldn't have it.

"No need for that, *bambina*," mother said. "I will take care of you." She beamed, though dark circles were still lining her eyes. It felt ridiculous to let my mother feed me. But if it eased her conscience, I would agree to it. Now more than ever, I was glad that Rico and Luna were not around.

My mother kept up a steady chatter the entire time. Problem was, I was getting tired. As soon as I took my last spoon, I leaned back into the couch and closed my eyes.

"Don't fall asleep just yet. You need to take another dose of your medication." I listened as my mother shuffled around to gather the pills and water from the kitchen. In another few seconds, I was shoving them in my mouth and forcing them down my throat. It took a minute for them to go down, but I managed to swallow them, though they left behind a nauseating taste in the back of my throat.

I detested taking pills.

Once they were down the hatch, I stood. "I'm going…" My mother lifted a hand to stop me from speaking.

"*Bambina*, you heard what the doctor said. No talking." She wrapped a hand around my waist. "Let me help you to your room."

Together, we walked up the stairs and down the hallway to my bedroom. Once inside, I kicked off my shoes while my mother peeled back the comforter. I slowly sat down on the bed, careful not to aggravate any of my injuries. I sighed burrowing my head deeper into my pillow. I'd missed my bed, my room, the familiar surroundings, all of it.

Mom brought blankets to cover my battered body then kissed my forehead. At the age of twenty-one, I was being tucked in by my mother. Who would have guessed?

"I can't tell you how grateful I am that God sent a Good Samaritan to help you that night. I just wish he hadn't run off so I could properly thank him for defending you." She smiled, running her hands through my hair. I could feel my cheeks burning red as they heated up from the thought of Marcel. I turned my face away, hoping she wouldn't notice.

Sorry, mom, he couldn't stick around. He's a gangster.

Of course, I didn't say that out loud. Maybe there was some good to not being able to talk for a while. I was certain Mother would want to know how I knew that much about my rescuer.

"And you'll be happy to know," Mom continued. "That two of the men who attacked you were arrested. Apparently, the man that protected you gave them a taste of their own medicine and left them unconscious beside you."

I nodded to acknowledge her words. She patted my hand and said, "Alright then. Get some sleep. I'll wake you up when it's time for dinner." I mouthed a thank you to her then closed my eyes.

As soon as she left the room, my eyes popped back open. I stared at the ceiling above me while my mind filled itself with thoughts of grey and black bandanas. Though I knew he was dangerous, for some reason, I wanted to see him again. He had been kind to me at the hospital. He was also demanding me to answer his questions. He wanted to know how I knew about him.

What exactly was I supposed to say to that?

The realization hit me that I didn't have to respond to his questions. I was out of the hospital now. As far as I knew, Marcel had no idea where I lived. He wouldn't be able to find me—but a little part of me wanted him to, maybe because I wanted to see his face again, hear his voice. I wanted him to check up on me once more.

My throat started to go dry as I recalled his dark, dark eyes, and how they had pierced through my very soul. I'd found other guys to be attractive in the past, but not like this. Every time I thought about this guy, my heart would jolt out of place. And it was strange because Marcel was a criminal. I was a Christian girl. This kind of attraction not only went against common sense, it went against biblical principles too. And yet, it was like invisible arms wrapping themselves around me with no intention of letting go. What would Pastor Archie think if he knew? What would my dad think? I supposed he would more than likely have a heart attack.

Guilt washed over me.

I needed to forget Marcel and any kind of romantic thoughts concerning him. After what happened with Brian, it was ridiculous of me to even consider these feelings. This was going to end now. I was a strong girl, and I was not going to let these emotions control me. I needed to get a grip on my heart. Christian girls didn't fall in love with mobsters.

With that resolve, I closed my eyes and forced myself to get some sleep.

My slippers made a flapping sound as I made my way downstairs. Halfway down, the smell of breakfast hit my nostrils. My feet took me straight to the kitchen, where I found Dad finishing up his meal, while Mother was cleaning up.

"Good morning." I chirped, feeling cheerier than I had in a long time. Both my parents glanced up, surprise in their eyes. They looked at each other, then back at me.

"Good morning. How are you feeling?" Mom asked, dropping the rags she was holding, she cocked her head a little to the right, observing me. "Maybe you shouldn't overdo it with your voice," she said in a concerned tone. "You don't want to hurt yourself."

"It's been a week, Mom," I reminded her. "My voice is doing fine. In fact, I'm starting to feel much better." The only thing that was still quite sore, were my ribs.

Mom didn't look convinced. "Maybe I should take you back to the doctor, just to make sure everything is healing up as it should."

I chuckled. "Mother, stop. I'm fine, really." Though I appreciated their concern, it was overwhelming. Just because of that, I acted extra careful in everything I did, just not to cause them worry.

Marissa Tesoriere lifted both hands in defeat. "Alright, alright. But if you feel any pain, tingles or whatever, please let me know. I don't want you overexerting yourself before the time."

"I will, I promise." To reassure her, I gave her one of my brightest smiles. She seemed to relax a little, going back to her cleaning.

Dad rose from his chair and pulled me into a hug. "Forgive us if we're smothering you. We're just worried about you."

With my head against his chest, I replied, "I know."

Luna had been dying to come home since hearing about my accident. She was worried about me. However, my dad had made it clear that she and Rico were to remain at our aunt's house until further notice. According to Dad, there had been an uprise in violent crimes in the area. He was concerned that our once quiet community was being pulled under by ruthless people. It made me think of Marcel. What was he involved in?

Until Dad figured out what was going on, he was not going to let them return. Rico, of course, didn't mind. He seemed to live in his own little world these days. Luna, on the other hand, was losing her mind.

"Dad is being paranoid," she had said this morning when we had last spoken together over the phone. "Those guys must have just wandered into the neighborhood."

That was my thought as well, but I knew better than to try to convince him. He needed to do what he could to protect his family, and I was not going to stand in his way.

"Since I'm starting to feel better, I'd like to go see Aunt Mariana," I told my parents. "I'd love to sit and paint on the beach again."

Aunt Mariana, my mom's older sister, lived on Tybee Island with her husband, Uncle Tony. She was a successful artist. I had lost count on the many pieces of art she'd sold over the years. She was my hero and the painter I wanted to be like in a couple of years. Oddly, she and my mother didn't seem to get along, and for the life of me, I could never understand why. Though my mother wouldn't let that stop us from seeing our aunt.

"Yes, that's a good idea," Dad replied. "Since you're feeling better, you should go."

"Thanks Dad." I lifted myself on my tippy toes to kiss him.

I was about to get myself a fresh plate of ham, eggs, cheese, and toast, but my mother beat me to it. I thanked her, grabbed myself a cup of coffee, then headed to the table. Where Dad was just about to finish his food.

"I'm off to work now." He planted a quick kiss on my forehead, and another much longer one, on my mother's lips.

"Have a great day at work, *mi amore*," Mom told him before he dashed out of the house. The food before me was divine, simple as it was. There was something about good food that always seemed to brighten one's day. I didn't even realize I was done till I had taken the last bite.

My mother looked over at me when she heard me let out a little burp. "Would you like more?" She asked as I reached for the glass of water on the table.

"Nope. It was delicious but I'm stuffed." I told her, bringing the glass to my lips.

"Good," she said, smiling. "Listen, I need to run a few quick errands this morning. I won't be long. Why don't you start packing for the trip to your aunt's? I'll drive you down to Tybee Island tomorrow."

I cringed. In times like these, I regretted that I'd refused to take driving lessons. Even though Mom was a housewife, she was busy all the time. Having to drive me to Tybee Island was going to steal a big chunk of her day. There was nothing I could do about it now, though.

"Okay," I replied. "Do you need any help at the store? I could come with you if you want." I asked, although I already knew the reply I was going to get.

"No." She waved a dismissive hand. "Finish your coffee and, if you can, pick out the clothes you need help packing. Do not overdo it. Your body still has a lot of healing to do."

Right.

After completing her morning routine, she grabbed her purse and headed for the door. I moved to put my plate and cup in the sink, then headed up the stairs to start packing. When I opened the closet, it seemed to contain more clothes than I'd realized. It was hard to pick out what I wanted so I opted to pull everything out one at a time and lay them on my bed. The first thing I selected was a yellow sundress that my mother had purchased for me a year ago. It was soft, light, and bright which was perfect for the summer. Still on the hanger, I held it in front of me and turned to face the mirror.

"That color suits you," I heard from behind me. I gasped, my heart slamming into my ribcage. Turning at the speed of light, I faced the last person I expected to see, standing there, on my balcony.

Marcel.

The dress fell to the floor. "How…how did you get up here?" I stammered.

"Did I scare you?" he asked, grinning. "I wanted to use the front door, but it appears you have surveillance cameras around the front and side of your house. I didn't think you'd want your parents to see me standing on their front porch."

The first thing I noticed was that he hadn't answered my question. I walked across the room to the balcony and glanced down. "You didn't climb all the way up here, did you?" I asked, turning back to face him.

"Of course, I did." He shrugged. "It's much easier than it looks, trust me." His eyes strayed to the pile of clothes on the bed. "What are you packing for?"

I followed his gaze to the pile. "I'm going out of town for a few days," I told him.

"Where are you going?"

"Tybee Island." I regretted my answer as soon as the words flew out of my mouth. Why was I even answering his questions?

It was none of his business where I was going. As much as I had wanted to see him, I said, "You shouldn't be here."

"I told you I'd be back, didn't I?" Marcel said. "Are you ready to answer my question?"

I did my best to mask my nervosity with fake boldness. Lifting my chin up in defiance, I said, "I'm not obligated to give you any answers. You need to go. My mom is going to be back soon." With my false confidence, I headed back inside the room to continue my search and finish packing. I hoped he would leave the same way he had entered before my mother arrived.

Marcel said nothing. He remained on the balcony, his arms folded across his generous chest. Despite his silence, his presence was so large and imposing it was hard to ignore him. I could feel his intense gaze on me the entire time. Only a few seconds back into my packing and I couldn't take it anymore. My fingers started to shake under the intensity of his gaze.

I could barely fold my clothes. I pretended to act like his presence didn't affect me, but that wasn't fooling anyone.

I marched back to the balcony. If he wanted to know, then I would tell him. "Look, I saw you a few weeks ago roughing up some guy in the parking lot of the restaurant where my friends and I were eating. I also saw you come into the restaurant looking for Sofia. I heard when she called you Marcel. That's how I knew your name. Are you happy now?" I placed my hands on my waist, looking up at him.

Slowly, a smile crept up his full lips. "So, you were watching me?" His eyes twinkled mischievously. My face burned with embarrassment, but I kept my chin up.

"You weren't exactly quiet. And you're one to talk," I threw back at him. "You're the one who's been following me around and *that's* creepy." I didn't add the fact that he was currently trespassing. "Seriously, you have to go before my mom gets back."

“Hmm. Is that any way to treat a sinner?” Marcel asked. “Shouldn’t you be introducing me to Jesus, say a prayer with me, or something like that?” This caught me by surprise. He must have seen the change in my mood because his smile slipped. “Hey, relax. I’m just teasing you.”

My lips quirked up in a half smile. “Yeah, you’re right. I should be introducing you to Jesus.” A thought popped in my head and my smile widened. I hadn’t thought of it before, but he had been the one to bring this up. “Would you like to go to church with me on Sunday?”

He looked confused for a moment. “I thought you said you’d be out of town?”

I flushed crimson. “Of course. Silly me. I almost forgot about that.” I rubbed the back of my neck, laughing nervously. “But I’ll be back home in about two weeks. You could go without me. I could tell Pastor Archie to expect you. He’s a wonderful man. He would take good care of you.”

He made a 'tsk' sound. “Uh, sorry, sweetheart, but that doesn’t work for me,” Marcel stated. “The only reason I’d ever go in the first place is to see you, so going while you’re not there would be an utter waste of my time.”

I dipped my head to hide my blushing face. “Marcel, whatever you’re thinking, it’ll never work.” My voice was small, vulnerable even. I had to make it clear to him. I was no fool to see that Marcel had some interest in me. A month ago, this would have scared the heck out of me, but now, I was almost flattered. For someone like me to have caught his attention was something I didn't understand. We were both from opposite sides of the world.

He kept quiet briefly, watching me, then asked, “Why?”

My head shot up. “What…?” I asked, stunned.

“Have you ever had a boyfriend?” Marcel inquired.

Did he really just ask me that...? He was still staring at me, waiting for an answer. “That’s none of your business,” I said, trying to avoid his eyes.

“Has anyone ever told you that you look stunning? I can barely keep my eyes off you.” His voice dropped low, and he took a step forward. We were now standing close to each other. He touched my cheeks with the tips of his fingers, and like an idiot, I felt myself leaning into it. I couldn't help it, his fingers brushed against my skin ever so gently, stirring up weird fluttering in my heart. It scared me, but at the same time I craved for more. “So beautiful,” he whispered, his words sending tingles through my ears to the back of my neck. I shivered.

Warmth spread to my cheeks. “Thank you,” I said quietly.

“Has anyone ever kissed you?”

I blinked in surprise. Another brazen question. “What?” I shook my head. “That’s none of your business either.”

“I bet you’ve never had a boyfriend, and no one has ever kissed your gorgeous lips,” Marcel went on, answering his own question. “You blush every time I ask you something.” There was no doubt in my mind that I was getting redder than the roses in mom’s garden. I opened my mouth to protest but then closed it again. I couldn't find the words to reply to him. How could he say stuff like this without even flinching?

Reality hit when I heard my mother’s car pulling up in the driveway. My heart started pounding in my chest as panic kicked in. “Oh my gosh. That’s my mom. You really have to go, Marcel.”

“How old are you, Norma?” he asked.

“Twenty-one. Why?” I didn't see how my age was important at that moment. I'd only responded thinking he'd budge after getting my answer, but he stood his ground.

“You’re old enough to bring a man home if you want, you do know that, right?” he said. I shook my head and rolled my eyes.

"Look, we come from two very different backgrounds," I explained. "It seems the way things work where you come from isn't the way it works here. I can't just take a boy home to my parents. It doesn't work like that." Inwardly, I cringed, remembering when my mother had walked in on me and Brian.

"I didn't say a boy. I said a man." His grin spread across his face. I eyed him from head to toe and back up again.

"You're a big guy, but I'm sure you're not that much older than me."

"Twenty-five," Marcel informed me. "Last time I checked, that's the age of a grown man." I stared at him for a beat as I registered his reply.

"Sounds to me like you had to grow up pretty fast," I told him.

He looked at me with a penetrating gaze before answering, "You have no idea."

The front door slammed shut and I knew my mother was already inside the house. "Norma," she called out. Pressing my small hands into his chest, I ignored the feelings that arose with the feel of the hardness I felt beneath his shirt and pushed him toward the edge of the balcony.

"Marcel, please. You have to leave." I begged.

He grabbed hold of one of my hands, which was still on his chest. "When are you leaving for Tybee Island?" he asked.

Why did he care? "Tomorrow. Now will you please go?"

He tilted his head a little to the right in thought. Then looked back at me, a mischievous smile on his face. "I'll go..." I sighed in relief when I heard that. "If you give me your number," he stated matter-of-factly.

I glared, but I knew it would do nothing to get rid of him. I stretched my hand out for his phone and he pulled it out of his pocket, unlocked it and slipped it between my fingers. I hit the screen aggressively as I typed the digits. I then proceeded to add my number to his contacts in less than twenty seconds, then handed the phone back to him.

"Now go." I demanded, pushing him again. Marcel only chuckled.

"See you soon, beautiful." With that, he stepped over the balcony and crawled down to the ground in record time. For such a big guy, he moved with the agility of a cat. It was fascinating to watch. As soon as his feet hit the ground, he glanced up at me, winked, then hurried away, disappearing through the garden.

Just then, the door to my room swung open, and my mother walked in. I turned to face her and found her watching me curiously. "What are you doing, *bambina*? I thought I heard you talking to someone."

"Oh. No," I lied with an undertone of fear. I didn't want to know what my mom would do, if she found out "a man" had been in the room with me. "I was just thinking out loud while packing, just like you asked me to," I told her, waving a hand at the pile on my bed. Mother's lips widened and it made me feel terrible lying to her.

Just then she lifted a shopping bag in my direction. "Bathing suits," Mother said, beaming. "I saw them and thought you might like them."

Translation: I went to the store specifically to buy you these because I couldn't help myself.

With a grin, I told her, "Thanks, Mom."

"You're welcome." Turning on her heels, she made her way back out of the room. I strode over to my open suitcase to toss the bathing suits in but stopped short when I spotted a dark brown Bible exactly like the one my attackers had damaged, sitting in one corner of the suitcase. My brows pulled into a frown. I remembered the sound of the pages being ripped out one by one and the sight of them falling to the ground like dead autumn leaves—I shook away the thoughts of the horrors of the night. My concern now was the Bible in my suitcase.

Where did it come from?

I took one more step toward the suitcase as my curiosity grew. Picking up the Bible, I realized it was new. I opened it to the fly leaf at the front where my father had written a lovely note on the copy he had given me.

There was a note in this one as well, written in beautiful cursive handwriting. The note simply said,

Norma,
I hope this makes you happy.
M.

"Marcel," I murmured. He had done this. He had gone out of his way, just to get me my Bible back, it wasn't the one my father had given me, but the gesture touched my heart just as much. It was really sweet of him to have done this. Despite his appearance, he seemed to have a good heart.

Unable to help myself, my face broke out into a smile. Marcel was getting to me even faster than I could have ever imagined.

Chapter Seven

Norma

The journey to Tybee Island turned out to be more exciting than I had expected. Even though thoughts of Marcel filled my mind almost the entire time we were on the road, I still enjoyed the bits of conversation I had with my mother. She'd been on a roll since we'd left the house. She told me about our neighbor and his constant war with his wife's old dog, and another neighbor down the street who was always singing at the top of her lungs. She even shared little snippets about the basketball game that the neighborhood kids played just a couple of blocks away from our home. Even though she barely understood the game, she always brought the kids little treats whenever she could.

It was unlike her to talk this much, as she was usually very reserved. This made me realize that she was nervous about letting me go from her sight. Of course she would feel this way. It was motherly instinct. Still, I was excited to finally be here. I was looking forward to having so much fun with my aunt.

"Well, we're here." Mom announced when we pulled up to the three-story Mediterranean house that belonged to Aunt Mari. I exhaled, delighted that we'd finally reached our destination. I couldn't wait to see my siblings. As soon as I stepped out of the car, my little sister bolted in my direction and threw herself into my arms. Never had I been so grateful that I was no longer in terrible pain. I wrapped my arms around her to tighten the embrace. I missed her so much.

"Ah, you missed me, I can tell," I said, giggling. She pulled out of my hold, nodding.

"More than you know," she exclaimed. "I've been so worried about you, and Dad wouldn't let me come home." She frowned. "It was so frustrating. How are you feeling? Oh no, I hope I didn't squeeze too hard? Did I hurt you? I'm so sorry." Ignoring my shaking head indicating I was fine, she kept on throwing questions at me. "Tell me how you feel."

Luna was talking a mile a minute. I laughed, shaking my head. She had always been the genuinely caring one who wasn't afraid to express how she truly felt. My brother, on the other hand, was like a mystery box. He kept things to himself a lot now, so it was hard to tell how he was truly feeling; he was nonchalant about most things. "It's okay. I'm fine. And I missed you too." I looked up, searching for my brother. "Where's Rico?" I asked, looking past Luna to the house. The closed doors prevented me from seeing in.

"I don't know," Luna replied, shrugging as her eyes traveled to the house, then back to me. "Probably somewhere moping around. He's been so weird lately. I don't know what's wrong with him."

Luna's shocking revelation about our brother hiding his relationship with God from his friends came back to mind. With all that had happened in the past couple of weeks, I hadn't been able to talk to him about it. But now that I was here, I was sure there would be time for that. My brother was obviously going through a rough patch, and as his big sister, I believed with all my heart that it was my duty to help guide him along as well as I could. He was a good kid at heart, I knew that, even if his actions spoke otherwise.

"Give him time. He'll come around." It was all I could think to tell my little sister. She mumbled a 'mmhmm' in the back of her throat before taking one of my bags from my hand and throwing the single strap over one shoulder. Right at that moment, the front door opened and the boy in question materialized in front of us, dressed in tan shorts and a white shirt.

Luna crossed her arms in front of her. “Speaking of the—”

“Luna!” I scolded her before she could finish. I didn’t have to look at her to know she was pouting. When Rico drew near, he ignored Luna and pulled me into a comforting hug.

“I’m glad you’re alright, sis.” He frowned and his lips pursed. At that moment, he looked so much like our dad. Though still young, Rico was turning out to be a fine-looking man.

“Thanks, little brother,” I said gratefully.

I heard the car door open then slam shut, suddenly remembering I had rushed ahead leaving Mom. “I’m doing well, too, thank you. In case anyone would like to know,” Mom commented, walking towards us.

Luna broke into laughter. She threw herself at Mom in much the same way she did me earlier. “Hello mother, glad you’re here too.”

“Thank you.” Mom said as they pulled apart. “At least someone appreciates my presence.” She eyed Rico, obviously waiting on him to give her a hug as well. He shook his head, knowing the jab was for him.

“So dramatic,” he mumbled under his breath before giving her a quick hug.

Luna walked up to her side again. “Are you staying with us Mom? I’m bored with grumpy Rico, who has been no fun might I add—” He shot her a look, but she ignored him, “and Aunt Mari is always busy painting,” Luna added.

Mom gave her a sad frown. “Uh, no *tesoro*. You know I can’t stay. I have to get back to the city to take care of your father. We don’t want him burning down the house now, do we?” She let out a chuckle as she lovingly patted Luna on the cheek. “Now wipe that pout from your face. You have Norma now; she will keep you company.” I raised my hands in a cheer, trying to make Luna laugh.

"Not really," Luna whined. "You and I both know Norma will be painting the whole time. It's probably the main reason she's here. She'll be with Aunt Mari in her studio the entire time. I'm sure if she had a bathroom and some food in that studio, she wouldn't step out at all." I chuckled because I knew she was right. "I still won't have anyone to talk to."

Rico sighed. "Maybe you should get out more and try to find other little whiny girls your age," he suggested, his tone dripping with sarcasm.

Luna was about to give him an earful, but the sound of approaching footsteps stopped her. We all looked up to see Aunt Mariana emerging from the house. As expected, she was covered in paint from head to toe. I dashed in her direction. It had been so long since I had last seen her and I had terribly missed her and her crazy stories. Her grin a replica to Mom's, she spread her arms wide to welcome me into a hug.

"Aunt Mari, it's so good to see you," I squealed. "I've missed you."

"Likewise darling." Aunt Mari replied. She held me out at arms' length and eyed me up and down. "Ah, even more beautiful. You must have all the boys back in Atlanta falling over themselves in front of you." I giggled, even though this wasn't the first time I'd heard these words from her. If only she knew that I'd taken after my mother and was living a pretty reserved life. Well, until lately.

"Don't be ridiculous," Mom said, furrowing her brows. "Norma is a good girl. She's focused on her studies and her faith."

"That doesn't mean she can't have a boyfriend," Aunt Mari retorted. "Tony and I dated while we were both in college and that never interfered with my education, or my relationship with Jesus for that matter."

"We both know Norma is not like you. Just because you chose to live your life down that road doesn't mean my daughter has to follow you," my mother shot back. Aunt Mari broke out in eccentric laughter.

"Oh, little sister," Aunt Mari said. "You've always been strung so tight." She let go of me and hugged my mother. Mom returned the embrace, but it was obvious she was still irked by Aunt Mari's boyfriend comment. I cringed inwardly. After Brian, I was sure my mother wasn't remotely interested in the idea of me having a boyfriend. And given the kind of men I found attractive these days, she would more than likely pull her hair out.

Luna and I glanced at each other, without saying a word. None of us understood why their relationship was so strained. Sure, Mom was a by-the-books kind of person while Aunt Mari was a world of beautiful chaos. It was hard not to enjoy her company. Mom had always disliked that her older sister was a rule breaker and had always warned us never to pick up that trait. 'Just because everyone is doing it doesn't mean it's right.' She would always say.

"I should get going," Mom said, when the embrace broke. "I have a long drive back into the city."

Aunt Mariana scoffed in disbelief, "Oh no you don't," she told her, shaking her head stubbornly. "You're not going anywhere until you've had lunch with us. I know you're in a hurry, but stay, just for lunch, please." I knew Aunt Mari only added the last word because she knew my mother was just as stubborn.

"Yeah, Mom, you should stay," Luna pleaded.

She hesitated, looking like she was going to say no, but in the end, she sighed and nodded in agreement. Aunt Mariana clapped her hands emphatically, like an excited little girl. This little gesture brought a smile to my mom's face. "Wonderful. Let's go in, shall we?" Rico reached over to help me with my bags before we headed for the doors.

As we walked into the spacious three-story house, I took notice of the many new paintings hanging on the wall. Aunt Mari was a professional painter, so I didn't expect anything less. They had increased since the last time I visited. A piano was standing at the other end of the bright and open room. I took in all the beauty around me. I couldn't help but notice how much more American than Sicilian Aunt Mari sounded. Unlike my mother. While Mom would occasionally speak Italian, Aunt Mariana hadn't used as much as a single Italian word in all my years of knowing her.

My siblings and Mom chatted with animation, while Aunt Mari and I went into the kitchen and made lunch together.

"You should go sit with your mom before she leaves," Aunt Mari suggested. I immediately shook my head. I loved this lady and enjoyed her company. She never missed a chance to talk about when she was my age, and I enjoyed her stories even though they were about things my mother wouldn't be happy about her telling me. Like her first *real* kiss, and some of her bizarre friends and the crazy things they had done together. It reminded me of my friends and I, though in my case we hadn't even done a quarter of the things she mentioned.

Soon, lunch was ready. It was a delicious mix of crab sandwiches with fruit drinks. "This is so good, *sorella*," my mother told Aunt Mariana as she took a bite of her food. "You always know how to make a mean sandwich," Mom complemented taking another bite.

"Thank you," Aunt Mari replied.

"So, Norma, will you finally tell me about the attack?" Luna asked out of the blue. I winced a little, avoiding her gaze. I'd just arrived, and the attack was the last thing I wanted to talk about, especially while eating lunch. I hoped Luna would understand that it was still a sensitive topic for me.

"*Bambina*, I'm certain Norma doesn't want to talk about that," Mom said, answering for me. "She just arrived and is tired."

"Right. Sorry." Luna deflated like a hot-air balloon, letting out a puff. When she glanced in my direction, I mumbled a swift, *we'll talk later*. That seemed to brighten her mood a little and she nodded. This reminded me that Luna had always been the curious one. At a really young age, she was already asking questions that those her age wouldn't even have thought about. It was why she was so smart. Sometimes it surprised me.

While we enjoyed lunch, we talked about several random things. By the time lunch was finished, Mom realized more than an hour had passed. She stood and attempted to take the dishes to the sink, but Aunt Mari waved her off. "Leave those. I'll take care of them."

"Okay," Mom replied, though she was still looking at the plates. "I suppose I should hit the road now. Lunch was wonderful. *Grazie, sorella.*"

"Any time, little sis." Mom frowned, disliking the endearing term. She never liked when Aunt Mari called her that. I knew Aunt Mari was aware of it, but it didn't stop her. Though sometimes it looked like my mom and Aunt Mari had the relationship of a cat and dog, they still held strong love and care for each other. She gave us all a final hug before heading for the door.

"Call me when you get home," I told her before letting go.

"Will do." She responded.

We stood outside, watching her walk to the car. After she climbed in, we waved again. Barely a split second after Mom drove off, Luna dragged me up the stairs. She only let go of me once we were standing in my room. "Will you please tell me everything now?" she started. She wouldn't even wait for me to rest my head or my food to settle. "I can't take the wait any longer. I need to know exactly what happened. And who is this mystery protector of yours that Mom keeps talking about?"

"Oh. That." An image of my Bear came to mind.

Whoa. My Bear? Really, Norma?

"Uh-oh, I know that look," Luna commented. I scolded myself mentally. Marcel was getting to me. I couldn't even control my thoughts about him. My cheeks were turning red too quickly and

I felt like my body was giving me away, betraying me. But Luna, just like Betty Ann, could always tell when I was keeping something from her.

"Spill. Now."

With a sigh, I flopped down on the bed in the center of the room. She followed me and taking a seat next to me, her eyes wide with anticipation. Since resisting was useless, I decided to just rip the bandage off.

"It was Sofia's brother. Marcel." I studied her face to see her reaction. It was just like I had expected, absolute shock.

Luna's jaw fell open. "As in, Marcel?" She asked in a fierce whisper.

"Yup." I said it so casually like it wasn't a big deal, even though just a few weeks ago, I was going crazy from the thought of him; I wasn't fearful of him anymore, though I couldn't say I fully trusted him—not yet.

"I…I don't understand," she stammered. "How…how is that possible?" Before I could reply, something clicked in her. She snapped her fingers, her mouth open. "Sofia?"

"Apparently, our little encounter with his sister did reach his ears," I explained. "He'd been following me around for a couple of days. That's how he ended up witnessing my attack and coming to my rescue."

She frowned. "That's kind of creepy, him following you around. You should be careful," Luna said.

"I know. That's what I said too. But...," I shrugged.

She gave a sad smile. "Still, I'm glad he was there. God knows what would have happened if he hadn't intervened."

I shook my head. "Honestly, I'd probably be dead," I told her, my voice dropping low. "Luna, it was awful. The guy who kicked me, it's like he was out of his mind. I thought I was going to die that night and..." I couldn't even complete my sentence as my voice failed me.

Tears welled in her eyes, reflecting my own emotions. She threw her arms around me and pulled me close. I relaxed in her warm embrace; the hug was just what I needed. When she pulled away, she announced, “We should go to the beach.” This was her way of moving past the retelling of my experience that night. She was always the one to think positive, washing away all the negativity and bitterness of the past. “It will be fun,” she said.

“Haven’t you had enough of the beach already?” I laughed, happy with the new mood that had awakened in her.

She gave me a look full of disbelief. “How can you say that, Norma? You can never have enough of the beach,” Luna replied. “It just doesn’t happen.” With that, she dove for my suitcase, dragging it to the bed and began rummaging through my stuff. “You did bring bathing suits, right? Please tell me you at least brought more than one.”

“You’re not going to try to dress me, are you?” I asked eyeing her suspiciously.

She laughed, refusing to look up as she continued to go through my clothes. “Of course not. Honestly, I’m looking for something I can wear.”

I wanted to laugh, but I scowled at her, pretending to be annoyed. “Little sisters. Always stealing your stuff.” Ignoring me, Luna continued to dig for her prize. I doubted I would ever get the swimsuit back if she found one she wanted.

With every stroke of my brush, the trials of the past few weeks seemed to dissipate into nothing. In this world, I was at peace, and nothing could break me away from my happy place. Aunt Mari was just as lost in her painting as I was in mine, and I didn't have to look at her to know this.

It was the day following my arrival and we were seated in Aunt Mari's home studio, where it was white, bright, and just overall ideal for painting. This was my favorite place in the entire house. Our model was lying still as a statue on the off-white couch in her silver dress, gazing out the window.

She was the perfect model. Her thick, dark hair was glossy, and just about flawless in the light of the sun coming through the gigantic windows. She had the fullest, reddest lips I'd ever seen, and her eyes were the color of a green meadow. She held that look I'd seen so many times on popular celebrities on television. Confident, courage, and charm. They were her weapons and she knew it.

The painting session was one of the many reasons why I loved going over to Aunt Mari's. It was her job to paint beautiful pictures, and she allowed me to sit in and paint with her, I felt honored. She would evaluate my work and give me pointers to improve. I was both excited and nervous about what her thoughts would be this time.

My aunt was a much better painter than I was. She was a professional after all, with years of experience I did not yet have. She had helped me a lot, since the first time I had sat down beside her to paint. Through the years, I'd progressed greatly.

"Alright, let's take a break," Aunt Mari announced.

"Uh-huh," I answered, without stopping. The model, on the other hand, was happy to oblige.

"Thank you," she said in a thick Russian accent as she shifted out of place to stand up. I was a little annoyed that she'd moved, I had just been working on her eyes, but I knew she was only following directions. I withdrew from my half-done painting and straightened myself. My aunt was already standing behind me.

Her face remained impassive the entire time so I couldn't tell what she was thinking. Aunt Mari had perfected the act of masking her true feelings from onlookers. If she hadn't been an artist, she could have been an actress. The longer she was silent, the more I became nervous, wondering whether I'd done a poor job of it. My work, though not yet completed, was looking pretty good in my eyes, but I still needed Aunt Mari's opinion and approval.

"You've improved, Norma," she finally said. I sighed with relief, only now realizing I had been holding my breath while waiting for her response.

"You really think so?" I asked with a bright smile.

"I do," Aunt Mari stated. "Last year, you were so focused on making your paintings perfect, you didn't give room for your creativity to bloom. Now you're more relaxed with your strokes. Not afraid to capture flaws where they lie. This is good."

"Thank you. You have no idea what that means to me."

"Believe me, I do know." She chuckled. "Now, go on, take a walk, stretch your legs, and have a drink or something. I'll call for you when I'm ready. I need to use the little girls' room." With a sassy smirk on her face, she headed for the exit. I chuckled, shaking my head at her. With one last look at my painting, I stood and left the home studio.

Downstairs, I retrieved a fruit drink from the refrigerator, slipped on my sunglasses, and started for the door. The walk along the beach was wonderful. Luna and Rico were already at the beach enjoying the water. The moment I started my walk, I spotted Rico in the distance, surfing with some of the local boys. I couldn't see Luna yet, but I was certain she was somewhere close by.

I wasn't sure how long I had been strolling, but the moment I spotted an empty bench, I perched on it, crossing my legs. The wind on my face was delightful, in contrast with the blazing summer heat. In my old jeans and blue camisole, I probably looked like a mess, but I didn't mind. It was the ideal outfit for painting.

Slurping on my drink, I closed my eyes and rubbed the back of my neck with the palm of my hand to alleviate some of the tension sitting there.

"May I join you?" a familiar voice asked.

Startled, I almost jumped out of my own skin. I opened my eyes and glanced over my shoulder to find Marcel standing there. I choked on my drink, and nearly fell off the bench, but steadied myself quickly.

"Careful now," he said, reaching out. "We don't want you hurting yourself."

I blinked twice, making sure he was really standing there next to me. "Marcel. What are you doing here?" I asked.

He had the audacity to look a little bashful. "Funny story. I was in the area, actually." He circled the bench and came to sit beside me. "What's this?" He reached for the drink in my hand and took a generous sip. "Hmm. It's good. Did you make it?" he asked. I looked from my drink in his hand back to his face. The whole thing felt surreal. First thing, I hadn't thought he would know where my aunt lived, but he apparently did. And then, I'd thought I wouldn't see him for a while, yet here he was, right beside me.

Questions were the only thing spinning around in my head. Why was he here? How had he found me? And why was he still holding my drink?

"Norma?" I blinked, realizing he was still waiting for a reply.

I had to think back to remember his question. "Uh, no. My aunt did." For the entire time, I couldn't stop staring at him. My Bear looked even more breathtaking than the last time I'd seen him, though he was only wearing simple black jeans and a white shirt. As usual, he had his bandana tied around his crown, giving him that fascinating look that drew me in. He smiled. He was so handsome. How was I going to resist him with this amount of charm?

Stop, Norma. Stop it right now!

I tore my eyes away from him before he could pull me in any further. A few more seconds, and my eyes would have been forever glued to him.

"You look like you've just seen a ghost," he said, gently touching my cheek with the back of his index finger.

He'd totally distracted me. I shook my head to gather my thoughts. "Are you still stalking me?" I asked. He blinked a few times, as if surprised by my question.

"No, not at all. Why would you think that?" he asked with a growing smile.

"I don't believe you," I said.

He chuckled. "I know that's how it looks but the truth is, I came here for a job. I remembered you said you'd be on Tybee Island, so I thought I'd come look for you."

My eyes narrowed. "What kind of job?"

"Sorry, sweetheart, but it's not anything I can discuss with you."

"Do you kill people for a living?" The words flew out of my mouth before I had a chance to stop them. I almost slapped myself for asking that, because I wasn't even expecting an honest answer. To my surprise Marcel broke into a deep quiet laughter.

"What if I did?" he asked, smiling sheepishly. I stared up at him. What exactly was I supposed to say to that?

"I don't know what you expect will happen between us, but whatever it is, it's never going to." I finally said.

Marcel turned slightly to face me; his dark eyes locked on to mine. All humor was gone, replaced by something I couldn't define. "Do you think so?" he asked tenderly. "I haven't been able to stop thinking about you, Norma, and I know it's the same for you."

My heart sputtered inside me. He was right. It was the same. Still, he didn't need to know that. I was determined not to give in to his charms. "You're a little full of yourself," I commented.

"I can tell you're attracted to me," he said simply, waiting for my reaction.

I let out an ungraceful snort. "Even if I was…" I paused, lifting a finger to correct myself, before I said something that could later be used against me. "…but I'm not, just so you know. That doesn't mean I should be around you. You need to go. You shouldn't have come here."

"So, you don't want to see me? Don't deny it, because we both know that would be a lie."

"Norma!" Aunt Mari's voice rang.

My heart leaped to my throat when I heard Aunt Mari calling my name. Whipping my head around, I spotted her in the distance coming toward us. "Oh my gosh, this can't be happening," I groaned running my hands through my hair as I sought for a plan. Turning my attention back to Marcel, I found him still watching me, unconcerned about the woman approaching us. He was too comfortable for my liking. I glared at him, expecting him to leave, but Marcel continued to look calm. I wanted to jump to my feet and meet my aunt before she could reach us, but that would draw too much suspicion.

"You have to go. Now." I repeated, praying he wouldn't be stubborn like last time.

"It's a little too late for that, don't you think?" he said. "Your mom is on her way over here. She's already seen me. If I go now, it'll look like you're doing something wrong. You wouldn't want that right?"

Begrudgingly, I had to admit that he was right. Aunt Mari had already spotted us. I could already hear all the questions she was about to fire at the man who was sitting beside me, so calm and collected.

"That's not my mother. It's my aunt," I corrected. My brain felt like it was running on a treadmill, groping for ideas to explain this. But I came up empty.

Marcel's face registered surprise. "Oh. She looks just like your mother. But now that I look again..."

"Sisters." I filled in for him. "They're sisters."

When Aunt Mari finally caught up to us, her eyes wandered over to Marcel. She eyed him with such shameless curiosity that I wanted to run and hide. I waited for her to say something, but she was too busy observing Marcel. "Well, well," she finally started. "Who is this handsome young man, Norma?" My mouth fell open, but no words came out.

"Umm…this is…ahh…"

"Hi, I'm Marcel," he said, interrupting me. Jumping to his feet, he held out his hand to Aunt Mari, who grinned from one ear to the next as she took his hand.

"Pleasure to meet you, Marcel. I'm Mariana, Norma's aunt, but you can call me Mari."

"Nice to meet you, Mari," Marcel replied. "And please, forgive me if I was imposing on your time with your beautiful niece." I rolled my eyes mentally. Here he was, acting like such a gentleman. Aunt Mari glanced at me, her face alight with a huge grin.

"You didn't tell me you made a new friend, Norma." I could feel my cheeks heating up, and it wasn't from the sun hanging above our heads.

"Umm, Marcel is from Atlanta, actually," I explained. "That's where we…uh…met."

"Atlanta?" Aunt Mari pressed, surprised. "What are you doing all the way out here then?" There was a gleam in her eyes that didn't sit well with me. Marcel, on the other hand, laughed. He seemed to be enjoying himself.

"I came here for a job," he said, giving her the same bogus story.

"Hmm," she murmured, her knowing smile not faltering for even a second. Obviously, she didn't believe him either. I was about to tell her Marcel needed to go when she suddenly asked, "Would you like to join us for lunch?" My mouth open. I'm not sure why her invitation surprised me. Aunt Mari was easygoing and chill, I should have known she wouldn't let Marcel leave without luring him in to eating with us.

"No." I blurted at the same time he said, 'Yes, I would love to, thank you.' My stomach churned.

"Good." Aunt Mari said. "Lunch will be served in the next half hour. Don't run away, Marcel."

"I'll be there," he promised her. With a smile and a wave, Aunt Mari headed back to the house, no doubt to make something extra fancy for Marcel. Problem was, she had no idea who she was about to feed. But I knew. Turning my attention back to him, I gave him the most intimidating glare I could muster.

"What do you think you're doing?" I all but growled at him. Marcel, undaunted by my outburst, took a step toward me, closing the already meager distance. He reached for a lock of my hair and tucked it behind my ear.

"I'm trying to get the girl," he whispered, staring into my eyes. His words sent shivers down my spine. But like the proper girl I was, I still resisted.

"That'll never happen, Bear," I whispered back. Marcel pulled away to look at me.

"What did you call me?" he asked.

Only now realizing what I'd just said, I flushed crimson. I stared at my hands as humiliation washed over me. With his index finger, he slowly lifted my chin.

"What did you just call me, Norma?" he asked, searching my eyes.

"It's kind of embarrassing...and stupid." Pulling my chin out of his hold. I tried to avoid his eyes, but he held my eyes to his.

"Try me." He was now standing so close I could feel his breath on my lips. I knew he'd heard what I'd said, he just wanted to hear the words from my lips again.

I sighed in defeat. "Bear," I said, looking straight into his eyes. "I called you Bear, okay?" He stared right back in silence, waiting for me to continue. "You're a pretty big guy and when I saw you for the first time at that restaurant, it was the first thing that came to mind. Bears are magnificent creatures, but they're so…big and dangerous…like you."

By the time I was through, Marcel was grinning from ear to ear. "So, you think I'm magnificent, huh?"

I had to close my eyes. Did he just ignore the other part of my explanation and focus on the part that pleased him the most? "Seriously, was that the only thing you heard coming out of my mouth?" I asked in disbelief.

"Pretty much," he said. I chuckled, but there in the back of my mind, I knew I was playing with fire. This had to stop here and now. As if he could sense my resistance, Marcel said, "Don't."

I backed away from him. "I meant what I said. It will never happen." I expected him to step into my space again. Instead, he took his own step back. I looked up at him, thinking this was him giving up. But his eyes were lit with more determination than I'd ever seen in someone.

"Maybe," he said, handing me back my drink. "But I'll never stop trying."

Chapter Eight

Marcel

Mariana's house was nothing short of a mansion. No surprises there. While walking to the house together, Norma had mentioned that her aunt was a successful artist. The three-story structure was mostly white with more windows than I'd ever seen in one house. I didn't know much about art, but I assumed it was to accommodate enough lighting for Mariana's work.

The moment we walked in, we spotted Rico sitting on the couch, munching on a bowl of chips. Dorito's if I had to guess, while watching TV. When he recognized me his eyes instantly went wide.

"Hey," I greeted in a friendly tone, trying to be a good guest.

The bowl almost fell from his hand, but no words came from his mouth. I could only imagine how his heart was threatening to escape his chest, with the way he looked at me. I guess he recognized me then. I wasn't surprised though.

I watched his initial shock turn into abrupt anger. He glared daggers at me. If looks could kill, I'd be in a pretty bad situation. His eyes told me he wanted nothing more than to toss me out of his aunt's house.

"Hey, are you okay?" Norma asked when she caught the look on her brother's face. He didn't get a chance to reply before a pair of feet came rushing down the stairs. A girl who looked almost exactly like Norma at first glance, made her appearance. The closer she got, the easier it was to spot the differences. It was obvious this one was younger.

I assumed this was Luna, Sofia's classmate. She was a pretty little thing with those big, curious eyes and jet-black hair cascading down her back. Still, she had nothing on Norma. She was just as shocked as Rico, minus the hostility. I didn't get much of a smile from her either. It was more wonder, curiosity.

"Oh, you're finally here," an excited voice said.

I whipped my head to the right to find Mariana waltzing in from the kitchen. She patted my hand with a bright smile. I sighed in relief. At least someone actually wanted me in the house and was excited to see me and it made me feel comfortable. "Kids, this is Marcel, Norma's friend. He'll be having lunch with us today. Marcel, this is Rico, and this is Luna. Norma's brother and sister," Mariana introduced.

I didn't have to look at Norma to know she was blushing; it was her habit to blush at even the smallest thing. It was cute to witness her innocence. I had never met a girl who blushed as much, especially at her age. It solidified my perception that she was the real deal. She was pure. For some reason, this excited me more than it should have. Deep inside, I knew I should leave her alone. But no matter how hard I tried, I couldn't go a day without thinking about her.

Was it crazy to believe in fate? Was it crazy to believe that Norma and I were actually destined to meet? Though we both came from different walks of life, what if everything had been aligned by some divine power? These questions haunted me every night as I lay awake in my bed, thinking about her. The more I tried to run away from her, the more I felt pulled closer by some force I didn't fully understand.

"Good to meet you both," I said with a nod in their direction. Luna stepped forward with a gleam in her eye and offered me her hand. As I took it, I realized Norma had told her about me. At that moment, it was easy to reciprocate her smile.

"Nice to meet you, Marcel." She said giving me a telling look. I made a mental note to ask Norma later what exactly she had shared with her little sister. It was the way she had said my name and, I hadn't missed the look she had given to Norma. There was something and I was sure of it.

To my surprise, Rico rose from the couch and stepped forward to shake my hand as well. I hadn't expected that from him at all, seeing that the anger was still simmering in the depths of his eyes, but no one else seemed to notice.

"Welcome," was all he said before trying to pull his hand from mine. I tightened my hold as a means of letting him know I had my eyes on him. His already brown eyes seemed to go a shade darker. I had to give it to the kid. He had spunk. More than his family could ever imagine.

Norma moved closer to me once Rico had stepped away. "Are you ok?" I smiled at her and nodded. I wasn't sure if she wanted me here, but it felt nice to have someone inquire after my well-being for a change. "Yeah, I'm good. Your siblings are nice." I told her. Luna was pleasant but I couldn't say the same about Rico.

"Shall we eat?" Mariana asked, a few seconds later. "I'm finished with the cooking."

"Yay," Luna said. "I'm starving."

Norma left to assist her aunt, while Rico sat back, meeting my gaze. I could tell his goal was to make me uncomfortable, since he couldn't actually do anything else more than glare at me. I smiled at him, which only seemed to anger him more.

For a moment, the whole place was busy as everyone helped to set the table. A few minutes later, the table was set, and we all sat, Norma to my left. Every time I glanced at her, she was watching me, and every time she realized she got caught, a blush appeared on her face before she could look away. Why that was so endearing I couldn't tell.

The food placed on the table had my mouth watering and I wanted to fill my plate. Then I realized no one else was reaching for their food yet.

"Norma, could you please say grace?" Mariana asked.

Norma straightened in her seat, seemingly excited about the prospect of blessing our lunch. I could not recall ever sitting at a table where people were praying for their food. We usually just went in, happy we had some good food before us. Though everyone closed their eyes, I observed Norma as she dove into her prayer, her head bowed.

"Lord Jesus, we thank you today for another meal to nourish our bodies. We consider, Lord, that there are many in the world who do not have this privilege, and it makes us so grateful that you have chosen to bless us. We ask that you strengthen our bodies and help us to always be appreciative for everything you have done for us, in Jesus' name."

Her voice was soft, sweet, and musical. I could not take my eyes off her as she spoke those words. By the time she was through, I was fighting back a smile. A resounding "Amen" followed. I only mumbled mine when everyone else had said theirs.

When the covers were lifted, the scent of homemade burgers and fries wafted out. My stomach growled. Norma didn't look at me, but a chuckle escaped her lips. She began to load my plate with the food before serving her own.

"Thank you," I murmured close to her ear before she turned her face away from me.

"You're welcome," she replied shyly. I could feel the eyes of the three other people around the table stuck on us, but I didn't care. Taking the giant burger in hands, I took my first bite. The flavors hit my tongue like a tornado. Honestly, I hadn't been expecting much. My own mother had made burgers at home for us before and they were never anything like the fast-food stuff. But Mariana's burgers were like eating at a five-star restaurant.

"Whoa. This is really good," I raved. I wasn't a man of many words, but I couldn't help but commend her for her cooking.

"Thank you," she answered with a chuckle. "That's very kind of you."

"How did you two meet?" Rico inquired. I'd expected him to ask this long before now. If I'd been in his position, I would have been a lot more hostile than he'd been so far, especially because we both knew the type of man that I was. Luna and Mariana leaned forward, equally interested in the answer Rico requested.

Since I didn't want to divulge any information that Norma wasn't willing to disclose, I turned my attention to her. "Uh...maybe you should tell him." Our eyes only locked for a second before she began blushing again.

Clearing her throat, she began. "Marcel was the one who saved me the night I was attacked."

Rico's brows pulled together as he stared back and forth between us. As for Mariana, a loud gasp came from her. "Norma. You never told me that. Oh my gosh." She put a hand to her chest. "I can't believe it. You were so brave taking on those guys on your own. Norma could have been killed that night, but you were there to protect her. Thank you. We owe you a lot."

"It was my pleasure to help," I replied waving my free hand, so she knew it was nothing.

"Yeah, he's my knight in shining armor," Norma said with a chuckle. It was sweet, but the images of that night flashed into my mind and the only thing I could think about was how she could have died. Even Rico's snort couldn't shake me out of that dark place.

"Rico," Mariana said in an astonishing tone to her nephew. Then she reached across the table to pat my hand. "Don't mind him and his hostility. His acting this way because he doesn't know you yet. The Sicilian men in our family are always protective when it comes to the females in the family."

"Totally understandable," I told her. "I have three younger sisters and I would crush anyone who tries to hurt them in any way." Translation; they'd be six feet under. I expected the woman to cringe in horror. But she only smiled, probably not realizing the seriousness in my voice.

"Of course, you would." She glanced at the two other girls at the table and grumbled, "Men." Norma and Luna broke into giggles. I was almost certain then that this aunt of hers had a rebellious streak and was more than likely watched like a hawk by every man in her family.

"I've heard Sofia talk about you at school before," Luna started to say. My ears perked up.

"Really?" I casually asked, aware that whenever I showed up at Sofia's school to pick her up, I would get strange looks from the students.

"Yeah. None of the guys at school mess with her because she constantly tells them about the things you would do to them if they touched her." Another Rico snort.

"Rico, quit with the grunts," Mariana scolded. "It's rude and really irritating. If you have nothing nice to say, keep quiet and eat your food."

"Sure, whatever," the boy muttered. Then pushed his half-eaten plate forward and leaning back against the chair with his arms folded across his chest.

"Look, I'm not trying to be rude," he said, after an awkward minute of silence. "Believe it or not, I'm grateful this guy saved my sister's life. But what I want to know is, why is he still around and how did he know Norma would be here on Tybee Island?" he questioned.

"Marcel is here to do a job," Mariana told him.

"A job? Oh, please," Rico said with disdain, shaking his head.

"Why don't you just eat like Aunt Mari told you to," Luna said.

"Why don't you just mind your own business and let him speak for himself," He shot back. She eyed him for a second before returning to her food. I noticed Norma tensing up a little.

All the humor I'd felt before was gone. This kid was starting to get under my skin with his obnoxious attitude.

"Come to think of it, you didn't mention what you do for a living, Marcel," Mariana said, her attention now focused back on me. The slight hugging of her brows told me that Rico's behavior was starting to put doubts about me in her mind. I didn't answer right away. I was thinking of a good reply to give her. So, she asked again, "What exactly do you do for a living?"

"Yes, please tell us, Marcel," Rico mockingly said. "What exactly is it that you do?" With my anger rising, I had to keep my controlled enough not to crush the drinking glass in my hand.

Luna was looking at her brother with scornful eyes. She obviously didn't like the attitude he was giving me.

I had to come up with an answer fast, or I would raise suspicion. I mean, who would have to think for so long just to answer a question on their occupation, unless they were thinking of a smooth lie. "I work in the shipping industry," I finally replied. "I'm into importing and exporting."

Rico burst into laughter. "Oh wow," he said, mocking tone still in place. I resisted the urge to stand up and crush this kid. If anyone had handed me some tape, I would have used it to shut his mouth. "And what exactly do you—"

"Aunt Mari, guess what?" Norma chimed in, cutting off her brother. He looked at her, irritated she interrupted, but she ignored him as she faced Mariana. "Marcel has agreed to come to church with us when we get back home."

"Really?" Luna asked, her eyes lightening up. "That's great."

"Wow, that's wonderful." Mariana commented. This seemed to distract her from Rico's earlier probing. She jumped into some speech about how good it was for young men like me to know God for ourselves, or something along those lines. My focus was still on my little nemesis trying to mess things up for me before it had even started. His eyes seemed to tell me, *you've won this round.* I found the whole situation ridiculous; he was barely older than Sofia. If he thought I was going to get in some brawl with a kid...well, he could keep dreaming.

While his aunt was raving about church life, Rico stood up, his chair scraping the floor. I cringed at the noise. "Aunt Mari, thank you for lunch. Please excuse me," he simply said walking away. We all watched him leave till he turned around a corner and out of our view.

"Seriously, what is his problem?" Luna protested, turning to look at everyone who was still seated at the table. Norma only watched her brother's retreating figure with a grimace.

"Maybe I should go talk to him," Norma suggested. As she started to rise from her chair, panic started to rise from me. It was pathetic.

"No, leave him be," her aunt told her. "He'll be fine. Finish your meal and go freshen up. We need to get back to the studio in another couple of minutes." Norma still looked like she wanted to run after her brother, but in the end, she sat down again to my relief.

"Going back to painting?" I asked, eyeing the two women covered in paint.

"That obvious? I just need to add one or two touches to what I've done so far." Mariana chuckled. "Painting is my one passion in life. The talent comes from my father. He was an excellent artist himself. Unfortunately, Norma and I are the only ones who inherited his gift, which is kind of sad. My daughters couldn't draw an apple to save their own lives."

Although I didn't need to see Norma's art to know it was good, I was still curious to see what she could paint. I stole a glance at her. One day, when she was more comfortable with me and would finally stop trying to push me away, maybe she could draw me. A naughty thought entered my head as I envisioned being her model and posing for her. She'd probably blush and leave the room before I could finish taking off my shirt.

"Rico and I couldn't draw a straight line to save ourselves," Luna commented, snickering. "We've left the painting skills to Aunt Mari and Norma."

Without Rico there, I started to actually enjoy myself. Norma, forgetting the earlier tension, broke into laughter. "You're exaggerating. It's not that bad."

"You're just being nice, Norma. It is *that bad*," Luna told her. She eyed me from across the table. "My sister is such a sweetheart. She always sees the good in everyone."

I turned to look at the intriguing girl in question. Though I sensed she had a pretty good idea about who I was and the kind of business I was involved in. 'Shipping business', Ha!. I knew she wasn't buying it. I turned to Luna who was still smiling at me like we'd been friends for years. There was something about her that reminded me of my twin sisters; her carefree nature and the crinkles beneath her eyes whenever she smiled. "I can tell," I told her.

Norma glanced up at me and I watched as a tinge of red spread across her paint-stained cheeks. Earlier, she had gone on and on about her aunt and how good she was as an artist. And yet, she'd never said a word about herself. I knew she was enrolled in an art school, but even though I've never been the guy to walk into a gallery, I still appreciated art. I couldn't wait to see Norma's work.

Mariana watched us with eyes as sharp as an eagle's. I could feel her dissecting me with her mind. Another man may have been alarmed about this, but not me. I had experienced harsher things than a woman's inquisitive look.

"How long will you be in town, Marcel?" Mariana asked. "My church is having a barbecue this coming Friday. We're all going together. Would you like to join us?"

Her words surprised me. I hadn't expected a second invitation. For a moment, I had been bracing myself for another interrogation, but her tone and words were nothing but kind. Regardless, I wanted to spend time with Norma, no one else. "I'm sorry," I answered. "I won't be in town on Friday. I'm actually heading home tonight." Norma looked at me when I said that. Was that disappointment I saw?

"Oh. Well, that's too bad," she replied. Mariana rose from her seat. "Norma, it's time to get back to work. Our model is waiting." With that announcement, Norma popped the last of her fries in her mouth, downed her drink and stood up as well. I followed suit.

"Thank you for inviting me to lunch, Mariana. It was the best I've had in weeks," I said earnestly. There was always something special about a home-cooked meal. Her lips quirked into a full smile. I was almost certain Rico's attitude would have messed things up for me. Not that I cared much about getting to know her. It was Norma I was interested in. No one else.

But based on how *my girl* talked about her aunt, I knew she looked up to her perhaps more than she did her own parents. I didn't need her aunt getting on Rico's side and turning Norma's heart and mind away from me. I almost had her right where I wanted, and nothing was going to stop me from having her.

"You're welcome. And it's Mari, or Aunt Mari if you prefer," she said.

I didn't have to think twice before I answered her. "Aunt Mari it is then," I told her. Actually, it was just what I wanted to hear. It meant that I had the chance to see Norma again. It meant Aunt Mari didn't oppose what Norma and I had going. With another grin, she patted my cheek the way my mother would have.

Then, looking at Norma, she said, "Norma, dear, you should escort Marcel to the door. You have five minutes. So, get moving," she said with a wink before turning on her heels and heading for the stairs.

“Yes, Ma’am,” Norma shouted after her. I expected Norma to spend her five minutes walking me to the door and saying our goodbyes. Instead, she reached for the plates on the table.

“Hey, forget about that,” Luna said, fanning her off. She tossed her head in my direction, sending me a quick glance, her eyes twinkling with approval. Innocent as Luna looked, she had a playful streak beneath it all. I decided I liked her, after all. She seemed more like her aunt in terms of behavior and perspective.

“Right,” Norma said, practically dropping the plates. “Thanks.” I realized then that she was nervous about being alone with me again. Together, we walked to the door in silence, while Norma fidgeted with her fingers. She was clearly nervous around me.

When I stepped through the open door, I turned to face her. “Your aunt is something else, isn’t she?” I commented, hoping to get her talking. Instead, Norma let out a nervous laugh.

“Oh yeah. She’s the quirky one in the family,” she explained. “By the way, thank you for the Bible you left me the other day. It was so kind of you.”

I rubbed the back of my head with a slight shrug. I had totally forgotten I had left that for her. “Don't mention it, it was nothing. It’s the least I could do after…well…after.” I forced myself not to think about it and instead, focused on the weird look I got from the man behind the counter. He probably didn’t expect to see someone like me purchasing a book, let alone a Bible. I couldn't blame him. The society we lived in was fond of judging people by their looks. People forgot that demons could dress as an angel and vice versa.

“It wasn’t nothing to me,” Norma stated. “It was one of the most thoughtful things anyone has ever done for me,” she said gratefully. “You should know how much this means to me.”

I smiled. “I only want to make you happy,” I admitted. She smiled back.

“I am happy,” she said. “Thank you, Marcel.”

That wasn't what I wanted her calling me. There was something about her calling me Bear that just touched my heart. "We're back to Marcel?" I teased, lifting my brows. She flushed crimson.

"You prefer me calling you Bear?" she asked, confused.

"Yes," I said, with what I hoped was an irresistible grin. She eyed me then, as if to gage how serious I was. Then she smiled. I wasn't certain how long we'd been standing there looking at each other in silence. Aunt Mari's five minutes had long passed. Leaving Norma was hard. Harder than I had imagined.

"Fine, we'll see about that." Her smile was teasing now. Then she quickly looked behind her. "I should get back to work," Norma said. "Aunt Mari must be wondering what's taking me so long."

"Yeah, sure thing."

"Promise me something," she blurted, her cheeks tinging red as if on cue. This piqued my interest. I took a step toward her. Nervous as she was around me, my girl stood her ground.

"What?" I probed.

"Stay safe, and please, don't get yourself killed," she said. Unable to resist, I swept a lock of her hair behind her ear again, using the opportunity to brush her cheek ever so gently. She leaned in closer to my touch, staring up at me with those innocent eyes.

She was irresistible. "I promise I won't."

"That kind of life isn't for you," she suddenly went on. "There is a better way. I know it might not be what you want to hear but Jesus loves you very much and He wants to change your life, if only you'll let Him."

I groaned. Why would she have to come up with this now? Of course, she would. She was a good girl who loved Jesus. Somehow, I'd ended up forgetting that, though I wasn't sure how. She wanted to win my soul to her God. Maybe this was the best time to come clean with her.

"Sweetheart," I started. "I have to be honest with you. I have no interest whatsoever in your religion. What I want is *you*. The only reason I came here is because I wanted to see you, Norma."

She finally took a step back then. "You're only saying that because you don't know better." A smirk crept up my lips. I wasn't going to argue with her about this. She was naïve. But even so, Norma Tesoriere had me practically on a string, and she didn't even know it.

Taking a step back myself, I reached for her hand and kissed the back of it. "I'll see you soon." Norma bit on her bottom lip. Once more, we stood there staring at each other. There were many emotions in her eyes, it was hard for me to focus.

"Norma!" Aunt Mari called from upstairs. She pulled her hand away from mine.

"I have to go." With that, she stepped back inside and shut the door in my face. I should have been offended, and yet the only thing I could do was shake my head and laugh at her behavior. Turning on my heels, I headed through the lush garden toward the beach.

"Marcel," I heard coming from my left. I looked over to find Rico sitting on one of the benches, his scowl still perfectly in place. He had been waiting for me.

"You need something, kid?" I spat out.

"What are you doing with my sister?" he asked. There was something about Rico that reminded me of myself. We both held that love and sense of protectiveness for our sisters.

I huffed. "You need to chill out. I'd never do anything to hurt her. She's a special girl." I had hoped this assurance would calm the boy. It seemed to do the opposite. Rico flew off the bench and was in my personal space in less than two seconds.

"You need to stay away from my sister," Rico growled, his finger poking into my chest. "She's good, with the purest heart and I don't need you messing up her life. Back off now, Maxwell. I mean it."

It took all I had to keep my fist from smacking that smug look off his face. I didn't like people touching me without my permission and with the number of times he had poked my chest, he should be paying with that finger. Usually, this blatant violation would have left my opponent on the ground, writhing in pain. This was different, however. This was Norma's brother. If I touched but a hair on his head, I would lose her forever.

Even so, that was not what held me at bay. It was this boy's willingness to stand up to a guy like me, whom he knew well enough could crush him aside with one hand, just to protect his beloved sister. Another smirk and I patted him on the shoulder. "Make sure you stay in school, Tesoriere. Your sister will be proud."

Rico's entire body stiffened, and he didn't reply. I could almost see the wheels turning in his mind's eye, digging up the buried secrets of the night he had almost lost his life. As the memories came flooding back, his rage melted, leaving only a simmering anger. Rico turned to walk away, his lips tight. After my last comment, it was clear enough to him now that his hands were tied. Rico would never tell his aunt or parents about who I really was because I held his little secret.

Knowing I had him where I wanted him, I backed away and continued on the path down to the beach. It had been a low blow, even for me. Still, I was the kind of guy who used whatever resources were available to get what I wanted. And I wanted Norma Tesoriere.

Chapter Nine

Norma

"Are you sure you don't want me to drop you off at work?" My dad asked for the third time.

And for the third time, I told him, "Yes, Dad, I'm sure." There was no way I was going to have him take me to work. Our jobs were in opposite directions. If I let him go out of his way, he would end up being late, and I didn't want that to happen.

"Alright then," he sighed. "Please be careful."

I gave him a quick smile before dashing out of the house. Mom was just coming down the stairs when I made it to the door. Honestly, I heard her calling after me, but I pretended not to.

Ever since the attack, my parents had become terribly overprotective. The only time I had been ever free of them were the couple of weeks I'd spent with Aunt Mari, and the relaxation had been fabulous. I'd been sorry when our vacation came to an end. Now that I was back, the worry for my safety had come right along as well. Even while at Aunt Mari's, mom had kept calling to check in on me; every morning when she knew I would be up, and at night, just before I went to sleep.

Before the assault, they had always trusted my judgement. But the incident had brought reality crashing down. I understood why. It did the same for me. I wasn't going to sit and hide in the house in fear, because if I did, it would've meant that evil had won. It was summer. I wanted to be out, I wanted to work, and I wanted to make my own money.

Hence the reason I was on my way to the Art Museum. It was my first day on the job. The receptionist had just had a baby and was on maternity leave. She wouldn't be back for several weeks, which worked out perfectly for me.

On my way to the bus stop, my mind was clouded with the thoughts of a specific guy who had promised to attend a church service with me. I wondered if he would stay true to his words. Even though he hadn't visited Tybee Island again throughout the time of my stay there, I'd regularly found myself thinking about him.

As I waited for the bus, I couldn't help but think of Marcel. Where was he? What could he be up to since the last time we spoke? I couldn't predict his movements, as he was quite mysterious.

A *honk* from a car driving by brought me back to reality and I got myself ready to hop on the bus. It was late, and if not for the reflections in my mind of Marcel, I knew I would've panicked and regretted not allowing my dad to drop me off. The one thing I didn't want was showing up late on my first day of work. I wanted to make a good first impression, even if it was only for a temporary job.

Not long after, I managed to get there just a couple minutes shy of 8 a.m., my scheduled time to start. I made a mental note to catch an earlier bus next time, even if it meant I would be too early. I hated being late. Especially for work.

The Art Museum building was a three-story structure with beautiful glass windows. I dashed to the double front doors at the entrance and hit the buzzer. When the doors stretched open, I spotted a large man with a big pot belly, dressed in a crisp white shirt and black pants with a baton tucked to the belt. The uniform looked a little intimidating, but when I caught sight of his face, he was beaming from one ear to the next, his eyes shined with warmth.

"Good morning, little lady," he started. "You must be Ms. Tesoriere?" My new face was probably a dead giveaway.

"Yes, I am." I nodded, relaxed by his kind greeting. "And good morning to you, too. I was told to ask for Ronald James." I added, suspecting I was already standing right in front of him.

"That's me." He said, confirming my thoughts. "But you can call me Ron. That's what everybody calls me." He stepped aside to let me in. "Your security pass is ready by the way," he informed me as I walked to the semi-circular front desk that would be my station for the next several weeks.

"Oh, good. Thank you. Where can I collect it?" I inquired.

"It's right there on your desk," Ron said, pulling at the waist of his pants. With his rounded belly in the way, the pants didn't get too far up.

When I found the pass, I waved it. "Found it. Thanks again."

"You're welcome, Ms. Tesoriere. If you need anything at all, I'll be right here." He pointed his thumb behind him to the small booth where he was stationed, near the door.

"Thank you, Ron," I said, realizing then that I would probably be saying it more often than I already had, since he was obviously a kind man.

As soon as he left for his booth, I turned on my computer and got to work. Half an hour later, other workers were filing in, as well as visitors to the museum. I dove into my work with tenacity, only coming up for air at lunch time when Ron came to my desk to check on me.

"Are you settling in, okay?" he asked.

I nodded. "It's been great so far. Things are going even more smoothly than I had expected."

"What are you having for lunch?" he asked, changing the subject.

"Is it lunch time already?" I glanced at the clock and noticed it was a few minutes after twelve. "Wow." I'd been so lost in my work, I hadn't seen time fly by. I looked around for my lunch container and found it sitting beside my handbag beneath the desk.

Snatching it up, I unzipped it and popped out a container with a turkey sandwich, baby carrots and *hummus*. My mother had packed it that morning and I hadn't even stopped to look inside. Twenty-one and mom is still packing my lunch, I thought.

"Oh, nice." Ron commented. "I was just checking to make sure you had lunch. My wife always packs mine and I like to share."

I grinned. "That's very kind of you," I said, smiling. "What are you having?"

"Rice, kale, broccoli." His lack of enthusiasm amused me.

"Oh?"

"Yeah, my wife and my doctor conspired against me," he explained in such a dramatic tone I almost burst out laughing but controlled myself. "Apparently, I need to lose some weight. She even packed me cucumber juice when all I wanted was a bottle of soda." He let out a deep sigh. "This is my life…for now."

I felt bad for him. "You can have my hummus," I offered. That was the first thing that came to mind. Poor guy. Having to eat stuff he didn't want. Luckily for me, my mother could make even the blandest of vegetables taste like heaven. She and Aunt Mari had a cooking talent to die for. It made everyone's mouth water.

He sent me a grateful look. "Thanks, but I'm not allowed to eat that either. Too much fat, they said." He shook his head this time. He looked so unhappy over his food restrictions, I wasn't sure if I was supposed to laugh or comfort him. Had I been in his wife's position, I would have done the same.

"Don't worry," I consoled him. "Not this one. My mom made it with *melanzana*."

He looked lost. "Mel- what? Is that English?" he asked.

A laugh burst out of me. Sometimes I forgot not everyone understood Italian. "Forgive me, Ron. I meant eggplant."

"Oh!" He joined me in laughing. "Never would have figured that one out on my own." I snatched up the carrots and hummus and handed them to him.

"You should try it. It's delicious." Ron frowned, skepticism written on his face. Still, he obliged me and swiped up a little bit of the eggplant hummus with the carrot. When his eyes popped open, I knew he was caught, hook, line, and sinker.

Ron handed the container back to me and leaned in. "Say, Ms. Tesoriere, would it be possible for you to get your mother to give up this recipe?"

My face split into a wide smile. "Of course. She would be overjoyed to share it. By the way, you can have all of this. I have more at home waiting for me in the fridge."

"Thank you so much, Ms. Tesoriere. You're a lunch saver. I'm spreading this stuff all over my kale salad, then I can digest it happily." With that, he headed off to his booth again.

Just then, my cell phone rang. *Dad* popped up on the screen. I hit the green button.

"Hey Dad, what's up?"

"Hi, sweetheart. I was on my lunch break, and I thought I'd reach out to you. How's your day going so far?"

"It's good. Really good," I told him honestly. I went on to tell him about Ronald and how wonderful a man he was. "He's the only one I've gotten to know so far."

"That's nice," he said, and though I couldn't see him, I knew he was smiling. "Listen, I was thinking that maybe I should pick you up after work. What do you think? I could leave work a little early so I could get to you on time."

"Uh, Dad, no. That's fine. You don't need to come all the way over here." His workplace was far from mine, and I didn't want him leaving his work early just to pick me up.

He let out a long sigh. "Norma, I don't like you walking by yourself, especially at that hour of the day. I'm going to leave work early to come and get you." I was about to argue when I heard him grunt. "Darn. I just remembered; I have a meeting at the end of the day. But I'll reschedule it."

"Dad, I've told you a hundred times, I'm fine," I replied with a firmer tone. "You're forgetting that I'm not a kid anymore. You just have to trust that God will protect me."

The phone went silent on his end for a little while. I knew he was processing what I'd just said. Most of the time, my parents seemed to forget that I was an adult. Some ladies my age were already living on their own, far away from their parents, and some had already settled down with a partner. At my age, my parents still had so much control over me.

Once more, he let out a long sigh. "You're right, honey. You're right. It's just that I can't stop myself from worrying. But I should be trusting God. Thank you for reminding me of that."

I sighed, rubbing my forehead. "It's no problem, Dad. I'll head home as soon as work is over." I told him.

"Yes, please do. Text me when you get home, yes?"

"I will." I said, smiling.

"Thank you for indulging your old man." I let out a little snicker.

"You're not that old, Dad." He laughed. He wasn't even in his fifties yet.

"Talk to you soon, honey. Bye."

"Bye, Dad."

When the call ended, I dove into my turkey sandwich while I continued to work. It was about an hour later when a text popped up on my cell phone screen. I expected it to be Dad, checking in on me again. It made me roll my eyes. Sometimes, when he forgot even the smallest detail, he wouldn't hesitate to call back.

It was from an unknown number. But when I opened the text, I knew exactly who it was from.

Are you free?

Three little words, yet my body was already pumping adrenaline. How did I come to this place where a guy like him could have this kind of effect on me? I took note that this was the first time he'd ever texted, even though he'd had my number for weeks. I hit reply.

Norma: At work.

His response was immediate. As soon as I'd sent my message, three little dots appeared, indicating he was already typing.

Marcel: Back at the hardware store?

My brows drew together. How did he know about the hardware store?

Norma: How did you know I worked at a hardware store?
Marcel: You told me, remember?

I frowned. For a moment, I almost believed him. Until I thought about it again and remembered I had never even mentioned the hardware store in any of our conversations.

Norma: I'm certain I didn't.
Marcel: OK, so you didn't. I found out before I started following you around.

I sighed. Just how long had he been doing that? And what else did he know about me. It freaked me out to think that the entire time I had been extra careful after Sofia's threat, Marcel had been following me himself.

Norma: You're creepy.

Marcel: Only when it comes to you, babe :)

This shouldn't have made me smile, yet it did. When I realized it, I swiped it off my face instantly. I had work to do.

Norma: I should go. I shouldn't be texting right now.
Marcel: Where are you working?
Norma: At a museum.
Marcel: Which one?
Norma: That you don't need to know.

The idea of Marcel showing up at my workplace was nothing short of disastrous. Not only would he scare people away, but he would distract me. I couldn't afford that. As much as my misleading heart wanted to see him again, I resisted the urge to send him the address to the museum.

Marcel: Alright, then. I'll figure it out on my own.

I snorted, decided to ignore him and get back to work. However, knowing my Bear, I knew he wouldn't give up without a fight, and I was a little nervous about him finding me, as he'd promised.

Norma: Good luck with that, Marcel.

I waited and when I got no reply, I moved to drop my phone. Just then, my phone buzzed again.
Marcel: Norma?
Norma: What?
Marcel: I thought I was Bear to you now.

Warm heat filled my cheeks as I read those words. I was glad that he wasn't here to see the way his words affected me. I typed my response and read my text over and over again before I hit the *send* button.

Norma: Fine. What do you want, Bear?

Marcel: I want to see you.

I bit my lips, palming my head, and couldn't help but smile. I knew the weird feelings stirring up in the pit of my stomach. Marcel was able to awaken things in my body I never knew I was capable of feeling. No guy had ever done this to me.

Norma: You can see me at church.

Marcel: That's not enough. I want to spend time with you. Every day.

Before I could reply, another text popped up.

Marcel: I feel like I can't breathe when I'm far away from you :)

I rolled my eyes. So, this was what they called sweet nothings. Despite that, I found that my hands were shaking while my heartbeat kicked up a notch further. How could he just say things like that to me? I was trying to be a good girl, to forget him, but this guy was bent on breaking me down.

Oh God, help me. I silently prayed.

Yet even though my heart was burning with desire to see him again, I held my ground.

Norma: You'll see me at church on Sunday.

Marcel: How about this evening after work?

I decided then that I wasn't going to prolong this conversation. I silenced my phone, turned it face down, then returned to work.

For the next couple of hours, I managed to push thoughts of Marcel out of my mind. By the time 5 p.m. rolled around, I'd completed more tasks than I'd thought possible.

"Time for me to hit the road, little lady," Ron said as soon as another security officer signed in for duty. "How did things go today?"

"Great," I told him. "I should get going as well. I need to get home too." My father's request came back to mind.

"Alright, then. Well, I guess I'll see you tomorrow?"

"Sure will," I told him.

When Ron left the building, I packed up my stuff. The other security officer seemed distant, but I waved in his direction when I passed the booth to exit the building. His response was a simple nod. *Nice*, I thought with sarcasm.

The moment I stepped outside, I spotted my Bear, and my mouth fell open. Marcel was standing there, leaning against the wall with his cell phone in hand. As soon as he spotted me, he pushed away from the wall and started walking in my direction.

"Hey, beautiful."

"What? How…?"

His mouth lifted in a wide grin. "I took a wild guess," he said, lifting his brows. "I'm pretty good at this, aren't I?" He shoved his hands in his jeans pocket, looking around the environment, before his eyes settled back on me. "You should be proud of me."

I swung my handbag over my shoulder and looked around me. People were moving about but no one seemed to pay any attention to us. "You shouldn't be here," I told him.

"But I *wanted* to see you," Marcel said. My earlier resolve to resist him instantly dissolved into thin air. "You look good in that dress." He took another step towards me.

With my cheeks burning, I glanced down at the simple pencil dress I was wearing. Not knowing what to say, I opted to walk away. I didn't get very far. Marcel snaked his hand around my arm, stopping me in my tracks.

I looked down at our intertwined arms.

"Norma, wait. Look, my little sister has violin practice right across the street from here. I'm on my way to pick her up and then we're going to grab something to eat. I was hoping you could join us."

I should've said no, but when I looked into his eyes and saw him, staring back at me, I didn't find it in me to turn him down. "Okay," I said, nodding.

The look of relief that crossed his face made me smile. Marcel gently took my hand and led me across the street and into the small studio. Inside, we found a group of young boys and girls playing their violins as they were directed by an older gentleman. All around the room, people I assumed were parents, were scattered here and there, listening. The sound of music permeating through the room was rapturous. These kids were good.

"Excellent work, everyone!" the instructor shouted when the music ended. "I will see you all next week." With that, the room erupted into shuffles as the kids began to pack up. I glanced around the room, though I had no idea what Marcel's sister looked like.

"Marcel!" I heard a little girl yell. Because of my height, this little one was almost as tall as me already. She ran toward us. Her dirty-blonde hair whirling around her. Marcel reached out to grab her as she leaped into him.

"Hey there, little princess," he said. "You were pretty awesome."

"Thanks." Her gaze shifted to me, and I found myself shifting from foot to foot under her intense stare. It was striking that her hair was dirty-blonde, and her eyes were blue as the ocean. I had assumed that all of Marcel's siblings would look like him. With his haunting dark but beautiful eyes, and jet-black hair, she looked nothing like him.

"Hey Juliana, I'd like you to meet my friend, Norma," Marcel said, evidently catching our stare down. "Norma, this is my baby sister, Juliana."

"Hi Juliana," I started. "It's lovely to meet you." She was still watching me intently and it made me want to back away from her.

I felt relieved when Juliana's face finally broke into a sweet glow. I had been wrong earlier; she had the same smile as Marcel. "You're Marcel's girlfriend, aren't you?" she asked, her eyes twinkling with that same mischievousness Marcel sometimes carried. I could feel myself turning red. Marcel, on the other hand, was amused by his sister's brazen question.

"Not yet," he told the little girl. "But I'm working on it." Juliana giggled then. I glared at him. Why would he tell her that? I wanted to slap him on the arm, but judging from his size, I suspected I would have been the one to feel the brunt of it, not him. "Come on, let's get something to eat." Marcel winked at me, and I melted under his gaze like a fifteen-year-old. It was ridiculous.

"Yes," Juliana said, beaming.

Together, we walked down the street to a nearby diner. I had never eaten there before, although I had passed by it a few times. Marcel led us to one of the booths close to the window, while Juliana kept up a steady chatter. It reminded me of when I first saw him.

"I like this class better than the last one, Marcel," she was saying when the waiter showed up. "I like this teacher better."

"You were in a different class before that one?" I asked her.

"Yeah. That teacher wasn't as nice as this new one, and he plays the violin better too. I've wanted to come here for a long time, but Mom didn't have the money. So, Marcel is paying for it. He also bought me a new violin for my birthday. He's the best brother in the world."

"Well, isn't that sweet?" the waiter said, his voice uninterested. When Marcel eyed him coolly, he cleared his throat awkwardly.

"What would you like, Princess?"

She bit her lip in a cute manner as she pondered about her order. Finally, she decided. "Pizza, please," she said, oblivious to the shift in the air. "Pepperoni," she pronounced the word in the slowest form I'd ever heard it being pronounced. She looked to her brother. "What drink do you think I should have?"

He smiled at her. "Anything you want, baby girl."

She nodded, then looked back at the waiter. "Ok, and a strawberry milkshake." The waiter wrote down the order with pursed lips.

"And you, sir?" he mumbled.

"I'll have a cheeseburger, loaded fries and a milkshake too," Marcel told him.

Before he could ask, I said, "I'll have the same, thank you." When he walked away, I gave Marcel a curious look. I hadn't failed to notice the unfriendly vibe between them. "Did something happen between you two?" I asked.

He tried to avoid my eyes, but I followed them, not allowing him to escape my unseen clutches. He finally sighed in defeat. "Not at all," he said. "Why would you think that?"

"Oh no. Something *did* happen," I told him, shaking my head. "Spill."

Marcel's brows shot up toward his hairline. "Do you really want to know?" My smile slipped then, as I remembered that this gorgeous man in front of me was a gangster.

"On second thought, maybe not." I turned my attention back to Juliana. "So, Juliana, you were saying earlier that you have the best brother in the entire world." Did she know about the things her brother was involved in?

"He is," Juliana stated matter-of-factly. "You know what the music instructor told me today? He said he's thinking of having me lead one of the songs in the next music program."

"Wow, that's great. Congratulations," I told her. Despite his status in life, I couldn't help but admire Marcel's relationship with her. It was quite the contrast from what I'd witnessed between him and Sofia, but I supposed that was somewhat different. Sofia was obviously an unruly teenager who wanted to have her way while Juliana was around ten or eleven, with a talent she was excited about.

The waiter returned with our orders in record time, despite his cold fish attitude.

"Thank you," Juliana and I said in unison.

The little girl was the first to bite into her pizza, while her brother sat there looking at her, his eyes filled with admiration.

He turned to me, and our gaze met. "Eat, Norma."

I reluctantly stopped looking at him and focused on what was on the table before me. Halfway into our meal, the sound of explosions reverberated through the air, sending the hairs all over my body standing on end. Stunned, I froze in place while other people dove under their tables, screaming.

I was so terrified I couldn't move. A strong hand reached for me, tugging me to the ground. I found myself wrapped up in Marcel's arms beside a terrified Juliana. His body was so much bigger than ours that he managed to shield us completely from the outside.

I expected to hear glass shattering around us as bullets flew. Were they shooting at him? Was this a retaliation for a dispute he had gotten involved in?

Why, oh why did I ever agree to come here to begin with? I'd promised my dad that I would go straight home after work, hadn't I? Now here I was, crouched down under a table while men were firing guns outside. He would have a heart attack if he knew what was happening right now.

The explosions ended abruptly, making the sounds of wailing around us more apparent. Juliana was sobbing all over my shirt. I wasn't even sure when she reached into my arms.

Marcel pulled us from the floor with his eyes trained outside. The restaurant's windows were perfectly intact, with no sign of damage anywhere. Clearly, those men, whoever they were, were not shooting at Marcel, or anyone inside the restaurant. Still, he looked worried. He dropped some cash on the table before dragging Juliana and I toward the restaurant's kitchen.

"Hey, you can't come in here!" a man I assumed was a manager, protested. Marcel didn't bother replying but shoved him aside. He opened the huge steel door that led outside and poked his head through.

"Marcel?" Juliana called through her tears. He only spared a glance at her before he continued walking.

"The path is clear. Let's go," was all he said. When he pulled us through the door, light hit the back of my eyes. They adjusted quickly enough though and I looked in every direction for signs of trouble as Marcel dragged us down the alley.

We were almost at the exit when we heard footsteps running towards us. Marcel stopped and pointed to a dumpster. "There. Hide. Now." He commanded. The area was messy, and it smelled, but we huddled into the corner behind it. Marcel stooped in front of us, with a finger on his lips, indicating for us to stay silent.

"Marcel, are they shooting at us?" Juliana asked, her voice and hands shaking.

"No, baby girl," he told her. "But we have to stay out of sight. Now be a brave girl and keep quiet for me, okay?" Juliana nodded, though tears were still streaming down her face. I was as terrified as she was, but I pulled her into my chest and hugged her tightly.

Just then, three men bolted past the dumpster with guns in their hands. My eyes went wide as saucers. I had only ever seen guns in movies. I'd always heard about the crime rate in Atlanta, but having lived in one of the better areas, I'd never experienced anything like this before. Not until my mugging. And not until Marcel came into my life.

Marcel stayed in place long after the men had disappeared. I wanted to get up and run and not stop until I was in the security of my own home. But I had no idea what I was dealing with here. Marcel understood this world. He was my best hope of getting out of this place alive.

In the distance, we could hear police cruisers approaching, their sirens blaring. Only then did Marcel stand. "Let's go," he said. I expected him to go in the direction of the sirens. Instead, he continued down the path where the three men had come from.

At the end of the alley, I could see several police cruisers spread out in front of the restaurant. There was a body on the ground, a man from the looks of it, and he wasn't moving. "Don't look," Marcel said, stepping in front of me. He flagged down the first taxi that came by and hurried us in.

Though I knew I wasn't supposed to look, my eyes strayed to the man's body yet again. Marcel caught me staring once more. He pulled my face into his chest and ran his fingers through my hair. All I wanted to do at that point was break down like Juliana and cry. Yet I knew it would only distress the little girl more. So, I held it in, opting to caress Juliana's arms for her comfort, and mine.

Vaguely, I heard Marcel give the driver my address. By now, I was perfectly aware that Marcel knew more about me than I wanted to admit to myself.

"I'm so sorry, baby," Marcel whispered into the quiet space. Somehow, I knew he was not talking to his sister. He was talking to me. I glanced up at him, catching the turmoil in his eyes. This man was not good for me. He was trouble, even when he tried not to be.

I should have ended things there. I should have told him that we should stay away from each other. The words were there, sitting on the tip of my tongue, but they died a thousand deaths the moment he looked into my eyes.

Chapter Ten

Marcel

I'd never hated myself the way I did after the incident at the restaurant. Not only had I gotten Norma and my little sister in a dangerous situation, but it could have gotten them killed. If those guys in the alleyway had seen us, chances were, none of us would have made it out alive. One bullet in our direction and before I could have had the chance to react, she or Juliana could have been lying dead in my arms. The thought of it ripped me to shreds.

I knew Norma had been trying to keep a brave face for Juliana's sake, but the terror in her beautiful eyes had been evident. There had also been a look of wariness. She was reconsidering her decision to spend time around me. And who could blame her for that? She had just started to become comfortable with me and trouble had already come knocking.

Had she gone straight home instead of having dinner with me, she would never have seen a dead body sprawled out on a cold Atlanta street. It was a wakeup call. I was a treacherous man. I wasn't right for this girl, even though I already knew my heart would stop beating without her.

When we turned the last corner that led to her house—the same one, unfortunately, where she'd gotten hurt—Norma pulled out of my arms and straightened her spine. "You can stop here," she told the driver. His brows crinkled with confusion, but he allowed the car to stop anyway. She didn't want her parents seeing her with me.

I was the last guy on earth they wanted around their daughter. I knew she respected her parents, and their decisions, so the fact that she was here with me meant a lot to me and I didn't want this to end. Not now, not tomorrow, not ever.

I slid Juliana from under my arm and stepped out of the car to get to the other side, but by the time I had reached her car door, Norma was already standing outside.

"Hey," I called before she could walk away. She turned to face me but didn't look into my eyes. I lifted her chin to look at me. "I can't tell you how sorry I am that you had to experience something like that."

"I know," she answered gently. "But it wasn't your fault," she said. "You couldn't have known."

"Right."

She forced her lips to curve into a half smile. Then she started to back away. I used my other hand to gently capture her arm. "Norma, wait. *Please*." I glanced back to see Juliana watching us from the window, with a sad look. I turned back to Norma.

She was already starting to shake her head. Consumed with emotions, she just said, "Bear, I'm tired. I just want to go home."

I could feel my girl slipping away from me. I couldn't afford that. Still, it was a lot for her to take in. I decided not to push her.

As she turned to walk away, she met my eyes with reluctance. "Thanks for bringing me home."

"It was my pleasure," I whispered to her.

"Good night." Norma slid her hand out of my hold and backed away. I didn't stop her this time. When she turned and walked off, her back toward me, she didn't look back even once. I watched her until she disappeared into her house not even a full block away.

"Where to next?" the driver asked as soon as I jumped back into the car. I gave him my address then settled Juliana next to me, holding her tight in my left arm. She fell asleep mere minutes into the ride. I glanced down at her and noticed the tear stains on her cheek. Terror gripped me all over again. The shootout had been too close for comfort.

Those men in the alleyway had been unfamiliar, but there was one thing that had made them stand out. All three had been sporting cobra tattoos. The Cobra Clan.

While the Cobras and Johnny's Boys had never actually been in any kind of conflict, there were allies of ours who were enemies of theirs. Chances were, they would not have been friendly with us. It reminded me of the reality of how dangerous the world I'd chosen was. The worst part was that, there was no way to get out of it. Once you started the game, you were *in*. Forever. No quitting the job, no retirement plan. I had seen guys try to defy the odds before, and it hadn't ended well for them. Most didn't live to tell their stories.

Minutes later, the car came to a stop at my house. "Wait for me," I told the driver. "I'll be back in about five minutes."

"No problem," he replied as I stepped out carrying Juliana in my arms. My mother was just setting the table for dinner when I walked in.

"Son," she started. "I hope you're staying for dinner."

"No, Ma, sorry," I told her. "Juliana and I already had dinner. I just came to drop her off."

"Oh." I purposely didn't look at her but continued to my sister's room. I didn't want to see the look of disappointment in my mother's eyes. Not today. I was dealing with enough right now.

Sofia and Isabella were just coming from their rooms when I entered the hallway. Isabella ran to me and hugged my waist, while Sofia stood still, staring.

"How are you doing, Isabella?" I asked.

"Good," she murmured. "I'm glad you're back."

"So am I, sweet girl," I answered.

"Where have you been?" Sofia said, her tone dripping with irritation. "I told you I needed to talk to you."

"I'm not in the mood to deal with your stuff right now, Sofia. Another day."

"That's what you said the last time. How many 'another day's' are you going to keep giving me?" she pestered.

"Can't do it right now," I replied, not looking her way. "I have some things to take care of."

"You always have something to take care of," she grumbled. I ignored her and headed into Juliana's room. Looking down at her and still seeing those tear stains made me realize that what she had experienced wasn't something that any kid should witness. I resolved to do something about it.

"I'm sorry, baby girl." I said, touching her face. As soon as I had her settled in, I dimmed the lights and exited the room. Not surprisingly, Sofia was still standing there, waiting for me, arms crossed in front of her.

"Marcel," she whined.

"No, I'm not buying you another tablet and no, you can't go to the dance Saturday night," I said before she could start. While my concerns were on more important things, all Sofia cared about was Sofia. She was always demanding something.

"You can't be serious!" she practically screeched. "I already made plans to go, all my friends are going to be there. You can't do this."

"Oh, I can."

"Are you kidding me? What's your problem?"

"You should check yourself first, before asking me that. Now, I have things to do. We'll talk later."

"Things like what? Cutting people's throats?" she commented. I turned on my heels to face her then, my brows creased. My sister seemed to think I was dropping bodies all day for a living. No wonder she continuously used me as her bargaining chip to get herself out of trouble.

Shaking my head, I went to the kitchen where I knew my mother would be. "Is everything okay?" she asked, reading the look on my face.

"I can't stay for dinner. I wanted to let you know that something pretty bad happened." All the blood started to drain from my mother's face. I held up my hand. "Just hear me out. Juliana is fine. Physically, at least."

"What happened, Marcel?" Mom demanded.

I sighed. "There was a shootout close to the restaurant where we were eating," I explained. "We weren't in the line of fire, but she was pretty shaken by the experience. I think we might need to get her into some kind of counselling or something... to help her get through it."

A hand flew to my mother's mouth. "Oh, my poor baby."

"I have to go, Ma. The taxi is waiting." I moved to walk away, but her voice stopped me in my tracks.

"Marcel." I turned to face her. "It didn't have anything to do with you, did it?"

I creased my lips and shook my head. "No, Ma, it didn't. Don't worry." I walked over to her and gave her a quick hug. As I exited the kitchen, Sofia came rolling in.

"Marcel." Sofia called again, anger lacing her voice.

"Go to dinner. I told you I don't have time right now." With that, I continued my way out the door. When I got back to the waiting taxi, I gave him another address that was about seven miles away from my home.

A few minutes later, I was standing in front of a stunning two-story house with dark walls and windows. The small gate to the side opened the minute the camera spotted me. Though no one was visible outside the gates, I knew well enough that there were guys scattered all over the premises. It was well secured.

Once I was inside, I nodded a greeting to a few of the men strolling about, smoking, drinking, and fooling around with some of the girls. As with the gate earlier, someone swung the double doors of the house entrance open for me and I stepped inside.

"Marcel, my man, where have you been?" I heard, coming from my right. I recognized the voice instantly. Kade, a tall, skinny man with a greying beard, was sitting on one of the couches, the women on either side of him wearing silk dresses that aroused the lust of men. He looked a little drunk.

"I'm here to see the boss," I told him, disregarding his question.

"Oh yeah. He's in his office. Step in." He let out a belch then broke into laughter. I scrunched up my nose in disgust. When I reached the boss's office, I knocked on the door once before stepping inside. Another unsurprising scene met me. Johnny was on his computer, more than likely checking on his next batch of shipments.

Johnny was not your ordinary "Boss". He had brains along with his knack for business. For all the years I'd known him, I'd never witnessed him wasting time, even though he allowed the rest of us to relax and have fun.

Although he only ruled from just over five feet, he was feared by all who worked for him.

"We have a problem," I told him when I shut the door. I slid into one of the chairs facing his desk. "There was a shootout involving the Cobras, close to Jack's Place. I was having dinner there with my little sister when it happened."

Johnny, who hadn't looked up once from his computer screen, met my eyes. His stare was as dark as my own but more intense. "I heard," he started. Of course he had. He had ears all over town. The news had probably reached him before I'd made it home. "Did any of the Cobras see you?" he asked, raising a perfect shaped eyebrow.

"No," I told him. "We almost ran into them in the alleyway at the back of the restaurant, but we managed to hide in time before they could see us."

"Good." He brought his attention back to the computer. "I don't need any of my boys on their radar. You already know how the game goes, son. An eye for an eye." A Bible phrase; his words reminded me of Norma. Norma. I needed to talk to her. I shook my head. I couldn't think of her right now. Especially not with Johnny here with me. If he found out I had my mind on other things and decided to dig into it, he would surely find out about her. I couldn't let that happen.

"I know." My throat felt like sandpaper saying the words. Swallowing to take the discomfort away, I asked, "Who does the corpse belong to?"

"He's the nephew of the Rioters' leader." Johnny replied. He paused before adding, "This is going to start a war between them. But we're not getting involved. It's none of our business."

Johnny feared no one. Still, he wasn't a man who played hard. He played smart; it was the one thing I admired about him.

"Got it, Boss," I said.

Johnny looked up from his computer screen a second time. "I'm going to need you to lay low for a while. The streets are going to get dangerous, and I don't want you or any of the guys getting caught up in it." He pulled out a drawer, took out an envelope, and then handed it to me. "This is yours. Good job on the last shipment."

I stood up to accept the envelope. "Thanks, Boss."

With that, Johnny returned to his computer.

The entrance hall of the house was rowdy when I got back out there. After receiving my envelope from Johnny, I understood the reason behind the boys' good mood. They didn't seem to have a care in the world.

"Come and have a drink with us," Kade called out to me. I tossed him a friendly nod but didn't mean it.

"Another time, man."

He groaned loudly. "That's what you say all the time. 'Another time' never comes. One of these days, I'm going to have to force the drink down your throat," he joked.

"Sorry, bro. I need to get home for dinner." Kade went back to his drink and his women who had their hands all over him.

I made a beeline for the exit, wanting to get home as soon as possible. I needed to talk to Norma. I had to know that we were okay, and that she wasn't going to run away from me. A few feet away from the door, one of the most gorgeous women I'd ever met in my life sauntered toward me. It was Tori, a woman I used to mess around with before Norma came into the picture.

"Where do you think you're going?" she asked. Snaking her arms around my neck and pressing her generous chest against mine. "I've been waiting for you all day, Marcel. Where've you been? I haven't seen you around lately. I've missed you," she whispered into my ear, then glanced up at me with a pair of sensual emerald eyes. A few weeks ago, I would've given in to her seduction. Now, I just found it bothersome. I unhooked her hands from my neck and stepped back.

She frowned, confused. "Not now, Tori. I have other things to take care of. I'm sure one of the other guys would love to accommodate you."

"Seriously?" she questioned. "Why would you even suggest…" she paused, eyeing me with suspicion. Then her mouth spread in a devious smile. "So, who's the lucky girl?"

"I don't know what you're talking about," I said, avoiding her eyes. How was it that women always knew when there was another girl? Her sharpness surprised me. Not that it mattered; we hadn't been exclusive. She had just been a woman for when I had wanted her. But she had latched onto me.

Her eyes twinkled with mischief. "I don't know half of what there is to know about you, Marcel, but I know enough to know there's definitely a girl. You've never said no to me before." That wasn't entirely true. I'd said no to her before countless times, though not directly. I'd give some excuses to escape her clutches when I wasn't in the mood for her.

"Maybe I'm just not interested anymore," I told her with a little shrug.

"Right," she replied with a knowing smile. Then she leaned in to me again and, in her low and suave voice said, "Don't worry, I won't tell Johnny. But I expect a parting gift," she added, backing away again and extending her slender hand. A golden bracelet was dangling from her wrist. Money for her silence. Of course.

Tori was a tall redhead with the most striking green eyes, full lips, a slender figure and perfect, porcelain skin. She was one of the few girls I'd gotten involved with while working for Johnny. I was now starting to regret it.

Knowing I wouldn't be able to get rid of her, I reached for my wallet and took out some cash, handing it to her. "Satisfied?" I spat out.

"Very." She gave me a quick kiss on the cheek. "Whoever she is, she's very lucky to have you." Then she walked away stuffing my money somewhere in her generous bosom. Quickly turning on my heels, I hightailed out of there before any disasters could happen.

As soon as I hit the streets, I jumped into another taxi. Fifteen minutes later, I was in my room, locked away from the rest of the house. I was feeling miserable, and I wasn't even sure why. I took a long hot shower, to wash the dirty feeling I had on me from the day. My muscles relaxed under the warm water as it trickled from my hair down to my feet. Once in bed, I couldn't keep my eyes off my cell phone.

All I could think about was Norma. I had to talk to her. If I didn't, I wouldn't be able to get any sleep. And my legs were already itching to go to her house. But what if she wouldn't talk to me?

I snatched up the phone, hating myself for how weak I was with this girl. I started to type out a message when Johnny's words replayed in my mind.

This is going to start a war between the Cobras and the Rioters.

War. I'd experienced a few turf wars over the past couple of years and none of them would be like this. Every side felt the negative effects of the battles. Anyone could get caught in the crossfire if they weren't careful. Norma and my family flooded into my head. While I wasn't going to get involved, I had to keep them safe in times like these.

But now I was distracted. I needed to stay away from Norma. Deep down, I knew I wasn't right for her, but my mind and my heart couldn't agree.

Norma had become my weakness. I hadn't lied when I'd told her that I felt like I couldn't breathe whenever I was away from her. Even while on my bed, my heart was racing just thinking of her, remembering her gorgeous smile, the way she blushed whenever I said something she wasn't used to hearing. My lips turned up in a grin at the memories.

Before long, I found myself typing out a message. I hesitated, my hand hovering over the send button for nearly a minute before I got the courage to hit *send*. The worst that could happen was her not replying.

Marcel: How are you?

A minute later, my cell phone beeped.

Norma: I'm alright. You?

Relief washed over me. I hadn't expected her to reply. After what had happened.

Marcel: I'm good. I'm sorry about what you went through today.

I bit my lips as I waited impatiently for her reply. I adjusted on my bed, to get more comfortable.

Norma: Stop apologizing, Bear. It wasn't your fault. How's Juliana?

She called me Bear, that was good.

Marcel: She's alright. Fell asleep on the way home. Told my mom we might need to get her into counselling.
Norma: That's a good idea.
Norma: I think I might need some myself :)

She sent the second text before I could reply to her first. She was joking, but I couldn't help but feel there was some underlying truth to her words. I was about to type out another *I'm sorry,* when another text came in.

Norma: Don't apologize again, Bear. You're not to blame.

It was like she was reading my mind. She didn't know a whole lot about me, but at the same time she already understood me. Her use of that term of endearment made me grin like an idiot. It proved she wasn't angry with me. My uneasiness was beginning to fade, but that feeling only lasted until another text came in from her.

Norma: I'm going to bed. Good night.

I wasn't ready to let her go. But what exactly could I talk about to get her to stay with me? There was only one thing that came to mind. Despite my lack of interest in the Jesus thing, I knew it was my only angle. I began typing out another message.

Marcel: What's your favorite Bible verse?

Norma: Interesting question.

Norma: It's Romans 5:8 "But God shows his love for us in that while we were still sinners, Christ died for us."

It worked. I had her right where I wanted her. With this, I could prolong the conversation. I typed out another message.

Marcel: Why that one?

Norma: Because it shows how much God loves us even when we are unlovable.

Marcel: Unlovable is not necessarily a word that suits you. I think you're very, very lovable.
Me, on the other hand. I'm an unlovable brute.

Norma: Ha! Don't be fooled. I've had my moments. I'm not perfect.

Marcel: I think you're perfect.

Norma: I make mistakes like everybody else. And I have my own inner battles. The worst part is that I can't talk to most people about it because they've already formed their own opinion of me. You're just another in that long line. I'm not as innocent as you might think.

My smile dipped when I read that last message and my brows pulled into a deep frown. I couldn't picture her doing something that bad.

Marcel: What battles?

Our conversation was taking another turn. My mind was running a mile a minute now, trying to figure out what she could have possibly done in her life to warrant the way she saw herself.

She had to be hiding something; there was no doubt about it. The urge to know Norma was so overwhelming, I *had* to know. For a while, I waited, my fingers fidgeting. I didn't want to blink as I stared at the phone, waiting for her reply.

None came.

I typed out another message.

Marcel: Norma?

Her message finally came a minute later.

Norma: Several months ago, I started dating a boy I shouldn't have. He came to visit me at home, and we ended up making out on my bed. It would have gone on to other things if my mom hadn't walked in on us. I'd never felt so disgusted with myself in my entire life.

Norma? Making out? With another guy? In her bed? The bare thought stung to the core of my being. At the same time, it made me laugh inside. For someone who could barely look me in the eye, I was surprised. I read her message half a dozen times before replying. She was disgusted with herself for merely kissing some boy. Wow. And here I was working overtime to keep my fifteen-year-old sister from sleeping with men twice her age.

Marcel: You shouldn't feel guilty. Most girls your age have done way more than just kissing some boy.

Norma: You don't understand. I'm a Christian girl. I should never have let that occur. I knew and yet I still let it happen.

This was an odd conversation. As someone who grew up on the streets, I didn't see anything wrong with two people having fun between the sheets. If both were in agreement, the pleasure was all theirs for the taking. My fingers moved frantically as I typed out my own opinion on the subject.

Marcel: I see absolutely nothing wrong with people having a good time. Maybe you shouldn't be listening to everything your Bible tells you.

The moment I sent that text, my phone started to ring. It was Norma. I answered immediately, excited to hear her voice.

"Hi, beautiful," I said.

I heard her sigh. "You really don't understand, do you?" she started.

"I suppose I don't," I admitted. "Pleasure is there for the taking. I don't have any guilty conscience about taking what I want."

"Right," Norma replied. "But we don't get to do whatever we want. As a believer in Jesus, my aim is to live a clean life before God. Of course, sometimes we make bad choices, but the goal is always to strive for a holy life, like Jesus did when he walked the Earth. I can't just go and sleep with some random guy, no matter how much my body might want that. You should also remember that just because everyone does it, doesn't make it right. Many things that are wrong have been normalized by society, and I won't follow in that line. Whenever I give myself to a man for the first time, it will be with my husband, in marriage."

As I listened to Norma boldly declaring her stance, I couldn't help but respect and admire her even more. Though her beliefs were putting an obstacle in my pursuit of her, she suddenly became the model I wanted my sisters to follow.

"Hmm," I replied, my tone teasing. "Does this mean I'll have to marry you before I get to kiss those succulent lips of yours again?" I understood exactly what she meant, but I couldn't help but ask.

Norma burst out laughing, the beautiful sound of it sending sweet tingles through my body. "You're so silly," she said. "I should go. It's getting late and I have work in the morning."

"Talk with me a little longer. Your voice is like a lullaby to me. We could fall asleep together," I joked.

"And if I do that, who is going to sing me to sleep?" She laughed. There were the tingles again.

"Fine, you win." I said.

As we said our goodbyes and hung up, my mind began to replay our conversation. Lying there, staring up at the ceiling, I came to the conclusion that, as much as I respected Norma's decision about how she lived her life, I couldn't give up on the chase. I had to have her.

One way or another, I was going to make her mine, even if it meant going to that little white church.

Chapter Eleven

Norma

"Bye, Reggie. Have a good night," I called out to the other security officer on duty. Reggie also happened to be a Christian. He attended another church in the city. Nothing felt better than learning that there were other believers at my workplace. Just like with Ron, Reggie and I became fast friends. I was already starting to regret that I would only have the job for a few more weeks. I had settled really well and was already getting quite comfortable; I would miss them when I left.

As soon as I stepped outside, I found Marcel waiting for me. He had been doing this for the past couple of weeks. Despite my refusal to go out on an "official" date with him, he was still determined to always escort me home after work. Each day, I would gather my belongings, secretly hoping I'd see him outside, and he never disappointed me. But I wasn't going to tell him that.

He's the most handsome man I've ever seen, I thought, as I walked toward him. I was dying to know what he looked like without his bandana. Would I ever know?

I often wondered what he would have been doing if not for picking me up, but I never asked him. During our walks I did my best not to question him. He wasn't ready to open up and I didn't want to push. After what I'd experienced a couple of weeks ago, I suspected I wouldn't like his answers.

It was stupid to keep entertaining him, but Marcel had been asking so many questions about the Bible, I didn't have the heart to turn him away.

Please. You know you want that guy as much as he wants you.

I ignored the voice of reason within me and waved a hand in Marcel's direction. "Hey."

"Hi." He said, strolling over to me. He had that same cat like swag to his steps, just as the first time I'd laid eyes on him. Marcel was getting more handsome with each passing day, and he definitely got the attention of the girls passing by. Often, when we walked down the road, I would notice other girls watching him in awe. I was surprised he never gave any of them a second glance. This always made me feel better, although I never mentioned it.

Marcel was next to me within seconds. For a couple of minutes, we walked together in silence. I had been expecting him to start up a conversation, but he seemed bent on remaining deep in his own thoughts. I would glance at him every once in a while, but look away quickly whenever he turned to me.

Wondering if something was bothering him, I broke the silence and asked, "No questions today?" His silence was awkward, and I could no longer stand it. He looked at me and merely smiled.

Sighing, I decided to do the talking. "How's Juliana?"

"Still seeing the counselor," he simply responded.

I nodded. Since the incident at the restaurant, Marcel had made sure she never missed a session with her therapist. I was touched. It showed how much he cared about his younger sister. It was awful that she had to experience such a horrible thing at such a young age.

"Did your mother ask you any questions about that night?" I asked.

He nodded. "Juliana talked to her about what happened. I'm sure I don't need to say she was horrified. My mom told me once I had left that evening, she had woken up and couldn't sleep again till my mother had comforted her and assured her nothing bad would happen to her." I nodded.

We continued walking in silence, with occasional glances at each other. Since I wasn't used to us walking together like this, it wasn't long before I spoke up again. "Is everything else okay?" I just needed to ask. Since he was usually the one to start our conversations.

"Sure," he answered. "Everything is fine." Then he fell silent again. I wanted to groan in frustration. "Why are you asking?" he asked.

"You're not your usual chatty self today."

"Hmm," he murmured. "I thought you didn't want to hear me speak so much." One side of his lips lifted up in a smirk. "Do you miss the sound of my voice, Norma?" he teased.

"Don't be so full of yourself. I'm just saying, it's unlike you. To talk so little."

"Just admit it, beautiful." He chuckled. "I won't bite you…not yet." He added the last part in such a low voice, it almost escaped my ears, but I caught it. I decided to ignore it. I wasn't going to let it get to me, not now.

"Fine, maybe I do miss your voice...just a little."

"Tell me about the seven deadly sins," he said out of the blue, surprising me.

I whipped my head up to look at him. "The seven deadly sins?" I would think he wouldn't even know anything about that, since I doubted, he had ever opened the Bible. "Where did you hear about that, Mr. I'm-not-into-the-Jesus-thing?" A deep chuckle reverberated in his throat.

"A colleague of mine, actually," he replied. "He told me that anger is one of the seven deadly sins. Since you know so much about things like this, maybe you could tell me more."

Colleagues. Right. I supposed that was a nicer way of saying fellow criminals.

"Your friend is right, but not completely," I told him. "It's wrath, not anger."

"Uh, sounds like the same thing to me," Marcel commented.

"They're not, though. Not really. Anger is normal. We all experience it. There are many examples, but for now let's keep it simple and I'll just give you, my opinion. If that's okay?" I paused waiting for a reply.

He only nodded. So, I continued, "I think it depends on the type and reason for the anger. Being angry is sometimes justified, sometimes not. But what matters, especially with anger, is your level of self-control. While you experience the emotion. Wrath is anger that's out of control. It's expressed with violence. Wrath consumes a person whereas an angry person can usually keep control of themself." I said. But Marcel stayed silent. I could see he was taking in each word I spoke.

After some seconds, he said, "Okay. That kind of makes sense," nodding only slightly. "But if someone hurt one of my little sisters, it should be within my right to exact vengeance on their behalf." I saw where he was coming from. Without a doubt, he would want to inflict pain on someone who had hurt one of his loved ones. I wanted to explain more but maybe this was too much too soon.

"Of course, *you* would think that. But God said that vengeance belongs to Him. When someone hurts us or the people we love, we have a legal system in place for it. Also, when it comes to taking vengeance, it's not our place either, it's God's."

Marcel came to a full-on stop and stared at me incredulously. I knew he genuinely didn't understand what I was saying. And now he looked confused; I wasn't surprised. After all, the lifestyle he appeared to lead required it of him. I didn't even want to think about the things he might have done.

"You can't be serious," he exclaimed, shaking his head. "So, you're telling me that if someone were to hurt you again, you wouldn't want me to kill the man who touched you?"

That night quickly flashed before me, but I replied, "Yes. That's what I'm saying." Though it was hard for him to believe, he needed to understand that it wasn't right.

"That's crazy, Norma. I don't think I would be able to stop myself. Sorry, but I can't follow all the rules from that book of yours. They're too much."

I smiled compassionately. "I understand," I said. "And I don't expect you to follow every rule from my Bible. But with time, Marcel, and when you come to know more, you will understand." I thought for a while. "Do you know any stories, or specific verses?"

"The story of Adam and Eve."

"That's a good one. Any others?" When he was silent in thought, I said, "How about any line you could pick out from the Bible?"

Marcel's lips pursed and he shook his head. "I think my favorite quote of your book is where it says *an eye for an eye*. That's one that makes sense to me. All these other things about not hurting those who hurt me or the people I care about, that stuff is just ludicrous."

Although I didn't need Marcel to tell me what he meant by that, still I proceeded to ask anyway. "So, what exactly are you saying?" I wanted to hear more.

Marcel shrugged. "It's something my boss always says. If someone hurts you, you hurt them back. An eye for an eye, an arm for an arm. That's the way things work in my life."

I shook my head. "You can't just choose the parts of the Bible that suit you."

He smiled at me. "I'm sure I can start from anywhere and I've decided to start from that part."

Marcel was definitely taking things the wrong way. "Do you know there's another Bible verse that says if anyone slaps you on the right cheek, you should turn the other side to him also?"

He frowned. "What for?"

"To show that you wouldn't yield to violence. Two wrongs don't make a right."

He looked at me wide-eyed and laughed in disbelief. "You can't be serious? If someone lays their hand on me, they get mine back on them. It's a give and take situation, sweetheart. So, if someone came up to you and slapped you, you would turn your other cheek?"

I shook my head. "Marcel..." I tried to explain, but words failed me.

"I'm still a work in progress. I haven't heard that part, yet. But let's be real. That one will definitely not work for me."

"But it's there," I assured him, standing and facing him. A simple gesture that was meant to drive home my point.

He nodded. We stood like that for a while, staring into each other's eyes. He took a little step forward, moving closer to me. I didn't say a word, mostly because I didn't know what to say. "You're beautiful," he said softly, his hand gently touching my face. My heart was beating faster than necessary, but I couldn't help it. With so much passion and intensity. I saw the raw and unfiltered desire that lay in them.

"Mar…" The words died in my throat when his fingers touched my lips. Our bodies were now touching. It was the smallest contact, but strong enough to create sparks in my heart. I wanted to say something, anything.

"I've wanted to do this, since the very first day I saw you." Marcel's head dipped lower, but I still couldn't let myself escape from his touch. I know I should, but I didn't want to. I'm trying to be good. *Jesus, help me here.*

"I'm…I'm…" I stuttered, my knees were going weak, my head felt light. "Please," I whispered. I didn't even know what I was begging for, I should be escaping his clutches, but I wanted his lips on mine more than anything else.

The earth seemed to revolve around this moment as every other thing faded into nothing. It was just this moment…just us…Marcel and me.

"Shhhh," he whispered, tenderly brushing the corner of my lips with his thumb. Then his finger left my lips. Without another word, Marcel's mouth caught mine. For a split second, I was frozen. My head was foggy, and I felt my legs weaken. I put my hands on his chest for strength. His hand reached out to grab hold of my waist, pulling me even closer to him. I kissed him back, returning it with as much intensity, satisfying the desires I had craved for so long. It was tantalizing.

As soon as his hands reached my neck, I came to my senses again. I raised my hands to push him back a little. He stopped, pulling back when he felt my resistance. Slowly, I stepped away from him.

"Norma," he whispered, his dark eyes searching mine.

I shook my head, trying to catch my breath before I spoke. "Bear, we can't do this," I said, my voice barely audible. I looked around as busy people passed us by on the sidewalk.

He smiled. "Are you concerned about the kiss, or the location? Because if it's the location, I can take you somewhere else."

Guilty as charged. Although I was certain my face was already red from embarrassment, because to be honest with myself, I wasn't upset about the fact that he had kissed me, or the location either. It had taken me by surprise, although it shouldn't have. The energy between us was hard to ignore. The kiss was bound to happen, it had just been a matter of time.

I was used to calling him Bear now. It rolled off my tongue like my second language.

He stepped even closer to me, and said, "You're breathtaking. I just couldn't resist kissing you anymore. I know I should tell you that I'm sorry, but that would be a lie. I'm not sorry. At all."

"It's fine, Marcel." I murmured, looking away. Afraid that if I stared at him for much longer, I might be the one leaning in for a second kiss.

He placed a finger under my chin, tipping it back, so I could look him in the eye. “I love your lips. That kiss, *with you*, was perfect.”

I bit my lower lip.

He looked down to my lips. There was conflict in his eyes. “I'm sorry Norma, but if you don't want me to kiss you again, you have to stop doing that.” Slowly he looked back into my eyes before he continued, “And you need to stop kissing me back.”

I let go of my lip quickly. I didn't realize it would have any effect on him. “Sorry.”

“Let's keep walking.” He reached for my hand but instead of allowing him to take it, I decided to put a little distance between us. I wanted to be alone. I wanted to think about the attraction, the kiss, and the consequences of this.

“Is there a problem?” Marcel asked, his tone filled with deep concern.

“No,” I simply answered and looked away.

“Kissing me doesn't change the fact that you're a good girl. I know you're beating yourself up over that,” he said, as though he was reading my mind. “My respect for you is still beyond what you could imagine. So please, don't push me away.”

To distract myself from the situation and the tension arising between us, I began to look for something that could catch and hold my attention. I spotted a hot-dog stand not far from us. The man under the big red umbrella was fixing an order for a customer. This was exactly what I needed for some diversion. I sent a quick and silent ‘thank you Jesus’ towards Heaven and pointed my chin in that direction. Marcel’s eyes followed my gesture.

“Would you like a hot-dog?” I needed a way of escape, to gather my thoughts, but *that* was so random. Probably the stupidest thing I’d ever said. *Would you like a hot-dog?* What a ridiculous thing to say.

Regardless, I began digging through my bag for my wallet. By the time I found the thing, Marcel was standing in front of me, holding two of them. I hadn't even seen him move.

"Oh. Let me pay you for those," I said. Another smirk grew on his lips, as he leaned forward so his face was somewhat level with mine. I thought he was going to kiss me again.

"You, Norma Tesoriere, are making me feel wrathful," he said barely above a whisper. I tried. I really tried to keep a straight face. In the end, I couldn't hold back the laugh that escaped my lips.

"You're kind of silly, you know that?" I said. When he smiled, his eyes lit up. I slid the money back in my purse then collected the hot-dog from his hand. I bit into it, realizing then that I was hungrier than I'd thought. At the same moment, I spotted a taxi coming our way and flagged it down.

"Thanks for the hot-dog," I hurriedly told Marcel. "See you tomorrow, I guess."

W*hy am I being so awkward*?

It had just been one kiss, yet I couldn't look him in the face. All the confidence I'd previously had was now gone. Now, whenever I looked at him, my heart doubled its pace. I could still feel his lips on mine even though they were long gone. As if they had imprinted themselves on mine. I wanted to taste them again, but I didn't dare.

Marcel didn't reply. Instead, he opened the back door to let me in, then slid in right beside me. "You really don't have to accompany me home every evening, you know. I'm a big girl."

"Of course, you are," he answered, with a hint of sarcasm.

We sat in silence for most of the drive. I was pulled from my thoughts when I noticed we were on the street where my church was located. I had been planning to go straight to my house, but it was a little late and our Bible study would be starting soon.

"You can leave me here," I told the driver. I turned to Marcel. "I need to stop here."

"I thought you were going home," Marcel commented, confused.

"I was, but I decided to stop at church instead for a Bible study," I explained. An idea formed in my head just then and I turned to look at him. "Would you like to come in with me?" Honestly, I was expecting a no, along with an excuse about work, or needing to get home to his family.

"Sure, why not." Marcel replied. Had I not been sitting I probably would have lost my balance.

"Really?" I asked, surprised.

He chuckled. "Yes, really. If that means I'll be sitting next to you for another hour, then I have no problem with that." Marcel paid the driver before slipping out of the vehicle. I sat in place, knowing he enjoyed helping me out of the car.

As we walked on the church grounds together, I perused the area, finding a handful of familiar faces here and there. I waved at each group as we continued toward the little white church that was my spiritual home.

Just before we reached the front doors, I spotted Betty Ann and Trudy standing to the side, deep in conversation. When the two saw me with Marcel, they gaped at us. Tugging at his arm, I led him towards them.

"Hey guys!" I called. They remained speechless watching us approach until we stopped before them.

"Who is this?" Trudy asked, her eyes trained on the giant of a man standing beside me. She looked from Marcel to me, then back to Marcel.

"Oh, uh, this is Marcel," I explained. "Marcel, these are my friends, Betty Ann and Trudy." The girls were more than eager to shake his hand and I almost cover my mouth to stop myself from cracking up.

"It's a pleasure to meet you, ladies," Marcel said, his voice deep and velvety as usual.

"Likewise," Trudy replied, giving him a friendly smile. "And welcome to our church."

"Yes. Welcome," Betty Ann choked out. I could see her brain spinning its wheels, lining up questions to throw my way as soon as she had me alone. She was just keeping her cool because Marcel was present.

Trudy shook her head from one side to the next. "Oh Norma, how do you manage to find these handsome men so easily?" I grinned at her, but my smile faltered a little when I found Marcel staring at me. Thankfully, he didn't comment on the subject, but I knew he was going to question me about it later.

"We should get inside," I told the girls.

"Sure thing. We'll talk later," Betty Ann said, throwing me an inquisitive look. With that, I led Marcel inside the church.

We headed to one of the pews on the right, halfway from the front and sat down together. For the first few minutes, Marcel was dead silent, but I knew it wouldn't last long.

"So, is there someone else?" he finally asked. He tried to sound casual, but I could hear the jealousy in his tone.

"Not that I know of," I told him, teasing. "Trudy was just referring to this other guy from my school. She met him at the same restaurant where I saw you for the first time. He was our waiter. My friends were trying to set me up with him, but I wasn't interested." I looked at him. "Relieved?"

He made a grunting noise in the back of his throat. Based on my experience with my teenage brother, I'd say that meant he was pleased. Though perhaps still irritated by the idea that there might have been another guy. He was probably feeling *wrathful* about it. The thought made me chuckle.

"No need to laugh," he said with a childish pout. It was so cute coming from him.

"You don't even know why I'm laughing," I said, trying to control myself.

"You're laughing at me," he grumbled.

I snorted. "Not sure why you're being so grumpy. You should be happy. Practically all the single women in the building are looking in your direction right now." Which was actually true; my eyes were not missing the glances they kept sending his way.

A smirk grew on his lips. "Maybe. But my heart is set on you."

I had no idea how to react when he said these things.

"Um, most of our members are women," I told him. "It's the same in most churches. More women than men."

"Really? Had I known that, I would have stepped into one of these buildings a long time ago," Marcel remarked.

"Says the guy who said only seconds ago that he only had eyes for me." I realized then that his words had bothered me more than I wanted to admit. Did he mean that? After the kiss we just shared?

"It was a joke, babe," he said. "But I'm glad to know you do feel jealous over me."

I stared at him. "Excuse me? I am not jealous."

"You are."

"You're incorrigible."

"And yet you still like me. Notice that's a statement, not a question," he said with confidence but beaming.

I didn't get the chance to reply. I could hear Pastor Archie calling my name. I looked up to see him coming my way, a smile as usual. I liked the fact that he didn't wear a suit and tie. He normally wore dress pants and a button-up shirt, but tonight he was dressed even more casually. Blue jeans and a polo shirt.

"Pastor Archie, hi," I said. "How are you?"

"I'm doing well, thank you. How are you?"

"Much better, thanks," I told him. "By the way, I'd like to introduce you to Marcel Maxwell. He's the one who protected me from those guys last month. Marcel, this is Pastor Archie."

The two men shook hands. "Good to meet you. And thank you for allowing the Lord to use you to protect our Norma." Marcel frowned at that. No doubt he was conflicted about the idea of God using him to protect me.

"It was the least I could do."

"Well, I'm happy you're here tonight. I sure hope you'll enjoy our Bible study.

"I hope so, too," Marcel replied.

When Pastor Archie moved on to greet someone else, I told Marcel, "I'm going to the altar to pray."

That signature frown of his was back. Being the good sport he was, however, he nodded. "Okay. I'll be here." He retook his seat while I headed for the altar. Usually, this was a much easier task for me, but for some reason, I couldn't get my thoughts together as my knees hit the cushion. Not only that, but I could feel Marcel's intense eyes boring into my back.

He made me uneasy at times. Still, I was delighted he was sitting in church with me. This was where I had wanted him for the past few weeks. Now, if I could only get him to see that this Jesus thing, as he called it, was good for him.

Chapter Twelve

Marcel

Church had never been an interest of mine. It still wasn't. And yet, there I was, inside a church building, my eyes glued to the back of a woman whom I hadn't been able to get out of my mind for the past several weeks.

Months ago, never would I have believed that I would one day be sitting here, facing an altar. Moreover, the people around me weren't giving me weird or judging looks like I had expected them to, instead, they all minded their own business. I twisted my neck, which seemed to have gone stiff as I froze in one position.

Norma was kneeling on a platform at the front of the sanctuary, with a few other men and women. Her head was bowed in prayer, her hands clasped together. Today, she was wearing blue jeans, a beautiful green blouse, and her long black hair laid perfectly on her back. This girl was stunning. Both on the inside and out. She was extraordinary.

The fact that she could be with anyone else, anyone much better than I was, but still chose to hang around with me just melted my heart. Sometimes it felt almost surreal standing beside her and listening to her speak. All her little habits, the ones she wasn't even aware she had were the cutest. The way she blushed over every little thing, the way she sometimes bit the corners of her lips when she was deep in thought, or the way she scrunched her nose whenever I gave her a cheesy reply, everything about her was irresistible.

For some foolish reason, I had started comparing her to all the other women I'd ever been with, and I had to laugh at myself inside. Seriously, was it even worth it to pursue this girl? Norma was pure, sweet, gentle, perfect in every way. Even though I wanted her badly, I detested the idea of corrupting something so amazing. I had strong feelings for her. They were becoming stronger with every waking moment I spent with her. She was doing something to me. Something I couldn't quite explain. Even with my eyes glued to her, I still hadn't decided if I liked what her presence in my life was doing to me. And I needed to decide fast, or I was going to fall in love with her. I just knew it.

There was a part of me that was compelling me to walk away while there was time. But there was another part that dreaded the thought of not being able to see her, talk to her or hold her hand the few times she would allow me. It was unimaginable that I was satisfied with those simple little things. For Pete's sake, how did I become so ensnared with this girl? It was ridiculous how hard I was falling for her.

I ran a hand over the back of my neck and sighed.

I felt a tap on my shoulders and turned to see an elderly woman standing behind me. I was confused for a moment; was I in her seat or something? "Hi," I said, in a low voice, to avoid disturbing the prayerful silence that had fallen over the room.

"The Hymn book." That's when I noticed her other hand was stretched forth holding a small burgundy book. The front cover simply read 'HYMNS'. I looked back at the woman. What exactly did she want me to do with it? It wasn't like I knew any of the songs in the book that I could sing along to, but then again, she didn't know that. "Do you already have one?" she asked after I didn't give her an answer.

Should I have come with one? Norma hadn't mentioned that. I looked around to see if Norma had brought one with her, but when I found none, I turned back to the woman. "No, I don't have one," I answered. I stretched out my hand to collect the book.

"Are you new here?" she asked. "I haven't seen you before." I nodded. "Oh, that's great." I watched her as she walked away to hand out the hymnal to other people. I'd never held one before.

I set it aside, turning my eyes back to Norma, as she rose and started to return to her seat next to me. She smiled shyly as she started to sit down, and I forced a fake smile. The questioning look in her eyes told me that she caught on to me. Was this a special gift women had to detect lies so easily? My mom was also good at this. They could easily see behind the mask I was putting on and could immediately tell if something was wrong.

"Are you alright?" she asked as she took her seat, grabbing my hand to give a little comforting squeeze.

There was no need to let her know how anxious I was feeling at the moment. No need to make her worry. I was here now and there was no going back. So, I put on a bigger fake smile and did one of the simplest things in the world to me. I did what I do best. I lied, "Yeah, yeah, I'm fine."

She studied me for a moment, choosing her next words as she bit the corner of her mouth. She looked down and her eyes caught sight of the hymnal. I seized the opportunity to distract her. "Some woman brought this for us," I told her.

"That must have been Mrs. Perez. She helps with passing these out," she said, and I just nodded.

"You seem nervous, Marcel, but you don't need to be. I promise. And I appreciate that you kept your word. But if you're not comfortable, you should let me know, it's fine." She said, her eyes filled with compassion. This pulled at my heart strings. Her soft tones were sending tingles all over my body. But I didn't want to worry her with my anxiety, it wasn't that serious and there was no need to make her fuss.

I shook my head. "Don't worry, it's nothing. As long as the ceiling doesn't fall on us, it's okay," I told her, hoping to make her laugh. And she did.

Pastor Archie was on his way to the podium. He didn't dress like I thought a pastor would, he looked so relaxed and informal. When I glanced around, I realized people were starting to file in from outside, so I assumed that the service was about to begin.

I attempted to clear my mind, so I could get through this experience without any preconceived notions. Kind of hard to do since I'd already had a lot of those long before meeting Norma.

"Hey guys," I heard her whisper. I turned, looking behind us to see Rico and Luna coming toward us. Rico turned red with irritation, and averted his gaze when he saw me looking at him, and faced his sister instead. The two slid into the bench on the other side of Norma.

"Hi, Marcel," Luna said, beaming from ear to ear. Her hair was pulled back with a black hair clip that matched the dress she wore. Though she was taller than Norma, this made her look much younger. "Nice to see you again."

"Hi, Luna," I smiled. I liked the girl's energy; I couldn't say the same about Rico. "Good to see you too," I simply replied. She nodded and turned quickly to face her sister, whispering something into her ear. Probably asking her how she got a guy like me to come to church with her.

You want to know, little girl? She stole my heart, that's what she did, I thought while watching them settle into their seats, a smirk pulling at my lips. I shook my head, holding myself back.

You're pathetic, Marcel.

A woman appeared in front of us, her presence casting a dark shadow. When I looked up, I was almost certain it was Aunt Mari because of the resemblance, until I caught the questioning look. This was definitely Norma's mother, Marissa Tesoriere. She did look a lot like her sister, but there were some things I noticed this sister did that the other didn't. Aunt Mari had had her hair in a messy bun when I'd met her. From the couple of times I'd seen Mrs. Tesoriere, she always wore her hair styled neatly. I understood why Norma had told me they were almost complete opposites.

"Hi, *Bambina*," she started, glancing back and forth between us.

"Mom," Norma said, her voice a bit squeaky. "I didn't know you would be coming for study today. I thought you said you were going to rest since you were so tired?"

"Yes," Marissa nodded. "But after I had a short nap, I felt better so here I am." She glanced at me. "Who is this?" She asked, assessing me from head to toe, then looking back at Norma.

Norma glanced at me then back to her mother. "Mom, this is Marcel Maxwell. He's the one who helped me when those guys attacked me," she added, surprising me with the clarity in her voice. But what stunned me even more was what she had just revealed to her mother.

Mrs. Tesoriere's eyes went wide and it made me wonder what exactly was going on in her head. She was as curious as her older sister had been, but in a different way. While Mariana was full of mischief, this lady seemed more… Level-headed.

"Well, it's a pleasure to meet you," she said decisively. "I must thank you a million times over for protecting my *bambina.* I don't know what we would have done if we had lost her that night."

I know what I would have done. But let's not talk about that.

Instead of telling her what I really thought, I said, "It was the least I could do, Mrs. Tesoriere. You have a little fighter on your hands, here. She didn't make it easy for them." I offered Norma a smile, and as if on cue, she blushed. Her mother was still watching us like a hawk. It was unnerving. Which was strange, considering not even Aunt Mari had driven the least bit of fear inside me. Mrs. Tesoriere was a tiny woman, but I sensed she could be a force to be reckoned with. I had to force myself not to squirm like a little boy being scolded by his mommy.

"Why did you run off?"

I whipped my head up to meet Mrs. Tesoriere's eyes. "I'm sorry?"

"Why did you leave that night after you helped my daughter?" she asked again.

"Oh. I'm truly sorry about that. I had an emergency at home. That's where I was headed, and I had no choice." The lie slipped past my tongue like butter on a knife. I did it most times without even thinking, and usually, I didn't feel any kind of guilt about it.

Under the scrutiny of Norma's mother, however, it was a different story. I took a peek at Norma who was also watching me. Her eyes did not bode any form of accusation in them, but I felt as guilty as if I'd killed a man. Where was this remorse coming from?

The answer came as soon as I asked myself the question. It was her. Norma. She was slowly changing me.

"Alright, everyone, let's come together," Pastor Archie said from the podium. "We need to get started."

The chatter in the room died down and all eyes turned to him. Mrs. Tesoriere finally ripped her eyes from me and took her own seat.

Thank God.

Pastor Archie led the group into prayer, followed by a reading from the Bible. Proverbs, I believe he said. As I listened, I realized that he was reading about the seven deadly sins. Memories rolled back as an image of Norma and I talking about this same topic came to my mind.

Momentarily, my face broke into a smirk. Glancing at Norma, I found that she was smiling as well but attempting to hide it.

After his greeting, Pastor Archie dove right into his teaching. I listened keenly to every word that fell out of his mouth.

"The wrath of man is cold, cruel, disastrous, and nothing good ever comes out of it," the preacher said. "But when it comes to God's wrath, it's filled with righteousness and justice. God, sometimes give us what we don't deserve, to test our faith. To make us stronger. Look at Job," He'd said, with a slight pause. Then continued, "And we'll read more about Job in next week's study. But know, if we do well, He will reward us. If we do bad things, He will punish us. It's just the way things work."

As I listened to the older man, I found myself agreeing with him. I was an example of how cruel a man could be. I couldn't begin to count on both my hands the number of people I'd hurt since I had chosen the path I was on. When I had just started out, I used to feel terrible about it. Now, it was like second nature.

"The Lord Jesus is the only one who can bring us goodness and hope," I heard him say when I zoned back in. "Without Him, our path will remain dark. No matter how difficult our situation, God always knows how to bring light and peace to our pathway. And isn't this why Jesus came to Earth to die for our sins? He did it so that we can escape His wrath and may be able to walk in His light."

Something about those words hit a sensitive spot in my heart. Although he wasn't looking directly at me, it seemed like his teaching had been only for me. Or was it just pure coincidence that this was the topic for the day, the same day Norma and I had a debate over the subject, just before we kissed? Was this a sign? Was this Jesus actually setting me up?

I was so startled by it, I stiffened in my seat. Norma must have felt my reaction because she turned to look at me then, her brows furrowed. "Are you okay?" she mouthed.

A giant lump formed in my throat, and all I could do was nod in response.

The experience was crazy. Why was I feeling like that? Like I wanted to break down and weep. Like I was feeling devastated over the way my life had turned out. Did I truly feel that way or was this some kind of voodoo action taking me over? I knew I was being ridiculous, over-analyzing this. Still, my anxiety rose like it had gasoline poured on it. Every word that came out of Pastor Archie's mouth seemed to be directed at me. As far as I knew,

Norma hadn't talked to him about me, and he and I hadn't had a real conversation. So why did it seem like he knew everything about me?

I twisted my palms into a tight fist, my nails digging into my skin as I struggled to calm down, but the moment Norma lifted a hand to touch me, I lost it. I jumped off the bench, surprising even myself. Norma turned to look at me wide-eyed. I needed to get out of this place. Church life was not for me. I knew that. And yet I had allowed myself to be dragged there by a pretty face. It was time to go.

With that decision, I spun away, rushed past the pews filled with people and headed for the double doors that led outside. I could feel everyone's eyes following me. Even Pastor Archie seemed to have paused his teaching for a split second. But they were the least of my problems. Unlike before, there was no one outside and darkness had already started to descend on the streets. I was almost on the sidewalk when I heard Norma calling my name.

I hadn't expected her to follow me, since her mother and siblings were inside with her, but she still had. I could hear her hurried steps as she ran to catch up with me, but I didn't stop. Maybe she would finally give up and go. I couldn't go back to that church; the words were like knives in my heart. I had been led into a room full of painful truths that filled me with a guilt I'd never known before.

"Marcel. Marcel!" I didn't stop. Her voice lifted to a higher octave when she said, "Bear." The term of endearment froze me in place. Her steps slowed when she saw I had stopped. Soon she was standing right in front of me. Her breath was a bit heavy as she looked into my eyes with concern. "What happened in there?" she asked. "What's wrong?"

What's wrong? What exactly do I say to that?

"Nothing. I need to go," I told her.

"It's not nothing, Bear," she said. "Please, just tell me what's wrong."

I growled, hating myself for what I was about to do. With a single step back, I told her with a firm but low tone. "I'm sorry, Norma, but I never should have come here. This is the last place I should be." I expected her to launch into some kind of explanation about how God wanted to save my soul. Instead, she stood there eyeing me with an odd look. Then she stepped closer to me. She paused for a moment before softly saying. "You feel Him, don't you? You feel the Holy Spirit. He's tugging at your heart right now and it's scaring the living daylights out of you."

"Scared?" I snarled. "I don't get scared, Norma. You should know that by now." My outburst seemed to do nothing to intimidate her. She closed the gap between us a little more by taking another step forward.

"You don't have to be afraid, Bear," she whispered. "He just wants you to let Him in. He wants to step into your life and change everything for the better. And I promise you, it will get better."

Peeved by her naïveté for the first time ever, I backed away from her again. "There's so much you don't understand. You're too innocent. Listen to me, this life, this world I'm in, nothing can fix it, not even your perfect, super awesome Jesus. There is nothing and no one that can save me from this. And I'm not going to drag you down with me. Do you understand?"

She was already shaking her head. "No, Bear, no." She closed the distance again, this time resting her small hand on my upper arm as if to stop me from backing away from her. "God can save you from anything, but only if you let Him. Don't walk away."

She was ripping me to shreds and she didn't even know it. I lifted a hand to her cheek and slowly stroked her face with my fingers. "You're a good girl. Too good for me. You are full of light. But me, I'm full of darkness. You were right when you told me in the beginning that we didn't belong together. I was just too selfish, and I didn't listen. I wanted what I knew deep inside I couldn't have."

"Bear, please, stop," Norma choked out, her voice hoarse with emotion. "Don't say that."

"I've done a lot of bad things in my life, baby," I went on. "Too much for me to ever be forgiven. Now more than ever, I regret choosing this path. For the first time in my life, I feel so incredibly guilty. About everything. About the people's lives that I've destroyed. But you know what? I can't back out now. This is who I am. And your Jesus can't change that."

"I understand how you feel, Bear, I do," Norma argued. "But you have to understand. God can fix anything. He can protect you." She reached for both of my hands and clasped them in hers. "Will you let me pray with you?"

"Norma, please listen to me —"

"I have, and you're not making any sense, Bear, why won't you listen to me?"

"Because I'll never be good enough for your religion, for your faith, Norma. Don't you understand? We're too different, you and I. We were never even meant to cross paths. I should have walked away sooner; it was crazy for me to chase after you." I couldn't look her in the eyes, couldn't bear to see her cry. I had promised to protect her from any harm, and here I was, the reason for her tears. This was proof enough for me that getting involved in Norma's story would only have a bad ending for her.

"Marcel, please don't say that. Let's talk about this."

Another sigh rose out of me. But she continued.

"Marcel, have you heard of Billy Graham?"

Hasn't everyone? I thought, but only nodded.

"In my opinion, he's the greatest evangelist in history, except for Jesus. He once said, *You can't change your past. But you can determine your destiny, by deciding for Christ. And when you do that, Christ changes your past. He wipes out all the sins of the past.* Marcel, please. Let Jesus do that for you too."

"Stop wasting your time on me, Norma. I'm not worth it, trust me." Her lips parted, no doubt to argue her point further. I lifted a finger and pressed it gently against her mouth. "No," I demanded. "I'm leaving now and I'm not coming back. You need to forget about me. Move on with your life and find someone who is worthy of the shining and sparkling treasure that you are."

She tried to pull away, but I pressed harder on her lips to keep her silent. "It's better this way and you know it." Lifting my finger from her lips, I pulled her into my arms for one last embrace. I wanted to kiss her so badly, but instead, I just kissed her forehead. The scent of her cherry blossom shampoo hit my nose. It was the hardest thing for me to let her go.

"Take care of yourself." It was the last thing I said before turning my back to her and walking away. I was glad that she didn't hold me back this time, but still her words pulled at my heart.

"Bear. Please. Don't." Norma cried from behind me. A sob broke out of her, wrenching at my heart. I wanted to turn around, scoop her into my arms and never let her go. But that was only a dream. I'd played this game for too long, dragging us both through the mud of deception. As difficult as it was, I didn't turn around. I continued to walk away from the girl I wanted with every last fiber of my being. I focused on keeping one foot in front of the other, ignoring the tremor in my limbs.

Chapter Thirteen

Marcel

"No, please! I'll pay him. I swear I'll pay him. I just need some more time. Please." A voice screamed out in pain. Calm and unflinching, I continued to do my job. Pale blue, yet unsteady eyes, glanced up at me, pleading for me to stop.

But I was in my groove. It was my job to straighten these guys out and I enjoyed every minute of it. At least, I thought I did. Something was burning inside of me. I wasn't sure what and didn't care to know why.

Nevertheless, I returned to work, balling my huge fist and connecting with force to the face of the idiot on the floor. Those eyes that were begging me mere seconds ago were now swollen shut. Crazy how this made me feel better.

The feeling didn't last long. Something was in my chest. Something heavy. It was scorching me from the inside out. I turned around to look at my partners, Kade and Scotty. To my surprise, they were not there. Other people stood there in their place. People I knew well. And other men I had also backed into a corner or beaten almost unrecognizable.

They were all staring at me accusingly. The guy behind me who looked like he could barely move, stood with them. His eyes were still swollen, yet he managed to pierce me with his pale, ugly eyes. It was unnerving. Feeling a little bit daunted, I took a single step back, only to collide with someone else. It wasn't just anyone. It was a little boy. I remembered his face well. He had watched from his closet, as I roughed up his dad for trying to skip town when he owed the boss money. Now here he was, staring up at me, tears in his eyes just like that night.

"Monster!" he cried. "You're a monster."

The bloodied men on the other side began to chant those words. "Monster. You're a monster."

Suddenly, I felt fear wash over me like I'd never felt it before. My knees wobbled. The metallic smell of blood assaulted my nostrils. I wanted to run, but they were closing in on me, labelling me for what I really was.

A cruel, heartless man.

With my heart racing in my chest, I started to run from them.

I sprung upright in bed and glanced around the dark room. My entire body was dripping with sweat. I gripped my chest, feeling my heart palpitating at a terrifying speed. For a moment, I was afraid it would break free from my rib cage.

"It was just a dream," I told myself, rubbing my chest. Still, that did nothing to calm me. For the past week, that's what my nights had become like. I ran my shaking hands over my face but pulled them away quickly when the iron smell of fresh blood hit my nose. I sprang out of bed, hurried to the bathroom and flipped on the light.

The smell of blood on my hands was so strong, I expected to be covered in it. But it was only sweat. This calmed me down a bit, but I was still worried. The stench must have been residues from my dream. It was unsettling. To fully wake myself up, I turned on the faucet and splashed cold water on my face. It felt good and did wonders to calm my nerves.

"You're okay. You're okay," I told the man in the mirror. "It was just a dream," I reminded myself. Still, I was convinced that something wasn't right.

I lowered my head again and continued to splash water on my face, while trying to forget the dreams I'd been having. They were more than disconcerting. When I was through with the water, I grabbed a washcloth and dried my face. As I put the cloth away, I made eye contact with the image in the mirror again. I didn't recognize that guy anymore.

The dark eyes that stared back at me were haunting. I wasn't certain how much time had passed when I finally returned to bed. I sat on the bedside for a minute, hunched over with my elbows resting on my knees, trying to get my wandering mind under control. Finally, I laid down and pulled the sheet up to my chest. I stared into the darkness, unable to stop myself from replaying the details of the dream in my head over and over again. Since the day I started working for Johnny, I had done my job and done it well. Whenever he needed to teach some unruly customer or debtor a lesson, I was the guy he called. Not only that, but I was the man who oversaw our shipments. Consciously, I knew these were things that destroyed people's lives every single day. But for the longest time, I hadn't struggled with guilt over any of it. In the beginning, I had; but as time passed, it somehow hardened me. Guilt had just been a blip in time.

Until now. Until I met Norma.

The past several days had been torture. Since visiting Norma's church and listening to that preacher, Pastor Archie, I'd been out of my element. It was good that Johnny had given me instructions to lay low until he needed me. I would have been of no use to him. I couldn't tell what exactly was messing with me, but I knew it had something to do with that night and a specific girl who lived in my mind rent free.

Thinking about the dream only reminded me that I missed Norma. Each day, I tormented myself by staring at her number on my phone, willing her to call or text me. When the phone remained silent, I would attempt to call or text her, only to pull back at the last minute.

What exactly would I say to her anyway? If I continued to pursue her, I was going to ruin her. I'd rather not have her, than bring her into my world, only to hurt her again. She deserved better.

Despite all that, I was physically aching just to see her lovely face, to say something naughty that would make her blush.

Disgusted with my pathetic state, I jumped out of bed once more and reached for my boxing gloves that were sitting in the top drawer of my nightstand. Still wearing my pajama bottoms and shirt, I stepped over to my punching bag and began throwing in a few hits.

It felt good. All my pent-up energy was being directed somewhere other than the face of one of my victims. As I thought about them, their accusatory faces appeared in my mind. I punched harder. I heard Norma's pleading cry for me not to go. It just about destroyed me.

I punched harder and harder, until I heard a knock on my door. Mom appeared, wrapped in the cream-colored silk robe I'd bought her for Mother's Day last year. Her hair was a sleepy mess, but she was still one of the most beautiful women in the world.

"Hey," she greeted, her voice a bit gruff.

"Sorry, Ma. Did I wake you?" I asked. I didn't think I was being too loud, unless she had gotten up to do something and was passing by my room.

"Something like that." She shrugged, rubbing her eyes with a yawn. "What are you doing?" She glanced around the room, before her eyes settled back on me. "What's with the gloves at this time of the night?"

"I couldn't sleep," I admitted. I didn't know the last time that I'd told my mother the truth. All the drowsiness seemed to disappear from her as she straightened to look at me, her eyes suddenly looking worried.

"What's bothering you, honey?" she probed. Of course, that was the first question she would ask. I was grateful for my mother. At times like these when my head was heavy and darkness seemed to be looming over, the love and care she showed me always helped keep me sane. I almost confessed the truth again but held back at the last minute.

"It's nothing, Ma. I'll be fine." There was no point in trying to fool her, she always seemed to see through it.

She tilted her head a bit to the right, studying me. "Does it have something to do with the girl?"

My heart skipped a beat. "How do you know about Norma?" My tone was more clipped and commanding than I'd intended. My mother didn't seem to notice. And if she did, she just chose to ignore it. A slow smile spread across her lips.

"Let's just say the walls in this apartment are pretty thin and you have a loud mouth, especially when you're talking to her," she answered. I grunted out loud, shaking my head. So basically, my mother had been eavesdropping on my conversations all this time. If that was the case, the girls were definitely as well informed as my mother.

"She seems like a nice girl," my mother observed. "A Christian girl, right?" She didn't show the least bit of remorse for having eavesdropped. "You should bring her home one of these days. I'm sure your sisters would like to meet her."

"That'll never happen," I commented. Annoyed that she'd frequently listened to my calls. "You shouldn't listen in on people's conversations, Ma." If she had listened in on my conversations with Norma, what other things might her ears have picked up on in the past.

She frowned. "Why?" She simply asked, ignoring everything I had said on snooping. "You don't want us to meet her?"

I shook my head. "Ma, let's just drop this okay? I don't want to talk about Norma, not now."

"Oh? Are you two having a problem? From the way I hear you talking to her, she seems like a nice girl. You must really like her."

"There's no problem. You should go back to bed. You have work in the morning," I told her. I returned to my punching bag, hoping she would just give up and go away. But, this was my mother. She didn't know what giving up meant, especially when it came to her children. It was one of the reasons why I had never mentioned Norma to her and had bribed my little sister into keeping quiet about it.

Pausing, I whipped my head around to look at her, irritated. "Is there something else?"

Mom took another step into my room, and standing on her tippy toes, planted a kiss on my cheek. "I just wanted to let you know that I'm here if you ever want to talk. Get some sleep, okay? It will do you good." With that, she turned on her heels and left the room. I let out a puff of air. My mother was the best of the best, but I knew well enough that she couldn't help me with this. So, I returned to punching, throwing all my effort into the bag. By the time I was through, the sun was starting to peek through the curtains of my window. It was morning already and I hadn't gotten any sleep.

I headed to the bathroom to refresh myself then went to the kitchen. It was a weekday, but since school was out, the girls wouldn't be up for another couple of hours. Mom, on the other hand, would soon be leaving for work. I decided to make breakfast for everyone, seeing I had nothing else to do.

Half an hour later, Mom joined me in the kitchen, dressed and ready for work. "Oh, you're such a good boy," she said when she noticed that breakfast was all done. I imagined my colleagues would laugh themselves unconscious if they ever heard my mother calling me a good boy. It wasn't a name that fit me. But she was my mother, always determined to see the good that might still be in me.

"How was the rest of your night?" she asked.

"It was good, Ma," I lied.

"Good." She nodded.

I handed her a plate of eggs, ham, and toast along with a cup of coffee. Knowing she was probably going to bring up Norma again, I disappeared from the kitchen right after, making up an excuse about doing laundry. All I really did, was walk back and forth in my room until I knew it was time for her to leave. Time had almost seemed to stop as I waited.

After a while, I headed back to the kitchen. When I arrived, I saw Mom was still in the house. She was putting her plate into the sink. "Leave that," I told her as I entered the kitchen.

She jumped a little, startled by my presence. She turned to face me, a hand placed on her chest. "Oh, Marcel, I didn't even hear you walk in."

"Sorry," I said. "Don't worry about the plate. I'll wash it."

"Thanks, honey," she said with a smile.

"By the way, I made you some lunch," I told her before she could leave the kitchen, handing her the paper bag that was left on the counter.

"Oh, thank you. You're on a roll this morning," she commented. She gave me another one of her motherly kisses. "I'll see you later?"

"Yep, you will," I told her. Another truth since I was laying low. "Have a good day, Ma."

"And you too," she said, walking away.

An entire hour after Mom had left for work, Juliana was the first one to drag herself down the hall, rubbing her eyes. When she spotted me, her eyes lit up, "Marcel, you're here."

"Yes, I am," I murmured dryly. Being home for the entire week had left my family stunned it seemed. Everyone expected me to disappear and not return for days. Who could blame them? This was the life I lived.

Leaving my half empty plate, I rose to get some breakfast for her. By the time I was through, Sofia stepped into the kitchen followed by Isabella.

As I watched all three of them, I couldn't help but entertain the idea of changing my life for good and surviving it. Literally. It would give me the opportunity to get a real job. One that would give me the chance to help take care of Mom and the girls without them ever having to worry about my safety.

Truth be told, although I played the tough guy who wasn't afraid of anything, I was consistently worried each time I stepped through our front door to go on a mission for the boss. In fact, I was terrified. Terrified that it would be the last time I would get to walk through that door. Terrified that it would be the final time that I would get to see my mom and sisters. Nothing was more dreadful than walking around with that kind of weight on your shoulder.

Like everyone else I was afraid to die.

Before Norma came into my life, I had resigned myself to this precarious way of living. Now that she was here, I entertained the idea of changing my life. How freeing would it be to walk freely on the streets without fear of a drive-by from rival gangs or an arrest. I would give almost anything to rid me of all these worries.

Norma had tried to convince me that it was possible, but I had shut her out and shunned all thoughts of it ever being true, simply because I knew it was ridiculous. But was it? I had a nagging feeling in my gut. Could I walk away from this life without any repercussions? It was foolish to even think that would be possible.

Still, I was tormented inside. I needed to make a decision and I needed to make one today.

I rose from my seat. "Hey, Sofia. I need you to watch the girls until I get back. I'm going on a quick errand. I'll be back before lunch time."

Sofia's plate was still full but her eyes were glued to her phone as she was typing away like a maniac.

“Sofia?” I called again. She didn't raise her head, only gave a mumbled response, words I couldn't hear. “Sofia, did you hear me?” I questioned again, my voice a bit louder. I was tempted to snatch the phone from her hands if she wanted to ignore me, but I wasn't ready for any kind of drama this morning.

“Yeah, yeah, sure, whatever,” she gave a grumbled response, without raising her head. I sighed, at least she had replied. I walked to where the twins sat, giving them kisses on the top of their heads.

“Marcel,” Isabella called me, grabbing the hem of my shirt before I could walk away.

“Yes?” I answered.

“When will you be back?”

“I'm just going to go see a friend. I’ll be back soon, I promise.” None of them looked like they believed me, but they nodded anyway. Their puppy dog eyes followed me straight to the door until I disappeared. Poor girls. I really hadn’t been around much over the years. Now more than ever, I realized that I left them worried every time I went through that door.

If there was a way to fix that, I wanted to do it. This was how I found myself standing in front of the little white church where I had last seen my girl. The taxi driver gave me a funny look when I had him stop here.

My feet felt like led as I walked into the church yard. There was a groundsman tending to some potted plants and when he spotted me, his eyes went wide with curiosity. He still managed to smile through it. “Good morning,” he started. “Can I help you?”

“I’m looking for Pastor Archie,” I told him.

“Ah, yes. He’s in his office,” he replied. “Let me walk you over there.” He stood, sliding his gloves off and shoving them into his back pocket.

“Thanks.”

In silence, we walked to the right of the building and headed almost to the back. There was a side door that led into a reception area. Though small, it was a cozy little spot, decorated with more plants. Behind the empty reception desk, there was a dark oak door that led to another room.

The groundsman waved toward the door. "There you go." After offering my thanks once more, I went to the door and knocked. The wait felt like an eternity, but it was probably only ten seconds. The door swung open, and Pastor Archie stood there with his glasses sitting on the bridge of his nose. His brows lifted when he saw me. Then a warm smile appeared on his face. I had only met the man once, but I considered myself a good judge of character. I knew this man was genuine. He was the real deal.

"Marcel," he started. "It's good to see you again." The fact that he remembered my name surprised me. Coupled with his smile, this made me feel a little better, a lot more comfortable with what I wanted to discuss.

"Am I disturbing you?" I asked. "You look busy." I pointed my chin to the large book in his hand. "I could...Uh, I could come back later."

"No, not at all. I was just catching up on some reading," he said, shaking his head. He stepped out of the way and gestured inside with the book. "Come on in."

Like the outer section of the office, Pastor Archie's space was humble but cozy. He had a wooden desk, cluttered with more books, along with a computer. There were two wooden chairs opposite his side of the desk. He motioned me to one. "Go ahead, take a seat. Would you like something to drink? I have soda and sparkling water," he offered.

"No, that's fine, thanks," I said, taking a seat. The pastor followed suit and sat behind his desk. The odd feeling of nervousness that I used to get back in middle school when I had to go to the principal's office over took me. The anxiety I had shoved deep down and tried my best to ignore was rising again. Something told me Pastor Archie wasn't the type to judge me, yet I still felt uneasy being there.

I stared at the walls, catching sight of a few pictures of Pastor Archie with other people, at different stages of his life. I assumed they were family members as well as members of the church. They all looked close, happy. In one of the photos, their eyes seemed to be looking right into my soul.

"So, what can I help you with, Marcel?" Pastor Archie said, pulling me away from my reverie. I turned to face him. "You left in a storm the last time I saw you. I was worried you might have a family emergency."

My eyes widened, although I shouldn't have been surprised by this. The way I had walked out, I was sure I had gotten the attention of the entire congregation. I was about to lie, and tell him that I did have a crisis at home or something, but what would that achieve in helping me find answers? I had come here to bring things into perspective. I had to be open and honest with this man if I was going to get any help at all.

Taking a deep breath, I said, "I'm not a good man." I waited for that to sink in before I continued. "I've done a lot of awful things in my life. Things I'm not proud of."

"Me too," Pastor Archie replied. I drew my head back in surprise.

"You're not taking me seriously, are you?" I asked, annoyance bubbling up. His brows drew together, as he leaned forward, placing his hands on the desk before him.

"Of course, I am, Marcel. Do you think the people in this church came here looking the way they do now? None of us were good when we came to the Lord. God didn't send His Son to this world for the righteous, but he was sent to save sinners. We were all a mess, until Jesus turned things around for us."

Like the good old pastor, my brows started to pull together. If only he knew half the things I had done, he wouldn't be speaking to me this way. “Okay. But I’m sure none of you have ever done the things I have. I’m among the worst of men, believe me.”

That made Pastor Archie subtly laugh. “Son, the fact that you’re here telling me this, means you are not among the worst of men. My gut tells me you’re just a young man who lost his way.”

“Maybe, but it was my choice to choose the wrong path instead of the right path. I chose wrong. That makes me…not good.”

Pastor Archie leaned back in his chair, eyeing me speculatively. “Alright, then.” He shrugged. “So, you’re the worst of the worst. Now what? Why did you come here, Marcel? What were you hoping to find?”

I don’t know, I wanted to say. But I did know. I wanted to get rid of the guilt. I wanted peace. I wanted to spend more time with my family, and above all, I wanted Norma in my life.

“Norma thinks there’s some kind of good in me,” I said instead. “She thinks that if I give my heart to Jesus, He’ll fix all my problems and change me. That doesn’t sound remotely realistic.”

“Is it just Norma?” he asked.

“What?”

“Is it just Norma thinking there's good in you? Don't you think so too? Yes, she may have planted the thought in you, but if you didn't believe it, you wouldn't be here. Am I right?” He waited for me to speak, but when I gave no reply, he continued. “Norma is on to something there. But tell me, do you already believe in Jesus, or did you just come here because you have your sights set on her?”

My eyes grew wide, then I burst into laughter. “You don’t pull any punches, do you, old man?” I really wasn't expecting such a question from him.

"I had to ask. Norma is a sweet young lady. I've known her all her life and I know she has a good heart. She sees good in people where others don't."

My laughter subsided as I let his words sink in. "I agree. That's why I walked away from her. I'm not going to lie to you, Pastor, I really, really like Norma. I've wanted her for weeks, but she kept resisting. She invited me to church a few times, but I wouldn't take her up on the offer. I never believed in all that church nonsense. I thought you were all crazy for believing in something you can't see. Until that afternoon."

"That afternoon?" Pastor Archie raised an eyebrow.

"Yes, that afternoon I came to church with Norma for the first time. I don't know what happened, man, but you said some stuff and it just tore me apart inside. I…well, I just had to leave. I thought that if I stayed there any longer, I would have broken into tears, which would have been utterly pathetic. So, I ran. The problem is, I haven't been able to sleep for the past week. I've been having these awful dreams about people I've hurt. And when I wake up, I feel so guilty about the evil things I've done, and it haunts me. I've never been a man to dwell on regrets or feel guilty." I paused. "So why am I feeling this way? Why do I suddenly feel so angry with myself?"

I ran my hands over my face, then through my hair. I must've looked like a mess.

"I know what you're going through," Pastor Archie said. I lifted my eyes again to meet his.

"You do?" For some reason, I believed he actually did know although he had never been in my shoes. Something led me here to him, because deep down, I knew he could give me the answers I needed to the questions I had. And also help...help rescue me from the darkness that surrounded my past.

"Yes," he replied. "God's Word has entered your heart. Now it's trapped inside you. The Lord is leading you to repentance."

"Repentance?"

"Yes," he stated. "You feel guilty because you're acknowledging to yourself where you've gone wrong. And the only way to find peace is to confess those sins and ask the Lord to forgive you and change your life."

I stared at him. Though I was trying to understand everything he said, this still didn't address my biggest problem. So, I asked, "What about my life?"

"What about it?" Pastor Archie asked.

"I'm part of a…" I stopped myself just in time from saying the word that almost slipped off my tongue. I quickly thought of something to replace it with, "Group of people," I said instead. "If I walked away, it just might cost me my life."

"That's why you need Jesus," he said. "There are many things that our human minds cannot understand. One of those things is how God can take an impossible situation and turn it around for good. You're afraid that by accepting Jesus, and walking away from this life, you might put yourself in danger. I hate to break it to you, but the moment you decided to become a criminal, you have been living in danger." Now it was his turn to pause before he added. "If you ask me, living without Jesus is more terrifying."

"More terrifying?" I asked, just above a whisper.

"Yes," he said. "Marcel, no one is completely pure at heart. You out of all people know there are men out there who are determined to bring you down. The evil in this world multiplies with each passing day. You never know who may be out to get you, or setting traps before your path. You don't know your tomorrow, only God does. That's why He sends His angels to guard and protect us. Now imagine a life without that protection. What's more terrifying than that?

"I'll have you know that the only reason you have been safe all this time, is because God saw that this day would come, when you would walk into my office to seek godly counsel. He knew you would be touched by His Word, and now He wants to lead you to repentance. You're going to have to exercise some faith in Him now. You're going to have to trust Him to continue to protect you. He has led you here Marcel. You meeting Norma wasn't just a mere coincidence. I don't believe in coincidences."

"Faith, huh?" Norma had mentioned that to me. One-or-two-times.

Pastor Archie chuckled. "It doesn't make any sense, I know. It's not supposed to, that's why it's called faith."

"Right."

"Well, son, what will it be? Will you answer God's call, or will you continue to live in torment, not knowing what tomorrow will look like for you?"

I ran another hand over my head. "Norma's told me about all this Jesus stuff. I thought it was complete nonsense at the time, but after what I experienced that afternoon, it's hard to deny. I think I want to try. I think I want to accept Jesus. Get to know this guy."

"Indeed, you can," Pastor Archie said. "You made the right choice, Marcel." He rose from his chair and pulled his glasses off to rest them on top of a stack of books. "Are you ready now?"

I figured there was no better time to do this. Exhaling deeply, I joined him in standing and nodded. "I'm ready."

"Father in the name of Jesus," Pastor Archie started to pray. "I..."

"Wait." I interrupted. He opened his eyes and looked up at me. "I changed my mind. I can't do this. I'm confused. I don't want to give in to something I don't understand and will later regret it."

Pastor Archie paused, then said, "Marcel, the Jesus has..."

Before he could finish his sentence, I quickly walked out of the room. I heard him call my name but played deaf. I needed peace. Too much doubt and fear overflowed my gut. It felt as though there was a war inside my chest. What if changing my life would cause even more damage? I had too many questions racing through my mind. I continued to walk as fast as my legs would carry me. The street life was the only life I knew. *It's where I belong*, I told myself.

"How would I survive?" I murmured.

I continued out the door and hurried to the front of the building. I paused on the walkway in the front that led to the steps. I needed to catch my breath. I felt as though someone was sitting on my chest. All I wanted was to be as far away as possible from here, this church, and Pastor Archie. I walked away without hesitation.

As I started walking back to the sidewalk and down the street, I suddenly felt as though an invisible force was dragging me back. The more I tried to keep my earlier pace, the more the peculiar feeling encircled me. The further I walked, the more urgent the sense was to go back. It was overpowering me. It was the same feeling as the night of Norma's attack. When I had to go back to her.

It literally hurt to get air in and out of my lungs.

What's happening to me?

At that moment, a thought crossed my mind. If someone was willing to forgive me and give me the peace I desired, why was I running from Him?

I wasn't sure, but it was like a voice whispered, "Go back."

Overcome with a strong impulse I knew nothing about, I turned and slowly began to walk back to the small church.

A few minutes later I was standing face to face with Pastor Archie again. He was standing outside the back of the church, near the door that led into his office.

His hands were pushed into the front pockets of his pants, and he was slightly rocking back and forth, as he gazed at the grounds surrounding him. I wasn't sure if he was surprised to see me or expecting me.

"I thought you might come back," he said.

I still didn't have all my questions answered, but I was convinced I needed this Jesus. One answer I did need to know was, how did he know I'd be back? And so soon that it seemed he was waiting for me?

"I asked the Holy Spirit for help." Pastor Archie replied as he searched my face. "Marcel, I know that feeling you were having when you left," he said. He went on to describe it flawlessly. "That's how I felt when Jesus chased *me* down. It's a feeling that cannot be ignored."

There and then, tears clouded my eyes. If Jesus was that powerful, so strong that He could bring me back, why then did I doubt He would give me the peace I craved? As I walked into the church once more, this time with Pastor Archie, I knew I was ready to take the bold step. I knew I wanted to give my all to this God whom Norma had constantly talked about.

I may not have had all the answers yet, but I knew now that I couldn't do life on my own anymore. And if Jesus was the real deal, I wanted to be a part of it.

Chapter Fourteen

Norma

"Ms. Norma? Ms. Norma."

Blinking twice as the voice drew me out of my thoughts, I lifted my eyes to gaze at Ron. He was standing in front of my desk, his lips crooked as he gazed down at me, concerned. I'd been getting that look since last Friday.

Ever since Marcel stormed out of the church, I hadn't set my eyes on him, or heard his voice. He had neither called nor texted. I would stare at my phone every hour on the hour, waiting for something, I just expected something, a call, text, or him showing up at my workplace again, but that never happened. I didn't feel like I had pushed too hard. Marcel had come with me on his own free will...maybe he just wasn't ready. I wanted to see him so badly.

"Ms. Norma," Ron called again.

The constant looks and questions didn't upset me, because I understood he was trying to play the role of a friend. With all the effort I could muster, I offered him a smile. "Sorry, Ron. What were you saying?" I really had to control my thoughts while at work.

He watched me for a while. "I know I've asked this already, but are you sure you're alright? You've been drifting off a lot these past couple of days. What's on your mind?"

I tried to give a small laugh, but it came out like a gasp for air. I cleared my throat. "It's nothing serious. What can I help you with?" The change of subject was sudden, but I needed to move on before Ron began to probe deeper.

"Nothing much, I was just saying how much I enjoyed the service on Sunday. My wife and kids did too. The kids liked their Sunday School teacher a lot. According to them, we have to go back next weekend." He chuckled.

Laughter burst out of me; this one was genuine. I knew very well who their Sunday school teacher was. So, it was no surprise his kids enjoyed her class. "Oh, yes. That would be my friend, Betty Ann. She has a way with kids and she's a good teacher." Betty Ann had this charm that always drew children closer to her, no doubt she would one day be an amazing mother. Speaking on Betty Ann being a mother, it just hit me that one day I would become one. The thought alone gave me goosebumps.

Who would my husband be?

The image that flashed across my mind shocked me. I didn't know why Marcel came to mind when I thought of a husband. When I was a young girl, my definition for a perfect husband had been like the prince from 'The Sleeping Beauty.' I wanted a man who would fight dragons for me and wake me up with a kiss. Though as I grew, my taste in men changed with each novel I read, moving from one male lead to another.

It was kind of crazy for me to be thinking of a husband when I didn't even have a boyfriend. I did want to have children one day, wake them up for school, dress them, prepare lunch for them. And I wanted a man by my side while I was doing all this.

The image of Marcel came to mind again. Funny how life could be going so well until you met someone who changed everything. Going back to the way things used to be is impossible after that.

Marcel filled a place in my heart, that I didn't even realize was empty.

"Ms. Norma?"

My mind had started to drift again, but Ron's voice forced me back to reality. "Yes?" I asked, blushing from embarrassment. What was wrong with me? I needed to get a grip on myself. I certainly didn't want to make Ron feel bad or think that what he was saying wasn't important.

"I don't mean to be a pest. I just want to be sure you're okay. You've been acting strange this week. We can talk about it if you want?"

"Oh no, it's nothing, Ron. Really, don't mind me. I'm just in a mood today."

"Did something happen? Something bad to a family member?"

"No, everyone's fine." I told him. "Nothing bad happened."

I didn't want to explain that I was hurting inside because a certain handsome gangster decided to walk away instead of trying. Trying a new life with Jesus.

And maybe one with me, my heart said. Could I have said or done something different?

My Bear walking away only made me realize how much I had enjoyed his company. I never knew how much I really cared for this guy until he left. Now it felt like my heart was cracked wide open. Not only that, but I was seething with internal anger. I just couldn't help it. How dared he shift on me like that? First, he followed me around, then showed up unexpectedly everywhere, was pretty much pushing himself on me, and made me care about him. Only to walk away? For all his big talk about how much he wanted me, I never imagined he would do something so unexpected and hurtful.

"You're doing it again," Ron commented, pulling me back from my thoughts. Embarrassment washed over me yet again.

"Sorry," I murmured. "I'm fine, just a bit tired."

He gave a small smile. "Nothing to be sorry about," Ron replied. "But you do need to talk to someone if there's something bothering you. Think about it."

I was tempted to just let it all out and tell Ron everything. He had such a big heart. There was no doubt in my mind that he would understand and probably offer some great advice. But then I thought of what he would think of me if he knew I was in love with a gangster?

In…love? Whoa girl! Calm down.

There was no way that I was in love with Marcel Maxwell. I liked him, yes, but love was a different story altogether. Love was a strong word. Love was a powerful feeling. So I was sure that wasn't the case here. I was aware that I liked him. A lot. But love?

"I'm a friend," Ron said, cutting into my thoughts. "Always remember that."

I almost broke my silence, until I remembered that this was my last week at the Art Museum. The receptionist on leave was coming back on Monday, which meant Ron would have someone else to share his stories with. What if he ended up telling that receptionist about me? I mean, he wasn't a bad guy or anything, he was a sweet man, but he did love to share stories and I wouldn't want to be another chapter in his book.

It was best to keep things under wraps.

"Thanks, Ron," I finally said. "I'll keep that in mind." Seemingly satisfied with my answer, he headed back to his booth. I glanced at my watch. It was close to eleven and yet I'd barely gotten any work completed so far. This was not like me. Usually, I finished my work for the day hours before the expected time. But here I was, my mind filled with thoughts I shouldn't be having, at least not right now. This was ridiculous. I needed to get my mind off this guy.

With that bitter thought, I returned to typing up the document I had been working on for most of the morning. Honestly, I was tired of staring at computer screens. There was nothing I wanted more than to go home and take a long hot bath. Vaguely, I heard the front door of the museum opening.

I didn't look up when I heard the footsteps approaching, until I felt a presence before me. "Hi, beautiful."

I froze, still staring at the screen before me. The familiar voice sent shivers down my spine. Though it had been days since I'd last seen him or heard his voice, I knew it like the back of my hand. With a gasp, I whipped my head up.

"Bear," I choked out, not believing the sight before me. His expression was radiant as he looked down at me. The next thing I noticed was that his bandana was missing. I couldn't take my eyes off him. Without the top of his face and head being covered, for the first time I was able to see how perfect his face was. This man's skin and features were flawless.

Realizing that I was just staring at him like a love-struck schoolgirl, I tried to regain my composure as best as possible. Clearing my throat, I straightened my back to look more dignified. "Hi. How have you been?" I asked, glad that my clear voice was hiding the emotion I felt. I wanted to run to him and throw my arms around him. But I controlled myself.

"Never better," Marcel replied with a smirk. My heart started to falter. What did that mean? Was he doing better being without me? If I were to be frank, he did look good. Different, too. I couldn't pinpoint where this change was coming from, but something was definitely there. Back then he had looked like a defeated man. The person standing before me was vibrating with positive energy.

"I see." My voice had lost some of the excitement. "Did something happen?" I asked, unable to stop myself.

"Something did happen, alright," Marcel answered. He paused, and a smile appeared on his lips. A full smile, not a smirk or grin. I couldn't believe it. This was just because Marcel was...happy? Happy about what? "I did it, baby. I gave in."

My mind was spinning like a whirlwind. *He had given in?* I had no idea what he was talking about. With a bewildered look, I murmured to him, "I don't understand."

"Jesus," was the only word he spoke. The change in his eyes was unmistakable. They sparkled with pure joy.

Marcel had…given his heart to Jesus?

A burst of excitement tore through me. I flew off my chair and ran around my desk to hug him. "Oh my gosh. Bear, you did it." I felt like I was going to cry. I couldn't contain the emotions whirling inside of me.

Marcel broke into a boisterous laugh that echoed inside the quiet space. He wrapped his big hands around me. I had never felt so happy in my life. "Thank you, Norma," he said. "Thank you so much. I'm really grateful."

I pulled away from him to gaze into his eyes. "Thank me?" I shook my head. "No Marcel, thank God. You walked away and I thought…well, I thought you didn't want to have anything to do with Jesus…or me."

"Oh Norma, you can't even begin to understand how much you mean to me."

"But you said so yourself, Marcel. I still remember your words clearly."

His laughter eased and he cupped my face with both hands. "I was stupid when I said those words, Norma and I didn't mean any of that, I just needed time to realize it. I know I hurt you. I'm so, so sorry. It's just that I had so much to think about. I'm here now, and I'm not going anywhere. What I meant earlier was, thank you for not giving up on me."

My eyes stung. Tears were coming. I blinked a couple of times to keep them at bay. "Thank you for coming back," I told him. Awkwardly, one of those pesky teardrops escaped. Marcel wiped it away with his thumb before I could get to it. As I looked into his eyes, the change was obvious. They were no longer challenging. His eyes shined. They smiled right along with his lips. "Oh, I have so many questions Marcel, there are so many things I want to know. How? Where? When? I want to know everything."

I was grateful to the Lord for having led Marcel right where he needed him. Everything had happened for a reason after all. God had a plan, and we just needed to trust Him. Then it hit me. If I hadn't gone along to the restaurant that night. If I hadn't gone to use the restroom after Rico's game. If I hadn't met Sofia and decided to stand up for my sister. If I hadn't opened my big mouth and mentioned Marcel's name. Then all of this, this moment, him accepting Christ, him standing before me, might never have happened. Pastor Archie had been right, there were no coincidences.

"I'll tell you everything later, baby." He glanced behind me, looking at what I suspected was my desk. "We can meet again and talk when you're done with your work."

"You know what I think? I think we should celebrate," I suggested.

"Hmm," he murmured. "I like the sound of that. What did you have in mind?"

I shrugged. "I don't know. Maybe we could go for pizza and ice cream?" His eyes brightened. I didn't know the types of food Marcel liked, but I did remember seeing him sneak some pieces of Juliana's pizza into his mouth the night we had dinner together.

"Nice, but I have to get back to the girls in a few minutes. I promised them I'd be back soon." My lips quirked up. There used to be a time when Marcel had seemed to avoid his home. Now he was in a hurry to his sisters. Change was a powerful thing. I was beyond happy for him; there were no words for how I felt.

"That's fine," I told him. "We can talk after work. Why don't you bring them as well? I'll take Rico and Luna along with me. We can share the news with them. I'm sure they'll be excited too." Marcel didn't look convinced, but he nodded anyway.

"So, where should we meet?" he asked.

"The park?" He nodded. "Great, I'll buy the pizzas..." I stopped when I noticed Marcel's brows creased and his demeanour changing. He shook his head. “You don't like pizza?” I asked, surprised.

“Oh, I love Pizza, but you are absolutely not buying the food,” he growled. “I’ll do that.”

“Please, let me get it. We’re celebrating *you*, remember? It’s only fitting that I buy.”

Marcel took a half step toward me, his scowl in place. “Norma Tesoriere, you are not buying the pizzas and that’s final. Now be a good girl and go back to work. I’ll see you in a few hours.” With a wink, he turned on his heels. “Text me and let me know what toppings I should get,” he added, waving a hand behind him.

As soon as he disappeared through the door, Ron trotted in my direction again. “Huh. Good-looking guy. Boyfriend?” he asked, tipping his head. I only gave him a smile in response and went back to my desk to continue my work.

Seconds later, I realized that I was finding it hard to concentrate. Only this time, it was for the opposite reasons. My excitement was overwhelming. Marcel was a Believer now. It was the news of a lifetime. The night he had stormed out of the church, I had thought I’d never see him again. I had cried myself to sleep for days. As difficult as it had been, I made up my mind to allow the Holy Spirit to handle it.

“I guess He never disappoints,” I murmured, pleased. I was happy about how the Holy Spirit turned around the situation. I honestly didn’t know how I would have managed, if Marcel hadn’t spoken to me again. I remembered a time when I used to push him away whenever he showed up. Now, I couldn't even imagine that.

I didn’t know if I spent more time daydreaming about Marcel or working, but the moment it was closing time, I picked up my bag and hurried out. I was eager to see him.

———

The moment my Bear entered the park, I spotted him. Our eyes locked; I felt a familiar tremble of excitement inside me. It happened whenever this man was near.

I continued to watch him, and stayed that way as he walked toward us, his siblings in tow. The heat in his eyes was intense, and I couldn't tear my eyes away from them.

"You've got to be kidding me," Rico commented, an annoyed look on his face. "I thought *we* were coming to the park for something special." I didn't bother acknowledging him, even though a part of me wanted to. Earlier when I got home, I'd broken the news to my entire family that Marcel had given his life to Jesus. My parents and Luna were pleased. But Rico, of course, had been unconvinced, even cynical. For some reason, he had taken a strong dislike to Marcel. I'd thought that he would have mellowed out since their first meeting on Tybee Island. No such luck. He was as adamant now as he had been then that Marcel was no good. It was getting ridiculous, because I didn't understand why he treated him so coldly when he hardly knew anything about him. Rico wasn't usually like this with other people, so I didn't understand why Marcel was different. *Normal* Rico was open, wanting to give people a chance. Either way, here and now, I wasn't going to let it faze me. I was going to keep my interest set on the man approaching us.

"Hey," Marcel said, when he stopped before us. His eyes took in my siblings, pausing a little longer on Rico before they settled back on me.

"Hi." For a few seconds too long, we stared at each other. Luna tried to conceal her smile, while Rico groaned with disapproval.

"Seriously, Marcel?" Sofia remarked. "You're literally making me sick right now." Her eyes shifted to me, eyeing me from head to toe and back. I assumed he hadn't told them who exactly they were going to meet at the park either. I gave her a nervous wave, but she returned it with a glare which brought my hand down.

Marcel cleared his throat. "Girls, you remember Norma. Well, not you, Bella."
He spoke. "Norma, this is Isabella. Isabella, Norma.

Isabella wasn't smiling like Juliana was, but she did seem intrigued. I swiped my hand down the side of my jeans before reaching a hand out to her. "Hi, Isabella. It's lovely to finally meet you. Your brother talks about you all the time." That must have been the right thing to say because a glow suddenly lit her face.

"He does?"

"Of course," I told her. "He talks about you and Juliana every chance he gets." Only when I said the words did I realize that I hadn't mentioned Sofia. I wasn't sure what to say, though. I couldn't lie. The truth was, whenever he mentioned Sofia, it was always with some level of frustration with her.

"I'm sorry, I…"

"Save it," Sofia said, cutting me off. "I know my brother isn't exactly proud of me. Nothing I'm not used to." She displayed a fake, more like mocking, smile that didn't reach her eyes, before treading off to sit on another bench close by. Marcel frowned as he followed her with his eyes. He looked like he wanted to drag her back so she could apologize.

"So, Isabella, Juliana, these are my siblings, Luna and Rico," I said, hoping to get things moving along. The two younger girls waved. Luna, being her cheerful self, pulled the two into a hug.

"It's so great to meet you both." she practically squealed. "I feel like we're sisters already."

"Oh man, will you stop?" Rico spat out with disgust. "You're just embarrassing yourself." Isabella and Juliana looked at him as if they weren't sure what to make of him. I took note of how less expressive Juliana was as well, even though she was very polite. It made me wonder if she was still struggling with what had happened that evening at the diner. I would have to ask Marcel about it later.

“Ignore the ogre,” Luna told the girls. “He just doesn’t know how to be human anymore.” Rico made another grunt in the back of his throat but didn’t reply. Like Sofia, he headed to a different bench from the one we were going to be sitting at. The two were now on their phones, plugged into their own world and effectively blocking us out.

Great, I thought, frustrated.

After the introductions were over, Marcel lifted the boxes of pizzas in his hand. “Let’s eat. I’m starving.” With that said, we all took our seats and began to hand out slices. Only at that moment did the two grumpy teenagers in our midst begin to eye us from a distance.

Marcel leaned in close while the kids munched on their food. “What do you say we let them starve while they watch us eat?” I covered my mouth to hide my laughter. It seeped out anyway.

“Funny. I was just thinking the same thing,” I told him. We glanced at each other before bursting into another round of laughter.

“What’s so funny?” Luna asked, her eyes big and full of curiosity.

“Nothing,” I replied. Then, before she could push any further, I handed her a plate with three large slices. “Take this to your brother, please. Thank you.”

“Seriously? He should get it himself.” Despite her outburst, she took the plate from my hand and stomped over to Rico. Without a word of exchange, she plopped the plate on the bench beside him then made her way back to us, eye roll in place.

“Thank you,” I told her once more.

“I did it for you, not for Mr. Grump. And you’re welcome,” she grumbled. Despite her momentary sour mood, Luna was beaming again when she returned to her conversation with Juliana and Isabella.

"Sofia." Marcel called out. Not knowing how this would play out, I touched his arm to let him know that I could send over her plate like I had with Rico. Nevertheless, Sofia shot from her seat as if she'd been waiting for the call.

Once she got to us, she took the plate with two slices Marcel had been holding for her. Another fabricated smile crossed her face before she grabbed another piece from one of the boxes and practically, stuffed half of it in her mouth.

"Hey," Marcel shouted after her. It was a hopeless call. By the time she reached her bench, the stolen slice had completely gone down the hatchet. I passed my eyes over her tall but slender frame. She was so small; one would think she ate like a bird.

"That's not fair. I only got two pieces," Luna grumbled under her breath.

Marcel let out a long sigh. "Here, have one of mine." He put the pizza on Luna's plate.

"Thanks." She said, shamelessly biting into it. I scowled at her. Geez. Why had I bothered bringing them with me?

"We should have just left them all at home." Marcel commented so only I could hear.

"My thoughts exactly," I told him. This time we didn't laugh. We watched as our siblings ate most of what was in front of us. Even Rico ended up coming for another slice. In the end, Marcel and I ended up with only two each.

After stuffing themselves, Luna, Isabella, and Juliana disappeared for a walk around the park, leaving Marcel and I alone with our two teens on either side of us. It only took minutes for Luna and the girls to befriend a group of kids who were playing with a football.

Somehow, while we watched them play, the space between us closed.

"Tell me about it," I whispered to Marcel. "How did it happen? What made you change your mind?"

"I wanted some things I didn't have."

His response was simple. When he offered no more, I knew I had to take the bull by the horn.

"What was that?" I asked, studying him with curiosity.

"Peace. Good relationships. Be a positive role model for the girls. Fill an emptiness inside I hadn't even realized I had. Until that afternoon at the church." He spoke each word slowly. His facial expression was relaxed, as he continued to observe the game.

My lips formed into a smile as I watched him. Once again, I was swept off my feet by his level of maturity. "I'm glad you took that step."

He turned his head towards me and sighed. "Does that mean you've forgiven me for hurting you?"

"I forgave you, even before you asked."

"Is that what Christians do? That's the expectation?" Marcel asked, his voice dropping a notch lower.

I nodded, wondering where the question was leading. "Yes, we forgive. We do what Jesus does."

"You're beautiful, Norma," he said, still maintaining the same low tone.

"Thank you," I answered, shyly.

A smirk touched the corner of his lips. "I didn't mean it as a compliment; I was stating the obvious."

Marcel's words affected me in a different kind of way. Whenever he spoke with that calm demeanor, my heart surged with happiness. Every part of me felt his words. I looked up and realized his dark smoldering eyes were fixed on me. I lowered my gaze. These feelings swirling inside me were all new. I'd never felt this before.

"Norma, look at me," Marcel said, lowering his voice until it was barely above a whisper.

I slowly lifted my eyes to his face. "You're incredible. The best thing that's ever happened to me. Without you, I wouldn't be where I am today. I love you, Norma."

My mouth opened, but no sound came out. Marcel placed a finger on my lips and smiled.

"Yes, I know it's crazy, but I do. I hope you'll be able to say those words back to me at some point. I've been wanting to tell you for a while, but I didn't want to scare you away. I knew you'd take my heart the first time I set my eyes on you. Remember when I promised I would come back to see you? When you were at the hospital?"

I nodded, gently.

"I had to force myself out that day because I was afraid I would confess my growing feelings to you, or even kiss you. The fear of doing that kept me away, even though you were all I could think of. And I didn't even know you yet. I only knew my heart was in trouble."

"I really don't…"

"Don't say anything right now," Marcel interrupted. Once again, all I could do was be drawn into his eyes and nod.

I turned to look around and realized that both Rico's and Sofia's eyes were glued to us. Neither look pleased. When Marcel finally lifted an arm across the bench behind me, Rico stood and started toward us. Before he could reach the bench, however, the ball from the game whist through the air and hit the side of his head.

Every player went quiet before they all broke into laughter. All except Isabella. Her hands covered her mouth, and she ran halfway in Rico's direction before stopping to say, "I'm so sorry."

Rico looked exasperated, but not angry, thank God. With that annoyed look, he kicked the ball in her direction. Though it wasn't with much force, Isabella ducked out of the way, letting out a high-pitched girly squeal.

Juliana, on the other hand, caught the ball with her left hand and began to juggle like a pro. We were all stunned, including Rico.

"Whoa. No way." Luna exclaimed.

"Did you teach her how to catch?" I asked Marcel. When I glanced up at him, he was smiling proudly.

"Sure did," he finally replied.

"I didn't know you played football," I admitted.

"I used to play before I quit school," Marcel started to explain.

"Really? You don't mean my high school, right? There's no way we went to the same school, and never met."

Marcel let out a deep chuckle. "I agree. Had I met you then, we would have been together a long time ago." It was an unexpected response and I felt myself already getting red-faced. I turned my head to hide it, but he had already noticed.

With a grin, he went on. "I went to a different high school."

"Yeah, and he was the best player. Way better than the losers from our school." That biting comment came from Sofia. We hadn't even been aware that she could hear us from that distance. Not only that, but she seemed so captivated by her phone. When we glanced at her, I realized that she was eyeing Rico with audacity. On cue, we switched to staring at Rico. He was scowling at Sofia.

"Huh," I murmured. "Isn't it odd that these two are both pretty popular at school and yet they don't get along? I'm sure there's a story behind it."

"Hmm," Marcel replied, a questioning look covering his face. "Knowing my sister, your brother probably said something that rubbed her the wrong way. She's not the most forgiving person in the world."

"Or they have secret crushes on each other," I laughed. Marcel pulled away slightly to scowl at me.

"They better not." That made me laugh harder. Always the big overprotective brother.

"So, you were the best player on your team, huh?" I asked. "Why didn't you try to go pro?"

Marcel lifted his shoulders in a shrug. "Stuff happened." I hoped he would say more but he remained silent. Part of me wanted to push the issue, but knowing Marcel, he wasn't going to talk about it if he didn't want to. I decided to drop the subject and move on to something else. The only thing that was on my mind was his talk about being in love with me, and the way he had looked at me when he had said those words. Mesmerizing. Alluring. I had a lot of thinking to do. I was falling in love with Marcel. Yet it scared me. As a Christian, I didn't want to get involved with someone who wasn't God's plan for me. What if our path had only crossed so I could help lead him to Christ?

I needed to distract myself from these thoughts. I made a drum roll on the top of my thighs with both hands. "I think I'm ready for ice cream."

"Me too," Marcel said. "Can you get the girls? I'll get rid of this trash." He stood and began to gather the boxes, bottles and cups. I headed towards the girls and waved them over, making sure to keep out of the way of the ball, because let's be honest, I was no Juliana.

"I hope you're ready for ice cream," I told them when they made their way over to me.

"Yes!" Luna said. I had to fight down my laugh. When it came to any kind of food she really loved, she was like a six-year-old kid.

After having all our garbage disposed of, Marcel took my hand and led us to the ice cream stand in the middle of the park. Though Rico and Sofia lagged behind us, they somehow managed to keep their distance from each other.

The stand was crowded and it took several minutes for us to place our order. When I tried to pay, Marcel handed the girl on the other side of the counter the money instead. Duly noted; I was not allowed to pay for anything.

"There's something important we want to tell all of you. Let's go sit under those trees," Marcel told our siblings, pointing to the south end of the park. There was a shaded area with a large group of trees. Surprisingly, no one was sitting there.

As we strolled through the park, ice creams in hand, Sofia suddenly came to a screeching halt.

"I need to understand something, well more like ask you something," she started glaring at Marcel, as we all turned to look at her. "Obviously, you both like each other, right?"

Marcel nodded in response. I didn't say anything. She was his sister, and I felt it was his place to answer her.

"Please tell me you didn't bring us here to tell us you're getting married." She asked with a bitter tone and with uneasiness in her eyes. I almost choked on my own tongue.

"What? No."

Marcel whipped his head around to look at me. "You don't want to marry me?" He put his free hand to his chest. "I'm wounded."

I smacked him lightly on the arm though I could not help laughing a little. "Will you be serious? Your sister looks terrified right now."

Marcel looked at Sofia. "No, we're not getting married. But God knows best. If he wants us to be together, it will happen. But not yet."

"Wait…What?" Sofia stuttered and came closer to us. Then she moved up close to Marcel, all the color drained from her face.

I noticed that Rico was glaring at him too. I ignored him, keeping my eyes on Sofia.

"When did you start talking like them?" She asked her brother. "Like a Jesus nut."

"There's nothing wrong with learning and talking about God," Marcel said, cautiously.

Rico let out a loud snort while Sofia continued to pale.

"Quit the whole con, Maxwell." Rico demanded. "Dude, get real. I know what you're doing. You obviously want my sister. That's the only reason why you're talking like that."

Marcel's lips curved into a smirk and his face glowed. "That was the plan, originally. But I'm interested in the things of God now. Hey, you're right Rico. I'm not changed yet. Not completely. But I feel different. Pastor Archie told me I'll be a work in progress." Marcel spread his arms wide as if to emphasize his point. "That's what we wanted to talk to you guys about." He paused again. "I gave my life to Jesus today."

"Right. Have you shared the big news with your boss?" Rico went on. "I'm sure he'll have a lot to say about that." When Marcel didn't immediately reply, Rico's eyes danced with humor. "Of course, you haven't. Because this is all crap. It's just another game of yours."

Stunned, I turned my attention to my little brother. "What do you know about all that? I'm sure I've never mentioned any of that to you."

An odd look flashed across his face before disappearing altogether. Had I not been staring at him, I probably would have missed it. "I know a lot more about him than he's willing to tell you," Rico said. "He's not a good guy, okay. He's only doing all of this to manipulate you, so you'll fall for him. In the end, he's just going to hurt you."

"You need to stop." The words flew out of my mouth with more force than I had intended. Rico cringed a little. Then he backed away.

"You know what? Fine. Do what you want. You're the big sister. But don't say I didn't warn you." With that, Rico tossed his ice cream in a nearby trash can and stormed off, exiting the park.

"Rico. Rico!" I called. But he continued without looking back. I started to take a step in his direction when Marcel wrapped a hand around my upper arm.

"Hey, it's okay. Just give him some time."

"He was rude."

"No, he was being your brother. He's only trying to protect you. I would have done the same."

When he put it that way, I understood Marcel's point. Still, I couldn't help feeling mortified by the way my brother had just behaved. Grouchy as he was these days, he was never hateful to anyone. It almost seemed like he had a personal vendetta against Marcel. If I hadn't known better, I would have thought the two had met before.

"I'm leaving too, before you try to talk me into accepting your God and your freak stuff." Sofia said, looking at me in a repulsive manner. The anger and hatred shooting out of her eyes were unsettling.

As Sofia stormed off, Marcel looked at me, as if to reassure me that everything was going to be fine.

"Hey," Marcel spoke up, looking at the twins and Luna. "Let's just enjoy our ice cream. Rico and Sofia don't know what they're missing. Who wants to go on the paddleboats?"

"Me!" All three girls squealed in unison.

In no time, the girls started chatting excitedly, like no altercation had ever happened. I admired the way Marcel kept his cool. I knew it wouldn't be easy for Sofia to accept his decision. But I had been so excited about it, I hadn't thought much about how his life would have to change. Was he ready for it? Was I?

It was early evening when I stepped out of the taxi with Luna and waved goodbye to Marcel and the twins. Now the only thought on my mind was how much I wanted to spend more time with him. As my sister and I walked up the concrete path to the front porch, passing the beautifully scented roses Mom enjoyed so much, I could feel Marcel watching me. It's what he did—staring until he could no longer see me. I suppose it was his way of safeguarding me from a distance.

The moment we got into the house, Luna went and sat by mother and began telling her about the afternoon. I waved at Mom, as I started up the stairs and I told her, "I'm going to change, I'll be back down in a few minutes."

When I got to my room, I closed the door and slowly leaned back on it. I closed my eyes, and instantly these new feelings I had for Marcel began to take hold of me. These feelings were wonderful. Strong. I was excited yet nervous at the same time. When I opened my eyes again, the first thing I spotted was the Bible he'd given me sitting on my nightstand. I walked over to my bed and sat.

I picked up the Bible and opened it to the note Marcel wrote in it. I slowly ran my fingers over those sweet words.

"I hope this makes you happy. Love, M." I whispered, pressing the book to my chest. *I am incredibly happy.*

"God, is he the one?

Chapter Fifteen

Marcel

It was the perfect day to be sitting in the park. It wasn't hot yet, and the sky was a clear, fascinating shade of blue, free of the usual rows and balls of clouds. God's creation never ceased to amaze me now. My wandering gaze stopped back on Betty Ann. She was undeniably a crowd-influencer, especially when the gathering was full of pre-teens and teenagers with never-ending questions. After a couple of weeks of being around her, I found that she had more energy than a border collie. As the Youth President at the church, she had invited me to join her team and reach these middle and high school kids. Being a person from the streets, she had thought I would be a good resource. I guess I was, at least in some ways. But I wasn't half as good as she was at holding their attention. I had witnessed this a couple of times, and at each event, she did it effortlessly. She seemed to connect with them in a matter of minutes. While I found my three sisters to be a handful. I was myself reluctant. Where would I even start? Another thing that made me insecure was that I was still new in the faith. Embarrassing myself wasn't an appealing prospect and I was afraid of saying something that wasn't appropriate for the kids to hear. And public speaking just wasn't my thing.

"You should join," Norma had said when I'd spoken to her about it. At first, I was against the idea. As far as I was concerned, I was still learning from them and didn't know enough to teach anyone, anything. But Norma's probing and encouragement finally motivated me.

"That doesn't matter, Marcel, the Holy Spirit will help you, He will give you the words, you just have to believe. You're going to be making much more of a positive impact than you ever imagined. Those kids need the right people to show them a better path. Someone they can relate to. And you're one of them. Someone once told me that experience is often the best teacher. And it only makes sense that you don't let these kids repeat the same mistakes you made. Work with the youth team, and help these kids make the decisions that are best for them."

"Like you helped me and didn't give up on me," was my reply.

When I first started out, I thought following Jesus would be a cakewalk and all my troubles would vanish. That, however, didn't happen. Apart from the fact that I'd been unnerved when Johnny had called just to check up on me, I found that I was still having some violent feelings. Not as many as I used to have, but thoughts of how I used to handle situations flipped through my mind now and then.

When I asked Pastor Archie about it, he pointed out that I would still experience struggle and encouraged me to read the Book of James. And pray. Pray every time I felt that way. The last thing I wanted was to disappoint Norma, myself, and most of all, Jesus.

The day Sofia angrily stormed out of the park, she had gone ahead to tell my mother that I was being influenced by Jesus fanatics and that I was starting to act like them. Even carrying a Bible.

That evening my mother had called me into her bedroom the moment I walked into the house with Juliana and Isabella by my side. The former me would have cooked up an excuse to avoid having that conversation with her, but the new me wanted to become a better friend, partner, and son.

"Sofia told me you 'found Jesus'," Mom had started, without mincing words. *Wow, that didn't take long. Sofia must have come straight home,* I thought.

"Yes, Ma, I did." I'd gone on to explain to her how I had come to that decision, and why I'd thought it was the best for me. "I was going to tell you about it, but apparently Sofia beat me to it."

"If this is what you want for your life, then you have my full support, Marcel. Just answer one question. Are you sure this is what *you* want and not the girl?" she'd asked, as she peered at me.

I had nodded in response, and added, "I've never been more sure of anything. Becoming a Christian removed the heaviness I once had in my heart. This is a new beginning for me and I'm glad I've finally found the missing piece of my life."

Rising to her full height, she had drawn me in for a long and gentle hug. "Good. Then I'm happy for you." That's how the conversation had ended.

Now the only person in my household who was finding it difficult to come to terms with my choice was Sofia. When she had realized that she couldn't get Mom to agree with her, she had called her dad to come get her. She had said she didn't want to share the same apartment with a Jesus freak. Mom had tried to talk her out of it, but she had been bent on leaving. Her stuff had already been packed, and the only thing holding her back was a ticket from her father to fly over to him.

Mom had become emotional about it, asking Sofia through tears not to make such a drastic decision. That was when I had finally stepped in. After all, nothing peeved me more than seeing my mother cry. "Sofia, you're being ridiculous," I'd told her. "The decision is mine and mine alone. What do you care anyway? This doesn't affect you at all."

She hadn't replied but had kept her hands folded across her chest while tapping her foot, as she sat waiting on the couch. Sighing, I had tried another approach. "Look, if you're worried that I'm going to push my new beliefs on you or whatever, don't. I won't force anything on you."

"I don't care about what you do with your life, Marcel. I just want to go live with my dad. I've said my goodbyes, you guys can do whatever you want to do, I don't care," she said stubbornly.

"Is this really what you want, Sofia? Because if it is, go. No one is going to stop you, not this time." She had kept holding the threat of her leaving over our heads, and now we could just as well let her go.

Although, I'd hoped my new faith would help her make better life choices.

Of course, I hadn't said that out loud, knowing it would have made the situation worse. She still hadn't replied right away, and I'd almost given up hope that she would change her mind. Then a text had come in on her phone and she had quickly read it. My best guess at the time had been that her father had finally replied to her. However, it seemed like the response wasn't what she had been expecting. She quickly regained composure, raising her chin, and faking a look of confidence, not knowing that I saw right through her. "Fine, then. I'll stay. For now," was all she'd said before yanking her luggage and dragging it back to her room.

I had no doubt that her father had told her to stay. Based on a little conversation I'd overheard while spending more time at home, her father seemed to have found someone special and was in the early stages of building a relationship with this new woman. More than likely, he didn't want Sofia around right now to complicate things. It was silly displays like these that proved how much of a child Sofia still was.

"Hey," Norma's soothing voice dragged me out of my train of thoughts, "Focus." She pointed towards the group of kids, but I shifted my stare to her face, finding myself drawn to those beautiful hazel eyes. All the thoughts that had been plaguing my mind vanished, and I was lost in the sight before me. My mind wandered once again, drifting towards the thought of where life might take us. We had only just started our relationship, but I couldn't wait to see what the future would hold.

She gave me a sweet smile and I tossed one back at her. My belly came alive with endless fluttering that felt like I had swallowed a dozen butterflies. Realising that I was losing myself already, I tore my eyes away from her and turned to take in all that was going on in our little area. Betty Ann was still interacting with a group of over twenty kids who were sitting in front of us; and as usual, all eyes were on her.

"Ms. Betty Ann, why did God create boys first? Boys are so…weird," one of the pre-teens said. I resisted the urge to laugh at her question. To me, it was so funny and innocent. Of course, the younger boys were more than a little put off by that, while the older, high school guys snickered, some almost uncontrollably. Betty Ann handled the question and the commotion with ease. While she was replying, as though my eyes had a mind of their own, I found myself stealing a glance once again at the lady who was standing on my left. She must have felt my eyes on her because she whipped her head up at me and caught me in the act, as I didn't have the chance to shift my gaze. I continued to stare at her radiant face, losing myself in it once more. I needed to stop this. After all, we were at the front where all the kids could see us. Yet I couldn't break my stare.

The dress Norma was wearing displayed pastel-colored flowers scattered all over a white background. The gentle breeze caused the knee-length summer dress to slightly sway from side to side. It was the same dress that Norma had worn a week ago when I officially asked her to be my lady. She had been gorgeous that afternoon, and her beauty was becoming more radiant every day.

When it came to persona, Norma was the complete opposite of Betty Ann, opting to stand behind all the other committee members, even though she had contributed so much to putting on these events. Norma didn't enjoy the spotlight and preferred working behind the scenes. It was one of the things that made me even more attracted to her. She wanted to do good, but she didn't seek to be praised for it.

The more time I spent around her, the more I craved being with her. She was the missing piece that I needed all this time, the one whose addition to my life filled the little void that was left. Norma was the one who helped lead me into my relationship with Jesus, and she was the one who hadn't given up on me, even though there were more uncertainties ahead than we could both begin to comprehend.

"Do we have to go to church for God to love us?" another girl asked, with those curious eyes fixed on Betty Ann.

Betty Ann turned to me, and all eyes followed the direction of her head. "Marcel, I think you should answer this one."

I nodded and smiled nervously. Some weeks back, I had asked someone the same question. "Alright, kids. God loves everyone but remember that the Bible says we should never stop hanging out together…encouraging and helping each other. We should be in church as often as we can with other people who love Jesus. We continue to learn more when we're there too."

I was surprised. No more questions were asked about it. It looked like they completely understood me. Deep down, I was happy about that. "Alright, everyone, we're going to end here for the day, but be sure to come next week with your notebooks, and your questions of course." Betty Ann threw a big smile in the direction of the kids. It was a smile so much like Pastor Archie's, it was a little uncanny. I'd learned a few days in that she was the niece of the pastor, as well as Norma's closest friend.

"Marcel, could you please do the closing prayer for us?" she asked. I glanced at her, my heart skipping a beat. Praying in public was not my thing either, but I was aware that saying no wasn't an option, so with all eyes on me, I forced the words, "Sure thing." When I closed my eyes, my mind went blank. I recalled a Bible passage I had read with Norma where Jesus said he would teach us how to pray.

Please, help me. I've got nothing. I said silently. Shortly after, I began, "Lord Jesus, thank you for another day with these precious kids…"

By the time I was through, I had surprised even myself. When I met Norma's eyes, she nodded with approval. I'd never felt so pleased in my entire life.

"Come along, kids," one of the other ladies called out. "Form a line over here." If I remembered correctly, her name was Alyssa. She pointed to the spot in front of the long table packed with refreshments. While the kids gathered, I moved behind the table to help with serving the meals.

Mere minutes into the task, my eyes caught sight of a black jaguar parked across the street. My happy heart did a nosedive in a split second. Without seeing inside, I already knew who it was. At this point, I only hoped that my face hadn't turned completely pale.

I waved a hand in Norma's direction. She was busy helping to seat the kids so they could eat but she caught my wave immediately and came over. "Everything okay?"

"Yeah," I replied. Looking toward the street, I added, "Could you take over for a few? I have something to take care of."

She squinted, obviously wanting to ask questions. In the end, though, she just said, "Sure." Relieved, I left the group and headed across the street. I could feel Norma's eyes on me the entire time. I hoped that she didn't get the bright idea to follow me.

As I reached the car, the passenger door swung open. Feeling vulnerable and exposed, I stepped inside, taking a seat and shutting the door behind me. Johnny was sitting in the driver's seat. He slipped off the sunglasses he'd been wearing, shifting his cold gaze to me. His blue eyes were frosty, nothing out of the ordinary. Sitting here together, Johnny looked like a mouse looking up at its predator. But I knew better than to ever believe this man was a prey. Short as he was in comparison to me, he could still cut me down to nothing in seconds—physically and otherwise.

Swallowing the lump in my throat, I met his stare attempting to look in control. Because fear was the strongest weapon of an enemy. "Why are you here, Johnny?" I asked. His brows shot up.

"Johnny? You haven't used my name in years. You've always preferred to call me "Boss". What's going on with you, son?" His tone was so fatherly, one would never be able to tell he was a coldblooded man.

"I already told you, I'm done," I replied. "I gave my life to Jesus, and He changed me. My old life is no more, which means I can no longer work for you." This was the same statement I had given him the last time, but he had probably just ignored it. Johnny wasn't going to make this easy for me.

"You won't work for me?" Johnny dragged out the sentence as if considering each word. Then he let out a long, slow sigh. "You know, the only reason I haven't taken you out already, is because you're like the son I never had. When you came to me weeks ago and told me all that crap about church and Jesus and whatever, I didn't take you seriously." Exactly as I had thought, no wonder he hadn't reacted back then. He had assumed it was all a farce.

"Johnny—" I tried to speak.

"To be honest," he continued, cutting me off. "I was convinced that this was just a game you were playing with that Christian girl. I know how those girls are. I've bumped into a few in my lifetime. They always play hard to get, but if you use the right approach, you might just score sooner than you think. You know?"

My lips thinned into a disapproving line and my jaw tightened. "Do not talk about her like that. She's not just some girl I need to score." Though I looked cool, calm, and collected, my heart was racing. What else had I expected? Of course, Johnny knew who

Norma was. I'd been praying he wouldn't find out, but deep down, I knew the truth already.

"It's been weeks," Johnny went on as if I hadn't said a word. "The war in the streets is dying down. I need you back on the job now. No more games." He tossed an envelope I hadn't noticed before in my direction. Out of reflex, I caught it. From the feel of it, there was a lot of cash inside.

There was a time when that envelope would have brought me happiness, especially when I thought of all the things I could use it for to make our lives a lot easier. Now, it held pain and regret. My fingers burned just holding it. Although I was apprehensive about the possibility that Johnny could very well put a bullet through me this very minute, I knew what I had to do.

"This isn't about the girl anymore, Johnny," I tried to explain, even though I knew it wouldn't result in much. "I really did experience a change in my life. I don't know how to adequately explain it with words. It's unlike anything I've ever felt before. You have to experience it yourself to fully understand it." I knew it was falling on deaf ears.

Johnny released a grating sound, resulting in laughter. The sound of it resonated in the car as he leaned his head to one side. "Have you lost your mind, boy? In case you've forgotten, I own you."

No, you don't. Not anymore. Only God does. That's what I wanted to tell him. But I still needed to tread carefully. *Choose your words wisely, Marcel, or say nothing,* I told myself.

"In the streets, you're feared, but also respected. What do you think will happen when word gets out you've turned into some religious idiot? Well, let me tell you, boy. Our enemies are going to see us as weak, and they're going to try to take us down."

"Yes, I do, but—"

"You have forty-eight hours," Johnny declared, cutting me off again. I almost bit my tongue off trying to stop myself from saying the words threatening to come out. "If you refuse to abide by what you signed up for, I'll have no choice but to come after you. Are we clear?"

My heart raced, pumping my blood more rapidly than usual. My blood shot through my veins, and fury like I had never felt before, bubbled up inside me. The temptation to grip this man by his throat and squeeze the life out of him grew strong. *He*...threatened...*me*. Usually, violence was the way for me. But I had to resort to other means. Like forgiveness. Love. This was the part of Christian life that was going to be the hardest for me. In my anger, solutions like these were like bitterness, poison, burning like acid in my mouth.

Somehow, I managed to keep my composure, despite my internal war. Norma had told me once, we should be slow to anger, so we wouldn't do or say anything that we might regret afterward. I tossed the envelope back into his lap before opening the door and exiting the vehicle without a word. I headed across the street without looking back. All the while trying to put on as neutral and calm of an expression as I could, so it would hide my rage and tremor. Also, expecting a bullet in my back, that didn't come.

"Who was that?" Norma asked when I halted in front of her. The meals had already been handed out to everyone and there were two plates sitting on the table beside her, which I assumed were for both of us.

As much as I wanted to, I couldn't lie to her. "Johnny," I told her simply. Her hazel eyes went wide with fear. Over the weeks, I had let Norma know about Johnny and my life. Only telling her enough, so she understood the impact it all had on me.

"Okay… What did he want?"

"You know what he wants," I told her, barely containing my fury. "He wants *me*. He gave me forty-eight hours. He says if I don't come back by then, I'm a dead man." My hands tightened into fists, remembering those callous, and heartless, words.

"What?" She paused, alarm written on her face. "What are we going to do, Marcel?" Her words were a soft whisper, but I could hear her as clear as day. I wanted to pull her into my arms and shield her from the evil in the world. But this wasn't the time or place.

"I don't know yet, sweetheart," I told her. "Before all of this, I would have ripped apart anyone who dared threaten me. But I can't be that man anymore."

"Maybe, you could leave town? Or the country? Or we could involve the police?"

I was already shaking my head before she could finish. "Oh no, not even maybe. Johnny has people everywhere. Before I could even take one step out of here, they would have caught me. I'm not going to run, Norma."

She gave me a sad and panicked smile. "Although this terrifies me, I suppose the only thing we can do is pray and trust God. He knows how to fix every situation."

I knew that what she said was the right answer, but that kind of trust did not come easy. Not when I was the guy who had always taken care of his own problems instead of depending on anyone else. And by Norma's expression she was still terrified, even after she'd said those words.

God. Please help me to trust you in all of this, I silently prayed.

Chapter Sixteen

Marcel

The sun was just starting to come up. I was lying in my bed, looking around my room. Strangely enough, I was thinking about the mundane that surrounded me. A bed, an unmatching nightstand, a TV on the wall collecting dust, a table with a single chair that I never used, and a clothes basket in one corner where I put my dirty clothes. The few pieces of dark brown furniture contrasted against the grey and picture-less walls. The curtains that had once been white were so old they had taken on a dusty shade of light grey. You'd have thought the landlord could have cleaned or replaced them.

What would Norma think if she were to see my room? I cringed at the thought. I couldn't help but compare the view of my room with Norma's. While hers was tidy, bright and welcoming, mine was… a grave waiting to bury me. Maybe later I could renovate the whole place. If I survived the next 48 hours. The walls needed fresh paint. What was left of the old one was peeling in some places. But before that I needed to puddy the small cracks. Maybe Norma could help me get new curtains and do a little fixing up here. She had such great taste.

Weeks ago, these would've been the farthest thoughts from my mind. In such a short span of time, I'd gone from one world to another and now things that had never crossed my mind, stared me right in the face. Sighing, I pulled the blanket off of me and slid to the side of my bed and onto my knees. I closed my eyes and began to thank God for all He had done for me. Things were going so well, not just with my new walk with God, but also my relationship with Norma.

I closed my eyes and whispered, “God give me wisdom and strength. I have no idea what’s coming my way. I need your protection. Not only for me, but for Norma too. Physical and emotional protection. I don’t know how to do this.”

Despite Johnny’s visit the previous day, there was a certain peace that washed over me. A calmness I didn’t fully understand.

I went downstairs to grab some water. My mother was already downstairs preparing breakfast. She was still in her nightgown. “Good morning,” I greeted her as I walked past her. “How was your night?”

She smiled, her eyes following me around the kitchen. “Good, how about you? You did get some sleep, right?”

“Yup.” I nodded as I closed the fridge door shut after taking the water bottle.

“Good,” she said. I could still feel her eyes on me as I walked around the kitchen. “Someone looks like they’re in a good mood. I like this new you.”

Shaking my head, I told her, “This will probably sound corny, but I’m just looking forward to taking Norma on a nice date tonight.”

“A proper date?” She clasped her hands with excitement. “Where are you taking her?”

“Some Italian restaurant that just opened, nothing too fancy. We're just going there to grab dinner. But still, this means a lot to me.”

She ‘oohed’. “Well, I'm happy for you, Marcel. I'm happy that you've found a good woman. Your life has changed so much since you’ve met her. I’m proud of you, son.”

“Thanks, Ma.” I said, turning and walking back down the hallway.

On the way, I passed my sisters' rooms. The doors were closed, which meant they were still sleeping. When I got to my room, I shut the door behind me and sat on my bed.

My heart had suddenly felt heavy. The threats from Johnny circled my mind. I knew what he was capable of. And I knew he would carry out his threat.

My thoughts were interrupted when an unexpected pounding on our front door permeated through the entire apartment. It was forceful, and my heart leapt in my chest. There was only one culprit that I could think of.

Johnny.

He'd given me forty-eight hours, but who knew what went on in that man's head? He probably woke up furious this morning, after deliberating my future and decided forty-eight hours was too much for a traitor. I had to get to the door before my mother did, before Johnny decided to show us why he was one of the most feared men in town.

With my heart in my mouth, I stood and headed out to face the music. Halfway down the hallway, I spotted my mother reaching to open the door. I was about to shout at her to keep it shut, but it was too late. As the door swung open, I stopped, and backed against the wall. Police Uniforms.

The police? Why are they here?

"Morning, Ma'am," the shorter of the two men said. "We're here for Marcel Maxwell. Is he home?"

They were looking for me. All my tracks were covered. Johnny and I had always made sure of that. So, what was this about?

Mom was nervously wiping her hands on her old, faded, pink apron. "What do you want with my son?" she asked with fear in her voice. Her voice was so soft, it hurt my heart to watch it.

My sweet Mama. If only she knew all the things I'd done. But I was grateful she didn't. The only question was, what did the cops know? And how much? During all my years of working with

Johnny, I'd avoided any serious confrontation with the law. I had been brought in for questioning a few times, but they had never succeeded in letting anything stick.

Something deep inside told me things wouldn't be the same this time around.

As my heart painfully beat inside my chest, the taller of the officers flashed my mother a smirk. There was nothing I wanted to do more at that moment than knock that look off his arrogant face, but that would only get me deeper into whatever problem this was.

"We have a warrant for his arrest. He's wanted for an assault and battery charge. We can do this chatting at the police station. Now, if he's here, get him for us. Or step aside and we'll get him ourselves." He gritted out the last few words.

Assault and battery. Either Johnny had turned me in, or it meant someone I'd beaten up for him had found the courage to report me. Before my life had turned around, I would have found the guy and nicely connected my fists to his face again until he withdrew his statement. But not anymore. I was no longer that violent man. That meant I had to do the right thing. It was easier said than done. The second the charge came out of the officer's mouth, dread crept up my spine and I stepped back. The officers must have spotted movement because they both looked my way at the same time. Without thinking, I turned around and bolted back down the hall.

It was undoubtedly the worst reaction to have, but I couldn't stop to think as adrenaline pumped through my veins. I couldn't stop my feet from moving. They seemed to have a mind of their own. Just as expected, the officers came after me.

"Stop right there!" one of them called out. I didn't stop. Instead, I disappeared into my bedroom, unlatched the window, dove right onto the fire escape, then ran down the steps. Several flights of the clanking metal stairs later, I got to the last flight and leaped over the side rail, landing on my feet with ease. As soon as I was flatfooted, I shot down the road in a run for my life. Somewhere in the back of my mind, I expected to hear bullets whizzing past my ears, or feeling some going through my back. Fortunately, that didn't happen. Nevertheless, I could hear the officers behind me yelling out my name and commanding me to halt.

I didn't know how long I ran before my legs wanted to give out. When I looked around me, I found that I was close to the museum where Norma had worked for several weeks.

Norma. What am I going to tell her?

What had I brought into her life? There was no way that she was going to be able to deal with all of this turmoil and chaos.

My feet began to lead me in the direction of her house, but when I began to think things through, I realized it was a bad idea. Even worse, I was dressed in my pajama bottoms and a t-shirt. How would I explain that? I couldn't involve her in this mess. But where was I supposed to go? Going to Johnny for help was no longer an option. For all I knew, he might have even been the one behind this. Regardless, he would surely turn his back on me, just like I had done to him. Besides, I had already washed my hands of that life. Going to Johnny would just get my hands stained again. That wasn't going to happen.

Though the guys I'd worked with in Johnny's gang had become somewhat friends, I knew their loyalty was to Johnny, so I didn't even bother entertaining the thought of going to one of them.

For a while, I wandered aimlessly through the streets, with no sense of purpose or direction. For the first time in a long-time, I felt…lonely. A lump began to form in the back of my throat.

After having walked for an unknown length of time, I turned into a familiar street. My hands in my pockets, I glanced around me. Everyone was in a rush to get to their destination; none of them taking notice of the barefooted guy in his pajama bottoms. They'd probably assumed I was just another homeless man. Many of them were expressionless as they hurried past me. Although there were a few people laughing and chatting together as they walked, there were also some businessmen and women barking instructions into their phones. Others held their heads high, walking like they owned the streets.

On the busy road, horns blared at each other like animals at war. Some even put their head out their windows, shouting curses to the vehicle that might have obstructed their path. Stopping and staring, I wondered if any of these people felt as lonely and worried as I was feeling right now.

I wished I could just go back to yesterday and warn myself of what would happen today.

You are not alone.

The voice was a mere whisper but very clear, even though I was in the midst of a crowd. Blinking in surprise, I paused in my steps as I glanced around to find the source of that voice. Whoever had said it, because I knew I hadn't imagined it, that person had to be very close. When I looked around, nobody was even paying attention to me. Like I was already dead.

I rubbed a hand over my face. "I'm going crazy."

Certain that it was my mind playing tricks on me, I continued walking. Then it happened again.

You are not alone.

Once again, I came to a halt, though this time I didn't look anywhere. This was starting to get a little creepy. My throat went completely dry as I tried to process what was really happening to me. Was I hearing…imaginary voices? Was this how madness started? A delirious chuckle burst out of me. Suddenly, I knew I had to talk to someone. The moment that idea formed, the first person that came to mind was Pastor Archie.

He might not be able to save me from this, but I knew just a few words from him, and I wouldn't feel so lost. With quick footsteps, I started in the direction of the little white church. Crazy as it was to hear that voice, I started to realize it was right. I wasn't alone. Pastor Archie had promised that his door was always open if I ever needed to talk. And right now, I definitely needed that. I prayed he didn't have any visitors and wasn't busy, but if he did, I would wait until he was free.

A sense of urgency overtook me, and I found myself picking up the pace, until I was full on running. When I jogged up the walkway of the church, I spotted Roger, the groundsman.

As I slowed to a walk, attempting to catch my breath, I noticed he stood up and waved a hand in my direction. When I got closer, he wiped his hands on his jeans before stretching it out to shake my hand.

"Brother Marcel," he said with a grin. "I wasn't expecting to see anyone so early today. Anyways, it's really good to see you." He eyed my current style of clothing with curiosity but made no comment. I was glad because I didn't want to have to explain that I had made a quick dash for it because the cops had come to my house to arrest me.

"Same," I answered. "Just on my way to see Pastor Archie." With that, I turned without waiting for his reply, and headed straight to the pastor's office. His secretary, whose name I couldn't remember, was sitting at her desk. She looked up with a prepared smile and curiosity in her eyes when she took in my state.

"Marcel?" she asked, surprised. It had only been a few weeks since I had started attending this church, but everyone already seemed to know my name.

"I'm sorry. Is Pastor Archie in?" I didn't have time to exchange pleasantries and just wanted to get to the point.

"Um…yes. Is he expecting you?" she asked. She picked up her planner and began sifting through it. "I don't think your name is here. If it was, I would at least remember writing it down."

"No, he's not, but I need to see him. Now, please." I told her. "It's urgent." Her eyebrows shot up in surprise, but before she could speak, I added, "Please." Again. The single word seemed to deflate her. With a gentle sigh, she nodded and stood.

"Wait here," she said to me. "Let me make sure he's available."

"Thank you."

She headed to Pastor Archie's office door, knocked, and went inside. I paced back and forth in the small reception area as I waited. It felt like forever had passed.

When Pastor Archie's office door opened again, I stared at Charmaine - yes, that was her name - with bated breath. "You're in luck, my friend," she said with a smile. "Pastor Archie can see you."

The breath I was holding whooshed out of me. "Thank God." If Pastor Archie wasn't able to see me, I was just going to sit in the church and wait until he could. Better here than on the streets. Charmaine smiled compassionately as she shifted to the side to let me in. I vaguely wondered if she would have given me that same smile if she had known the cops were hunting me.

Stepping into Pastor Archie's office, some of the weight began to fall off my shoulders. If there was one thing I had found out over the past couple of weeks, it was that this man had the answer to most things. He was a wise man who had clearly learned from his own life experiences, as well as from standing firm with Jesus. Whenever I was with him and heard him speak, his words always seemed to make everything clearer. They opened my eyes to things I didn't even know existed. It became exciting to get information and answers to understand things that questioned my new faith.

Pastor Archie stood with his usual grace and smiled. "It's good to see you, Marcel. Come on in. Close the door behind you." He was dressed in his usual button-down shirt and dark blue jeans. He waved me over to one of the chairs in front of his desk and I slid right in without hesitation. "I didn't expect to see you here today..." He eyed my clothing. "What's going on, Marcel?" I liked how he was able to see something was wrong immediately. He was a smart man, but any idiot could have seen something was wrong. I'd been in my pajamas for Pete-sake.

"I messed up," I started before he could settle back in his own chair. His eyes warmed with thoughtfulness. I knew what he was going to say to this. Anytime I tried to tell Pastor Archie about the crimes I had committed in the past, he would always reply with the saying 'No one is above sin' and that I should stop feeling like I'd committed the worst crimes in the world.

"Haven't we all?" he commented, just like I had expected. I chuckled a little but shook my head.

"You don't understand. I mean, I've really messed up." I ran my hands through my hair as my frustration grew.

He leaned forward and gazed directly into my eyes. I was waiting for him to comment on my clothes as well, but nothing. This man must really have 'seen it all'. He asked, "What happened?"

Taking in a deep breath, I began my tale. When I paused to gage his reaction, contrary to what I had expected, he looked neither shocked nor appalled. But I should have known better. This was Pastor Archie. He didn't seem to be surprised by anything I said or did. He only tilted his head, waiting for me to finish before he spoke. Another thing I respected about this man. He actually listened.

"I panicked," I continued. "I panicked and I ran. I didn't know where to go so I came here to talk to you. Pastor Archie, I don't want to go to jail. Not at this stage of my life. I've given up everything for God, so I don't understand why this is happening now." I was confused. I had thought once I accepted Jesus and started following Him, all this would pass.

"I see," Pastor Archie replied. "I understand this must be stressful for you. Tell me something, though, Marcel. The crimes you were accused of, are you guilty of them?"

My eyes dropped to the table between us. "Assault and battery? Yes." I confessed. I stared down at my fists in front of me where a few scars from my previous life were still visible. "I'm not proud of any of those things. In fact, I loathe myself sometimes when I remember the things I've done. But I never thought I'd have the cops breathing down my neck. Johnny was the only problem I anticipated, and I was ready to deal with that. But this…this is something else."

"Johnny, that was your boss, right?" Pastor Archie asked and I nodded. "Marcel, do you believe with all your heart that God has forgiven you?" Pastor Archie asked. It wasn't the question I had expected, but I nodded.

"Yes, I do." I answered. I truly believed it. I knew the Lord had forgiven me because, though I still carried guilt for all the people I had wronged in the past, my conscience didn't condemn me anymore.

"Good. Because He has. The problem with sin is that it always comes with a cost. While Jesus died on the cross to save us, there are some things that we do in our lives that come with major reactions. Take, for example, a kid who steals money from a family member. He may apologize after the deed, but the fact is that the money is gone. The consequence that comes with this is that he will have to find a way to pay it back and earn back the trust that was lost. In your case, you assaulted someone. And though you're sorry for what you did, it doesn't change the fact that you hurt them. Going to jail to do time is the consequence that comes from your action. At this point, you have no choice but to face it and let the Lord help you through it."

My heart hammered in my chest, and I could feel my hands start to tremble. "Pastor, I can't go to jail. What about Norma? I want to...I want to be with her. I really think she's the one. And this can really mess things up. I don't know what to do."

His lips quirked up in a sad smile. “I know. Believe me, I know. But you have to turn yourself in. It’s the right thing to do.”

The right thing to do. Of course, deep down I knew it, but I had been hoping there would be a way out of this. “Is there no other way?” I asked. The thought of going to jail was unbearable. The palms of my hand went clammy with anguish. I wiped them clean on my pajama pants.

I had never been to jail before but was certain it wasn’t a place I wanted to be. I'd heard stories from some of the guys that had been there before. It also didn't help that some guys that I had roughed up were also there. I could already predict that things weren't going to go smoothly for me. Since I had accepted Jesus into my life, all I wanted was to be with Norma, have a better and a more stable relationship with my family, and also have some level of inner peace. Now, all of that was quickly slipping through my fingers.

“In this walk with Christ, you are going to be faced with some difficulties. Difficult choices, difficult circumstances. But in all of that, always make the right decision. That will ensure you come out victorious. Marcel, I’m certain you know the right thing. Do it.”

I nodded, but only to show I’d heard all he said. Deep down, I wasn’t convinced yet. “I know I did a lot of terrible things but going to jail isn’t something I want to do. If I didn’t have Norma, I would be okay and face the music. But…”

Pastor Archie attempted to smile again, but tight-lipped. “Trust Jesus in all of this. He will never abandon you.” With some reluctance, I nodded. My head began to spin as I thought of all the changes that would come to my life as a result of this.

Even though my mother worked hard to take care of herself and the girls, it had always been my desire to ease the pressure off of her. For the past couple of weeks, I’d been working odd jobs to keep the cash flow going. The plan was to get permanent employment and earn a stable income. That way, Mom wouldn't have to worry about every little bill.

As it related to Norma, I already had big plans for us, even though we had only recently started dating. I could already see her being so much more to me than a girlfriend. But with this new problem, it was highly possible that she would slip right through my fingers. Norma might be forgiving, but I wasn't sure if her family would see me as the best choice for her. There was already some scrutiny from her parents toward me.

"Although it might feel like it's the end of the world, Marcel," Pastor Archie said, pulling me from my depressing thoughts. "And although it may look like your life is about to end, it's not. It's just the beginning. God will use this situation for His glory, and for your uplifting and spiritual growth. If you allow Him. Jesus has plans for you Marcel. You can't see it now, but you must have faith. It's what we live by."

Pastor Archie rose from his chair and came to stand beside me. "Come, let me pray with you. Then I'll drive you down to the police station."

I'd never felt this anxious in my life. Even Johnny's threats hadn't broken me down like this. Still, I stood with Pastor Archie to go and face my fears. The biggest was losing Norma. He rested a hand on my shoulder, and I closed my eyes.

"Lord Jesus, you promised us that when we are afraid, you will be with us," he started. Just like earlier in the streets, tears burned the back of my eyes. It was embarrassing. Crying wasn't a habit of mine, but by the time my pastor ended his prayer, my face was damp. I wiped the streaks away quickly, hoping he wouldn't spot them. If he did, he made no mention of it.

"Ready?" he asked. There was a lump in my throat. I swallowed hard before replying.

"No, but let's go before I change my mind."

The walk from the office to Pastor Archie's vehicle barely registered. It was like I'd been tossed in another world that I didn't recognize. I was in a thick fog. I had no idea how long the journey to the police station took us, but the moment we got there, Pastor Archie cleared his throat. "Maybe you should call your mom. And Norma of course. They'll want to know what's going on."

"Right," I choked out. Clearing my throat, I reached for my cell phone. First, I started to dial Norma's number. Halfway through the digits, I stopped and deleted them. My heart had never raced this much before. In a split second, I decided it was probably better to call my mother first.

"Sweet mercy, Marcel, are you okay?" Mom started when she answered the phone and realized it was me.

"Yes, Ma. I'm fine. Listen, I'm sorry about what happened this morning. I shouldn't have run, but I panicked." The phone went silent for a bit, and I knew the question was coming before she even asked it.

"Son, is it true? Did you hurt somebody?"

I huffed out a breath. "Yes, Ma, it's true."

"Marcel." she squeaked out. "What is wrong with you? You can't go around harming innocent people."

Innocent? I wasn't sure about that. Either way, it was still wrong. "I'm so sorry, Ma. I did a lot of things I'm not proud of. But I'm a changed man. Which is why I'm going to have to turn myself in."

The phone went silent.

"Ma?"

A sob echoed through the line then. "Oh honey…"

"It's okay, Ma. Don't cry. Everything will work out. Just make sure you take care of yourself and the girls, okay?"

"Yeah, yeah, of course. We'll be okay." I could hear her sniffling and I knew she was wiping away tears. It broke my heart to know that I was putting my family through so much pain. They didn't deserve it, especially Mom. She worked so hard to make sure we had a home and were fed. Now here I was, repaying her with the consequences of my criminal life.

"I'm sorry Ma. For *everything*." I paused, and heard another heavy sob come from her. "I should have been a better son for you. A better person. You raised me better than this."

"Oh Marcel, you've made some mistakes, yes. But you've always been good to us. Your heart has always been in the right place. I love you, son."

"I have to go, Ma. Tell the girls I love them, and I'll see them soon." I didn't wait for her reply but ended the call. If I heard another sob from my mother, I'd probably change my mind.

Like before, I started to type Norma's number into the phone. It must have taken me a full minute. When her sweet, melodious voice came over the phone, tears began to form in my eyes again. "Hey, Bear," she said, with a gentle tone. "To what do I owe the pleasure of this call?" The tears threatened to spill again hearing her lovely voice.

"Norma," I breathed out. My voice came out strained, like I had been shouting all night long.

"Marcel? Marcel, what's wrong?" The sweetness in her voice was gone, replaced by concern.

"I'm sorry, baby," I told her, sniffing lightly. "I messed up."

"What do you mean you messed up?" she asked, her voice raising a tad bit. "What happened?" I glanced over at Pastor Archie. He nodded once in encouragement. Small as it was, it gave me the strength I needed. From the beginning to the end, I spilled the entire story to my girl.

"No. No," Norma kept saying when I was through. "It can't be like this. There has to be another way."

"Baby, I wish there was, I really do. I just called to let you know that I'm turning myself in."

"No, Marcel, this can't be happening. You can't...we can't... Where are you right now? I'll come meet you. We'll figure something out. There has to be another way."

It touched my heart to see how much she cared about me. If I was going to stay in prison for a long time, knowing that Norma was out there praying for me it might make things a little easier. At least that was my hope. "There's no other way, sweetheart," I told her. "I have to turn myself in. It's the Christian thing to do, right?" The voice on the other end was silent.

"Bear, this is too much," she finally said barely above a whisper. "I don't know how to deal with this."

"I know, baby. But you'll just have to have faith and trust that God will work things out. This is hard for me too, but things *will* work out."

"How?" she asked. I wished I had a reply to that. I knew it was all she needed, some words of hope that everything was going to be fine. But I couldn't give that to her. I didn't even know myself. So instead, I told her honestly, "I don't know."

The line went silent again. Neither of us knew what to say at this point. We hadn't anticipated this. Certainly not Norma. I'd banked on the idea that all the guys I'd beaten up in the past were too afraid of me to ever report anything to the police. I couldn't have been more wrong.

Pastor Archie gave me a nudge on my arm when he saw I had been quiet for a while. "We should go." He stated.

"Yeah," I replied. "Sorry, Norma, but I have to go now. Okay?"

"Okay," she muttered.

"I'm leaving my phone with Pastor Archie. Please, get it from him and hold on to it until I get back. Can you do that for me?"

"Umm, yes..." My heart plummeted at her reply. She was crying silently.

"Oh, sweetheart. Forgive me for putting you through this. It was never my intention."

"I know," she sobbed out. "But it's hard. I don't know how I'm going to go through this."

"You can. You're stronger than you think." Her replying snort told me she didn't believe a word of it. "Goodbye, Norma. I love you." Like I'd done with my mother, I ended the call before she could reply.

I specifically chose those three words to be the last thing I said to her. I thought she needed to be reassured of my feelings, because, in all that was happening, what scared me the most was losing her.

I turned to look at Pastor Archie. "Alright, let's get this done before I get out of the car and run the other way."

Chapter Seventeen

Norma

It was my first time ever sitting in a courtroom. I had watched things like this on television shows and movies, but never thought that one day I would sit here myself, observing someone who meant so much to me being judged. I had never had a reason to come to a place like this. But we can't see into our future. Before Marcel, my life had been ordinary. At that moment, I wished it still were. Although I was in love with this man, I wasn't ready for the sudden turn my life was taking. Marcel had brought out feelings and emotions that had been foreign to me. He had made me feel things no other man could.

When Marcel had called to tell me the police were after him, I had thought I was going to lose it. With all my heart I'd hoped that at some point he would tell me he was only teasing. I was so worried about him. I hadn't got much sleep the past two weeks, since his arrest. Last night, I just stared at my ceiling for hours. Praying. At one point, I got up to take a hot bath hoping that would help. But instead, I found myself breaking down into uncontrollable sobs. The last three words he had told me over the phone had been one of the reasons for my sleepless nights. He had told me that he loved me.

Breaking away from my thoughts, I looked around the courtroom, searching for Marcel's mother, but she wasn't here. He had probably asked her not to come.

My dearest Marcel, I thought. *He doesn't want any of his family members to see him in this situation.*

There were so many people in the courtroom. I wondered what their stories were. How they had ended up here. No smiles, no laughter. Only worried and troubled faces. It made me wonder whether my life really had been *normal?* Or had I been sheltered and shielded from what now appeared to be the default lives and stories of all these people around me that didn't know Jesus? My heart hurt for them.

Before I turned back to my Bear, I prayed for these strangers that were sitting around me. I prayed that they would seek God's grace and mercy; turn to Him for guidance; realize the need they had for Him. Lastly, I prayed for Marcel. I prayed that all this would go well. That he would soon be able to hold me close to him. Prayed that he knew, without a doubt, how much I cared about him, even though I hadn't said those words back.

When I looked up at him, his head was bowed. As the victim, Trevor Graham, walked up to take the stand. I couldn't see my Bear's eyes, but I knew they held remorse. The victim, dressed in a black suit was a tall, thin middle-aged man with greying strands and very dull eyes. It was hard to tell whether or not they had any color.

Once the man had taken the stand, he told his story, as his attorney led him with the questions he asked. He started out speaking slowly and quietly. But it didn't take long before we could hear the intensity in his voice. Pointing his finger at Marcel, he declared, "That man came into my brother's house along with his accomplices and attacked me," he fired. As Mr. Graham described the beating he'd received, I cringed in shock. At the end, his scrawny hands were shaking in fury and his dull, lifeless eyes blazing with anger.

Outside of the first night I had seen Marcel, I hadn't seen that side of him. I had only witnessed a kind, gentle, and loving man. A man who had saved me from those violent men; a man who had visited me in the hospital when I was hurting; a man who kept me company; a man who had become a friend and, if we were given the time, maybe even more than that. Part of me wanted to jump out of my seat and scream, "It's all a lie!" But I knew better. Marcel hadn't walked with the right crowd or been a good man before Christ came into his life. Though my every encounter with him had been filled with tenderness on his part, I was well aware of the person he could turn into if he was triggered, and it was that person that was sitting here today, facing trial.

The image of Marcel that night at the restaurant throwing that man against the van replayed in my mind. He had done it so easily; had looked so fierce. That was the Marcel that had attacked Mr. Graham.

Sadly, I had no doubt that he could do the harm that Trevor Graham was describing. That man had experienced first-hand the gruesome violence my Bear had been capable of.

I didn't even know what to think. All I wanted was for things to return back to normal once again. Marcel had given his life to Christ. He had turned his back on that life and everything had been going so well. So why this, why now?

I quietly sat in my seat as the proceedings went on. Marcel had already pleaded guilty in the beginning, which seemed to have shocked the entire courtroom. Apparently, they believed him to be a cold-hearted beast with no remorse. If that's what they thought, they didn't know my Bear at all. He might have been a criminal once, but he was sweet, and kind, and so loving now. Above all, he had changed. He had fallen in love not only with me, but also with Jesus. He was now eager to know more about God, study His word, and do His will. He was no longer the Marcel whose name Sofia used to 'use as her bargaining chip', as Marcel had once put it. He was the man who had saved my life.

"Thank you, Mr. Graham," the district attorney said when the man was through. While Mr. Graham continued to sit silently on the stand, his attorney paced back and forth in front of the judge's desk and narrated the events of that night with explicit detail. When he was done, he planted himself in front of the judge and concluded, "So, you see, Your Honor. This man, Marcel Maxwell, is nothing but a violent criminal who deserves to be locked up for a long time. He assaulted my client, Mr. Trevor Graham, thinking him to be his twin brother, Mr. Tyler Graham. And while we're unaware of the doings of Tyler Graham or the circumstances that led to Mr. Maxwell's rage toward him, the fact remains that Marcel Maxwell assaulted a harmless man. It's the responsibility of this court to lock him up so he won't harm the innocent again."

With each word, my chest grew tighter, and my hands more clammy. The way he had said 'locked up' like Marcel was some sort of wild animal stung me. The district attorney was obviously good at his job. Nevertheless, he had one thing wrong. My Bear was no longer a hardened, violent criminal. He was a man with a bright future ahead of him. I remembered the sound of his voice when he had called to tell me about what he did. It was obvious he regretted hurting Mr. Graham and every other person he had hurt in his former life. There was no question in my mind that Marcel's conversion was real, true. However, what he had done to this man was also real and true. And wrong.

"...no criminal deserves to go unpunished." the district attorney rambled.

Still, the compassion I had for Marcel left me feeling a little upset that Trevor Graham was doing this to him. I knew it was foolish—no, selfish—for me to think like that, especially in the light of what had happened to me months ago when I was attacked by criminals. That's what Mr. Graham must have endured at the hands of Marcel, maybe even worse. Although Mr. Graham's hand was no longer in a cast, the scars on his face were still visible.

With a heavy heart, I decided to focus on what was going on in the courtroom rather than diving deeper in my thoughts. The room was silent as all eyes were watching, and every ear was listening.

After the attorney had finished presenting his case, Marcel was asked if he had anything to say. He did. I held my breath as Marcel slowly stood to say his peace. He was wearing an orange jumpsuit, handcuffs still on his hands and restraints on his ankles. His hair was longer now, his eyes looked tired, carrying bags under them. At that moment, I had wanted nothing more than to be in his arms. The pain in my chest was agonizing. I had been certain my heart would crack open. Never in my life, had I imagined I could care so much for a man.

Marcel spoke and it shook me from my thoughts.

"Yes, Your Honor," he started, looking back and forth between the judge and the defendant. "First of all, I very much want to extend my regrets and apologies to Mr. Trevor Graham for what I did to him. I wasn't a good man until recently. I started out as a kid walking with the wrong crowd and doing the wrong things, struggling to fit in somewhere, trying to prove my worth. The night I assaulted Mr. Graham, I caused unimaginable pain to an innocent man. I also realize that even if it had been his brother, I had no right to do the things I did."

With a sigh, my Bear shook his head. "I'm deeply sorry for hurting you, Mr. Graham, you have no idea. A few months ago, I met the Lord Jesus, and He changed my life. Things that I didn't understand, or care about, I do now. He opened my eyes to see that the life I was leading wasn't the life He wanted for me. For anyone. I needed to change. And I did. I made a complete turnaround and now I'm a different man. I know it's hard for many people to believe, but it's the truth.

"I'm aware that I will have to do jail time. Honestly, it's something I've feared, but anticipated would come for a long time. Still, as I committed a crime; I have no choice but to face the consequences of it. I'm prepared to do that. I only hope that, at the end of my sentence, I will have found God's purpose in all of this." Then he slowly sat back in the chair.

My heart bled for him as I watched him retake his seat. The judge, a woman with sharp eyes, put both arms on her desk. I wasn't sure how much time passed as she sat quietly, looking at Marcel then around the room. I wished I could have read the thoughts going through her mind. But she did a good job of concealing them, as well as any emotions she may have had. Finally, she closed the session for a thirty-minute recess. The moment she slammed her gavel down and left the room, I started toward Marcel, ignoring the eyes of everyone who was watching me approach him.

"Bear." I whispered. He turned around to look at me and his dark eyes widened in surprise.

"Norma? You're here."

"Of course, I am." Suddenly, I felt the strong urge to touch him and assure him that everything was going to be fine. I tried to close the gap between us. I just needed to hug him. If this was going to be for the last time in a long time, I needed to feel him. But just as I was about to reach over the wooden gated area for him, the officer stretched a hand out in front of me.

"Sorry, Ma'am, but you're not allowed to do that." I took a hasty step back to avoid his meaty hand knocking me over.

"You're saying I'm not even allowed to give him a simple hug?"

"No." The officer shook his head, looking at me like I was foolish. Then he looked from me to Marcel, then back at me. "I'll allow you just a few seconds to speak to him, though. Make it quick and take a step back."

"Thank you." I nodded. Feeling like a fish out of water, I looked back at Marcel. "Are you doing, okay?" I asked in a rush from where I stood, on the opposite side of the wooden gate. They would come for Marcel any time, I just needed to make sure he was okay first.

"Yeah, I am," he said, which surprised me. His physical appearance wasn't the best but there was peace in his eyes.

"Are you sure?"

"Yes. I'm trusting God to take us through this, and I want you to do the same." My throat tightened as a lump formed there. Since I couldn't find my voice, I just nodded.

"I will." I assured him. He was right, this wasn't the time to shed tears as they would do nothing to help him. It was the time to trust in God. I didn't know the sentence Marcel would get, but I prayed it was going to be something that wouldn't take him away from me for a big piece of my life.

Then the officer reached for Marcel's arm, helped him from the chair and slowly led him from the courtroom. My insides tightened, as I watched my heart walk away from me.

When the door closed behind him, I turned and walked into the corridor to stretch my legs and get some different air. I would say *fresh* air, but it wasn't. It was only a different kind of air; musky and sour. As I looked out the window, I saw dark clouds building in the sky and getting darker in the distance. *How fitting for the day,* I thought. The hall would have been empty if it weren't for a few wooden benches alongside the walls and the two small groups of people that were standing and chatting outside the different courtrooms.

I paced the hall for several minutes. I should have been praying, but what could I say that I hadn't already said? I had already told God everything I was feeling. I had nothing different to share with Him. God knew my thoughts and my heart. He had a plan and I needed to have peace and accept whatever He would allow to happen. Like it or not.

I noticed people walking back into the courtroom. Had half an hour already passed? As I followed them and went back through the double-wooden doors, a whirlwind of emotions came over me, and my entire body started shivering. I took my seat and waited the last few minutes for the session to start again.

"All rise," was announced as the judge marched back to her desk. It was time for sentencing. My palms were sweating, and my heart was racing.

"Please, Jesus." Was all I could breathe out. When the judge turned her eyes to Marcel, I held my breath.

"Mr. Maxwell, what you did to Mr. Graham was an unthinkable and serious offense. As such, you deserve to be put in jail for your crime. Nevertheless, it's appropriate for me to acknowledge that you have been very cooperative with this court. I'm also pleased that you've decided to turn your life around. It will be a positive start for you, to what I hope will be a new beginning as a productive citizen. I hope that by the end of your sentence, you will have figured out what you would like to do with your life and pursue it with all your heart. The important thing is that you have changed; learned a better way. So, you should be successful in integrating back into society after serving your time."

The words were touching, and it made me wonder which way things would go. Five years? Ten years? How long would my Bear be put away?

"Mr. Maxwell, this court finds you guilty of assault and battery. You will therefore serve a *minimum* of eighteen months in prison and be fined res..." Before she could finish her next sentence, Mr. Graham flew off his chair and glared at the judge.

"A year and a half? Are you kidding me?"

"Mr. Graham, be silent and sit down," came the harsh statement from the judge.

Trevor Graham slowly retook his seat, but I imagined the scowl was still glued to his face. The judge continued to issue my Bear's sentence. To be honest, I was just as stunned as Mr. Graham. What I'd expected was years of waiting. Countless times, I had imagined myself aging away, without Marcel by my side and the pitiful looks I would get.

Not only that, but I was certain my parents would have discouraged me from waiting. They were already wary of the obstacles that came with Marcel. The only thing that had kept them from outright lashing out against my relationship with him, was the fact that they had met the guy, and knew he was genuine about his new walk with the Lord.

Marcel turned to look at me as the judge moved on with another case and looked to the other side of the room. Two officers came, one on either side of him, and began to lead him away. I stood and stared in his direction, my face wet with tears.

"Oh Bear." I murmured.

When he looked back at me, his face was expressionless. It was a bittersweet victory. Although we both felt unspeakable pain over the separation, I knew we were both thankful for the favorable sentence.

"I love you," he silently mouthed. I froze in place as I watched them lead him away. At that moment, a hand touched my shoulders and I turned to see who it belonged to. I came face to face with Pastor Archie. I had no idea he was even there.

"He'll be alright, Norma," Pastor Archie assured me. He squeezed my shoulders and smiled down at me. Sniffling, I leaned into him. He put an arm around my shoulders and we both stood side by side watching the officers lead him away. Tears continued to roll down my cheeks. The shock of what was happening made me unable to utter a single word.

When he disappeared through the door, a sob broke out of me. Pastor Archie turned me to face him and held onto my shoulders. "Stay strong, Norma. This is no time to break. I know you can do it."

Then it hit me.

I love you.

Once more, Marcel had told me that he loved me and I hadn't seized the chance to say it back. "I didn't get the chance to say it,"

I mumbled. I wished I had said it, so he would know and take those words back with him.

"Say what?" Pastor Archie asked curiously.

"Nothing. Excuse me," I choked out and walked away, out into the corridor. I was staring out the window when I noticed Pastor Archie approaching me. I was grateful that he gave me a few minutes to have my pity party. I had to laugh inside as I thought, *how does he put up with all of us?*

After a few minutes of silence, he asked, "Do you need a ride home?"

"Thank you, but no. I think I'll walk. I need to clear my head. Thank you for coming. It means a lot to me. And I'm sure Marcel is incredibly grateful for you." Then I said a quick goodbye and slowly turned around the corner to head for the exit.

As I walked through the glass doors under the dark clouds outside, I heard someone growling, "It's ridiculous. After all I endured, a year and a half are all she gave him?" I lifted my head to find Trevor Graham standing just outside the courthouse with his lawyer and two other men. His face was red with anger and his eyes were filled with disbelief.

Despite my uncalled-for irritation with him earlier, I felt a note of sadness for him at this moment. He had suffered much, and even though I felt like a martyr in this situation, the truth was, he was the only victim. He'd been innocently attacked.

At this point, the only thing that I could think about was that this was the goodness of the Lord toward my Bear. Even though Mr. Graham may have thought Marcel deserved to be in prison a lot longer, the judge had determined to give him the least amount of time permitted, according to the law. I believe God used that judge to bestow mercy on him. It was a miracle, really. To be honest, I was happy and thankful. But there was a weight of sadness that was covering me, and I couldn't shake it off.

A wave of fresh tears threatened to well up in my eyes. I pushed them away, then started toward Mr. Graham. He and the other men were still fuming over the case, but I ignored the harsh words and stepped in closer to them.

"Excuse me, Mr. Graham?" I called.

The men grew silent and eyed me with interest. I ignored them with the exception of Trevor Graham. Even the shortest one in the group towered over me. I'm sure my hesitance was apparent to them.

"May I help you?" Mr. Graham asked curiously.

"Forgive me for disturbing you," I told him. "I just wanted to tell you how sorry I am for what you had to endure that day. It must have been awful. But I'm happy that God brought you out alive and well." I glanced at his injured hand then. "Um, I'm sorry. I just wanted you to know that." That said, I turned and quickly walked away and rushed down the steps of the court building. It had started to rain, and I hadn't brought an umbrella. Though the rain wasn't heavy, I knew I was going to get drenched if I stayed without cover for much longer.

"Who was she?" a man from the group asked. I didn't hear the reply because I was moving almost at the speed of sound, my shoes making a slapping sound with every step I took, coupled with the chattering from the people around and the *pit-pat* from the rain. Instead of walking, I quickly flagged down a taxi, opened the door and got in. I gave the driver my address. Twenty minutes later, I walked through my front door. I needed something to do. Something that would get my mind off the dark thoughts about my life.

My only answer to that was painting. My mother was in the kitchen, busy baking fresh bread for dinner. The smell was heavenly, but I had no appetite. My stomach ached and grumbled, yet I couldn't swallow anything. My steps were heavy as I went up the stairs. When I entered my room, I dropped my tote bag on the bed and walked to the closet. All my art supplies were on the shelves to the right. I pulled out my canvases, brushes, and paints, shutting the door behind me.

As I was putting on my old painting blouse, I heard my mother say, "Norma?" She knocked on my door softly before pushing it open.

I didn't bother turning to look at her but continued to set up my workstation closest to the window. "Yes, mother?"

"Are you alright?"

Was I alright? What a silly question. How could anyone be alright when someone so close to their heart had been taken away? I couldn't even think straight, and honestly, I didn't want to think at all. A year and a half were five hundred-and-forty-eight days. But I would count down one day at a time as I waited for him.

"Norma." My mom said my name again. I heard her take a step forward.

"No." The word flew out of me before I could stop myself. I set my paintbrushes down and turned to face her. With agonizing pain in my heart, I continued. "No, Mom, I'm not alright. And I won't be until Marcel comes out of that horrible place." I didn't even want to picture Marcel in jail, I wondered what he was going through.

"*Tesoro…*" she started to say, but I cut her off, shaking my head.

I was trying my best not to cry. I needed to be strong for Marcel. He said I was one of the strongest people he had ever met and though I found that difficult to believe, I wanted it to be true, for him. My heart was palpitating so hard I could feel and hear it in my ears.

"I'm worried about him, Mom. What if he gets hurt in there? How is he going to survive?" How am I going to survive? I thought as I moved to sit on my bed. My legs were getting weak, and it felt like they couldn't carry my own weight anymore. My chest hurt, my head, everything hurt and all I wanted was for the pain to stop. But it wouldn't. Would it ever go away?

Mom walked over and sat on my bed next from me. “It’s going to be difficult, yes. I understand. But you know that through all of this, God is working out His own will. Marcel will be fine. I have no doubt he can take care of himself,” she said. “But I have also seen such a transformation in him, I’m certain Jesus is walking right beside him. You have to trust that.”

“I hope so,” I said, my voice barely audible. “Because if something happens to him in there, I don’t know what I’ll do. I...” A small knock interrupted. It was Luna.

“Hey,” she said, walking into the room. Without another word, she came and sat down at the other side of the bed, putting her hand on my arm. “God is with him.”

She moved even closer. I laid my head on her shoulder, closing my eyes.

“He’ll be fine, don't you worry.” As we stayed in that position, listening to the pitter-patter of the raindrops on my bedroom window, I couldn’t help but think about her words. Would Marcel really be okay? Would *we* be, okay?

Chapter Eighteen

Marcel

I was a strong man, but prison life was still tougher than I had imagined. Some of these characters were even more heartless than my old boss.

Right after I stepped out of the courtroom, heart shattered from seeing those tears drop from Norma's eyes, one of the officers leading me out told me to brace myself for the terrible experiences ahead. I wasn't certain if he was trying to scare me or prepare me for it. Either way, I hadn't replied, but had kept walking, my eyes fixed forward, and my mouth shut.

Even though I knew I could take care of myself, the moment those words left his mouth, my heart started to beat unsteadily. But that was nothing compared to how I felt when I walked into the prison for the first time. The cell they put me in was so small, I feared I wouldn't be able to breathe. I couldn't imagine how I was going to survive a year and a half in that tiny box that was designed for two. There was also the fact that the guys who surrounded me looked like they wanted to rip my eyes out. Or worse.

"New boy!" a man had called on my first day. His voice was rough. His eyebrows together in a frown as his eyes watched me. He must have been in his early forties.

My name wasn't 'new boy', and had I come here before my life had changed, the outcome would not have been pretty. But I knew I had to be careful. Life in here was nothing like outside. I attempted to ignore him, but he called again.

"Hey, new boy!" This time, his eyes were fixed on me from the bench where he sat. I only took a brief glance at him. He was sitting up now. I faced my front and continued in the direction I was going. It wasn't wise, but going to meet him alone wasn't either.

"Are you deaf? The man is speaking to you," another guy who was standing next to him said to me.

I had heard of guys who strutted themselves around the prisons. Often instructing men and giving them commands to do their dirty work. I'd also heard of people who disobeyed those orders. The stories were not good. I cringed at the thought and the horror those men went through day after day.

At that point, the two guys who had spoken to me, plus a third guy who was standing there, were now glaring in my direction. I stopped in my tracks and turned toward them, praying for peace to handle the situation. If I was going to be here, I didn't want to make my time here any worse than it already was. I started walking towards them.

The first guy, who looked like the leader, said in annoyance. "I don't have any time or patience for this."

My first instinct was to slip back to my old ways, but instead, I continued my pace and approached them, while asking God to lead the way. *Jesus, I can't do this on my own. I'm about to snap. Lord, please take control.*

I stopped a short distance from them. The leader kept quiet for a while, watching me. Then he said, "You look familiar. What's your name?"

"Marcel," I answered curtly. I looked closely at his face, he said my face looked familiar, but he didn't look familiar to me. I was sure of that. I would remember a face like his.

"Marcel what?" He cocked his head. "What's your last name?" He asked, but I didn't answer. I was focused on not losing my temper and worsening my case.

"Answer me. Did you fall from the sky?" he asked again, visibly trying not to laugh.

At that moment I wished I had, because I had no words; nothing would come out of my mouth. What was wrong with me? Then, Proverbs 15:1 – *A gentle answer turns away wrath, but a harsh word stirs up anger*—filled my mind. I didn't know many verses by memory yet, but when Pastor Archie had mentioned this to me one day, I had gone to my Bible to read the whole passage, and this particular verse had stuck.

I took in a breath and calmly said, "Maxwell." The struggle to keep my cool was becoming overwhelming.

The leader stood up from the bench and stepped forward, only stopping a couple of feet away from me.

"Don't mess with me," he warned. "That attitude is gonna mess you up in here." Though he was an arm's length away from where I stood, I could feel his breath.

What attitude exactly was he referring to? He had asked a question which I had provided an answer to. I think he was just trying to break me down.

Trying to focus on Jesus and attempt to not sound like a smart-Alec, I simply stated, "You called me. I'm here." Oddly enough, he didn't look provoked by that.

He smirked. As big as I was, he looked at me eye-to-eye. We were about the same height. I managed to conceal my anger and, I admit, my fear. The other two guys hadn't moved an inch, but their eyes were both locked on me.

At that moment, from the corner of my eye, I noticed another guy starting to approach us. Great, another one of his partners, I thought—He was shorter, heavily built, and sporting strong neck muscles. With his beard that reached to his chest, he reminded me of the stereotypical biker. His facial expression was hard, but he seemed calm, in control of all emotions.

"Let him be, Trey," he said to the leader of the group with an accent I didn't recognize.

"Stay out of this," was all Trey managed to say before some officer announced that *yard time was over*. Trey looked like he wanted to say something else, but decided against it. He sneered at me once more then turned, walking back to his guys. I heard him mutter some words as he walked away, but they weren't loud enough for me to hear.

As we walked, the guy who had intervened turned to me, and with a tight-lipped frown he said, "Be careful in here. No one's got your back."

I nodded.

He held out his hand for a handshake. "I'm Greg," he said.

I stared at his hands, wondering if I should accept. Although he had just helped me by easing the situation, that didn't make him any less dangerous than the rest of them. I didn't know who I could trust, nor who belonged to which group. In this place, any kind of trust seemed foolish, if not downright reckless. I took the outstretched hand. "Marcel," I said. "Thanks," I added, unsure about the protocol of politeness here.

"You're new here?" he asked. "You should stay away from Trey. He's not the type you want to mess with." After a few seconds, he added, "I can't protect you, but you should stick with me. You'll be at least a little safer."

From that moment on, Greg was at my side. Over time, he even became a friend, something I hadn't had in…I don't remember how long ago. He helped make life in prison a little more bearable while I was serving my time. I knew God had sent him.

A familiar voice pulled me out of my reverie. I sighed. I had been so deep in thoughts, I had lost track of the moment.

"Did you know that slothfulness is one of the seven deadly sins?" Greg reiterated.

My lips quirked up as I eyed him. The rest of the guys chuckled. Rafael, unaffected by the jibe, stretched both arms over his head and yawned, revealing two missing teeth.

"Don't judge me. I'm not slothful, I'm only tired," he defended himself, his tone laced with a hint of sarcasm.

"Right," Greg said with a sneer. "You're tired because you sleep too much."

"Watch it, Greg," Rafael warned. He wasn't looking at Greg, but I knew well enough that he could shoot off that chair in a split second to attack. I'd seen it happen before. It was time to calm things down before they escalated.

"Alright," I called out. "Let's settle down and get to our Bible study." That said, the guys began to pull their chairs toward me, until a circle was formed. I passed my eyes around the group of hardened criminals and had to force back another grin. Hard to believe that in a place like this…this hell on earth…I could have a little peace. But since the first day I had been tossed in there and Greg had introduced me to them, these guys seemed to have sensed something in me.

It was Greg who had first asked if I was a Christian. That had surprised me. As far as I could tell, there was nothing about me that stood out. Yet, somehow, he had managed to see the light of Jesus in me. Never would I have imagined these men would be gathered around me for Bible study, the day I heard the judge's sentence. I had had images of violence flashing through my mind, and though things definitely weren't a bed of roses, it wasn't as bad as it could have been.

To be quite honest, for the first couple of weeks, even with Greg's comradeship, I'd been depressed, especially when I thought of Norma. She and Pastor Archie had been the only ones there to support me that day. Not because my mother didn't want to come. More than anything, she had wanted to be there, but Isabella had fallen ill on the same day and had to be taken to the doctor. Mom had been distressed by the way things had worked out, but I hadn't been. It had been a blessing in disguise. No way I would have wanted my poor mother witness me being hauled off to prison. It would have broken her, and I needed her to be strong for the girls.

The first few days in prison had been the worst of my life. This had to be as close to hell a person could get while still alive. Even for me, this place was horrifying—it still was. The worst of thoughts came to me. I'd been hanging on by a thread, worried that my family wouldn't survive without me. That Norma would break under the pressure. That I would lose my mind.

Until one day, something happened.

An inmate had fallen ill. Grievously ill. Some of the guys had pleaded to get him help, but for whatever reason, their request was ignored. Perhaps he was the guy that *cried wolf*, who knows. Everyone, including myself, thought he would die. We had no idea what illness he carried, but we knew it was bad. It was this concern that led me to visit him.

I wasn't certain how my hand ended up on his shoulder. I felt like I was in a dream. I had no idea what I was doing, but what I did know was that I was to pray for this man. So I prayed like I had never prayed before, asking God to heal this stranger in front of me, and to give him a testimony.

To my dismay, nothing happened after I had prayed. In fact, he seemed to grow worse as the night progressed. I didn't understand why God would lead me to pray for him, only for him to die. But he didn't die. The next day, he got out of bed, healthy and whole as if nothing had ever been wrong with him.

That guy was Rafael.

It was amazing. More than amazing. It was a miracle. A real-life miracle that God had done through me, a prisoner. From that day on, my name was known throughout that cell block. Not a day went by that someone didn't ask about my faith. It was then that I started to realize what my purpose was, and why God had allowed me to be there.

I had been placed here to be a light to these rough men. God wanted to use me to harvest some of the darkest souls for His Kingdom. The moment I understood that, I started His work. Now, months later, I was still being used by God to change lives.

With the help of Pastor Archie, I managed to get many of them who had been paroled integrated into churches in the area. It was the greatest feeling in the world to know that I was being used by God to help change so many lives. The depression I had been struggling with at the beginning was now gone.

"What are we studying today, Preacher?" Rafael asked, his eyes still closed.

Preacher. That was what everyone called me since Rafael's miraculous healing several months back. I smiled at him. He had been one of the first to inquire about my religion and had started meeting me on a daily basis to find out more. Before long, other men followed.

"How about, *'Go to the ant, you sluggard. Consider her ways and be wise'*?" Greg snickered, to Rafael's annoyance. My lips started to twitch but I suppressed it. For as long as I'd been here, Rafael and Greg had never gotten along. I didn't understand why. They had probably had an altercation long before I arrived. Playing referee was a constant task for me.

"How about: *'Do unto others as you will have them do unto you'*?" I asked Greg. "That's Matthew 7:12, by the way. Since you always ask." Greg ran a hand through his beard but didn't answer. He was a rough guy, but he had so much interest in Scripture that it was the only thing that could silence him. This time around, I let my smile break through. We continued with our study, the guys bringing up questions when they were confused and I tried my best to explain. At other times, these men would put their heads together and try to explain things for themselves.

A couple of hours later, I retired to my cell for the day. Tired, my mouth widened in a yawn, and I stretched my aching muscles.

I was dying to roll over into my bed and fall asleep. Still, I fell to my knees and closed my eyes. I opened my mouth to begin my prayer, but the words died on my tongue when someone approached me from behind and ripped my Bible from my hand.

I shot to my feet and turned to face my attacker. My eyes widened a little when I realized it was Micah, one of the guys who had beat up Norma many moons ago. Striker, his partner in crime, stood only a few feet behind him. I remembered how I had once sworn to destroy them if I ever crossed their path again and right now, I was tempted to do just that. The looks on their faces woke nothing in me but anger and I didn't like it.

From the moment I had been incarcerated, these two had had their eyes on me. Naturally, they harbored deep resentment against me not only for having beaten them up, but also for having gotten them arrested. Vengeance had been flashing out of their eyes every time I had dared to look into them. Despite that, they had never made a move on me. I suppose it was the respect I had gained from the other men that kept them at bay. But what had given them the idea that it was time to approach me and settle the score?

As if to answer my question, two other men walked up behind Striker, their faces solemn. Scotty and Kade. My former colleagues.

Oh, God. This isn't looking good.

Despite my fake appearance of calm, my heart was racing. They were the last men I had expected to see, and if they hadn't stood right here before me and I had just heard rumors about them being here, I would have called it bluff. What were Scotty and Kade doing in prison? And when did they get here? Even though I asked myself the question, I already knew the answer. I turned my attention back to Micah and Striker.

I cleared my throat. "Is there something you need?" Micah's chuckle grated the back of his throat. The unmistakable sign of a chain smoker.

"What we want is your blood, *Preacher*." He spat my prison name out like something bitter on his tongue. "But, apparently, we're not the only ones. Your friends here are not very fond of you either. I think they want you dead even more than we do." He let out another grating laugh that soon turned into a vicious cough. I cringed at the sound of it. Under more favorable circumstances, I would have told him to have that checked out, but I was certain none of these guys wanted to hear a smart mouth.

Adrenaline was already surging through my body, preparing me for a fight. Even my fists were starting to form. I only realized because Striker, Scotty, and Kade all dropped their gazes to my hands. Catching myself, I loosened my fingers, doing my best to stay calm.

"Hand it back and walk away," I told Micah, stretching out my hand for the Bible. He looked like he wanted to say something clever, but his friend tugged at his arm then whispered something in his ear. The smug look on Micah's face faded, replaced by a hint of doubt and fear. God only knew what was going on in their heads. Did they think I was going to fight them? Four against one? Perhaps. After all, that was the guy they knew, not this new Bible reading, Jesus lover who now had morals and meaning to his life.

I had known Micah and Striker were here since I had first arrived, and I had done my absolute best to avoid crossing paths with them. The look in Micah's eyes told me he wanted to press my buttons. I prayed he wouldn't. I wasn't sure how I would react if any of them attacked me. My instincts would be to fight back, but I didn't want to give in to violence.

In the end, he tossed my Bible onto my bed and turned to walk away with Striker close behind him. Scotty and Kade glanced at each other then back at me. Unable to help myself, I stepped closer to them. To their credit, they stood their ground.

"Why are you here?" I asked, though Micah had made that gruesome remark earlier.

"Don't act so surprised, Marcel. You know why we're here," Kade replied. "You should've known this was coming. Don't play stupid with me. You thought you'd get away by getting yourself locked up? I thought you were smarter than that. You know nobody walks away from Johnny. You're going to pay for disrespecting him. And for disrespecting us. I think you know the price."

My stomach somersaulted. "So, Johnny wants me dead, huh?" Understanding there was nothing he could do to make me change my mind and get me back, Johnny had turned to his second option: eliminating me. Me being sent to prison wasn't enough for him. He couldn't tolerate rebellion and didn't rest until he put an end to it. One way or another. It was his way to protect himself, and to warn the other members of the gang under him.

"Don't worry," Scotty chimed in. "It won't happen today." I relaxed a little at that but was still tense as I knew what was going to come next. "But it will happen. You won't see us when we're coming, I promise you that. I guess, expect us, when you least expect us." Of course they would strike when I was least anticipating it. It was their way to provoke apprehension in me, and to make the wait more enjoyable for them.

I passed my eyes back and forth between the two. At one point, these guys hadn't just been my colleagues. They had become my friends. They had both feared and respected me when I was in my element back then. It was hard to see how they could kill me that easily. And yet, I knew better. If you walked away, you paid with your life. Friendships didn't matter in this regard.

It was sad that they may never break from this and if they ever chose to, they would face the same thing I was going through right now. I wondered if they had ever considered leaving, but had discarded the idea when they thought of the consequences. It saddened me to think that most men never realized this when they signed up; or maybe they did, but just didn't care at the time. I had followed Johnny, because at that time, I had all that anger I was holding onto, and he used it to trap me. Luckily, I had found Norma, I had found God and I knew with His help, I was going to get through this.

I had been hoping to find some amount of humanity in their eyes, but to no avail. There was none. Scotty and Kade were serious about their mission. Fear wrapped itself around my heart like a poisonous snake.

"It doesn't have to be like this," I found myself saying. "I've never told the cops anything about Johnny or the business. You know me. You have to know that."

Scotty shook his head, clicking his tongue. "No, we don't."

Then Kade answered. "Johnny doesn't care what you reveal or what you don't. Bottom line, he doesn't trust you."

I didn't say it out loud, but I was sure Johnny trusted no one. Kade continued, "And neither do I. You're a loose end that needs to be tied up. Plain and simple. You never should have walked away in the first place; you were just lucky, and Johnny was kind enough to give you time so you might realize your mistake. You brought this on yourself, Marcel. Now you'll just have to bear the consequences of your decision."

"Like I said, it won't be today," Scotty added. "You have our word. Now go on back to your little prayer session. Let your God know you'll be meeting Him soon." Kade broke into a soft chuckle. It almost made me laugh too, but not out of mirth. How on earth had I ever come to consider these guys family?

"Try to eat well, too. You'll need some strength when you take your last breath," Kade added before they both walked out.

When you take your last breath.

I exhaled deeply. I had held my breath without realizing it until I could no longer see their backs. I closed my eyes and said a short prayer. I knew it was only God who could get me out of this inextricable situation. Despite Scotty's continuous promise that they wouldn't touch me just yet, I was certain that if I let my guard down at any point, I was a dead man.

Chapter Nineteen

Marcel

After Scotty and Kade had left the room, I dropped onto the small mattress I'd been sleeping on for almost a year, and sighed. It wasn't surprising that things had come to this. Still, I couldn't stop myself from feeling betrayed. For ten years of my life, Johnny had become somewhat of a father figure to me. In fact, I was the only one among the guys that he ever called son. For some reason, I thought that fondness that he had for me would have somehow prevented him from taking vengeance on my walking out on him.

How naïve I had been.

Johnny wasn't my father, and I wasn't his son. He was nothing near a father figure. Johnny was just a criminal with a cold heart who could kill a man without batting an eye.

Was that what I'd been looking for? A father figure?

When he had picked me up and taken me under his wings, giving me money to help my family and offering advice I should never have listened to, I did look up to him as such. I had never had a father figure in my life before, and though I didn't voice it to my mother because I didn't want to worry her, it was still something that bothered me. Nothing had broken my heart more than to see other dads come to watch their boys play ball and cheer them on.

The memory of the first time I saw Johnny came back to me. It had been at my last football game in high school, a decade ago. At the time, he'd been looking for one of my teammates whose dad had run from town when he couldn't come up with the money he owed Johnny. Incidentally, I'd had a beef with that same kid and was more than willing to crush him. Victor was his name. Ever since I had taken his title as best player, he had been my plague in high school. Not that I carried revenge in my heart for Victor anymore, but I still remembered everything that had led me to join the gang, like it was yesterday.

During that game, Victor had intentionally tripped me, and almost busted my knee. He'd made it look like it was an accident, but I'd seen the look of satisfaction in his eyes. The problem was, he never knew the fury that I had inside me. I was the cool, calm, collected guy who got along with most people. He'd never really seen me lose my temper, and that must have been the reason why he did what he did. Unfortunately for him, his plan didn't work out the way he had wanted. I shined in that game. The crowd went crazy each time I scored a touchdown. My hidden rage helped fuel my energy.

When the game was over, I'd waited until all the guys had cleared out of the locker room before I made my move. I had been waiting for that moment.

"You," was all he said with a growl when he saw me. His hatred for me had been evident, but no different from the disgust I had had for him. Victor wasn't a small guy. He was tall, ripped, and according to the girls, handsome. Thing was, I was bigger. Maybe not as handsome, but definitely bigger. I hadn't been in the mood for a conversation. All I wanted was for him to pay for everything he'd done to me during that year. So, without a word, I grabbed him by his throat and held him to the wall with one hand. That was when I'd offered him some choice words. Words I won't repeat now that I'm a Christian. Victor was gasping for air, trying to pry my fingers away from his throat. It only made me squeeze harder.

After a while, he'd stopped fighting, his legs barely kicking. I'd been so mad at the time, I hadn't considered that I might be killing the guy. A hand on my shoulder was what had brought me back to my senses. When I turned to look at the intruder, he was a short man with an intense gaze set on me. There was something about him that reminded me of a character in a comic book, one of those people who come off as timid and innocent, but turn out to be the fiercest of all. There was something about the gleam in his eyes that almost made me tremble.

That man had been Johnny. Standing just behind him was another guy, a cigar hanging off the corners of his lips. It was Kade.

I remember thinking I was in trouble and wondering if they worked for the cops, but one more look at Kade told me they didn't. That day had been the beginning of something new for me. Johnny had recruited me to be his muscles. He also got the location of Victor's father through me. In fact, finding this man had been my first job. I'd done it, and done it well, even though I was terrified of what I was doing at the time, and worried that my mother would find out. As the years went on, my lifestyle hardened me, changed me into a different person, and not a good one.

Now, after ten years of doing his dirty work, he was going to kill me, simply because I didn't want to be his muscle anymore. I understood his decision, but it didn't lessen the sting of betrayal. The heart of man was indeed filled with wickedness. At this point, although I was terrified, the only thing I could do was put my trust in God. After all, He was a better Father to me than Johnny had ever been. Because unlike Johnny, I knew God would never turn his back on me.

"I trust You," I said into the darkness. "You won't fail me. No matter how this turns out, I trust you. Save me from the hands of these evil men."

I stayed awake for a while, just staring at the ceiling, my mind numb. I don't know how much time passed, but my eyes started feeling heavy and my eyelids began dropping. Before I knew it, I was caught in a dream. In the dream, I was at a funeral. A group of people dressed in black were standing a couple of feet away from me. I recognized each of them. My mother, my sisters, my church family. They all had a solemn look on their face.

As I started toward the group, I saw Pastor Archie speaking at the front, but I could barely focus on a word he said. Between him and the small crowd was a dark brown casket, more than six feet long. As I drew closer, the sight of the woman I loved came into my periphery.

Norma.

She was also dressed in black, and she looked stunning. Forgetting everyone else, my lips quirked up as I walked over to her, excited to see her. My hands itched with the desire to touch her and hold her close to me. The closer I got, the louder the stifled sobs became. She was crying. Not only her but my mother and my sisters. I blinked in surprise. Whose funeral was this?

I stepped closer to Norma. Reaching out, I touched her shoulder. I touched her, but didn't feel like I made contact. I reached out again, but the same thing. “Babe, are you okay? What’s going on?”

Norma didn’t look at me. In fact, she gave no indication that she had even felt my touch. I tried to turn her to look at me, but I couldn’t move her. Perplexed, I stepped completely in front of her. She didn’t as much as blink. She couldn’t see me, none of them could. It was like I was invisible.

My heart sprinted. My throat went dry.

Turning, I looked at the casket one more time. A troublesome thought pressed against my mind, but I did my best to shut it out. It was impossible. It couldn’t be…

My legs propelled me forward. I noticed then that the top half of the casket was pure glass. As my eyes landed on the figure of the man inside, my knees went weak. I’d only seen such scenes in the movies. And yet, here I was, looking down at myself in a casket, face pale, body rigid.

It was me. I was…dead.

I stared in shock as everyone stared back at me now, tears rolling from their eyes. I glanced down at myself, then looked at Norma. “Baby, I’m right here.”

It seemed she could finally see and hear me because she answered, “It’s you, Bear.”

“What do you mean?” I stammered.

“You're dead, Marcel. You died and you left me. You promised you would never leave me, Marcel. But you’re gone.”

“No, no, it's not possible, this can't be.” My words froze in my mouth as I felt the floor begin to give way as it pulled me down, trying to swallow me up. I reached out to grab something, but then...everyone was gone. The only thing in the room was *my* casket. It was open now. And the only thing looking at me was ... Marcel.

“No!” I shouted.

I woke up gasping for air and flying into a sitting position. I was drenched in sweat and my heart was beating dangerously fast. I rubbed my chest as I looked around me, realizing that I was still in my tiny cell. Relief overtook me but that didn’t last for long. Replaying the dream in my head, I didn’t have to wonder what it meant, I knew.

I was going to die.

At this young age, I was going to be taken from this world. No, it couldn’t be. The gorgeous face of my girl popped into my head and my hands trembled. Norma.

Was this just my mind playing tricks on me because of the threat I had received earlier? Or was this a premonitory dream?

It couldn’t mean anything else. It was clear as crystal. I took it as a sign that I wouldn’t have much longer to live. The thought tore me apart. I’d prayed and asked God for His protection, but I guess He had other plans for me. He wanted me home. He wanted me with Him.

A sermon from our associate pastor came back to mind that instant. "Sometimes our loved ones die so young, and we wonder, why? Why did they have to go so soon? Why can't the good-hearted people in our lives live long, happy lives themselves? But have we ever stopped to think that maybe, just maybe, they've already fulfilled God's purpose?

"This is why it's important that we always watch for Him. That we know God's purpose for our lives and pursue it with all our hearts," he'd gone on to say. "None of us know how much time we have left on this Earth. Death is appointed to every man and there's no way to escape it. But if we know the plan for our lives and fulfil it, we can leave this world knowing that the reward for our good works is waiting for us in heaven."

Purpose.

Had I fulfilled my purpose here on Earth? Was this the last chapter of my story? Speaking of purpose, what had mine been? Had I been fulfilling it unconsciously, or had I missed it altogether?

Lord, I have only just started my journey; it can't be the end already.

I was still new to the Christian faith, and there were still a lot of things I still didn't understand. However, I hoped to God that whatever I'd been doing with my life while in prison was part of it. I hadn't done much, but I'd helped in bringing a few souls closer to God. He had allowed me to get incarcerated. I'd thought it was the worst thing that could happen to me, until He used me as a vessel to heal Rafael, and some of the men began asking about my faith.

Despite my apprehension, my heart filled with joy at the memory. All one needed was faith, trust in God, and with his help, one could experience some amazing things. There were several guys who got saved through the ministry that God had given me here in prison. This had to be part of my purpose, right?

Needing answers and some supernatural strength that exceeded my own, I slid to the floor, got on my knees, and began to pray once again. Usually, my prayers were short and to the point. This time, I found myself weeping before God, begging Him to help me through all of this. I wasn't ready to die. I didn't want to leave my family, or Norma, just yet. I wanted to come out of prison, alive and well, and ready to take on the world. I wanted to live for a long time, be happy with my loved ones by my side.

Was that too much to ask for?

For the rest of the week, dreams of my impending death continued to plague me. It was hard to step out of my cell and do Bible studies with the guys while these visions haunted me at every turn, and especially when I closed my eyes at night. Even though the Word of God was reaching them, I knew well enough that if they as much as smelled a rat, sensed my life was in danger, chaos would break loose.

I didn't want that. I didn't want a riot. I didn't want any more dead bodies. I wanted them to change. They watched me from afar whenever we did a Bible study, or when I read my Bible on my own. I wondered if anything I was saying was making an impact on their lives. I hoped it did. I prayed for them. I didn't know how many years they were given, but I prayed they would be released one day. And most of all, I prayed they would accept Jesus like I had.

When Saturday came, I was told I had a visitor. Happiness washed over me when I heard it was my angel. As soon as I joined her at the table, she beamed at me. "Bear," she breathed out. After all this time, that nickname she had given me still did things to me, always bringing out that silly love-struck feeling. I reached out my hands to her across the table, palms up. Without hesitation, she rested her smaller hands in mine. Momentarily, I'd forgotten about the horrible week I'd had, as I drank in her loveliness. Not only her features, but her fragrance.

Today, her hair was up in a French-braided ponytail. I loved when she had her hair pulled back. It accentuated the perfect line of her high cheekbones, her chin, and the curve of her neck. I wanted nothing but to trace my fingers softly across her skin, while whispering sweet nothings into her ears. Everything about this woman was mesmerizing.

A blush started to creep up her skin. I smiled, she always flushed at the smallest things. "Why are you looking at me like that?" she asked shyly.

"You know why," I told her. "You're so beautiful."

Her blush deepened, her lips spreading in a shy smile. "Thank you." She lifted one of her hands out of my hold and swiped a hand through my overgrown hair hanging just above my eyes. "Your hair has grown really long," she pointed out. "You look kind of rugged, but still handsome." Before pulling her hand away, she lightly brushed my cheek with the back of her hand. Realizing what she did, she looked embarrassed. Norma was never one to initiate a touch in public. My girl was as old-fashioned as they came. This only made me realize how much she missed me.

The smile on my lips waned as I recalled my dream and the dreadful week I had had. Norma noticed the change immediately, and her eyes grew wide with concern. "Bear, what's wrong?" she asked.

I didn't bother answering that question. No doubt, she wouldn't like the answer. "How are things with you, babe?" I asked instead. Norma blinked a couple of times. "Tell me what's been going on."

"Uh, well, Aunt Mariana sold two of my paintings." Another smile grew on her face, though not as radiant as the first. "She's been getting calls from two museums. They want to showcase my paintings. Can you believe that?" She looked really excited.

"Of course, I can," I told her matter-of-factly. "You're very talented, Norma. This shouldn't be surprising to you. I'm so proud of you." I gave her another smile that was much more genuine than the first. Despite what I was going through, I was proud of my girl. I knew well enough how hard she had worked to get where she was. She had earned this success. The only shame for me was that I couldn't be there to celebrate with her. And I wasn't sure I would ever get the chance to, judging by what was going on.

"Thanks, Bear. That means a lot to me," she replied, beaming. "I was so happy when Aunt Mari told me the news. I couldn't wait to tell you."

"This is what you've always wanted," I reminded her. "No matter what happens from here on out, I want you to grab your dreams and success with all your might and never let go. I know Jesus is with you every step of the way."

My words were meant to bring her comfort. They did the complete opposite. Norma's brows gathered into a frown. "Something's wrong. What happened? And don't blow me off this time, Marcel. I deserve to know the truth."

Closing my eyes and lifting them toward heaven for just two seconds, I huffed out a breath. There was no way that I could keep this from her. Like she had said, she deserved to know. Still, I hated to make her worry. But it couldn't be avoided much longer, so I spilled the beans.

"There's a hit on me," I told her. "Johnny wants to tie up loose ends to protect himself. And by loose ends, I mean me."

I watched as Norma's blood drained away from her face, a gasp escaping her lips.

"I don't understand," she said, when she finally found her voice. "Can't you talk to the warden about it? He can't just send his people in to…to…"

To kill me, baby, I thought.

Of course, the words never made it out of her mouth. "Talking to the warden wouldn't work. In fact, it would make things worse for me. This place doesn't take anything seriously until it's too late."

"But we can't just sit around and do nothing." she cried. "There has to be something we can do. Someone we can at least meet with to help you."

"There's nothing to do, Norma," I told her. "At this point, the only thing we can do is pray and trust God. If it so happens that He doesn't deliver me and I die, at least I'll be with Jesus on the other side."

Tears welled up her eyes. "Are you crazy?" she cried under her breath. "You can't die. How do you expect me to live without you?" A lonely tear trickled down her cheekbone.

I gave a sad smile. It was bittersweet to know that she felt this way about me. It was all I wanted. But I had to prepare her mind and her heart for what was coming. There was no other way. "You're strong, Norma, it might take time, but you'll heal, and you will learn to move on." I spoke.

Then I thought silently, *with someone else.*

"Are you listening to me? Or better yet, are you listening to yourself, Marcel?"

"Baby, don't underestimate yourself. If it comes to that, you *can* and you *will* live without me. You're one of the strongest people I know. *You* are amazing." I took a deep breath. "The reason why I have this peace deep inside me is because of you. You, Norma Tesoriere, came into my life when I needed you most and you led me on the right path. I love you with every single fibre of my being and I…I'd always imagined…having more time with you."

"Bear," she choked out. "Don't speak like you've given up; you will get out of here and I'll be waiting for you."

I could feel a lump building in my throat, but I pressed on anyway. "I really want to have more time with you. But if we don't end up getting that chance, I want you to continue to live for God and shine like the beautiful person you are. Inside and out." My heart had started picking up the pace with longing for her.

Suddenly, I rose to my feet, knowing I had to end this visit right now. I was almost at breaking point. It was hard to watch the tears continue to build in those beautiful eyes. God, why had I pulled Norma into this life? Besides Jesus, she was the best thing that had, or would, ever happen to me.

"Two more minutes and visiting time will be over!" A guard called out.

"Over?" Norma whispered. She began to shake her head. "No, no, no. Bear, I'll be waiting for you, okay? You only have a handful of months left and you will be a free man. We will be together again."

"You don't know how badly I want that, Norma. It's all I've been looking forward to ever since I stepped foot here. But this isn't something I can control, with Johnny still out there, I can't..."

"No..."

Suddenly, I felt the need to say this to her. Although I didn't want to, the words spilled out, "Norma, it's time for you to go. In fact, maybe you should just consider leaving me, ending it. Maybe you should run. Run and never look back." I whispered.

Even as I said the words, my knees started to grow weak. Norma's eyes went wide, and she flew out of her chair just as I had. "What?" she whispered.

"I love you." Those were the last words I said before I turned and walked away. I heard Norma call to me, just like that evening at the church, when I had stormed out of the Bible study.

"Marcel? Bear, please…"

Her words were only a murmur yet they ripped me to shreds. Again. All I wanted to do was fall on my face and weep. But seeing me like that would have distressed her even more. So, I kept walking, until I was out of her sight.

I wanted to be glad, glad I had seen Norma, spoken to her again, poured out my feelings, so that if I was to die, I could die in peace.

But I wasn’t. I thought of my mother. This had always been her greatest fear and now it was becoming reality.

As soon as I was back in my cell, my knees gave out. I fell before my bed and the tears I’d been holding back began to pour out of me, along with my prayer. “Oh God, please...”

Who knew how long I had been on my knees and cried like a little girl? Somewhere along the line, I ended up falling asleep. The sound of my cell door opening pulled me out of my slumber. I wasn’t sure who it was, but when I looked up, Scotty and Kade were standing over me. Vaguely, I made out silhouettes of Micah and Striker just behind them.

Cowards. You could trust them to come like thieves in the night. Four against one, even if they did kill me that night, I wasn't going to give them the satisfaction of seeing me beg for mercy.

Before I could make it off my knees, Scotty and Kade came after me. The only thing I saw was the flash of something sharp before they both began to dive their shining blades into my flesh. Sleep left me completely as pain and adrenaline shot through my nerves and veins. I shoved them both away with every bit of strength I had left. The two flew into the wall opposite my bed. But they had stabbed me multiple times and the pain hit in places I'd never felt before. I felt myself bleeding out fast as warmed blood gushed out of my veins, soaking my clothes and dripping to the cold prison floor.

My vision started to blur. Everything became surreal. The pain, the blood, the men holding the knife before me. Adrenaline was still helping keep the pain bearable.

“Idiots.” I heard Scotty yell. “Help us hold him down.” I assumed that was meant for Micah and Striker. My vision continued to blur, and my head became light. The darkness that filled the room didn't help, but I could still make out all four men coming at me. I tried to get to my feet, but it was an impossible task. Micah and Striker held on to both my hands. Someone else, whether Scotty or Kade, wrapped an arm around my neck from behind.

The plunge of a weapon came at me again. Despite my fighting, they managed to overpower me this time. After a while, there was no more strength left in me. As soon as I stopped fighting, all four men let go. I tumbled to the floor, my blood pouring out.

Weak as I was, I managed to straighten myself into a sitting position. I leaned my back against the bed with a hand to my stomach. My entire body felt numb.

Scotty and Kade stooped down in front of me watching me gasp for air. At one point, they stared at each other. Was that remorse I saw in their eyes?

"I'm sorry, kid," Kade said, confirming my suspicion. "Sorry it had to be this way. You know I always liked you, Marcel. And it was a pleasure working with you. But this is business."

It was almost funny that my own killers were sympathizing with me. I opened my mouth to reply as a pool of blood made its way up my throat and out of my mouth. I coughed a few times before my throat cleared enough for me to speak.

"I…I forgive…you." I lifted my eyes to look at Micah and Striker. "All…of…you." My voice was scratchy, but at least I got my message out. All four men looked at me as if I'd grown another head. The guilt on Scotty and Kade's face made me feel sorry for them. They'd been assigned to end my life. If they failed at the job, Johnny would kill them both. It was the way of the game. Even though they may not have wanted to kill me, it was a choice between my life and theirs.

"Kid, if you want, I can make this easier on you." Scotty lifted his knife. The shining blade was dripping with my blood. His look was sheepish but I knew exactly what he was saying. He wanted to make my death quicker so I wouldn't suffer anymore. Something about that offer made me laugh.

"I'm…fine," I told him. "I…deserve…this. I've…hurt…too…many…people." A round of coughing overtook me again. Scotty and Kade stayed put, waiting on me. To die, I supposed. After all, they did have to report back to their boss that I was dead. There couldn't be any mishaps.

"You know," I went on when my coughing subsided. "I never…got a chance… to tell you… this…before. Jesus died…for you. You…should…give your life…to Him…before… it's…too late."

A chuckle rose in the small cell. I wasn't sure who it came from, but my best guess was Micah. "Can you believe this guy?" he commented.

"Shut up you fool." That voice was definitely Striker's. Even with my hearing dying, I could make out his somewhat high-pitched tone. Scotty and Kade, on the other hand, shook their heads and emitted long sighs. They finally rose to their feet.

My vision was getting darker with every passing second. I could barely make out the figures of the men as they turned and walked away. The creaking sound of the cell door opening and closing sounded strange. As if I'd been far down a tunnel. As if it was final.

I wanted to sleep. My entire body felt tired and drained. This must be what death felt like. Of course. I was dying. I was going home. To be with Jesus. No. I wasn't ready to die. Norma. I wanted her. For the rest of my life. My wife. Our children. My beautiful bride.

These were my last thoughts as I slipped away from the land of the living. Then everything went dark.

Chapter Twenty

Norma

Despite my mother being an incredible cook, and her *Caponata* undoubtedly tasting as delicious as always, I tasted nothing when I put my fork to my lips. All I could think about was the depressing conversation I'd had with Bear earlier that day. His ex-boss wanted him dead, and Marcel had resigned himself to that turn of fate. *Run*, he'd said. *Run, and don't look back.*

How could he expect me to do something like that? After everything we'd been through together, did he think I would just roll over and give up? Had he lost his mind? I would rather remain single for the rest of my life than walk away from him. I wanted to tell him that, but he'd walked away before I could speak my mind. He had looked so beaten. I wondered how long he had tortured himself with this before he had finally settled with what he believed to be his fate.

My Bear really believed he was going to die.

I couldn't allow myself to believe that for one second. Why would God pull him from that life, only to let him be murdered? He was a good man now, with a good heart. Jesus had changed him, and he was better than what he used to be. There was no way that God was going to allow my Bear to die such a horrible death. No, I just knew the Lord had a bright future planned for Marcel.

Right?

I wondered what he was doing at the moment. I would have given anything to be beside him, to comfort him, reassure him. Marcel needed to know that I wasn't going to leave him. Ever. But he had walked away. Had I known sooner that we only had two minutes of visiting time left, I would have used that little time to try and make him believe God had a different plan for him.

"*Bambina*," I heard my mother say, slicing through my thoughts. "You're not eating. And you're lost in space. What's the matter?" Luna and Rico had already stopped eating to look at me once they heard my mother's words.

"Yeah, Norma, you've barely touched your food." Luna pointed out. "And this is your favorite dish."

"It's nothing, Luna. I just...got lost in my thoughts." I forced a smile for her benefit and turned to my mom. "Sorry, Mom. I'm fine." I dug my fork into the food for another bite. I had no appetite, but I ignored that and swallowed it. When the food hit my stomach, I could feel it churning violently. I could feel my mom's eyes as well as Luna and Rico's, glued to me. Despite my stomach's discomfort, I continued to eat until half of what was on my plate was gone. Now she wouldn't worry as much if I stopped eating.

"Thanks for the food, Mom," I said before excusing myself and heading to my room. Grabbing my phone, I noticed that there were a couple of texts from Betty Ann. My best friend had been so supportive since I had met Marcel. I was so grateful to her. However, there were days when I just wanted to be by myself. Today was one of those days.

When I got into my room and closed the door, I'd started to dial Pastor Archie's number. Before I was able to finish, a knock sounded on my bedroom door. Luna came in, eyeing me with curiosity. "Hey sis," she started. "Can I come in?" she asked, even though she was already in. I wanted to be alone. I wanted to talk with Pastor Archie, but I didn't have the heart to say no to her. Giving her a tight smile, I nodded. She made her way over to my bed and plopped down beside me, cross-legged.

"I know something is bothering you," she said. "Do you want to talk about it?" she asked.

Usually, I felt better when I talked to my sister or my friends about things that were bothering me. But I didn't think there was anything she could say or do, that would help with the situation. And I wasn't sure, outside of Pastor Archie, who Marcel would want me to share this with. At least not yet. Although I did want to open my heart to her so bad, I couldn't. Not yet. I needed to call Pastor Archie. "I need to make a phone call first."

Just then, my cell phone started to ring. We pulled apart and I glanced at the screen.

Alexia Maxwell. Marcel's mom.

My heart skipped a beat. Since he had been incarcerated, she and I had kept in touch. I'd even met her and the twins for lunch a few times. She was a nice lady, passionate about each of her kids. With Bear not around, I did my best to keep her company, making sure she didn't worry too much. But since my last conversation with him, I didn't know what to expect.

I glanced at Luna. "I have to take this." She nodded and left my room. Once she was gone, I hit the green button. "Ms. Maxwell, hi. Is everything—" I started, trying to sound bubbly but failing miserably.

"Norma," she said, interrupting me. The first thing I noticed was how hoarse her voice was. She had been crying. "Can you meet me at the hospital?"

I flew off the bed. "I can, I'm on my way now. Are you okay?" I asked fearing the worst.

"I'm fine," she replied. "Marcel's not. He's hurt. They've taken him to the hospital. I'm on my way there now."

Marcel. Hurt?

My heart threatened to burst through my chest. I didn't have to look in a mirror to know all color had drained from my face. "What do you mean he's hurt? What happened to him? How bad is he?" Even as I asked the questions, the answers already hit me like a brick. Only hours ago, Marcel had told me there was a hit on his life. I knew exactly what had happened.

Johnny. That's what happened.

Pain like never before pierced through me. My entire body shook as fear encircled me.

Run, and never look back. Those had been his words to me. Suddenly, the memory of a certain dream hit me. The same dream I had had in that Youth Committee Meeting on the evening I'd seen Marcel for the first time in the parking lot.

Run, and never look back.

It was him. It was Marcel. Tears welled up in my eyes. Was it crazy that he had warned me to run in the other direction before we had even met?

"He's unconscious and needs surgery." Surgery? What did they do to him? How bad was he? "That's all I know." Ms. Maxwell's voice pulled me back.

"Oh my gosh…" The tears that had welled up in my eyes now rolled down my cheeks. My Bear. What had they done to him?

"I know it's hard, Norma, but this is no time to fall apart," Ms. Maxwell said. "Meet me at the hospital. We're going to need to stay strong, together, to get through this. For Marcel's sake." I nodded, then realized she couldn't see me.

"Yes, Ma'am," I managed to choke out. Ending the call, I reached for my purse on the nightstand. I dashed out of my room and down the stairs. There, I found my mother laughing at something Luna was saying. Rico made a smart comment, but it went right by me. When I reached the landing, all eyes turned to look at me. My mother put her cup of tea on the coffee table and jumped to her feet.

"Norma?" I didn't answer her and kept heading for the front door. "Norma what's wrong?" she asked again, her voice louder and a bit panicked this time.

"I can't right now, Mom," I told her. "I have to get to the hospital." I got to the front door and was about to open it when Rico grabbed my hand, stopping me. I didn't even hear him as he came up to me, or maybe my brain just didn't register it.

"Norma, you're not wearing any shoes." His voice was soft, merely a whisper. "You can't go out like this." I looked down and saw my bare feet. I loved walking barefoot around the house. Luna and Mom met me at the door as well, their faces burning with concern.

"What happened?" Mom asked. Upon hearing her question, my legs threatened to give out from under me, so I sat down on the small, padded bench by the door.

I tried to calm down because I knew that if I said another word, I was going to burst into tears. I didn't want to cry again. I needed to be strong. Marcel had said I was one of the strongest people he had ever met. It was time I proved him right. But I couldn't help the ache in my heart, and the looks on my family's faces just pulled the strings.

"They tried to kill him. They tried to kill Marcel." I said, almost breaking down. "He doesn't want to be a part of them anymore, so they tried to kill him." Through the haze of my distress, I heard Luna gasp.

"We have to get to the hospital," Luna said. "And you can't drive, Norma." She was right. I didn't even have a car to begin with. I wasn't thinking straight. But I needed to get there, one way or another.

"I'll take you, Norma," Mom said. To my siblings, she added, "You kids stay home. Your Dad will be here soon."

"I'm not leaving my sister," Luna practically snapped. "I need to be by her side," she added, her tone much softer this time.

"Neither am I," Rico added. "We're coming with you." Mom was silent for a split second, then she sighed.

"Fine. Go get her shoes." I assumed she was talking to Luna because she dashed off up the stairs. When she returned, I slipped the shoes onto my feet. They didn't match what I was wearing, but I didn't care. I just wanted to get to him.

The drive to the hospital was mostly silent, except for my sniffling and the whispered prayers coming from Luna and my mother. The simple words helped me to calm down a little. Halfway into the drive, I glanced up at Rico, who had pulled out a box of tissues and handed it to me. I cleaned my eyes and blew my nose.

When Mom finally turned into the parking lot of the hospital, a burst of energy hit me, and I grabbed the door handle before she even came to a full stop. "Norma!" I heard my brother yell, but I ignored the call and bolted out the door. With quick steps, I made it to the hospital's double glass doors before my family had parked the car and caught up to me.

At the front desk, I noticed there were two police officers standing there conversing with a nurse across the counter. I stepped between them so I could see and speak to her more clearly.

"Excuse me, I'm sorry to disturb you, but I'd like to know if a Marcel Maxwell was admitted," I said. She glanced at me with a slight furrow of her brows.

"Are you family?" she asked.

"No, but—"

"Then I can't disclose that kind of information to you," she stated. There was something about her that I didn't like, even though I knew she was only doing her job.

It was like a knife was being twisted in my gut. I wouldn't leave till I had laid my eyes on Marcel, or at least got words to reassure me that he was going to be alright. I was about to make another plea when a hand came to pull me away. Certain it was my mother or one of my siblings, I turned, only to find Ms. Maxwell standing there, her eyes red-rimmed and swollen, just like mine. Without saying a word, she pulled me into a hug.

"Thanks for coming," she said. She pulled away almost immediately. "Marcel is still in surgery. Based on what I've been told so far, he may be in there for a while." The two officers were staring at us. I didn't even have to look; I could feel their eyes on me. I assumed they were Marcel's guards, but I didn't bother asking. Ms. Maxwell, realizing they were listening to our conversation, pulled me away from the counter, and led me to a waiting area where Sofia and the twins were seated, looking wide-eyed and alarmed. It was the first time that I'd seen Sofia in this rumpled state, as well as the first time without her phone in hand. She had to be worried sick.

"What happened to him in there?" I asked her when we were away from the prying officers.

"Well, according to the doctors, Marcel was stabbed several times with a sharp object," she replied, her voice a little choked.

"Oh no," a familiar voice exclaimed from behind.

It was from my sister. They'd finally caught up to me. I walked a short distance away from them as the words swirled around in my head. My breathing was getting heavy, I tried to calm down, but a pain struck my heart. I found myself having to sit down again, as my hands gripped my chest. With each breath I took, it got worse. Someone said my name, but I wasn't certain who. It sounded like the voices around me were far away. I could feel the darkness coming, like heavy clouds above my head. The next instant, I fell to the floor with a thud.

When I opened my eyes again, I was on a bed. A hospital bed. Flying into a sitting position, I glanced around me. My mother and siblings, as well as Ms. Maxwell, were all at my side. "Norma. How are you feeling?" Mom asked.

"Marcel," I breathed out, ignoring her question. "Where is he? I need to see him."

"You can't see him yet. He's still in surgery," Mom informed me. "I'm sorry, *bambina*, but I think you should let me take you home. It will be another couple of hours before the doctors are through with the operation and—"

"No." I told her, insisting. "I'm not going anywhere." From the corner of my eye, I noticed my brother and sister glancing at each other. They were worried about me, but they shouldn't be. I wasn't the one lying on an operating table, battling for my life. It was my Bear. I was fine. He wasn't.

"You can go home if you want," I told mom. I could see the stress in her eyes, and I didn't want her worrying about me. "I understand that you have things to do, so I don't expect you to babysit me."

"Norma, why would you say that?" Mom started, looking surprised. "Do you think I would choose doing house cleaning instead of staying here with you?" As soon as she said the words, I regretted what I had said. Of course my mother wasn't like that. She always put us first no matter what. I was upset and I was taking it out on her.

"I'm sorry," I said. "I'm just scared for him right now. I don't want to lose him." Her eyes softened as she looked at me.

"I know, honey." She pulled me into a quick hug before continuing. "I know you're worried, but you have to trust God. He is the only one who can help us through this. He's the only one who can save him."

"Marcel is strong," Ms. Maxwell said. "My son is a fighter and I know better. He won't give up easily. Like what your mom just said, trust in your God. Marcel's going to get through this."

I nodded, knowing she was right. I hadn't been doing much trusting lately. Mostly, I was full of sadness. Marcel was still alive and fighting for his life. I had always been the one telling Marcel to trust in God, and here I was acting like all hope was lost. Shame washed over me.

Lord, please forgive me for not trusting you.

Just then, Sofia and the twins broke into the room and announced, "Mom, the doctor is here. He wants to talk to you." Hearing this, I pulled out of my mother's hold and leaped off the bed. Neither she nor my siblings bothered trying to stop me. Together, we all left the room to see the doctor. He was a small man with dark hair and kind eyes. When he noticed how many people were in front of him, he blinked in amazement. Probably surprised we were all here for Marcel because he was a prisoner.

"It's okay, they're all with me," Ms. Maxwell told him.

He nodded. "Alright. I just wanted to update you. We've managed to stop the internal bleeding. But the injuries Marcel received are life threatening, and to be very honest with you, it's not looking good. The next twenty-four hours will be crucial. I wish I could give you more positive news. I am truly sorry." No one was moving; everyone was silent.

Marcel might die? I thought.

My heart beat fast in my chest. Before the doctor could leave, someone whispered out softly, but clear, "No." I didn't even realize it was my voice until all eyes were on me. "He's not going to die."

"Norma, calm down," Rico said. "The doctor never said that." With a small head nod, the doctor then walked away to go back to the operating room.

For the next couple of hours, we sat together in the waiting area, mostly praying for Marcel's recovery. Not even Sofia made a snide remark about us "Jesus freaks." She mostly stared at the floor. At some point, Dad had come in and Mom had given him the details of what we knew. He instantly called Pastor Archie and asked him to contact the church prayer-chain.

Dad stayed with us for a while, but ended up falling asleep and almost fell off his chair. The comical moment and the soft laughter resulting from it, gave us all some emotional relief from the tension we were feeling.

It was then that I told Mom it was time for all of them to go home. None of them wanted to leave, but I stood my ground and forced them out the door. "I'll call if anything changes. I'm okay, Mom," I assured her.

"I'll take her home after we see Marcel," Ms. Maxwell stated. That must have done the trick because my mother finally agreed. By that time, the twins and Sofia had also fallen asleep. Ms. Maxwell and I sat in silence, lost in our own thoughts, until the doctor came to us, about midnight, to give us an update. The surgery was finally over, and they had moved Marcel to his own room to recover. Despite our relief, the doctor made it clear that Marcel still wasn't out of danger.

"Please, can I see him now?" I asked the doctor. He looked at Ms. Maxwell for her approval.

"Yes, of course she comes in with me," she said.

The doctor then turned and led us toward Marcel's room and gestured to the door.

Ms. Maxwell thanked him, and we headed inside. My heart was in my throat. When I caught sight of him, my hand flew to my mouth. The doctor had warned us earlier that Marcel was not in good shape. But I wasn't prepared for this. He wore so many bandages, and was tied to tubes. And his face. He looked so pale. As pale as...I couldn't finish the thought.

I slid into the chair next to him and slipped my hand in his. "Hey, you, I'm here, Bear." The moment I said that I felt kind of silly. I didn't even know if he could hear me, or even sense my presence. His hand laid limp on the bed as I rubbed the inside of his palm. This was the first time that I'd ever touched him and not gotten a reaction. It solidified the horrible reality in more ways than I could express with words. If the movies were right, then maybe he could hear me. Then I could offer words to assure him that I was here and that I wasn't going anywhere.

"Oh, Bear, I'm so sorry this happened to you. You mean the world to me, and I don't want to lose you."

I wondered what was going on in his head. Was he in a peaceful place? Did he feel me by his side? Or was he somewhere dark and cold, somewhere that spelled fear? I intertwined our fingers together, rubbing the back of his palm gently. Or was he safely wrapped in Jesus' arms?

Hot trails of fresh tears rolled down my cheeks as I looked at the bandages that wrapped him. Physically, he was a mess. So much different from the man I'd seen just this morning, tall, strong, and so unbelievably handsome. They'd managed to bring my Bear to his knees. Something I didn't think was possible.

I reached out to run a hand along his jawline. "I wish you would wake up. I want you to look at me again with those magnetic dark eyes of yours. Have I ever told you, how much I love the way you admire me, make me feel like I'm the only woman in the world, the only one your heart beats for?"

Jesus, please, don't take him from me.

I heard someone sniffling behind me. I'd forgot Marcel's mom was there in the room. When I turned around I saw her eyes wide and broken. Knowing it was time for me to get out of the way so his mother could see him, I stood. "I'll be back soon, I promise," I told him before kissing his forehead and walking out. Ms. Maxwell squeezed my hand as I walked past her.

"Keep praying to your God for my son," she whispered. That said, she went to Marcel's bedside.

As I left the room, the pain in my heart intensified. Memories of that dream came back to me.

Run. Run, and never look back.

Was this a message from God that Marcel was going to die?

Chapter Twenty-One

Norma

Three days later, Marcel still hadn't woken up. I hadn't left his side. His mother was standing on the other side of the bed, her hand tucked away in his left hand, while both of mine were in his right. One hand was still handcuffed to the rail, which seemed ridiculous to me. Even if Marcel woke up right now, he wouldn't be getting out of this bed on his own any time soon.

An officer was sitting outside the door, which I understood since he was still an inmate. I had wondered several times why we were allowed to see him. To stay with him. They must have thought he was going to die.

My mom was standing right behind me, her hands on both my shoulders. She squeezed every other minute or so, to comfort me I suppose.

"I don't understand," I said. "Why is he not waking up?" This situation with Bear had taught me that I wasn't as patient as I thought I was. I felt myself on the brink of insanity, and was doing my best just to keep it together. Even though his condition was slowly improving, I was agitated most of the time that he was still unconscious and unable to talk to me. I missed him so much it hurt to even breathe.

"He *will* wake up, his body needs time to heal," Ms. Maxwell said. "It's just a matter of time." Her voice was soft as she looked down at her son. Even though Ms. Maxwell wasn't a Christian, she still had more faith and confidence in her son's strength and recovery than I had.

To say her faith put me to shame would be an understatement, and it didn't help that my faith in God had dwindled over the past couple of days. Most of my days were spent at Marcel's bedside, begging him to wake up; and my nights were spent sleeping in the chair next to him, holding his hand. All the doctors and nurses knew me by name now.

The door to Marcel's room opened, but I didn't turn to see who it was. A foreign hand touched me. "My dear, you must be very tired. You've been next to Marcel since the day he got here."

The voice was familiar. It was Marcel's nurse, Miss Gomez. She paused, as if expecting a response from me. I pretended not to hear her. I suspected she wanted me to go home, and I was hoping that she would drop it if she didn't get a reply. She sighed. "You can't stay like this. You need to go home, eat, shower, and rest. I'm sure Marcel wouldn't be happy to learn that you have been neglecting to take care of yourself."

I tore my eyes away from my Bear to look up at her. Her light brown eyes were bright, alert, and so full of kindness. Still, I wasn't interested in hearing any more of what she had just said. Staying beside Marcel was the only thing that mattered to me. "I'm not leaving him," I told her.

"Oh no, sweetie. I'm not telling you to leave him," Nurse Gomez tried to explain. "I'm just saying you need to take some time to take care of yourself so that you'll have enough strength to take care of him."

"I'm not leaving him," I repeated. "He needs me here; I want to be here when he wakes up." She glanced helplessly at my mother.

"Honey, the nurse is right," Mom started to say. "You do need to take care of yourself. Your father and I are worried about you. Not to mention your sister and brother. We should go home so you can at least shower and eat. A break would do you good."

Never before had I as much as raised my voice at my mother. But in that moment, I was filled with so much hurt and anger that I bolted from the chair I was sitting on and glared at her. "I said

I'm not leaving. I get that you're concerned, and I appreciate that, but *my* concern is for Marcel. Do what you need to do, but I'm staying right here. I know without a doubt that if the tables were turned, he wouldn't leave my side." I dropped my eyes to the bed. "So why would I leave him? I'm not letting him out of my sight," I whispered.

Bending forward, I ran my fingers through his long, jet-black hair. Though Marcel had kept his hair short before going to prison, it had gotten so long I feared it would soon be as long as mine. He was so beautiful. Inside and out. I couldn't imagine not having this man in my life. If he were to die, I would die right along with him. Maybe not physically, but emotionally.

I heard my mom give a sigh of defeat. "I'm just worried about you."

"Don't be, Mom. I'm not the one lying on a hospital bed."

I vaguely noticed Marcel's mother coming around the bed and pulling my mom aside. They were probably trying to come up with a plan to get me to leave. I couldn't hear what she said to my mother, but her sigh made it clear that she had given in.

I was beginning to get annoyed. If Ms. Maxwell thought she was going to get rid of me, she had another thing coming. Marcel might be her son, but I loved him more than anything in this world, and I would have to be dead first before they got me out of this room.

"I'll be outside if you need me," Mom said after their whispered conversation ended. Mumbling my irritation out loud, I plopped back into the chair like a poorly behaved child. The room door opened and closed, signalling that my mother had left the room. The nurse must have walked out at some point as well because Ms. Maxwell was the only other person left behind me when I turned around. I avoided meeting her eyes and focused on Marcel instead.

Like my mother had done earlier, she stood behind me and rested her hands on my shoulders. I stiffened at the contact.

Whatever she was up to, I wasn't going to fall for it. I wouldn't go down without a fight. I would stand firm by my words.

She seemed unfazed by my reaction. "Let me tell you a story, Norma."

That was the last thing I was expecting to come from her lips. "A story?" I asked, irritated.

"Yes," she replied. "Marcel might not remember this, but when he was four years old, I had a terrible accident at home," she said. "I was in the kitchen preparing his breakfast, and I was feeling weak. I remember being exhausted that morning. A few minutes later, I slipped on one of Marcel's toys that was lying on the floor, and I fell. I hit my head pretty hard on the cold tile and started bleeding."

"Poor Marcel, he was such a tiny little thing." She gave a small laugh. "But that kid was smart. When he heard the thud, he ran into the kitchen and found me lying on the floor. And you know what he did? My little hero went to the living room, grabbed the phone and called the police. He told the officer, 'Mommy's got an *ouchie.*' Ms. Maxwell laughed. It made me feel fuzzy and warm inside, like when my mother gave me a well needed hug. Something about it made the walls of my heart begin to crumble.

"He never stopped saying that," she continued. "He needed them to know that Mommy had an *ouchie*, and luckily, they quickly understood the message he was trying to convey. Being only four, he hadn't yet learned his address, but thankfully, they tracked the call to our apartment. If my boy hadn't called for help that day, who knows what might have happened. Marcel saved me, Norma. He'll forever be my hero."

By the time she was through, I was bawling my eyes out again. "Why are you telling me this?" I sniffed, grabbing a fresh tissue to blow my nose.

"Ever since that time, he's been my fearless protector. And when his sisters came along, he became theirs too. Truth is, I've made many mistakes in my life. I ended up having kids with three different men. I hate that my poor choices in life left them without a proper male role model. It's one of the reasons why my son made some poor life choices himself. He had no father to help him understand what it meant to be a man. That left him in a place where he had to figure it out on his own. I'm not stupid. He tried to hide it from me, but I always suspected that he might be involved in a gang. I tried to talk to him, but I wasn't the voice he needed. What I'm happy about, is that he did finally find it. I don't really know much about Christianity, but I'm ever so grateful for your pastor, who has made such a big impact on his life. He talks about Pastor Archie all the time."

She chuckled, and I had to giggle along with her. "Yeah, he does look up to him." I thought about my dad and the few times he had sat in the same room with Marcel. Unlike with Pastor Archie, the two were taking forever to warm up to each other. I couldn't quite figure out why. Although they were very different from one another, they were both wonderful men. I was sure it was only a matter of time before the two would learn to get along.

"But it's not just the pastor," Ms. Maxwell continued, pulling me back to the conversation. "It's you, Norma. You were the key that opened the door to this change in him. You encouraged him to wash his hands clean, and he chose to follow a different path, a good path. You have no idea how proud I am of the wonderful man my son has become. I knew a long time ago that he had it in him. He just needed the right guidance. All Marcel wants to do is protect those he loves. Everything he did in his life was for that one single reason."

"I know," I muttered.

"He's a strong man, Norma. I have no doubt that he's going to pull through. And I'm telling you, if he wakes up and finds you looking like this—because, dear, you need to at least brush those teeth and take a bath—Marcel is going to be very upset. Not with you, but with himself. His protective streak will make him blame himself. Do you really want to add to his stress?"

My heart thundered in my chest. I knew she was right. This wasn't what Marcel wanted to see when he woke up. "You're right, I don't want that," I said quietly.

"Of course, you don't," she said with a compassionate smile. "Which is why you need to head home, eat, freshen up, and sleep a little."

I nodded, my shoulders slumping in defeat. "I know. Truly, I do. It's just so hard to walk away. I don't want to be away from him. What if he wakes up and I'm not here? Or what if…"

She cut me off, not allowing me to utter the words on the tip of my tongue. "When Marcel wakes up, you'll be the first person I'll inform. I'm sure Marcel wouldn't mind. All that concerns him is that the people he loves are safe. And now that we both know how much you mean to him, you're his concern too."

I nodded again. "Okay." Ms. Maxwell beamed at me, her dark eyes twinkling in much the same way Marcel's would. I hadn't taken notice before how much the two looked alike. I hadn't seen it at first, but by spending more time with her I was starting to notice little things about her features and actions that were similar to Marcel's.

Standing, I reached out to run my fingers through his hair again. "Hey, I'm going home for a little bit. But I'll be back soon. Just, please, keep holding on for me, okay?" I gave him a long but gentle kiss on the forehead before pulling away.

"Come on," Ms. Maxwell said. Without hesitation, I stood up, and together we walked out of the hospital room, past the police officer that sat guarding the door. The moment we stepped out, I spotted Luna, Rico, Isabella, and Juliana sitting together. They were having a conversation of their own and from the looks of it, whatever they were telling the little girls was making them laugh.

This touched my heart; I was glad for the siblings I had been blessed with.

Sofia was standing a few feet away from them, but surprisingly, her phone was still not in her hand. She was looking off into space, with an unreadable expression, her hands tucked in her jean's pockets. On the other side of the long hallway, my mom was sitting and conversing with my dad. I was surprised to see my father there. He should have been at work. He never missed work, except when he was sick or had to tend to something that was important. Maybe he had come to check on my mom or give us a ride back home. It was good that I had come out now. It was perfect timing.

"Norma," Luna called the moment I walked into the waiting room. She tore away from the group and came over to hug me. Isabella and Juliana followed right behind her, each watching me with curiosity.

"Hey." I tried to pull her in closer, but Luna pulled away. "Oh…my…gosh. Norma, I'm sorry to tell you this, but you stink." Her nose was scrunched up, as she looked at me from head to toe.

I chuckled. "Yeah, I know." Luna gave me a look of sympathy.

Juliana and Isabella made their way around Luna and threw their arms around me. I expected them to pull away like my sister had, but they didn't seem to mind. So, I hugged them back, wrapping my hands around each of them. Regardless, it was embarrassing. What had I been thinking? Ms. Maxwell was right. Marcel would scold himself for my not leaving his side. I had to take care of myself. It would be one less stress for him while he recovered.

"Is Marcel okay?" Isabella asked, her blue eyes blinking up at me with such innocence. "Has he woken up?"

"No, not yet, but he's doing a little better today," I said softly.

"Okay," she said.

"I need to go home for just a little while. But I'll be back soon." I told them.

"Be sure to take a shower," Luna added, rubbing a finger under her nose. I couldn't help but roll my eyes.

"Come on, I'm sure I don't smell as bad as you're making it."

"Fine, maybe I'm exaggerating a bit. But let's get you home and cleaned up before the building starts melting," Luna joked. I ignored her and walked over to my parents. I needed to greet my dad.

"Hey, Dad," I said as I stopped just a few feet before them. "I didn't expect to see you here." His lips pressed into a hard, disapproving line. I could see the disappointment in his eyes and my head dropped. "I'm sorry," I started to say but he pulled me into a tight hug, squeezing the air out of me. I didn't mind. There was nothing more comforting than being draped in love. I wrapped my arms around him, laying my head on his chest. We stayed like that for a while before he pulled back.

"If you hadn't come to your senses, I would have come in there myself and dragged you out," he said with a firm voice. He was worried.

I sighed. "I'm tired, Dad. Please take me home," I told him. He held me out at arms' length.

"You bet," he said. With that, my family and I started toward the exit.

Rico ruffled my hair, then scrunched up his face, "Luna was right. You do stink. You smell like a rotten egg."

"Well, at least you two finally agree on something for once," I grumbled. Then my eyes landed on Sofia who was still leaning against the wall, all by herself. She was watching me, her face neutral. Ever since Marcel and I started our relationship, she had become even more distant with him. She clearly didn't approve of his new lifestyle, which was sad because there was nothing that would have made my Bear happier than seeing his mother and siblings come to Jesus as he had. "I'll be right back," I said to my family. "I just want to hear how she's doing." They nodded, and I walked over to Sofia. We hadn't exchanged many words even though we had come across each other several times in the hospital. We were barely speaking to each other as it was.

"Sofia," I said, stopping beside her. "Are you doing okay?" Her eyes roamed from my messy hair to my shoes and back up again.

"You should get some sleep," she commented. "You look like something that escaped out of a zombie movie."

That made me smile. The comment itself might have sounded awful, but it was possibly the nicest thing that she had ever said to me. "Thanks," I replied. "I'll definitely do that." Then she pushed away from the wall to walk away.

Even though I had no idea how she would react, I pulled her in for an embrace before she could leave. Sofia stiffened—even I was surprised by my action—but I knew that if I had overthought the hug, I wouldn't have had the courage to give her one. I expected her to push me away and storm off; maybe tell me in more colorful words than my sister how wretchedly bad I smelled. Instead, Sofia patted me awkwardly on the back.

Wow.

I let go of her, not wanting to make her feel too uncomfortable. The moment I did, she dashed out of the waiting area.

Oh yeah. I was definitely winning her over.

The ride home from the hospital was mostly silent with only the occasional chatter of my little sister permeating the air. My body was so drained, I soon gave in and rested my head on Rico's shoulder. I had no idea that I had fallen asleep until I woke up in my room.

It was dark outside. I wondered how long I had been sleeping. Someone had taken me to my room. That had to be either Dad or Rico. Dragging myself out of bed, I headed to the bathroom for a much-needed shower. I didn't want to take a bath because I knew that once I laid in the tub, I would be tempted to lie there for hours. I still couldn't believe I had allowed myself to be so consumed with grief, that I got to this point. I smelled like I had fallen in a sewer.

I stepped into the hot shower. I let out a sharp breath as the water washed over me.

A half hour later, I walked out of the bathroom feeling fresh and smelling more like a human being. Once I got dressed, I headed down the stairs in search of something to eat. My stomach had been growling like an angry animal the entire morning. I hadn't been eating much. I remembered my mother's caponata which I had barely touched a few days ago. What I wouldn't give to have that meal right now. As soon as I hit the last step, I spotted Rico sitting on the couch, watching TV.

I walked over to him. "Hey, little brother. Were you the one who carried me upstairs?" Rico tore his eyes away from the sports news channel he was watching to look at me.

"Yeah," he replied. "And you almost broke my back in the process. For someone so little, you do weigh a ton."

I gasp. "I do not." I snatched up one of the sofa pillows and tossed it at his head. He only laughed, catching the pillow easily.

"I'm just kidding. You were light as a feather. Seriously." He pointed his chin to the kitchen. "You really need to eat. You're hungry, right?" he asked.

"Famished," I replied. Rico tossed the TV remote and stood.

"Come on, this is a job for the chef." I raised an eyebrow to that; Rico was the opposite of a chef. "Let me get you some food."

He headed to the kitchen. For a couple of seconds, I stood there motionless as he walked to the refrigerator. *He* was going to make me something to eat? I had never even seen my brother boil water before.

"Thanks, but I can do it," I told him, dashing in behind him. Rico pointed to one of the high stools at the kitchen island.

"Don't be stubborn, Norma, sit."

There was such a command in his voice, I had to grin. "Fine, I'll sit." My little brother wasn't so little anymore. It was easy to forget that sometimes. I sat on one of the stools and waited to see what he would do. The stove was clear of any pots, so I was intrigued. "What do you have for me today, chef?"

Rico pulled out two large containers and began to put the food on a plate for me. Chicken stew with white rice. I could already smell it even in its cold state and my stomach grumbled with approval.

After filling the plate, he put the containers back in the refrigerator, then popped it in the microwave, pushed a few buttons, and hit *start*. With that, he came around to where I was, and sat on the stool beside mine. He looked down in his hands, and for the first time, I realized that my brother was nervous.

"Rico, are you okay?" I asked. My heart started pounding in my chest even though he hadn't said a word yet.

He exhaled, then said. "I have something to tell you, but you have to promise me you won't tell anyone," he said. My eyes narrowed as I watched him.

"It depends on what it is. You didn't murder anyone, did you?" I was joking, of course. I knew Rico wasn't capable of that.

Rico looked at me as if I had lost my mind. "Of course not."

"Good. Your secret won't leave my lips, then. I promise," I told him. I could see he was relieved.

"Thank you."

"Sure. Now tell me what's bothering you."

His eyes fell again. "Alright. Here goes. When I was fifteen, I tried drugs for the first time."

It took a while for me to process what he had just confessed. When I finally had, I was in pure shock. That was not the confession I had expected to come out of my brothers' mouth. In fact, it was the last thing I had expected to escape Rico's lips. "Drugs? Did you just say drugs?" He nodded. I gasped and looked at the entrance to the kitchen to make sure no one was coming. "Have you lost your mind? What were you thinking? If Mom and Dad ever found out…"

"They won't," he said, cutting me off. "That's why I asked you to promise me. I know I can trust you to keep your word."

I let out a long sigh. "Of course, you can." I wanted to kick myself for leaping into the promise I had just made before knowing what it was about. If this situation turned out to be disastrous, I had no idea how I would keep it from my parents. I wouldn't be able to look them in the eyes. I wouldn't be…

"Norma," Rico called, pulling me from my web of thoughts. "Relax and hear me out."

"Uh-huh," I murmured. "I'm listening, tell me everything."

He continued. "It happened when I had one of the weekend sleepovers with some of the guys on the team. It was a stupid dare, but I felt like I had to do it. I mean, these guys were my friends." Of course, it had to be his friends who pushed him to this. Peer pressure. I knew they were getting to Rico, but I hadn't thought that it had gone this far. Then he continued, "I didn't want to look like a wimp. All I had to do was go out there and find a drug dealer to buy the stuff from."

Rico ran both hands through his hair, leaving some of the strands standing on end. "They told me about a guy from Johnny's Boys who'd be willing to sell to us."

My ears perked up at the name 'Johnny'. "Johnny's Boys? That's the gang Marcel was in." The wheels in my head began to turn faster than I could keep up with. “Oh no. No. Do not tell me it was Marcel who sold you those drugs.” I couldn’t imagine my Bear doing something like that, selling drugs to an underage kid. Even as an unbeliever.

“No, it wasn’t him,” Rico confirmed, shaking his head. “Anyway, the guy was supposed to sell me ecstasy. Obviously, he gave me something else.” His eyes took on a faraway look, as if recalling the day itself. “I thought I was going to die that day, Norma. When I took the pill, it sent my heart racing so fast, I could barely see straight. I was sweating, my hands were clammy, I was struggling to breathe.” He sighed. “Everything that could go wrong… went wrong. I blacked out. My friends actually thought I was going to die.

“By their own admission, they were considering leaving my body for the cops or some random passer-by to find me. They didn’t want to get in trouble with their parents or the police. Can you believe that?”

“Rico,” I breathed out. “That’s awful.”

“Yeah, tell me about it. When you’re scared, you do stupid things sometimes. Anyway, the guys told me the dealer just watched me. He did nothing to help.”

I was speechless.

Rico shook his head and continued. “I mean, I wasn't so surprised. The guy was a drug dealer. All he wanted was his money. Anyways, uh... Marcel showed up then. I guess he had been with him the whole time, just staying in the background.”

“Marcel was there?” I practically screamed.

“Yep, that’s what I just said,” Rico said between his teeth. His dislike of Marcel was apparent. His facial expression showed that. Reality came crashing on me like a bucket of ice water being poured over my head. Marcel and Rico *had* met each other before.

“He’s the one who helped me,” Rico went on reluctantly. “He stayed with me until the effect of the drugs started to wear off.

After I woke up, he left, and my friends took me back to our hangout spot so I could sleep it off. The next day, they told me everything that had happened, including the part where Marcel beat the crap out of that guy for selling drugs to kids."

I should have been horrified. Instead, I was relieved and even proud that Marcel had been angry about the drugs being sold to teenagers. Like his mother had said at the hospital, he was a good man inside. He had just been stuck and needed to be led in the right direction. Now more than ever, I was grateful that he had given his heart to Jesus.

"Okay," I said. "I don't understand, though. If Marcel saved your life, why do you dislike him so much?"

"I don't dislike him," Rico argued. I gave him the look and his shoulders slumped. "Okay, fine, so I don't like him. But I have my reasons. He did come to our hideout the next day. I don't know how he found it, but he did. You know what he said? He gave me a lecture about not doing drugs. Can you believe that guy?"

My face started to relax. But Rico scowled at me. "Your boyfriend is a dangerous man."

"Was," I corrected. "Marcel *was* a dangerous man."

"Right. Sure." Rico grumbled, then added. "I have to admit, he does seem different, but only time will tell. He appears to care about you. I honestly don't know what to think of him though. I have mixed feelings. He told me that I was a fool for trying to ruin my football future. He said I should focus on my education and my football career. Not throw my life away. Honestly, I see him as a hypocrite. I mean, his gang was selling drugs to people every day and he knew about it. I bet he even took the drugs himself. So, who was he to tell us not to?" Rico shrugged. "I just couldn't stand him, okay. So, when he showed up in your life, claiming he liked you, I didn't trust him. There were so many times that I wanted to tell you about his dirty deeds, but I couldn't. Because he knew about my secret."

He paused, then added, "I'm sorry I acted the way I did. But I didn't want to see you get hurt. I'm still not sure about him."

My lips quirked up into a sympathetic smile. Rising from my stool, I leaned over and hugged my brother.

"I know, and I appreciate it. I would have been more concerned if you didn't have a problem with us."

As we pulled apart, a thought came to mind. I looked him in the eyes. "Rico, can I ask you something?"

His brows pulled together with curiosity. "Sure."

"Your experience with using drugs, is that the reason why you've been so distant from God lately?" I asked. Rico flinched as if I'd burned him with a match. As before, he lowered his eyes.

"Something like that." He puckered his lips, then continued. "I was depressed after that weekend. Marcel's words kept replaying in my head. The part about ruining my life with drugs. Even though I disliked the guy, I never forgot what he said. I thought about Mom, Dad…you and Luna, and what could have happened. I just couldn't bear the thought of disappointing any of you. Even worse, hurting you guys with my stupid choices."

We sat in silence for a minute.

"I felt guilty for not telling any of you. I was so angry with myself. I lost my connection with God. After a while, I didn't feel Him anymore. Honestly, it was easier to just pretend everything was okay than to try to find my way back. I fell into peer pressure. I'm still not sure where I fit. I've played so many roles over the past couple of years, I don't even know who I am anymore."

"Well, it's good that you're talking about it now," I told him. "It's the perfect start on the road to your healing."

"Healing," Rico said, savouring the word. "I'd really love some of that." Just then, *the beep beep beep* of the microwave cut through the air, signalling that my food was piping hot and ready to be devoured. Despite my hunger, I ignored the beeping and took Rico's hand in mine.

"If you want, I can pray with you. You don't have to face this alone. In fact, God has never expected any of us to bear our problems without help. Which is why He encouraged us to bear each other's burdens. Even though you feel like God will never forgive you, in your head and in your heart, I know you know better than that. You and I both know that God has been waiting for you to come to Him and ask for His forgiveness. You're just too embarrassed to ask."

My heart broke when a tear slipped from my brother's eye. "Yeah, something like that," he said in defeat. "Yes, I do want you to pray with me. I've wanted that for a long time, but you're right, I was too ashamed to ask."

I nodded in understanding. "Come on, let's pray." I slipped my other hand in his free hand and closed my eyes. I wasn't the best with words, but I knew how to talk to God, especially when it was on someone else's behalf.

So, I prayed.

"Lord Jesus, you are the God who knows all our needs. You are not indifferent to our pain, our hurt, our internal struggles. Today, I give you my brother…"

I wasn't sure how long we were at it, but when I finally opened my eyes again, it was as if I was looking at a different guy. Despite the tears on his cheeks, Rico looked happier. Lighter.

"Thank you," he said. "You have no idea how much I needed this."

"This is what big sisters are for, right?" I told him. I rubbed my stomach. "Now feed me before I die of hunger."

Chapter Twenty-Two

Marcel

Voices.

I could hear people all around me. I just couldn't tell who they were. It was almost as if I was in a tunnel and they were at the end of it, whispering words I couldn't make out. I could feel someone holding my hand. I tried to move it in response, but was too weak. I tried again, wanting to make contact to let the other person know I was awake.

"He moved his fingers," a voice exclaimed. "I just felt it." I knew this voice. Was it my mother? I wasn't sure. The voice and words still sounded unclear and muffled.

"Are you sure?" another voice asked. This voice I didn't recognize.

"Of course, I'm sure," the first voice said.

Where am I? I thought.

A sharp pain hit the back of my eyes as brightness pierced through the long tunnel without warning, slapping me out of the darkness. It was bright, too bright. I groaned in discomfort, shutting my eyes again quickly to take refuge in the darkness.

"The blinds. Close the blinds." The familiar voice snapped in almost a whisper. The light began to ease. Someone in the room must have read my thoughts. My eyelids fluttered as I tried to open up to the world. The familiar voice continued to call my name.

Then a hand touched me. Fingers ran through my hair with such gentleness, it sent a feeling of comfort through my body. This had to be the touch of a woman. I didn't want it to stop. "Marcel, open your eyes. Look at me," she spoke again softly.

I was hesitant at first, but I opened them slowly. As my eyes adjusted to the light, the first thing that came into view was the ceiling above me. Then the face of a woman suddenly appeared. A whirlwind of memories flooded my mind, and just like that, I knew. Of course, I knew. How could I ever forget one of the closest women to my heart?

"Ma?" I croaked out. My throat felt dry and scratchy, and my voice was hoarse. Happiness and surprise came over me. What was she doing here? Where was I? I glanced around the room. These weren't the grey walls of my prison cell. And that bed was so comfortable.

"Yes, it's me, honey," she said, still stroking my hair. "I'm so happy to see those beautiful eyes of yours." She laughed but it sounded choked, like she was trying not to cry. Then I could see the spotted tear marks on her cheeks.

"Why were you crying?" I asked. "You look sad."

"Forget that. All that matters is that you're awake."

I glanced around me again. Nothing looked familiar, but it didn't take long for me to figure out I was in a hospital. The machines, the needle in my hand and the constant beeping, left no doubt in my mind. I hated hospitals.

"What happened?" I asked Mom. I tried to lift one of my hands, but found that it was restrained by handcuffs. The dull ache around my wrist made me groan. My whole arm hurt and felt stiff. How long had I been in that position? And why was I still in cuffs if I wasn't in prison? "How did I get here?" I asked.

"You're in the hospital," Mom replied. "You were…hurt." The glow in her eyes dimmed a little. It was at that moment that my memories returned to me like a train wreck. Scotty and Kade. They had attacked me in my cell, stabbed me to death. No, not to death. I was still alive.

How was that possible? I had felt their blades plunge into me so many times I had lost count. I had been certain that that was the end. But here I was, staring into my mother's beautiful face. They hadn't succeeded. I was alive.

This wasn't luck; this was a miracle. God had done this. He had shown how powerful He was and that only His decisions over my life were final. Scotty, or Kade, whoever Johnny had chosen to send, whatever weapon they had used, if God said it wasn't my time, then it wasn't. I couldn't begin to explain how grateful I was to be alive, to see my mother, and to know that I would see Norma again.

I tried to shift from my current position, but a sharp pain shot through my gut, knocking the wind out of me. My face contorted in pain. "I'm so sorry, son." Mom said, touching my shoulders to steady me, then proceeded to adjust the pillows my head was resting on. "You were badly hurt."

"Stabbed," I moaned in clarification, my free hand going to my bandaged ribs. I winced at the pain. "I was stabbed." I tried to bring both of my hands to my stomach but the shackle around one of my wrists prevented me once again. A hard, cold reminder that I was still a prisoner. My mother didn't flinch at my words, but her eyes showed how much they affected her. She gave me a warm sympathetic look.

"How are you feeling?" she asked softly, though the answer was obvious.

"I feel like an animal. A weak and helpless animal. And the pain is killing me all over again," I answered.

She tried to smile. "That's to be expected. You went through quite an ordeal. I'm just glad that you're alive."

So was I. When my former colleagues attacked me, I had no doubt that my time on Earth had come to an end. As I had leaned against my bed that day, my life slowly draining away from me, I had done my best to prepare my mind to meet my Savior. I had also tried not to think of Norma. It would have broken my heart.

I forgive you.

That was what I had told them. All of them. And I had meant each word. *Have a forgiving spirit, be slow to anger.* At first, when Pastor Archie had told me I had to forgive and forget those who had wronged me, I had found it hard. But the change in me over time made it easier. I could forgive, but how was I to forget? Even if I tried, the scars engraved in my flesh would remind me of that night for the rest of my life. My life. Norma.

"Where's Norma?" I asked. The last time I saw her she had been pleading for me not to go. I had been sure it was the last time I would see her. Now, I couldn't wait to lay my eyes on her again. To touch her again.

"I want to see her." My mom brought a glass of water to my lips, then put the glass back on the nightstand when I had quenched my thirst.

"She's on her way back to the hospital," my mother said, wiping some water from my chin. "The poor girl was glued to your bedside the entire time. We couldn't get her to leave until yesterday evening when I told her the story of you saving my life when you were just a little boy." She ran the back of her fingers over my cheek. "You were my strong, little hero."

Usually, it made me smile whenever Mom talked about my four-year-old self saving her. But not today. At this moment, all I could think of was Norma. I couldn't stop myself from worrying.

"Is she okay? How is she doing?" I asked.

"Of course, she is," Mom replied. "Yesterday, she looked like she was about to join you, but we finally managed to reason with her and get her out of here, thank God. Poor thing needed some rest and food."

Were those words supposed to comfort me? They only made me flinch. I knew my girl. She was a worrier, especially when it came down to the people she cared about. I imagined her here at my bedside, talking to me without getting a response, and praying even more when she realized the dire state I was in. Now more than ever, I wanted to kick myself for having caused her, and my mom, so much distress.

"Hey, don't go there," Mom said. She could read my face like a book. "Stop beating yourself up. Be grateful you have such a special girl who adores you so much."

"I know. But that doesn't answer my question. How is she?"

She shook her head with a smile. "Norma is fine. She's eaten, she's showered, she's slept. Trust me, she's doing much better. You'll see for yourself when she gets here." I nodded, satisfied with her reply.

When the door opened, I turned my head with some difficulty to see who it was, hoping it was the face I longed to see; but it was just the doctor. His face brightened when he saw me. "Oh, this is good news. It's nice to see you're awake, Marcel, just like Nurse Gomez just informed me."

I didn't know how to respond, so I only nodded.

My mother moved so he could take a look at me. He checked my vitals and asked some basic questions about how I was feeling. When he was done, he turned to my mother.

"I'll leave you and your son alone for now. Nurse Gomez will be back to give him some medication to ease the pain."

"Thank you, doctor," my mom said gratefully. "Thank you for everything you've done. I'm truly grateful."

"You're welcome." Then he left, leaving us alone in the room again.

My eyes looked around the small room once more. Whoever had been in here with my mother was gone. On the wall directly in front of me, was a TV running with the volume turned down. I stared at the screen. I caught sight of a familiar warehouse and my heart began racing.

"Ma, could you turn that up?" I asked. She glanced behind her, then back at me, as if she hadn't noticed there was a TV in the room. When she found the remote, she increased the volume.

The voice of a female news anchor filled the room. "It's a devastating time for local gangs as the bodies continue to pile up. Sources have confirmed that the gang wars that began a year ago was a result of the killing of nineteen-year-old Theo "Shacks" Langley, several months prior. Shacks was the nephew of the alleged leader of the Cobras gang, only known as "Cobra". Shacks was said to have been killed by a rival gang, The Rioters, led by Toby Barkley. Our sources have also confirmed that the war has spread to other gangs as well, including what's only known as Johnny's Boys, one of the vilest gangs in the area, the police stated. It was also reported that forty-eight-year-old Johnny Martin of an Atlanta address has disappeared. Authorities have so far been unable to trace him and confirm his whereabouts. They presume that he fled the country. More details on this in the evening news."

The news anchor moved on to another matter at hand, but I was stuck on the gang feuds.

"Marcel?" Mom called my name; she must have noticed the startled look on my face. "Is something wrong? Do you know those men?"

I nodded. "Yes, Johnny was...He was the man I used to work for."

"How horrible," she said. "I will forever be grateful to Norma for pulling you out of that life. Who knows what would have happened if..." She sighed, her eyes still glued to the television.

If this was true, then it meant things were worse than I had thought. I had learned about the clashes while in prison. The amount of outside information known in a penitentiary was surprising. Once the news was released, it spread like wildfire. Still, I never expected the wars to escalate to this level. Johnny had done his best to stay out of the disputes, even when Toby had demanded that he honor their treaty and fight with the Rioters. Johnny, being the guy he was, hadn't complied. As a result, Johnny's men began dropping like flies. Even more dismal was the fact that I knew the guys who lost their lives. At one point, they had been my friends, until I had chosen a different path. I briefly wondered whether Scotty and Kade were safe. Even though they had done what they had, I didn't wish harm to come to them. Above all, I wanted them to know Jesus like I did.

Had this happened a year ago, I would have been on the path of revenge without a doubt. That was the man I had been. I protected what was mine and those guys were mine. I would have killed for them if I had had to.

God was truly amazing. He had really changed me, fixed my heart, made me a new person. This knowledge was overwhelming.

Having been a member of a gang before my life changed, I assumed this was one of those seasons when old gangsters were dying out to give way to a new generation. I should have been worried, but I couldn't help but be grateful to God for saving me from it. I would probably have been among the dead too, had I not walked away. I had always been at the forefront of most of the operations and would have been an easy target. I closed my eyes and said a quick, heartfelt prayer of thanks to God for sparing me from this judgment. I was in a hospital, but it was better than being in a morgue. My family and Norma would have been devastated if something as terrible as that had happened to me.

Johnny's entire operation had crumpled. The men who wanted me dead were, or soon would be, dead themselves or in prison. It was tragic, and yet I could see the hand of God in all of this, protecting me. Protecting my family. Protecting my gorgeous girl.

Thank you, Jesus.

I was pulled out of my thoughts when the door slowly opened again. I looked up just in time to see the woman who held my heart walking in. Norma was beautifully dressed in jeans and a simple light blue top. How I loved this girl.

As soon as she noticed that I was awake, Norma bolted to my side. "Oh, Bear, you're awake." she cried out. With that, she broke into tears, snaking her arms around me. My body was sore from the stab wounds I was sporting, but I would rather have died than told her to let go.

"It's okay, baby. I'm okay," I told her.

"Marcel," she sobbed. "You have no idea how happy I am right now. I thought I was going to lose you. I thought…Oh, I'm sorry. I forgot you're in pain," she tried to pull back, but I held her with my one free hand.

"Shh, it's okay. I don't mind, it's fine," I soothed, smiling to calm her. It would have been so much better if I hadn't been restrained; then I could have wrapped both my arms around her. I could have held her in my arms the way she deserved to be held. I wasn't sure if my lulling worked, but after a couple of minutes, she finally got some resemblance of control over her tears and pulled away to look at me.

"I can't tell you how grateful I am that you're awake," she said in a shaky voice.

"You haven't been eating," I scolded her. It was hard to keep the words in any longer. She glanced over at my mother who was standing on the other side of my bed before meeting my eyes again.

"Uh...I ate last night. And this morning."

I scowled at her. "Last night and this morning? Really, Norma?"

"I was worried about you, Bear," she said barely above a whisper. "Food was the last thing on my mind."

Despite my irritation, my heart melted. The scowl on my face dissipated and I sighed. "No need to worry any longer, babe. I'm okay. Just sore." I glanced at the TV on the wall. "Did you see the news?"

"No. All I've been doing is thinking and worrying about you. Did something happen?" she asked in alarm. As soon as I saw the fear in her eyes, I wanted to kick myself for worrying her again.

"It's the gangs on the streets," I told her. "From the looks of things, everything is falling apart. Even Johnny is nowhere to be found. They suspect that he's left the country."

Norma went still, her eyes boring into mine. I was expecting her to find comfort in this news, but it seemed to do the opposite. Knowing her, she was probably worried about where Johnny could be, and whether my life was still in danger. To distract her from the thoughts that were plaguing her, I told her, "I've missed you, baby. I'm so sorry I've put you through all of this. If I had had my way, things would have been different."

"I'm fine, Bear. God allows things to happen for a reason. I don't need to understand His ways, or even to like them. But He's making us better."

I nodded. I had meant what I had said. If I could go back in time, I would have chosen a different path. Not the dreadful one I had. "Come closer," I whispered. Immediately, I saw curiosity growing in her beautiful eyes. She leaned forward until our faces were mere inches away from each other.

"Kiss me." I told her. For the first time since she had walked into the room, a blush crept up her cheeks. Norma turned to look at my mother, who was still standing on the other side of me, clinging to my hand for dear life. My lips curved into a smirk.

When my mother caught on to Norma's pleading eyes, she let out a little chuckle. "Um, okay, that's my cue. I'll be outside if you need me." She finally let go of my hand and disappeared behind the door, leaving me alone with Norma.

"Marcel," Norma called my name the second my mother left. "Your mother was here." She giggled.

"Well, don't keep a starving man waiting any longer," I told her. "Let me taste those delicious lips of yours." I smiled when I saw the shade on her cheeks deepen. I loved teasing her with cheesy lines to get this reaction from her. There was nothing more satisfying to me than to know I was affecting Norma the same way she was affecting me.

Norma chewed on her bottom lip. The sight was endearing. Now more than ever, I wished I could move both my arms. She was looking at my lips as if she was trying to figure out a math equation.

"Norma, I need you," I pleaded. She must have heard the longing in my voice because her eyes locked with mine. She ran her small hand down my now scruffy face, her fingers softly tracing invisible lines on my skin. I shivered under her touch, closing my eyes as I let out a sigh. Then, without any further hesitation, she slowly leaned down and captured my lips with hers.

It was heaven.

Being the gentle person she was, she moved slowly, exploring my mouth, and savoring every single moment, sending off fireworks throughout my body. My chained hand started to lift, only to be pulled back into place by the handcuff. At that moment, I fell even more in love with her. If there had been any part of me that had ever hesitated to be with her, that kiss had crushed it.

I wanted her. It was a good thing that I was inhibited after all. I needed to get my emotions under control. The moment I asked her to be my girl, I made a vow that I would never defile this precious woman. No matter how much I longed for her, I wouldn't touch her inappropriately. She would remain pure. It didn't matter how long I had to wait for her. I would wait. In the meantime, I had to break that kiss before I lost my mind. With all the willpower I could muster, I pulled my lips from hers.

"Whoa," I breathed out. Norma blinked down at me, innocence brimming in her eyes.

"What's wrong?" she asked, looking at me shyly.

"Nothing. That was perfect." I told her, without taking my eyes off her. "You take my breath away." She straightened then, with a look of satisfaction.

"I'm glad you approve, Mr. Maxwell," she said, giggling.

"I do," I told her. "I should let you do the kissing more often." She blushed crimson.

"Stop it. You say things like this all the time just to make my face turn red."

"I'm not going to deny that. You're beautiful. It's a sight I love to see." I started chuckling, but stopped with a gasp when a sharp pain sliced through my abdomen.

"Are you alright?" Norma winced, looking at me with concern. She looked down at my bandages then back at me.

"I'm fine." I told her. "Just a little discomfort, that's all." She looked at me with wary eyes. To distract her again, I returned to our conversation.

"I love you, Norma. I love you more than anything in this world," I whispered to her.

"I love you too, Bear," she replied softly.

It took a second or two after the words left her lips for my slow brain to process what she had just said. She had said the words back.

I needed to hear her say it again. "Tell me again." I told her.

She bent down and laid a small peck on my lips, pulling back to look me in the eyes. "I love you, Marcel. More than you can imagine."

My mouth now in the biggest grin I'd ever worn. I couldn't help it. This was the first time she had ever told me that she loved me. I had always been the one confessing my love. I knew she was shy, so I had never pushed the issue, hoping that one day she would find the courage to tell me. Because I had no doubt she would. Now that day had finally come, and I couldn't be happier.

"Thank you, Norma," I told her.

Her brows furrowed. "Did you say, 'Thank you'? For what?"

"For loving me, that's what. I don't deserve you, but I sure am happy I have you." That made her smile. Yet I could still make out a tinge of sadness in her eyes.

"The police officers are still outside the door. They're going to take you back to prison, aren't they?" she asked. "I don't want you to go back to that place, Marcel. I want you to stay here with me."

I chuckled, though there wasn't much humor in it. "I don't have a choice."

"I know that," she said. "I know there's nothing you can do."

"Don't be sad, baby. Yes, I still need to finish serving my time. I have about five or six months before they let me go. But don't worry. It'll be over in no time. And then we can start our lives together." Our lives together. Oh, I couldn't wait for that to come.

She reached out to play with the stubble on my chin, a look of hope now touching her lovely face. "I'd like that, Bear. I'd really like that."

Epilogue

One Year Later…

Norma

It was that time of the year again—summertime. Tybee Island was warm and sunny. Still, it was a welcome reprieve from the cold we had endured months earlier. As I stroked my canvas with my brush, I thought about all the things I wanted to accomplish. I always had a list of events and activities for seasons of the year, and summer was no different. To make things even more exciting, it was one of the happiest years of my life. My career as an artist had taken off in more ways than I had thought possible. I have God to thank for that. There was also my amazing Aunt Mari, who never ceased to push me in the right direction. With her birthday coming up in a couple of months, I wondered whether a surprise party would show her how much I appreciated her. She did love drama and excitement after all. I chuckled, remembering the last time she and Mom had a quarrel over her inability to keep certain thoughts to herself. As grown up as they were, in times like these they turned into teenagers.

"What are you laughing about?" I heard his steps as he approached, stopping only a few feet behind me.

My smile spread wider, though I didn't turn to look. "Just a memory of my mom and Aunt Mari being the *Felix and Oscar* we know they can sometimes be. What are you doing here? I thought you were out swimming with the girls."

"I came back about a half hour ago," he said. "The girls are downstairs watching a movie."

"Oh." I finally turned my head to look at him. He was dressed in red shorts and a white T-shirt. His hair was damp from what looked like a shower. He was the most handsome man I had ever set my eyes on. Hard as it was, I needed to peel them away and get back to work, although I would rather have continued to stare at Marcel. Sometimes I found it hard to believe that this fine specimen of a man was mine. I brought my gaze back to my painting. With every stroke of my brush, I could feel him there, looking at me.

When I couldn't take it anymore, I asked, "What are you looking at?" Before he replied, I already knew what he was going to say. Whenever I asked that question, he usually had the same reply.

"The most beautiful woman in the world," Marcel replied. When he said things like that, I couldn't help but beam from the inside out. The number of times Marcel had called me the most beautiful woman in the world had started making me feel just that—*like the most beautiful woman in the world.* He was always boosting my confidence, and sometimes I pretended to be oblivious, just to hear him repeat the words.

I rolled my eyes. "You flatter me, Mr. Maxwell," I said. "However, I can't afford to be distracted while doing this piece. It has to be perfect for the show next month."

"Oh, I love when you speak like that. So demanding and so in control," he said, chuckling.

I bit my cheeks to hold back the laughter that threatened to explode from me. "I'm serious, Marcel."

"Come on," he whined. "Come walk with me." Marcel could be needy at times; not that I was complaining. I loved it when he was like that. I felt flattered whenever he made me know the kind of effect, I had on him. "I promise I won't take much of your time and you can get back to your work later." I made no reply and continued painting. Maybe he would give up if I stood my ground.

Instead of backing down, Marcel made his way further into the room to stand right behind me. He rested his hands at the sides of my waist, coming so close that our entire bodies touched. "Norma, come walk with me," he whispered into my ear, his voice sending tingles all over me, as I relaxed into his chest. My eyes closed, drinking in the sound of his voice, the warmth of his breath on my skin. This man. He knew how to get my attention when he wanted it. I should have been annoyed that he was distracting me from my work. But all I could feel was excitement from being so close to him.

"I suppose a break with you wouldn't be so bad," I teased, delighted to spend some time with him. Setting my brush aside, I took his hand. A smile of victory now on his face. "Fine, I'll come with you. But after that, I'm coming back here."

He nodded. "No problem." Because we both knew that wouldn't happen. Once I stepped out of the studio with Marcel, I knew I wouldn't come back here until the next day.

Together, we walked hand in hand down the stairs, where my Aunt Mari and her husband were having drinks and conversing with my parents.

They all looked up when Marcel and I appeared on the landing. Aunt Mari leaned over and whispered something in my mom's ear. Given the scowl on my mother's face, her older sister had more than likely said something that burned her ears, and I knew it had something to do with Marcel and me.

"You guys going out?" Aunt Mari asked, her eyes twinkling with mischief.

"Don't mind us," I told them. "We're just heading out for a walk." They all grinned at us as if it was an inside joke we weren't privy to. Even my father was smiling. I was thankful that he and Marcel had gradually warmed up to each other, even becoming friends. Still, I wasn't used to that cheeky smile on Dad's face. Before I could question the meaning behind their odd behavior, Marcel pulled me through the door and into the fresh summer air.

"Let's leave them," he chuckled.

"Why do I get the feeling those four are up to something?" I asked. "Did you see the look on my dad's face?"

"No, not really," he replied. "I was busy looking at you. Did I tell you how lovely you look today?"

This man was going to turn me into a puddle of melted chocolate at his feet.

"Only about a dozen times," I told him. "But I don't mind hearing it again, and again, and again."

Marcel threw his head back in laughter. It was the most beautiful sound in the world. I smiled at that. I loved seeing him so happy.

"Fine then," he said. "I'll tell you again." He pointed to a sandcastle on the beach that must have been made by some random kid. "Right over there."

"Hmm. I think entering someone else's house without permission is called trespassing," I teased.

"Ah," he said, using his other hand to tap his chin in a thoughtful manner, a dramatic look on his face. "Then we had better make it quick," Marcel said before running off toward the sandcastle. I couldn't help laughing at his shenanigans as I followed him. I was a twenty-three-year-old woman, but right now, I felt like a mischievous little kid.

The sandcastle was gorgeous. It was the biggest and most well-structured I had ever seen.

"Wow, this is beautiful. Whoever made it spent quite some time on its design. The kid must have really taken his time on this. I would feel bad if we ruined it for him." I said, looking around but not spotting anyone.

To my surprise, Marcel fell to one knee in front of the castle. The waves were very close, but not close enough to touch our feet. I looked down at him with a look of surprise. "What are you doing?" My heart was beating dangerously fast now. When men got down on their knees before their lady, it could only mean...

"I'm telling you how beautiful you are," Marcel said with a smile. "Don't you want to hear it again, and again, and again?"

I relaxed a little, a girlish giggle bursting out of me. "I do," I answered.

Marcel took both my hands in his. The wild ocean breeze was blowing some of the strands of my hair in my face, but I refused to pull either of my hands away from him. I couldn't get enough of his tenderness toward me, and I was shamelessly going to soak up every drop of it.

"You, Norma Tesoriere, are the most delightful, amazing, wonderful woman I've ever known," he started. "Your beauty, your gracefulness, your gentleness, they won me over the day I first laid eyes on you. I tried to ignore what I felt, but it was impossible. The more time I spent with you, the more I wanted you. And I can't even put into words how thankful I am that you chose to give me a chance."

My heart was hammering in my chest. This wasn't one of Marcel's random endearments. This was different. My earlier thought hit again. Was it possible? Could the moment I had been dreaming of for the past two years be about to happen?

"Oh my gosh," I breathed out. "What are you doing Marcel?"

He grinned from ear to ear. "What I've wanted to do for a very long time." Letting go of my hands, he reached into the pocket of his shorts. I covered my mouth with both hands, speechless, at what was unfolding before me.

Is Marcel really going to ask me to…?

He came up with a black box in his hand and flipped it open. At that moment, I almost lost it. The gold ring inside was stunning and set with a beautiful diamond. I was blown away.

"Oh, Bear…" I started to say as joyful tears filled my eyes, but I couldn't even voice the words with the emotions swirling in me.

"I've been waiting to do this for a really long time now. Norma Tesoriere, you are the only woman that my heart beats for, and the only one I want to spend the rest of my life with." I stared down at him, looking into his dark eyes that had captivated me since the day they had first looked into my soul. I was mesmerized. I couldn't look away, I didn't want to. I wanted this moment to last forever. "You are the one I want to be the mother of my children. Would you do me the great honor of being my wife?"

I couldn't hold back any longer. I broke into tears, releasing the floodgate. "Bear, I…I..."

Even through my blurry eyes, I could see anxiety start to creep onto his face. I was such a sobbing mess. I needed to get myself together and give the man his answer before he had the chance to backtrack, thinking I wasn't ready.

"Sweetheart?"

"I'm sorry," I said, wiping my face with my hands. "Of course, I'll marry you." I laughed through the tears. "You're the only man I've ever loved, the only man I want to spend the rest of my life with, Marcel. Yes, and yes again, I'll marry you."

Relief washed over his face. "Oh, thank you, Jesus. For a minute there I thought…"

"That I wouldn't say yes?" I asked. "That's impossible. You're stuck with me forever." He laughed. "That's right, it's always going to be us. Marcel and Norma, always." His dark eyes shone up at me. Were those happy tears? Marcel wasn't one to cry so I knew he wouldn't let one of those tears escape, but I was pleased that his heart was mine, just like mine was his.

He pulled the ring from the box and slipped it on my finger. It fit perfectly. Rising from his knee, he pulled me close. "I love you, babe."

"I love you too, Bear." The words slipped off my tongue easily. It made me realize how far we had come. Together. He was such an amazing man. He pulled me against his chest, and I stood on my tippy toes, wrapping my arms around his neck. Burying his free hand in my hair, he leaned down to kiss me, and there they were again, the fireworks. I could almost hear them blast over my head as I drowned in the love Marcel poured into me through his lips.

I pulled him closer and deepened the kiss. After all this time, the feeling kept growing in intensity, even when I didn't think it was possible.

I couldn't believe it. I was going to be Marcel's wife.

As we pulled back, a beautiful image flashed before my eyes. Marcel would soon be the last person I would see before going to bed at night, and the first I would see in the morning when I woke up.

Although I had believed this moment would happen one day, it still felt surreal. After Marcel had been released from prison nine months ago, things had been tough on him as it related to going back to school and getting a job. Being an ex-convict, people seemed to judge him by his record, and not for the wonderful man he was. But we kept praying, and he kept trying.

A lot had happened, but our faith didn't waver. We both believed that God was in absolute control. And He proved He was. One thing I came to realize and appreciate was that God never left us without hope. Despite his cold attitude toward Marcel at the time, my dad had taken it upon himself to recommend Marcel to his boss when he learned how skilled my Bear was with a computer. Though Marcel hadn't gone to college, he had acquired good technical skills growing up, and that really helped him.

By some miracle, Dad's boss overlooked the fact that he had gone to prison. He gave Marcel an assignment on the day of his interview to see if he could handle and complete it, and my Bear had nailed it. I was so proud of him. It had been the beginning of a promising career.

Now my dad and my fiancé worked for the same software company. Chances were, my father would become the next CEO when his boss retired. As for Marcel, who knew what he would do next? Whether he decided to stay with that company or move on to another, I was extremely proud of him, and confident that he would succeed at whatever he set his mind to.

More than anything, I couldn't wait to be Mrs. Marcel Maxwell.

———

Marcel

Grabbing my hand, Norma dragged me back to the house to share the good news with her family. What she didn't realize was that everyone already knew about my proposal, and that's why they had looked at us funny when we walked out. It was also why I had to drag Norma out fast before my surprise was spoiled. Even our siblings knew about it. They had helped build the sandcastle. I'd made sure to go to her dad to ask for her hand in marriage. That had been six months ago. Mr. Tesoriere hadn't made it easy for me. Like any father should, he had laid down his terms.

I wasn't surprised. It was something any good father should do. Norma was his little girl and she deserved nothing but the best. Those had been his words and I had totally agreed with him when he said that. As such, he had helped me secure a good job that paid me well enough that I could save up, get my own apartment, and move out of my mother's place. He had also been one of the people who pushed me to go back to school and get my GED.

I had finally done it. I had finally asked Norma to marry me. And she had said yes! There was nothing that could stop this union because I knew God was the one who had brought us together.

As we neared the house, we caught the shifting of curtains and bodies scooting away at lightning speed. Norma glanced up at me. "Let me guess, they already know."

"Yup," I told her.

She shook her head and smiled. When we opened the door and stepped in, Rico and Luna were already in the room, along with the twins. Sofia was missing since she was spending time with her dad for the summer. They all pretended to be busy with something.

Norma held up her hand and waved it. "You can stop pretending now. I said yes." The room erupted into squeals and laughter.

"I helped with the sandcastle," Luna was quick to say as she pulled back from hugging her sister.

"Lies," Rico said. "I was the one who did everything, you barely did any of the work." He pulled Norma into his arms, hugging her.

I watched as everyone took turns embracing my beautiful wife-to-be. I was disappointed though that my mom couldn't be here because of her job. Even with my having a better job to help support my family, Mom was still adamant about working and supporting our family her own way. She wasn't the type to sit at home and depend on anyone else to take care of her.

However, I was thankful that she had at least gotten some time off to help me pick out Norma's ring. I knew a beautiful ring when I saw one, but Mom had a good eye when it came to fashion. I had wanted her to be the one to help me decide on the perfect one. And she had truly outdone herself. Norma adored that ring. She couldn't stop looking at it, as if to ascertain herself that it was really on her finger.

Since everyone was busy with Norma, I slipped away, deciding to call my mom. She picked up on the third ring. "Hello?"

"Ma, she said yes." I announced, unable to wait another second.

"Of course, she did." She bellowed through the phone. "I'm excited for you."

"Thanks, Ma." I answered. "Also, thanks for helping with the ring. She loves it."

"Anything for you, honey. You're welcome," she said. "I'm so proud of the man you've become, Marcel, you have no idea. You're going to be an amazing husband. I have no doubt about it. And perhaps in another year or two, you'll be a dad. I am sure you'll be a wonderful father."

My heart kicked up a frantic pace at that. Despite my excitement about becoming Norma's husband, I wasn't sure I was ready to be a father. Sure, I'd gained two good men in my life who had become great father figures. Pastor Archie and my soon-to-be father-in-law. They had quickly become the men who I wanted to emulate: loving husbands and great fathers. While I was continuously eager to be Norma's everything, I cringed at the thought of subjecting a little baby to my gruff and inexperienced person.

As if on cue, the memory of my little sisters, Isabella and Juliana, wailing as my mother exited the car with both of them in car seats, hit me. I was thirteen at the time and frightened by how small they were. Even worse, I couldn't picture myself ever holding them. It took me a little while, because I feared I would do the wrong thing and break one of them. They were so small, they fit perfectly in my big hands. At the time, my mother was in a relationship with the twins' father. He had seemed excited about the babies at first, but after a couple of months, he had left.

Just like *my* father.

"Son, I can feel your mind wandering away," Mom commented, breaking me out of my dark reverie. "Stop overthinking. When the time comes, you'll be a wonderful father as well." It was like she could read my mind.

"How can you be sure?" I asked, genuinely needing to know. After all, my father was pretty much a deadbeat. What if I had some of his lackadaisical nature inside me? My blood turned to ice as a feeling of dread crept over me. "I want to be the kind of man my child will look up to. I want to do things right. What if I make stupid mistakes? Or give the wrong advice?"

"Marcel Maxwell, you listen to me," she said, her voice going stern. "You are nothing like him, do you hear me? Nothing. You are a sweet, kind, and wonderful man who lives and breathes to protect those he loves. There is not a selfish bone in that body of yours and I am proud to call you my son. So, whatever you're thinking right now, stop it. You will be a great husband, and you will also be an amazing father. Think about your sisters. Who do you think they look up to? Who do you think stands as the father figure in their lives'? It's you."

"Me?"

"Yes, you. And you've done an amazing job with them. You were always here, protecting them, advising them, going to their activities, making them smile. You've been a good big brother. Fatherhood is not much different than what you've already been doing with them. When you get there, it's a stage you will forever cherish. Now," she said, going back to her strict tone. "No ifs, no buts. Do you understand?"

My throat tightened with emotion. It wasn't very often that my mother used that tone. But when she did, she meant business. I cleared my throat before replying. "Thanks, Ma," I said. "I feel much better now." And I wasn't just saying that for her satisfaction, I did feel better. My mother had opened my eyes. Fatherhood would certainly have its challenges, and I would certainly make mistakes, but I was going to be fine, and my children were also going to be fine. And if I ever had any trouble, I would have the most amazing wife at my side, and together we would get through it.

"You're welcome," she said. "By the way, I was thinking… I'm going to pop in at church on Sunday. I heard you would be sharing a short message."

"Really?" I asked, surprised. Over the past months, I had often tried to get my mother to come to church with me. There had always been one excuse or another, so much so that it had become obvious to me that she just wasn't interested. Now she was finally starting to show a little interest.

"Really," she confirmed. "I've been thinking about it; and when Norma told me you would be sharing a message, I thought, 'why not?'. I would love to hear it."

"Thank you, Jesus." I spoke.

"Alright." She gave a small laugh. "Get off the phone now and go have fun with your beautiful fiancée. I need to go check on my cooking in the kitchen. I'll see you when you get back."

"I love you, Ma," I told her before she could end the call.

"I love you too."

As soon as our call ended, I turned to find a pair of intense hazel eyes watching me from across the room. Norma's mother and aunt were talking to her about an engagement party, but she didn't seem to be listening. Her eyes were locked on me; eyes that were full of love. Love that not only overwhelmed me, but also challenged me to become a better man, and to prove worthy of such love.

It was love that had changed me. In every way. And though I still bore the scars of my commitment to One, I knew He bore eternal scars as a sign of His love and commitment to all who would follow Him.

It was at that moment that the last of my apprehension melted away because I knew, without a shadow of a doubt, that as long as Norma and I both followed Him together, we would continue to be changed, and fulfil our purpose here on Earth.

Norelle's first book

Lightly inspired by events and people from the past, this book will lead you through the innocence of youth and then into a dark reality. It will also touch your heart and remain in your thoughts for years to come.
Everyone has a past. Everything changes. Some for the better, some for the worst.

Francesca Romano's life is no fairy tale. Hers is an uncontrolled world of silent tears and torment, where love crumbles and tragedy looms because of things left untold — because of the secrets that are kept. A world where honesty is obsolete, and youthful rebellion turns into total chaos. Francesca tries to gain control when she disappears to a new place, hoping to never be found. To a place where she can start anew, and escape the despair, emptiness, and fear of her former world.
When she finds new love and new faith, she feels she is finally on the path to redemption and healing. Until one morning she gets a call, and all that which was left, returns to her, to satisfy an unfulfilled promise...
Trigger warnings: sexual assault, drug and alcohol use and addiction, violence, abuse, emotional control and addiction, obsession.

Other releases to watch for –

That One Day by Norelle Smith and S.P.W. Mitchell
Hiding Behind 'I'm Fine' by Norelle Smith

Book Review Request

If you enjoyed *The Gap Between Us,* please leave a review and comment on Amazon and Goodreads.

I will read every review. They not only help readers find my books, but they also help new readers discover the books that are right for them.

The Author

Norelle Smith is an American author with a passion for helping those in need. After working in the corporate world for more than two decades she decided it was time to move on. Norelle retired early and sought out her next adventure. Somewhere along the way, lost among the trails with her horses, she discovered the direction she needed to continue evolving; writing.

Norelle was asked why she writes under a penname. Her response – "Each book I write, although they're fiction, have pieces of my life in them. I'd like to tell my story through several books, through different characters and different situations, and remain unknown. I'm hoping to help someone else…hoping to show others there's a way out, and a better way to live. I believe some things should be kept a secret, but not left *untold*. Norelle is also donating half of her royalties and buys new backpacks and school supplies for kids in need. She's always preferred to remain anonymous when 'giving'."

The Gap Between us is Norelle's second novel. She's dedicating her time to writing books meant to inspire and motivate readers. Already, two more books are in the making. She has no ideations of getting rich – Norelle's writing career remains grounded in the fact she wants readers to feel from her books. Without evoking a deep emotional response, her writings would be incomplete.

www.norelleandmitchell.com
www.instagram.com/norelleandmitchell
www.facebook.com/IFUntold
IFUntold@yahoo.com